About the Authors

Lenora Worth is a Carol Award finalist and a *New York Times*, *USA Today*, and *PW* bestselling author. She writes Southern stories set in places she loves such as Georgia, Texas, Louisiana, and Florida. Lenora is married and has two grown children and now lives near the ocean in the Panhandle of Florida. She loves reading, shoe shopping, long walks on the beach, mojitos and road trips.

Jessica Hart had a haphazard early career that took her around the world in a variety of interesting but very lowly jobs, all of which have provided inspiration on which to draw when it comes to the settings and plots of her stories. She eventually stumbled into writing as a way of funding a PhD in medieval history, but was quickly hooked on romance and is now a full-time author based in York. If you'd like to know more about Jessica, visit her website: www.jessicahart.co.uk

A New York Times bestselling author, **Christine Rimmer** has written over ninety contemporary romances for Mills & Boon. Christine has won the *Romantic Times* BOOKreviews Reviewers Choice Award and has been nominated six times for the RITA® Award. She lives in Oregon with her family. Visit Christine at www.christinerimmer.com

A Cinderella Story

COLLECTION

A Groom for Cinderella

LENORA WORTH

JESSICA HART

CHRISTINE RIMMER

MILLS & BOON

First Published in Great Britain 2020
By Mills & Boon, an imprint of HarperCollins*Publishers*
1 London Bridge Street, London, SE1 9GF

A GROOM FOR CINDERELLA © 2020 Harlequin Books S.A.

Hometown Princess © 2010 Lenora H. Nazworth
Ordinary Girl in a Tiara © 2011 Jessica Hart
The Prince's Cinderella Bride © 2014 Christine Rimmer

978-0-263-28157-6

MIX
Paper from
responsible sources
FSC™ C007454

This book is produced from independently certified FSC™ paper to ensure responsible forest management.

For more information visit: www.harpercollins.co.uk/green

Printed and bound in Spain
by CPI, Barcelona

HOMETOWN PRINCESS

LENORA WORTH

To my sister-in-law Kathy Baker

Chapter One

It was all about the shoes.

Carinna Clark Duncan stood in front of the store window, staring at the pair of red pumps winking at her through the glass. She wanted those shoes. But she couldn't have them. Not now. Maybe not ever. Her days of extravagant shoe shopping were over. *Lead me not to temptation, Lord.*

She glanced around the quaint main street of Knotwood Mountain, Georgia, and then looked to her left at the old run-down turn-of-the-century Victorian house she'd inherited after her father's death a month ago. Duncan House—that's what her parents had called it. Now it had a dilapidated old sign that said Photography and Frames—Reasonable Prices hanging off one of the porch beams. Her childhood home had been reduced to a business rental, but the last renter had left in a hurry from what she'd been told by her father's lawyer.

The house was the only part of James Duncan's vast estate she'd received. The bitterness and pain rose up like bile inside her. But it wasn't because she wanted the whole estate, even though some cold hard cash would be good right now. No, her deep-seated resentment and anger came from another source. And her prayers for release hadn't worked.

This anger and jealousy was toward the woman who'd swooped in and wooed Cari's still-grieving father into marrying her just months after Cari's mother had died. That woman, Doreen Stillman, and her two children, had managed not only to fool Cari's vulnerable father for the last few years; they'd also managed to turn him against his only daughter. The daughter who'd loved and adored him and still grieved for her mother and him so much it woke her up in tears in the middle of the night.

Once the apple of her doting father's eye, Cari had soon become the outcast, the troublemaker who stood against Doreen. And Doreen made sure James Duncan knew this, made sure he heard all about how horribly Cari treated Doreen and her children. Even if it wasn't true, even if she'd been the one who'd been mistreated, there was no way to convince her besotted, grief-stricken father. No way. And now it was too late to make amends with him. Cari only hoped she'd been able to get through to him enough before he died to make him understand that she loved him.

Staring at the shoes with a Monday morning moroseness, she thought it was pretty ironic that a pair of shoes had started the whole chain of events that had eventually caused Cari to fall out of her father's good graces in the first place. Cari and her younger stepsister Bridget had been fighting over a pair of blue sandals. They belonged to Cari, but Bridget had insisted she wanted to borrow them. Cari had refused, saying Bridget was too young and her feet too long for the narrow, strappy shoes that Cari intended to wear to a party that night. But Doreen and Cari's father had sided with Bridget. Cari had not only lost the shoes—Bridget never gave them back—she'd also lost a lot of respect for her father. And apparently, he'd lost respect for her, too. Things had gone from bad to worse after that. Her once storybook life had become miserable.

But he had left her the house.

That alone had sustained Cari after his death. He'd left her the one thing she remembered with happiness and joy—the house where she'd grown up with both her parents. It had been a loving, wonderful, faith-filled home back then, full of adventure and all the things a little girl loved, including a turret room. Cari used to pretend she was a princess; she'd dreamed big dreams in that round little room just off her bedroom on the right side of the two-story house. Now, the pretty memories faded and she was left staring at a harsh reality.

Doreen had immediately moved the family out to a big, modern house on the Chattahoochee River and convinced James to let the town rezone this house for commercial use. Only she'd neglected to take care of this particular piece of property. Doreen wouldn't know a house with good bones if it fell on her.

The old house was still solid, but it needed a lot of cosmetic work, Cari thought. And so did she. Maybe she could make some sense of things, redoing this old place. Maybe. By leaving her the house, her father had given her a new lease on life. She once again had big dreams—for herself and for the house she had opened up earlier today. She planned to renovate it room by room. And she planned to open a quaint little boutique to showcase her jewelry and trinkets on the first floor. She could live on the second floor. It would be a great arrangement if she could make a go of it. *Please, God, let me do this right.*

But she did have another big problem. A definite lack of capital. She had to figure out a way to find the money to do everything she envisioned. From the research she'd done, a loan didn't look possible.

She turned back to the shoes, a longing bursting through her heart. She was a material girl—or at least she used to be. She reminded herself that those days were gone and so she couldn't afford the shoes. But she sure did admire them anyway.

Just keep on admiring, she told herself. And remember why you're here. You have something else to focus on now besides shopping. You have a home.

Cari thanked God and thanked her father. Maybe this was his way of telling her he had loved her in spite of everything. And she knew in her heart God had never abandoned her, even if it had felt that way since she'd become an exile from Knotwood Mountain.

The sound of shifting gears caused her to turn around. The bright summer sun shone brightly on the battered old brown-and-white open Jeep pulling up to the curb. The man driving downshifted and cut the roaring engine then hopped out, heading toward where Cari stood in front of Adams General Store and Apparel.

"Go on in and try them on," he said with a grin, motioning toward the shoes.

And Cari turned and faced another dream she'd forgotten. Rick Adams. In the flesh and looking too bright and way too good with the early-morning sunlight glinting across his auburn-brown curly hair. Did he remember her? Cari doubted it. He'd been a few years older and he'd run with a different crowd in high school. The fun football and cheerleader crowd. While she'd preferred reading sappy fiction on most Saturday nights and observing him from afar on most school days. The classic tale of the plain Jane wanting the handsome prince, with no happy ending in sight.

"Hi," she said with a stiff smile. "I can't try them on. I can't afford them." Honesty was her new policy.

He gave her a blue-eyed appraisal but she didn't see recognition in that enticing stare. "Too bad. I think they'd fit you just right."

She shook her head. "I don't think so. And don't tempt me. I've got to get going." She didn't give him time to talk her into trying on the gorgeous shoes. Cari hurried to the rambling house next door and quickly went inside.

"Did you see Cari out there?"
Rick looked up at his mother's words, spoken from

the second floor of Adams General Store and Apparel. Gayle was leaning over the timbered banister holding an armful of women's T-shirts with the words *I rode the river at Knotwood Mountain* emblazed across them, grinning down at her son.

"Cari? Cari who?"

"Cari Duncan. I thought I saw you talking to her."

Rick glanced outside then back up at his mom. "That pretty strawberry-blonde looking at the red shoes in the window? That was shy little Cari Duncan?"

"That's her—back home and about to open up her own shop right next door in the old Duncan House, according to Jolena." Gayle put the shirts on a nearby rack and came down the stairs. "Jolena told me all about it when I went by the diner this morning."

Rick looked up at his mother, his hands on his hips. "Why didn't I know about this?"

Gayle let out a chuckle. "Maybe because you missed the chamber of commerce meeting last night—again. Everyone was talking about it, Jolena said. And apparently, Doreen was fit to be tied because she planned to sell the house and turn a tidy profit on that corner lot."

Rick groaned. "I completely forgot the meeting. I had to get all this fishing gear and our rafts and floats ready for the summer crowds." He couldn't believe he'd just talked to Cari and hadn't even realized it was her. "Well, I'm glad someone's taking over the old place. It's an eyesore and last time I did attend a meeting, everyone on First Street agreed something needed to be done about it."

Gayle busied herself with straightening the bait-and-tackle rack by the cash register. "Doreen didn't worry about the upkeep on the place. I'm sure she's unhappy that it no longer belongs to her." She pursed her lips. "You know, that's all Cari got from the inheritance."

"You're kidding?" Rick went back to the window. "Her father owned half the property in town and she got stuck with that old house. That building needs to be overhauled. It's gone to ruin since the last tenant left."

"Doreen kicked the last tenant out," Gayle replied as she poured him a cup of coffee off the stove at the back of the store. "She's not an easy landlady from what I've heard."

"Then she probably wasn't an easy stepmother either," Rick countered. "I hope Cari can stand up to the woman. She was always so passive and shy in high school." Not that he hadn't noticed her pretty turquoise eyes and nice smile back then. But that was about as far as Rick had ever gotten with Cari. His girlfriend hadn't liked him being kind to a girl she considered "a boring little spoiled princess."

The girlfriend was long gone, and well…Cari was back and right next door, and she didn't look boring at all. The hometown princess was all grown-up. He'd have to go and visit her, apologize for not recognizing her.

"I can't believe I didn't know it was her," he said to his mother. "She's changed."

"Yes, lost weight and cut her hair. She's downright

spunky-looking now," Gayle said as she grabbed one
of Jolena's famous cinnamon rolls and headed back up
to the women's department of the sprawling store.
"And she'll need to be spunky if she intends to renovate that place. We'll have to offer her some help. Be
neighborly."

Rick grinned then headed to the stockroom. He'd
have to be neighborly another day. He had lots to do
today. Only a few weeks until the Fourth of July and
the flood of tourists who'd come to Knotwood Mountain to camp, fish, swim and go tubing and rafting on
the nearby Chattahoochee River. And hopefully shop
at Adams General Store and Apparel for all their outfitter needs.

They'd made this store a nice place since he'd come
back five years ago. His mother had taken over the top
floor for her women's apparel, knickknacks, souvenirs
and artwork and he had the bottom floor for more
manly stuff like rafting and fishing gear, rugged out-
door clothes and shoes and cowboy and work boots.
And since his older brother Simon designed handmade
cowboy boots in a studio just outside of town on their
small ranch, Rick also had the pleasure of selling his
brother's popular boots both retail and online. A nice
setup and, finally, one that was seeing a profit. He
wished his father was still alive to see how he'd turned
the old family store into a tourist attraction.

But…wishes didn't get the work done, so he went
into the stockroom and headed to the back alley, intent
on unloading and inventorying stock in between customers for the rest of the day.

First, he had to gather the empty boxes from yesterday and take them out to the recycling bin before the truck came cruising through. Always something to do around this place, that was for sure. But Rick liked the nice steady work and the casual atmosphere. It sure beat his hectic, stressful lifestyle back in Atlanta.

He'd put all of that behind him now. He'd come home.

He stopped at the trash dump and stared at the leaning back porch of Cari's place, wondering what had brought her back. Surely not just this old Victorian diamond in the rough.

He was about to turn and head back inside when the door of the house creaked open and he heard a feminine voice shouting, "Shoo, get out of here."

Out swooped a pigeon, flapping its wings as it lifted into the air.

The woman stood on the porch with her hands on her hips, smiling up at the terrified bird. "And don't come back. I'm the only squatter allowed on these premises now."

Rick let out a hoot of laughter. "Poor little pigeon."

Cari whirled, mortified that Rick had heard her fussing at the innocent pigeon. "Oh, hi. Sorry but it was either him or me. He's made a mess of what used to be a storage room, I think. And I'm pretty sure he's had a few feathered friends over for some wild parties, too. First thing on my list—fix that broken windowpane."

Rick strolled over toward the porch then looked up

at her. "Cari," he said, his smile sharp enough to burn away all the cobwebs she had yet to clear out of the first floor. "You've changed."

Cari pushed at her shaggy, damp hair. This pleasant morning was fast turning into a hot afternoon. "Same old me," she said, wondering if he was even taller now. "I figured you didn't recognize me, though." And he'd aged to perfection, curly brown hair, crinkling, laughing eyes.

"No, sorry I didn't. But it's sure nice to see you again. It's been a while."

She leaned on the rickety old railing, the sound of the river gurgling over the nearby rocks soothing her frazzled mind. "Yep. Last time I saw you, you were off to Georgia Tech with a cheerleader on your arm. How'd that go for you?"

He shook his head, looked down at his work boots. "Not too well at first. I partied more than I studied and the cheerleader found her one true love—it wasn't me. Just about flunked out. My old man didn't appreciate my lack of commitment, let me tell you. But I finally got things together and pulled through."

Cari nodded, noting the darkening in his eyes when he mentioned his father. "I did the same thing—didn't party too much, just didn't much care. I did flunk out at the University of Georgia. But I eventually went back and studied design and got a major in business. Little good that did me, however." She didn't want to elaborate and she hoped he wouldn't ask her to.

He didn't. Instead he looked off into the ridge of mountains to the west. "But here you are, about to open a business right here in Knotwood Mountain." He moved a little closer, one booted foot on the battered steps. "What's the plan, anyway?"

Cari eyed the old porch and the broken steps. "The plan is to get this house back the way I remember it." Except it wouldn't be the same. Nothing would ever be the same. "Why is it when a house is shut down it seems to wither and die?"

Rick lifted his gaze to the dormer windows and the gabled roof. "I guess because houses are a lot like people. They need to be needed."

Surprised that he'd turned all mushy about things, she decided to stick to a safer conversation. "I've got my things stored in Atlanta but I'm bringing them here in a few days. All the inventory left over from the shop I had there. And I want to order lots of other things. It'll take a while to get it going, but I think with the tourist traffic I might be able to make it work. I checked around and Knotwood Mountain doesn't have a shabby-chic boutique."

He squinted up at her. "That's a mighty big plan."

"Yes, it is. And I have a mighty tiny budget."

"You been to the bank for a loan?"

"Working on it." She wondered if the local banker would even talk to her. Doreen carried a lot of weight in town. But the Duncan name still stood for something. At least Cari had that. That and about two nickels to rub together.

Rick looked up and down the alley then back up at her. "Well, maybe it'll work out for you. What about your business? What kind of establishment will this be? And what exactly is shabby-chic?"

That was a subject she could talk about for hours. "I design jewelry. I take old estate jewelry and rework it then resell it. I also carry unique women's clothing and I fix up picture frames and jewelry boxes, trinkets—I like to take old things and make them pretty again. Sometimes I redesign tote bags and purses."

"Purses?" He grinned up at her again. "Maybe you can make one to go with those red shoes in my window."

"I told you, I can't afford those shoes."

He pushed off the steps. "Nobody can. My mother ordered them at market on an impulse and now they're just sitting there waiting for the right feet—and the right amount of money. Maybe those pumps have been waiting for you. And something tells me you'll work hard until you *can* afford them."

Cari's heart soared. It had been a while since anyone had expressed belief in her. A very long time. "You think so?"

He tipped a finger to his temple in salute. "If you can take on this old house then I'd say you can do anything." Then he smiled and walked back toward the open double doors of the general store's stockroom. But he turned and gave her a long, studied look. "Good to have you back. And if you need anything, anything at all, you call me, okay, Princess?"

"Thanks." Cari watched him go back inside then looked up at the mountain vista just beyond town. The Blue Ridge Mountains had always brought her peace. Even while she'd lived in Athens and later in Atlanta, she'd often come up here to the mountains just to get away. Of course, she'd never come back here to Knotwood Mountain, but there were other spots nearby she loved, where the rhododendrons bloomed in bright whites and pinks and grew six feet tall. She stood listening and silent, the sound of the river gurgling through the middle of town continuing to bring her a sense of peace and comfort.

"Can I do this, Lord?" she asked. Had she made the right decision, leaving Atlanta to come home? What choice did she have? she wondered.

After all, this old house was all she had now.

She'd pretty much wasted away her bank account and she'd maxed out her charge cards. All in the name of looking good, looking up-to-date and in style while trying to keep up with a man who never intended to settle down and marry her. All in the name of a facade that could never quite fill the void inside her heart.

Turning to head back inside, she thought about the red shoes and all they represented. Once, she would have marched inside the store and bought them without giving it a second thought. Just to make herself feel better.

Looking over at the general store, she whispered, "Sorry, Rick, but I'm not a princess anymore."

Once, when she'd been frivolous and impulsive and careless, she would have spent money she didn't have. But that Cari was gone, just like the passive, shy Cari from high school. This new, more assertive Cari was going to have to reinvent herself, one step at a time and on her own two feet.

Only this time, she wouldn't be wearing fabulous shoes or be hiding behind a carefully controlled facade when she did it.

Chapter Two

The next morning, Cari opened the door to Jolena's Diner and smiled at her friend. "Hello."

"Well, look what the cat dragged in," Jolena, big, black and beautiful, said with a white, toothy grin, reaching to give Cari a tight hug. "How was your first day home, suga'?"

Cari sat down on one of the bright red stools at the long white counter. "Different." She'd managed to get the kitchen clean enough to boil water and make toast and she'd slept on an air mattress in a small room upstairs. "I cleaned all day and unpacked enough clothes and essentials to get me through for a while. I'm going to pick up a few groceries and toiletry items. And I'm praying the bathroom upstairs will stay in working order until I can have a plumber check the whole place."

Jolena looked doubtful. "You could have stayed with us, you know."

Cari took the coffee Jolena automatically handed her, the hustle and bustle of this bright, popular diner making her feel alive. The smell of bacon and eggs reminded her she hadn't eaten much since early yesterday. The buzz of conversation reminded her how lonely and isolated she'd become in the past few weeks. But Jolena's smile held Cari together.

"I appreciate the offer, but I didn't want to put your girls out of their bedrooms."

Jolena grunted. "Those four—honey, they're always in each other's way so one more wouldn't even be noticed. Even a cute one with freckles like you."

"I did just fine on my own last night," Cari said. Never mind that she hadn't actually slept very much. But the moonlight coming through the old sheers in the room had given her a sense of security at least. "I have a bed and I scrubbed the kitchen and the storage room yesterday. Of course, I need a new stove and a refrigerator. That ice chest isn't going to work in this summer heat."

Jolena nodded. "I can hook you up with my friend down at the appliance store. He'll make you a deal."

Cari laughed at the woman who'd been friends with her mother, Natalie, since they were both little girls. Finding pen and paper, she wrote down the name and number. "You always have connections."

Jolena let out a belly laugh then waved to two departing fishermen. "Yes, I sure do. And speaking of that—you need a makeover, honey. You look a little peaked."

Cari pushed at her hair. "I guess I do look bad, but

I wasn't too concerned with my appearance this morning. I don't have any groceries yet and I just needed coffee, badly."

"And so do I," said a masculine voice behind her.

Cari pivoted so fast she almost fell off her perch. "Rick, good morning." Pushing at her hair again, she wished she'd at least bothered to put on lipstick.

Jolena leaned over the counter, her long thin braids tapping her robust shoulders. "Rick, you remember our Cari, don't you?"

Rick sat down next to Cari and took the cup of coffee a waitress brought him. "I do now. Didn't at first but we talked a bit yesterday afternoon. Good to see you again, Cari. Hope you had a good first night home."

"It was okay," she said, the warmth of his dark blue eyes washing over her. Could it be possible that he had matured into an even better looking man than the boy she remembered? Highly possible.

Jolena's gaze shifted from Rick to Cari, her grin growing with each blink. "You two went to school together, right?"

Cari felt the crimson moving over her freckles. "Yes, we did but Rick was the big man on campus. He…we…didn't hang out together too much."

"And that's a shame," Rick replied, winking at Cari. "But high school's always hard, you know. I'm sure we've both changed since those days."

When Jolena's overly interested eyebrows shot up, Cari slumped on her stool, wishing she could just dive under the counter. Did the man know the effect he had on women? Or did he just do this to her? She felt all mushy and soft-kneed. Which was just plain crazy. She wasn't in high school anymore. And she *had* changed. She didn't trust pretty boys anymore and she sure didn't indulge in adolescent crushes these days.

Finally, because he was still smiling at her, she said, "So why'd you come back to Knotwood Mountain, Rick?"

The smile softened and his rich blue eyes went black. "That's a long story and, unfortunately, I don't have time to tell it right now. I've got people waiting to rent tubes for the day." He got up, took his to-go cup of coffee and lifted it toward Jolena. "Put it on my tab." Then he turned to Cari. "I'll see you around, neighbor."

Cari waited until she heard the screen door slap back on its hinges then looked at Jolena. "What? Did I ask the wrong question?"

Jolena, known as much for her gossip as her soul food, leaned close, her dimples deepening. "I heard it had something to do with a bad breakup. I think the man was heartbroken and hurting when he came limping into town. But he's good now, real good. And *real* available."

Cari almost spit out her sip of coffee. "Yes, so available that he practically ran out of here. If he can't talk about her, then he ain't over her."

"He might get over her better if he had someone sweet to talk to, know what I mean?"

"I do know what you mean, but I'm not here to find a man, Jolena. Just like Rick there, I, too, went through a bad breakup—with the man and with my money that the man took." She pointed across the street. "You see that wilted wedding cake of a house sitting over there. I'm here to fix that house up and get my boutique going. That's about all I have any time or energy for. And I don't want a man standing around telling me what to do and making me feel guilty about everything from the shoes I wear to the friends I have. I want to do this my way."

Jolena wasn't to be hushed. "You got a point there, honey. But you need to take time to be friendly to the other merchants along the street. We stick together around here. You'll see. Don't be all mean and stand-offish with Rick Adams. You might need a friend, too. But that attitude will surely scare people away."

Cari couldn't deny that she needed to make a connection. But with Rick? Friend and neighboring merchant, maybe. But that would have to be it. Still, it wouldn't hurt to know more about him—just so she'd know what *not* to ask him next time she saw him.

"Okay, so he is good-looking," she admitted on a low whisper. "It won't be very hard to be nice to him. But that's as far as it goes."

Jolena made an exaggerated frown. "Girl, that man is so pretty, well, as my mama used to say, you could spoon him up like sugar."

Cari had to laugh. "Your mama would tell you to put your big brown eyes right back inside your head, too, if she were here—since you're married and have four children."

"You are so right," Jolena said, waving a glitter-nailed finger in Cari's face. "But what's your excuse, honey? Beside thinking all men are the scum of the earth, I mean?"

Cari frowned right back at her friend. "Me? I am not the least bit interested, especially in someone like Rick Adams. From what I remember back in high school, he had a new girl on his arm every Friday night."

"This ain't high school, girl, and you've changed since then. Maybe he has, too. He said as much himself." Jolena fluffed her heavy reddish-brown weave, her words echoing Cari's own earlier thoughts. "His mother is a good Christian woman, you know. Gives to the local food bank and works there, too. Helps out with the youth at church just about every Sunday night. And my mama says Rick has settled down, changed his wild ways since his father passed."

That caught Cari's attention. Had Rick had father issues just like her? "Tell me more," she said, smiling over at Jolena. "And while you're at it, can I have a short-stack with fresh strawberries?"

Jolena was more than happy to oblige.

Rick Adams. The second son of the late Lazaro Adams and widow Gayle Miller Adams. After her husband's death, Gayle Adams had turned her husband's Western and outfitter store into a haven for artists and craftsmen, including herself and her oldest son Simon. Then she'd put in a women's clothing department on the second floor. According to Jolena, the big old store had struggled after Mr. Adams had died, but now her good-looking second son was back from the big city and working hard in the family business.

Wonder what the whole story there is, Cari mused as she waited for Jolena to ring up a customer. She knew why she'd come home, but Rick? Could a woman have messed him up that badly? From what she'd heard from Jolena, he'd had it made in Atlanta. Big-time marketing guru, all-around business tycoon, etc. While she'd been mostly miserable and alienated from her father, and definitely messed up from too many bad relationships. But maybe being successful didn't help in the love department. It sure hadn't helped ease her misery and unhappiness.

"So that's supposed to make me sit up and take notice?" Cari asked when Jolena came back. "Just because he's successful in business does not mean he's ready for a relationship, especially if he's been burned before. And we can't know if he's changed from high school. Some people change, some people don't."

"You gotta have faith, honey," Jolena said, rolling her eyes. "Haven't I told you, if you turn it over to the Lord—"

"The Lord will turn it all to good," Cari finished, her voice low so she wouldn't attract attention. "Well, you know how I feel about that. The Lord hasn't provided me with the answers I need lately. Not since the day Doreen Stillman and her two spoiled children walked into my father's house."

Jolena's dark face turned serious and somber as the conversation shifted to the subject Cari couldn't get off her mind. "Cari, honey, it's been over eight years and your father has left this earth. You need to make peace with what happened. And with what *didn't* happen."

Cari shook her head, causing sprigs of curling strawberry-blond hair to fall around her face. "I can't do that, Jolena. I barely got to visit him when he was ill, and that's because of Doreen's hovering over him. He never once told me he'd forgiven me. And I prayed for that every day. I tried to tell him that I loved him, but I think it was too late. He was too sick to understand."

"I know things were rough," Jolena said, her sequined mauve sundress flashing with each wave of her hand. "Prayer is good but wanting to get back at your stepmother even after the man is dead and gone is not so good. Eight years is a long time to hold that kind of grudge, honey."

"The woman used my father."

"You think. You haven't seen anything to indicate that and she did stick around for all those years you were gone, remember?"

Cari cringed but held firm. "I lived with them before he kicked me out. I saw her in action. She married him for one reason. She wanted his money. And now, she has it."

Jolena twirled a plump dark ringlet. "She might have his estate, but if what you say is true that woman will pay her dues one day, mark my words. I just don't want you to be the one who gets hurt all over again trying to see that she does."

"I understand," Cari said, the words a low growl, her fork stuck to a fluffy chunk of pancake. "But my mother had only been dead three months when Doreen moved in on my still-grieving father. I became a stranger in my own home, and she somehow alienated my father from me to the point that he practically threw me out on the street. I left before that happened but things sure went downhill from there."

Jolena's dark eyes filled with understanding. "So you made a few mistakes, did some things you're not proud of. We've all been there, suga'. But look at you now."

"Yes, look at me," Cari replied, her voice shaking in spite of her stiff-necked pride. "I don't exist anymore, Jolena. I didn't exist to my father and we lost precious time. Now I have to do something to honor him. Renovating this house will do that. And give me something solid to focus on, at least."

Jolena grabbed Cari's hand and held it in hers. "I understand you're in pain, you're hurting, baby. But I promised your dear mother that I would watch over you. I can't do that if you keep insisting on giving me the slip and going off to do foolish things."

"You mean, like trying to confront Doreen?"

"Exactly," Jolena said through a sigh. "I like it better when you're positive and purposeful. You know the Lord wants you to have a purpose."

Cari laughed at that. "A purpose is one thing, but not having the funds to make purposeful things happen is another."

"Are you going to the bank?"

"Yes, in a couple of days. I have to get everything together and ply my case."

Jolena put her hands underneath her chin and smiled over at Cari. "Eat your pancakes and let me do the worrying. You want that old house to shine? Well, you can't do that all on your own. Just let Jolena here do some thinking. I might have an idea to help you out."

Cari was afraid to ask what that idea was, but knowing Jolena, it would be big and bold. And it would probably involve a certain handsome business-man, too. Jolena never tired of matchmaking and being bossy for a good cause.

Could she allow that to happen? Could she become a true part of the town she'd fled all those years ago? Could she ask for help, knowing that Doreen now held the upper hand? If Cari wanted her business to work, she'd have to learn to be more decisive and assertive instead of hanging back in the shadows. That would be the only sure way to get even with Doreen, to prove the woman wrong. She'd have to work at getting to know people she'd long ago forgotten. And that might mean being civil to a woman she detested. And be-coming close to a man she'd never really forgotten. Fat chance of anything other than friendship with Rick Adams, however.

She needed to find the strength to stand on her own two feet, once and for all. Self-control and fortitude—that was what she needed now. And if that meant being nice to her neighbors, including Doreen Duncan, and working for the good of this beautiful little village, then she could do that, too. Her father had left her this house for a reason. It was time Cari tried to figure out that reason.

She'd play nice with the community leaders and

she'd work hard to make a go of her business. She knew how to do that, at least.

And one day maybe she could finally be proud and self-assured enough to accept that in his own stubborn way her father might have loved her and believed in her after all.

Chapter Three

Armed with a cheeseburger for lunch, Cari headed back to the house to get busy. She had to call the contractor she'd hired and find out when he could start the renovations, that is, if he could give her a good quote. Then she wanted to call the phone company to get a landline for the boutique. Eventually, she'd need a computer for both the cash register and for placing orders. She'd also need to rebuild her Web site with the new location. But for now, her old laptop would have to do for some of that.

If she could get the bottom floor repaired and updated over the next few weeks and generate some revenue, she'd worry about the upstairs later. She'd read up on renovating old homes and all the advice said to take it one room at a time, starting with the most urgent ones. Maybe she could save some money by starting the preliminary work herself and leave the hard stuff to the contractor.

Doreen had left several pieces of antique furniture scattered throughout the house. The woman didn't know a thing about high-quality furniture but that would work to Cari's advantage now. She'd dusted and polished the old Queen Anne buffet she'd found in the parlor. That would make a nice display table and she could use the drawers to store jewelry and small items such as scarves and belts.

There was an old four-poster oak bed upstairs. It was rickety and needed some tender loving care, but it would be a jewel when Cari refinished it. She'd put it in the turret room and make it her own. With the few other pieces she'd found, she had enough to do some sparse decorating.

"Well, I'd say the kitchen and bathroom down here are both really urgent." But they were both clean now and she had the callused, rough hands to prove it. The bathroom was in fairly good working order, but it needed new fixtures and, well, new everything.

She put the cheeseburger bag on the now clean but chipped linoleum counter then turned to admire her handiwork in the old kitchen. The rickety white table and chairs had been scrubbed and looked halfway decent, but the old cabinets needed to be completely redone. They were high and big with plenty of good storage space. That was a plus. She'd gone through them and wiped them down then placed shelf liners in each one. She had a few mismatched dishes she'd unpacked and her coffeepot. Fresh daisies in a Mason jar made the old white table seem almost happy.

Some groceries would help. And a refrigerator.

Standing in the long wide kitchen, she called the man Jolena had suggested. He immediately gave her some quotes on various sizes and styles. Cari thanked him and told him she'd be out to look this afternoon. Having taken care of that, she surveyed the kitchen again, memories washing over her with a gentleness that reminded her of her mother.

The room was long and wide and filled with windows that had once looked out over a vast backyard that ran all the way down to the nearby river. That backyard had been sold in increments as First Street commercialism had continued to grow right into the old suburban Victorian neighborhood built along the Chattahoochee River.

Duncan House was one of the few remaining original homes built here at the turn of the century. Most of them has been razed or renovated beyond recognition to make way for progress. And while Cari was thankful that her small town was now a tourist mecca, she sure wanted to bring back some of that Victorian charm that had once colored the place.

"Starting with Duncan House."

Maybe she'd update the kitchen to make it functional for events and turn it into a nice sitting area for customers. She could bring over some cookies and pies from Jolena's Diner and serve them with coffee and tea from the old antique sideboard shoved up against one wall. Just like her mother used to do when they'd invited company over for Sunday dinner.

"And where will I get the money for that?" she wondered, thinking she only had a few thousand in her bank account and her one remaining charge card was for emergencies only. Getting a bank loan scared her silly since her credit history wasn't the best, but she had to try.

Determination and the financial budget she'd worked so hard to create and maintain over the past couple of years driving her on, Cari put away her bag and decided, now that she'd cleared and cleaned the downstairs open area, she'd give the bathroom one more thorough cleaning. She could then tackle the upstairs again, just to make sure she hadn't missed anything.

First on the list would be to make sure the stairs were safe. They'd seemed a bit wobbly yesterday when she'd ventured up to see her turret room. That was another thing on the list—the turret room was intact but dirty and waterlogged from broken window-panes. The pigeons seemed to love to roost there, too.

"Too bad about that."

She remembered the room when it had been all bright whites and feminine blues and yellows, with a tiny little table and chairs and a real porcelain tea set where she'd entertained her dolls and, sometimes, her father and mother, too. Cari had clopped around in a big hat and a pair of feather-encrusted plastic high heels, a princess content in her own skin. And very innocent and naive in her security.

"Too bad about that, too."

But she intended to restore the room in those same sky-blues and sunshine-yellows, using a hydrangea theme since the old bushes out front were still intact and blooming to beat the band.

Hearing the front door squeak open, she wondered if the contractor was here already.

"Ye-hoo? Anybody home?"

Doreen. Cari gave herself a mental shake. She wouldn't let that woman get to her. Taking a deep, calming breath, she called out, "I'm in the kitchen."

Doreen came through the arched doorway to stop just inside the empty kitchen, her gaze sweeping the room with distaste. "I just had to come and see for myself if all the rumors I kept hearing were true." Patting her bright red teased hair, she shook her head and rolled her eyes. "You can't be serious, Cari."

Cari prayed for patience. Putting her hands down beside her jeans so she wouldn't use them to do physical harm, she lifted her eyebrows. "Serious? Oh, you mean about reopening Duncan House? Yes, I'm very serious."

Doreen dropped her designer bag on the table. "I heard about it at the chamber of commerce meeting the other night and I just couldn't believe my ears. I mean, I knew your father left this old place to you—why, I'll never understand. But honestly, I expected you to call me, begging me to list it, just to get it off your hands."

Cari couldn't believe the audacity of this vile woman. "Why would I do that, Doreen? This is all I have left. You managed to get the rest."

Score one for Cari. The woman bristled to the point of turning as red as her dyed hair. "Your father left everything to me because he knew you'd just squander it away. I mean, c'mon, now, Cari, you don't actually think you can make a go of things in this old building, do you? The last tenant found out pretty quick that this place is way too far gone to run a business in. The utilities alone are over the top."

"From what I heard, you charged the last tenant too much rent and made too many demands for him to keep his photography and frame business going. I heard he moved to a new strip mall out on I-75 and he's doing great."

"That obnoxious man—I was glad to be rid of him. Always calling wanting something fixed, something changed. Impossible to deal with."

Doreen wouldn't give an inch, Cari knew. So she didn't try to argue with the woman. "I'm here to stay, Doreen. Get used to it."

Doreen grabbed her purse. "We'll see how long you last. You know, if you get desperate and want to sell, I'll cut you a deal. I'd planned to have this place torn down and if we both play our cards right, that can still happen. I'll be glad to take it off your hands and for a fair price, too."

"Why would you want to do that?" Cari asked. "Especially since you didn't take care of it when you were the landlord?"

"I had other priorities," Doreen shot back, the crow's feet around her eyes lined with too much concealer. "But now that your father is gone, well, I'm being a bit more aggressive in buying up more property." She swept the room with a harsh glance. "This should have stayed mine anyway. But I'm willing to buy it back and then maybe you can get out from under that mound of debt you brought back with you. If you change your mind, you know where to find me."

"I won't," Cari said, seething underneath her calm. Buy it back? Over her dead body.

She waited until the annoying clicking sound of Doreen's pumps had left the building then turned and ran out the back door to catch her breath. Leaning over the old railing, Cari felt sick to her stomach. Feeling tears of frustration she didn't dare shed, she held her head down and stared at an efficient ant trail moving steadily along the crack in the steps.

"We have to stop meeting like this."

She looked up to find Rick standing there staring at her, his smile friendly, his eyes calm.

Cari inhaled a deep breath. "You mean out in the alley, while I'm having a hissy fit?"

"Is that what you're having? I would have never guessed." Even though he was smiling, she appreciated the concern in his eyes.

Cari shook her hair off her face. "The wicked stepmother just paid me a friendly visit. Offered to buy me out. Can you believe that after the way she let this place get all run-down?"

Rick could tell she was hanging on by a thread, so he decided to keep things light. "Interesting that she'd even suggest that. I saw her taking off on her broom a couple of minutes ago so you're safe for now. If it's any consolation, she looked madder than a wet hornet."

"That does make me feel better," Cari replied, her eyes brightening. "I shouldn't let her get to me, but she does. She always has."

He sat down on the steps. "Got a minute to chat?"

She looked back inside. "Sure, none of this is going anywhere soon. And if I don't get a bank loan, it's not going to change anytime soon."

Rick understood she had a lot on her mind, but he needed to clarify something. "Look, Cari, about earlier at the diner when you asked me why I came back here?"

She put a hand over her eyes. "Oh, you mean when I was being completely nosy and out of line?"

"You weren't out of line. Nosy, yes, but out of line, no. It's just that I don't like to talk about my reasons for coming home. It's…complicated."

She slapped him on the arm. "Tell me something I don't know. I'm the queen of complicated homecomings."

His expression relaxed as he let out a long sigh. "Seems we both came back here to prove something to somebody, maybe?"

"Now who's being nosy?"

"Okay, I admit I'm wondering why you did come back and especially to such a challenging project?"

She put her head in her hands and stared down at her pink toenails. "My father left me this house. After our rocky relationship, that was enough reason for me."

Rick knew right then and there that Cari Duncan was someone special. And he could certainly understand the concept of needing something to hold on to, some sort of validation from a loved one. "Well, my father left the general store to my mother and my brother and me and one of the reasons I came home was to make sure we kept the legacy of his hard work alive and thriving. My brother Simon is an introverted artist, a boot maker who lost his wife a few years back. He didn't want anything to do with running a retail store and, honestly, he doesn't have time. And my mom tried her best to keep things going but she was working herself into an early grave, just like my dad. I had to come home to help. And…I needed to get away from Atlanta. You know, that same old crowd—hard to shake."

She didn't respond at first. She just sat looking at her feet. Then she said, "Funny, I loved the crowds. I lived in Athens after college and then moved to Atlanta. I had a good job—a career, with my own boutique and employees who worked hard selling my designs and other brands. I was in an upscale part of town and I was making pretty good money. I partied and laughed and played and spent way too much money trying to keep up with the crowd, trying to live up to this image I had of myself. It caught up with me when I fell for the wrong man. He decided he liked my cash flow a lot more than he loved me. I carried him after he lost his job—bad idea. I went into debt trying to buy his love. But I got rid of the slacker boyfriend and I got help from this very strict financial advisor who put me on a tough budget. I've managed to pay off a lot of it and I've even saved a little bit—a first for me."

"So you came home to start over."

She looked up finally, her eyes glistening like

muted turquoise glass. "Yes, and to fix the mistakes I made with my father. Only, it's too late, I think."

Rick looked around at the pines and oaks out beyond the honeysuckle vines lining the alley wall. A cool breeze moved over the oak trees and played through the wind chimes his mother had hung at the back door of the general store. "I'm sorry you lost your father, but if he left you this place then it has to mean something, right?"

"That's what I'm hoping," she said. "And that's what I want to figure out. Why did he leave me this house when he seemed so distant in life? Is that too weird?"

The little catch of doubt in her words held him. "Not weird at all. I think it's rather noble to want to fix this place up, to honor your parents."

"But foolish?"

"Nope. Just as long as you don't let she-who-won't-be-named get to you. That kind of distraction can derail you."

She stood up, her hands on the splintered banister again. "That will be the biggest challenge." Then she smiled down at him. "But thanks for explaining things to me about why *you* came back. I don't think my reasons are nearly so clear-cut, but here I am."

"I didn't explain everything. There was a woman involved. She wanted more than I could give, so we parted ways. Took me a while to get my head straight. So just like you, here I am."

"Who would have thunk it, huh?"

He got up, shaking his head. "I guess we're the next generation."

"I guess so. Knotwood Mountain has lots of potential. I never planned to leave here. I was just kind of driven away. And I thought I'd never be able to come back. But this opportunity came along at the right time."

"And so now you're back and you seem to have a lot of potential yourself," he said before he could hold back. Then he turned to get back to work. Even a good distraction was still a distraction, after all. "I guess I'll see you out here a lot, considering how I deal with women every day in the store and I have one very temperamental mother. I know how many hissy fits a woman can throw."

"You got that right," she said. "I'm pretty sure this won't be my last one. I'm waiting to hear from the contractor then I'm going begging at the bank. If I can't get a loan for an overhaul, I guess I'll just fix up the downstairs and open for business. Start out small and work my way up, hopefully."

Rick took in that bit of information. He had connections down at the bank, but Cari would be insulted if he offered his help. Still, he wanted to help. "Good luck," he said, his mind spinning as he watched her head back inside.

Then his cell phone rang. "Hello?"

"Rick, how you doing?"

"Jolena, what's up?"

"I need to talk to you. About a mutual friend."

"Oh, yeah, and who's that?"

"Cari Duncan," Jolena replied. "I've got a plan but I need your help."

"Name it," Rick said, wondering what Jolena had up her sleeve. And wondering why her timing always seemed to be just right.

When he heard her idea, he had to smile. This just might work and if it did, Cari would have to go along with it. She'd be crazy not to.

Chapter Four

Cari sat down with the bank officer, her palms sweaty, her breath held. Feeling the cool bump of the old leather chair against her legs, she waited for her fate, a sensation of ultimate doom sifting in her stomach. "So, Mr. Phillips, what's the verdict?"

The older gray-haired man stared through his bifocals at her, his stern expression and apologetic discomfort shouting out the answer she already knew. Clearing his throat, he glanced down at the papers in front of him. "Well, young lady, you seem to have a long history here. Lots of credit problems." He put the papers down and leaned back in his squeaky chair, the tuffs of peppered hair on the top of his head looking like twisted fence wire.

"Carinna, I have to be honest with you. It doesn't look good. Especially in this economy. Any kind of business loan is risky these days, but this…well…the boutique idea is a good one and it worked for you in

Atlanta, but while we always want to help new businesses here in Knotwood Mountain, financing a major renovation of that old house, well, that's just not something we're ready to do, I'm afraid."

"But you've seen my business plan," she said, ready to fight for herself. "It's solid, based on my success in Atlanta. I've paid off most of my credit card debt and I even have some start-up money saved. I know it's not much, but I'm willing to do a lot of the work myself to save money."

"What about your projections? We need to be sure you can make your monthly payments."

"My cash flow projections are low, but I did a conservative estimate on that. I fully expect business to pick up once I get some advertising out there. I'll find a way to pay back the loan." She hoped.

"All good points, but you don't have anything for collateral. Or anyone willing to cosign on this."

Cari didn't like his condescending tone or the implication that she didn't have another soul willing to take a risk on her. "I have the house sitting on a prime corner lot on First Street. That should be collateral enough."

"Not in this day and time," he replied, his ink pen thumping against his desk pad. "But you could probably sell it for a tidy sum and start over in some other location within the town. Your stepmother could help you there, I'm sure."

Cari sat still, refusing to have a meltdown in front of this grumpy old man. She'd done her homework, learned all about small business loans, talked to her financial advisor about the risks. She'd even joined the Small Business Association and found lots of online tips. And there was the slight possibility of getting grant money if she registered the house as a historical landmark.

All of that aside, it seemed this man was going to be her biggest obstacle, because he controlled the purse strings. But, she reminded herself, he was just doing his job. "I understand, Mr. Phillips. And I was shocked at the amount the contractor quoted me on the renovations, too. What if I did a little bit at a time? I don't have to do everything he's suggesting. I can just get the bottom floor updated and in working order so I can open my boutique. If I have it up and running before the Fourth, I know I'll clear enough to make the monthly loan payments as the year goes by. Christmas is always a good season here, too, with the winter tourists."

"You can't predict that," he replied, taking off his glasses. "Look, I knew your father. He was a solid businessman—knew a good piece of real estate when he saw it. Maybe he left you Duncan House so you could sell the whole thing and turn a nice profit. It's in an ideal location for a new business."

"Just not the new business I'm proposing," Cari replied, disappointment coloring her words.

"I'm afraid so. I can't lend you money on your name alone, although the bank did take that into consideration."

"But my good name just isn't enough, is it?" she asked, her finger hitting the report in front of him. "I got myself into a financial mess. But I worked hard over the last couple of years to straighten things out.

My business plan worked in Atlanta. I just let my personal finances get out of control."

"It takes longer than a couple of years to clear up bad credit and you know it," he retorted. "I do admire your fortitude, however."

Cari stood, her fingers grasping the strap of her bag. "And I admire your complete and unwavering honesty. But I'm not going to give up on this. I came to you first because this is where my father did his banking. I'll just try somewhere else."

"You'll have a tough row to hoe, Carinna. I wish you luck."

Cari turned to leave, dignity and the Duncan name making her spine straight. Too bad she hadn't considered coming to the bank *before* moving into the old house. But she wanted to live there, remodel or no remodel. She'd find a way to make this work, if she had to redo the house in square yard increments. And if she had to find a job somewhere else until she could get the boutique going.

She was on her way out the double doors when they swooshed open, the morning heat and sunshine warring with the sterile air-conditioning and doom and gloom of the annoying bank. Cari looked up and found herself blocked by Jolena and—

"Hi, Rick, what are you doing here?"

"He's with me," Jolena said, lifting a thumb toward Rick. "I mean, we're together—here to see you." She looked past Cari to Mr. Phillip's office. "Let's go back in and talk to the man, honey."

"What?" Cari tried to protest, but Rick's strong

hand on her elbow stopped her. When he guided her back toward the big office, she asked, "What's going on?"

"We have a plan," Rick said, not bothering to slow down. "Just be quiet and listen."

Not sure she liked being ordered around, even if he did look yummy and forceful in his white shirt and crisp jeans, Cari glanced from Jolena to Rick. "Jo, what's about to happen?"

"You getting your loan approved," Jolena replied, her dark eyes wide with intrigue and triumph. "Let Rick do the talking, okay?"

Cari didn't have much choice. Rick was already shaking hands with Mr. Phillips. What were they going to do, hold a gun on the man and demand he give her some money? Not a half-bad idea, although that would look like bank robbery to all the other customers.

"This is…highly unusual," Mr. Phillips said, his expression bordering on perturbed. "Rick, care to explain this unexpected visit?"

Rick directed Cari to a chair and gently pushed her down. "Yes, sir. Mrs. Beasley and I are here as concerned citizens of Knotwood Mountain. Since we're both business owners on First Street and since Miss Duncan wants to renovate Duncan House and move her already successful business here, and since she is the daughter of one of the town's most prominent citizens—now deceased—we're here to make you an offer you can't refuse."

Both Cari and Mr. Phillips asked the same question. "Which is?"

Jolena grinned and nodded toward Rick. "Tell him, Rick. Go ahead."

Rick pressed his hands onto the big desk, his knuckles splayed across the unfortunate report regarding Cari's finances. "We want to cosign a loan for Cari Duncan."

"What?" Cari gasped, shaking her head.

"Impossible," Mr. Phillips retorted.

"Not so quick," Rick said, finally sitting down to talk business. "Think about this. Jolena and I both have a vested interest in the upkeep of First Street, and let's face it, Duncan House had been an eyesore for years now. While we appreciate that Cari's father was ill for many of those years and that his wife, Doreen, did her best to run his real estate company, we couldn't help but notice the second Mrs. Duncan tended to neglect Duncan House."

He gave Cari an encouraging look. "It's been vacant for over a year now and, well, it just doesn't sit well with us that the house has become so unappealing and run-down." He sat up, his tone going from conversational to serious. "It doesn't sit well with the chamber of commerce or the city council either. And I'm sure it doesn't impress the locals and the tourists, not at all. I get complaints on a daily basis."

Mr. Phillips lifted a hand. "But—"

Rick went right on talking. "I've thought of buying the place myself, but you know I have my hands full with the general store. And Jolena has a good thing going with the diner, but her customers have to stare at that boarded-up old house all the time. And that's a shame."

"A real crying shame," Jolena added, her chin bobbing.

"Why, just the other day, Mrs. Meadows asked me what we intended to do about that old house. And when I told her none other than little Cari Duncan herself, the daughter of James Duncan, was coming back to fix up the place, well, I can't tell you how excited Mrs. Meadows was. She even said she'd get the Garden Club in on helping with the landscaping. Something about getting the place on the National Historic Registry, too. And you know she's one of those Daughters of the Revolution—those women can sure stir up a stink when they want something done. And Mrs. Meadows really wants something done about Duncan House. But only if she knows someone is willing to invest in the renovations. And do them up proper, of course."

"But—"

Rick went in for the kill. "No buts, just a good solid plan to keep First Street pristine and tourist-ready. That's why we're here, Mr. Phillips. To do our civic duty."

Cari tried to speak. "But—"

"No buts," Jolena said, elbowing her in the ribs. "Work with us here, suga'."

"I can't let y'all do this," Cari said, trying to stand. Two strong hands grabbed her and put her back in her place.

"Yes, you can," Rick replied. "Because we're not actually doing this for you—although we like you and we're glad you're back. It's for the overall good of this community." He winked at her then turned back to Mr. Phillips. "I'd hate to have to take this matter before the city council later this month. You know how revved up those good old boys can get when they think we're losing tourist dollars."

Mr. Phillips looked like a whipped puppy. "This is highly unusual and a bit unorthodox."

Jolena let out a bubbling giggle. "It's all about a good cause, Mr. Phillips. Just think what a glowing report we could give for the bank, knowing that you took a risk on a hometown girl and her dreams? Her daddy would be so proud. And I'm sure it will make a favorable impression on others who might want to do business with you."

Rick nodded. "Cari gets the loan and we both cosign as collateral. If things don't work out and she can't pay, Jolena and I will take over the payments and co-own the property then we'll decide what to do with it. How's that for a solid plan?"

"I just don't know," Mr. Phillips said.

But Cari could see the wheels spinning in his head. The man knew he was sitting across from two prominent members of the community, two people with a lot of pull and power. Two people with determined looks and a lot of name-dropping to back those looks. As surprised and shocked as she was, Cari was glad to have them in her corner. Not sure if she should be thankful or full of denial and refusal, she had to speak up.

"I can't allow this," she said. "I just can't."

"You don't have any other choice," Mr. Phillips

said. "If these two are willing to take the risk then I guess I'm willing to loan you the money. But not the whole amount, Cari. I'll give you fifty thousand to get you started—that's half, and that's generous for a small-business loan. If you fail, your friends here will be out twenty-five thousand each. Unless you can find a way to salvage this crazy plan."

Cari couldn't breathe. She'd just gone from being broke and with no hope to having money and a lot of new hope. But it would mean she owed Jolena a great deal. And Rick Adams, too.

Was she so pathetic that the best-looking man in town felt sorry for her? Sorry enough to float her a loan? That didn't make a bit of sense, but it was so sweet. Wasn't it?

"I don't know," she said, shaking her head. "I wanted to do this on my own."

"You will be doing it on your own, honey," Jolena said, her hand touching Cari's. "It's a loan from the bank—and that's what you needed. We're just the insurance policy. And we talked this over good and thorough and we both agree you won't let us down."

Before Cari could form another protest, the handshake agreement was in place and the paperwork was being drawn up.

"You can all meet back here in a few days to sign the papers," Mr. Phillips said, smiling at last. He reached out a hand to Rick. "Good doing business with you."

Rick pointed to Cari. "You're doing business with this woman, Mr. Phillips. She's the boss. Don't forget that."

Cari appreciated the way he'd shifted the power back to her. But she wanted to have a long talk with him when she could find her pulse again.

"Thank you, Mr. Phillips," she finally said. "I'll be in touch."

The old man nodded and gave her a grudging smile. "You must be a lot like your father, Cari. He always had champions, friends willing to vouch for him no matter what. That's how he formed such a solid business." He glanced down at his desk and mumbled, "Too bad his current wife can't be the same way." Looking embarrassed, he quickly amended that. "But it seems *you* have two very high-up champions of your own. Not a bad way to start out, let me tell you."

Jolena pointed a finger toward the ceiling. "She has one very, very high-up champion—the Lord wants Cari to grow and prosper. I think that's why He brought her home."

"I can't fight that kind of power," Mr. Phillips replied with a grin. "Now, if y'all don't mind, I do have some *scheduled* appointments today."

Cari waited until they walked out onto the sidewalk before she turned on them. "I can't believe you two. You steamrolled me into this. Now I not only owe the bank, but I owe both of you, too."

"A simple thank-you would be nice," Jolena said, giving her a stern look.

"Thank you," she said, letting out a long breath. "But honestly, I don't know how to thank you. I feel like a charity case."

"You are no such thing," Rick replied. "Jolena and

I had a long talk and decided this would be a good business decision. Doreen purposely let that house go to ruin. This is our way of taking care of business. So don't go all noble and self-righteous on us. We intend to see a return on our investment, let me tell you."

Jolena chimed in. "Yeah. Our best hope is that we never have to take over that loan, honey. While we'd love to own rental property on First Street, we'd rather just sign off and be done with it when push comes to shove."

"No pressure there," Cari said, wondering how she'd managed to get herself in this fix. "But I am grateful. I can't begin to tell you what this means to me."

Jolena gave her a quick hug. "I've got work to do." Then she leaned close. "Your parents gave me a start twenty years ago. They sold me the diner at a rock-bottom price and even did owner financing for me. I owe them both, honey. This is my way of paying back a grateful debt."

A grateful debt. Cari liked that concept. And she was grateful. "I'll work hard to make sure I do the same, then."

She watched as Jolena pranced down the flower-lined street toward the diner. Then Cari turned to Rick. "Okay, I get why Jolena helped me. She's obligated since she's my godmother. But you, Rick? I don't understand that part. You barely know me. Care to explain why you just put your neck on the line for me?"

He started to speak, but she interrupted him. "And

don't give me that good-business-good-neighbor-good-for-the-community speech, even though it's a very persuasive speech. Just tell me why you'd take a chance on me like this? I'm thankful and I'm humbled, and I'm going to work hard to show you how much I appreciate this. But I really need to know why you stood up for me in there. What's in it for you?"

Chapter Five

Rick couldn't believe what she'd just asked him. "What do you mean, what's in it for me? You make it sound as if I deliberately bullied you into getting your loan because I had a hidden agenda."

"Well, you sorta did, didn't you?"

Wondering if he had made a mistake—a big one—he couldn't decide if she was thrilled that she had a chance to fix up Duncan House or if she detested him for trying to help. "You don't trust me, do you?"

"It's not that. Okay, maybe I just don't trust your motives. We haven't seen each other since high school. And we weren't exactly chummy back then."

He hit his head with his hand then scrubbed it down his face. "You can't be serious? You think I have ulterior motives?"

"Do you?"

Rick grunted, trying to think of a retort. "I called

myself trying to help another human being. Who messed you up this much?"

She shifted, throwing that ridiculously large leather bag over her shoulder. "Okay, so I have trust issues. I trusted my father and look where that got me. I've had one bad relationship after another and I almost went to the poorhouse just trying to impress the last man I dated. You'd think I'd run screaming from any man who offers me help. And yet, here I stand, taking handouts on the street." She shrugged then let out a long breath. "I came back here to learn to stand on my own two feet. And already, I've been rescued. Do you know how that makes me feel?"

So that was it. She was shielding herself by second-guessing him and accusing him. Maybe because he'd embarrassed her by springing this on her? "Hey, this is *not* a handout and I didn't do this to rescue you. You've had some tough breaks so Jolena and I wanted to give you a fair start by backing you on this one thing. But if you feel that way just march right back over to the bank and tell old man Phillips you don't want his money. It'll sure be a big worry off my mind."

She stared up at him with those iridescent eyes, her humility clear on her tightly drawn face. Rick watched as she frowned then looked down at her gladiator sandals, her freckled skin blushing a becoming red. "I'm so stupid," she finally mumbled. "Look, Rick, I don't mean to sound horrible and unappreciative. What you just did in there for me is so incredible, but it's hard to believe."

He shouldn't have fussed at her, but at least she was

calming down a little bit. "Is it so hard to believe that people around here are willing to help other people?"

"Yes," she said, nodding her head. "Yes, it is. I left here broken and afraid—an outcast—and I missed my father so much. I couldn't come back though. I just couldn't. I guess I built this protective shell around myself. And I forgot what real kindness is all about. I'm sorry. So sorry."

Rick wished he hadn't been so impulsive and harsh with her. "Look, it's okay. Maybe we should have discussed the plan with you before ambushing you at the bank. You think it's charity but it's not. It's just a cosign on a loan. A business decision. You don't owe me anything and I don't expect you to grovel every time you see me."

She actually grinned at that, her features relaxing. "I never planned on groveling. Maybe baking you a pie or something—even if I can't cook very well."

"You could just buy me a pie from Jolena. I love her strawberry icebox pies."

"That I can do, whenever my loan comes through that is."

He reached out to shake her hand. "Then we're square, you and me?"

"I guess so. It's just so odd, knowing you helped me like this."

"Oh, I cosign loans with a lot of the women I meet. It's just my way of doing things. And it's a great way to break the ice."

She slapped at his arm, her smile genuine. "You make me laugh. How is that possible?"

"Because I'm a clown? Maybe a clown with little forethought on some things?"

"No, because you're a good, sweet man. An old acquaintance, but new friend. And it's been a long time since I've had a friend I could really trust."

He had to laugh at that quick turnaround. "Oh, so you trust me now?"

"Yes, I do. I don't know why, but I do." She moved away. "Do you trust me—to make good on that loan?"

"I'm going to try. It'll be mighty hard explaining to my mom and brother if you don't. I don't know how they'd go for being co-owners of Duncan House."

Her eyes widened. "You didn't discuss this with them?"

Rick grimaced. He hadn't meant to let that slip. "We didn't have time, and besides, I don't discuss a lot of what I do with them. They both tend to lean on me for the big decisions. And with this, it was today or never at the bank. Jolena and I had to move fast, especially when we saw you coming out of the bank, looking disappointed."

Because she looked so worried now, he said, "Hey, I have a hefty sum of money at that bank. Mr. Phillips knows that. It's okay. I sold a lot of my stock and set up some certificates of deposit when I moved back here. All of my investments flow through the bank, so they owe me one."

"You never cease to amaze me," she replied. "You are a smart businessman. I can learn from that."

"I can't complain," he said. "But if I don't get back to the store, my mom's gonna send out the stock boy to find me. Even smart businessmen still have to answer to their mothers sometimes."

She hesitated then smiled at him. "Thanks again. I mean it. I won't forget what you did." Slanting her head to one side, she said, "I guess this makes us partners in a way, right?"

Rick hadn't considered that angle. "I guess it does at that. But I'm more of a silent partner. Now, Jolena, that's a whole 'nother thing."

She smiled again. "I can handle Jolena. And I owe you both a big debt of gratitude."

When she reached out her hand, he took it, shaking it with businesslike precision. And with an acute awareness of how tiny and dainty her fingers felt against his.

She must have felt the same strong current. Her eyes lifted to meet his, surprise pooling inside their depths.

Rick let go then started walking backward toward the store. "Maybe, just maybe, you can reward me for my good deed one day."

"Oh, yeah. How's that?"

"By wearing those red shoes. I'm going to save them just for you—size seven. Sort of like a housewarming gift."

"Hey, how do you know my size?"

"I have my sources," he said, grinning at the pretty glow in her eyes. "See you later, Princess."

Her laughter echoed after him, making him glad he'd stepped up to help her. Cari was a nice woman. Maybe she just needed someone to show her that same nice so she'd recognize it in herself.

* * *

A few days later, Cari was busy unpacking the rest of the stuff she'd brought from Atlanta. She'd sold off most of her furniture and a lot of her clothes. She'd kept only what she could put in her midsize economy sedan and a small rental trailer hitched to her car. Since she couldn't do much upstairs right now besides sleep, she put her old leather love seat in what used to be the dining room, across from the big parlor that would serve as the main space for her shop.

The big bay window had a window box, so she cleaned and scrubbed that inside out to make sure no cobwebs or other critters were inside. She stored some clothes and books there for now. A couple of chintzy chairs she'd salvaged from a garage sale and re-covered finished the make-do room. Thankfully the windows had drapery—old and ugly—but the bright blue heavy curtains did allow her some privacy at night and they picked up the blue flowers in the chairs.

After she'd tidied up her temporary sleeping quarters upstairs by placing a favorite quilt over the air mattress and setting out an old fern stand for a nightstand, she tackled the small downstairs bath again, hoping to add some flowers and a couple of botanical prints to make the room brighter. It had been installed long after the original house was built in what must have been a storage closet in a long hallway, but the plumbing worked fairly well if she remembered to jiggle the handles on everything. She'd just finished scrubbing it down for the third time and putting out some toiletries when she heard footsteps hitting the porch.

Peeking up the hallway, Cari saw a teenage boy peering inside the beveled glass on the old front door.

She hurried up the hallway then cracked open the door. "Can I help you?"

"Cari?"

It took her a minute. A familiar sensation swept over her as she stared at the young man. His blond hair was long and shaggy and his blue eyes wide with a hopefulness that tugged at her heart. "Brady?"

He grinned. "Yeah. Can I come in?"

"Of course." She opened the door and instantly hugged him close, tears forming in her eyes. "You've gotten so big."

He stood back, obviously uncomfortable with the hugging situation. "I was only eight when you left. I'm sixteen now. I just got my driver's license."

"You're driving. Oh, wow."

Her stepbrother had grown up. She called him her stepbrother even though she'd only lived in her father's house for a couple of years after he'd married Doreen. But she'd been the built-in babysitter during that time and while Brady's sister Bridget had been a brat at fourteen, Brady had been a confused little boy who needed some attention.

"Mom doesn't know I'm here," he said, looking down at his big feet. "I just wanted to say hi."

"I'm glad you came by. Want a soda?"

He nodded then glanced around. "I can't believe you're gonna live in this old place. You know Mom hates this house."

"Yeah, I kind of gathered that," Cari replied, careful

not to say anything derogatory about Doreen to her son. "I've always loved it, I guess because I grew up here. I felt like a princess living in a big castle." But she'd learned that fairy tales were just that—tales that never had a happy ending in reality.

Brady slung his shaggy hair off his face. "Bridget thinks it's lame, you living here. She listens to whatever Mom says. And Mom isn't happy about it. She wanted to keep this property and sell it for a profit or something like that."

Cari let that slide as she reached into her ice chest and took out a drink. "How's Bridget? Is she off to college yet?"

He popped the top and took a swig of his soda. "She was in school but she flunked out, only Mom doesn't want anybody to know that. She's home for the summer. I don't see her much so I don't know if she's going back to school. She likes to hang with her friends and party a lot." He rolled his eyes. "And she has like this major crush on your neighbor next door."

Cari furrowed her brow. "Who's that?"

"Rick Adams," he said. "Have you met him? That older dude who runs the general store? Mr. Goody Two-shoes—always doing something to 'help give back' as he calls it. Bridget thinks he's so all that. She's always going in there to buy stuff so she can flirt with him. Mom tells her he's a *fine catch,* whatever that means."

Cari's heart did a strange flip. Trying to wrap her mind around Bridget and Rick as a couple, she decided she'd have to withhold judgment until she actually saw Bridget. "A bit young for him, don't you think?"

"She likes older men. Especially men who can buy her things."

"Oh, I see."

She did see. Bridget had always been self-centered and shallow and it sounded as if that hadn't changed. The younger girl had taken Cari's place in James Duncan's affection. Cari had witnessed that right from the start. Remembering her pretty blue sandals, she wondered how many pairs of shoes Bridget had now. It didn't really matter, except for the principle of the thing. It wasn't fair but then, she'd learned that a lot of things in life were not fair. Besides, what Rick did with his spare time was his business.

Did he return Bridget's affections?

Putting that burning question out of her mind, she focused on Brady. "Hey, I was about to get a bite to eat over at Jolena's. Want to come?"

Brady looked hesitant at first then finally bobbed his head. "I could go for a burger, yeah."

"Okay then. Let me shut things down here and we'll walk over."

He waited for her to grab her purse and cell phone. "So you're gonna open a shop here? Mom said it sounded like junk to her."

Cari gritted her teeth at that remark. "Not junk." She wasn't in the mood to keep explaining. "I design things—and redesign other things. Plus, I go to market and find clothes and accessories that I know women will love. It's fun and I did pretty good back in Atlanta."

Until the rent went up in the quaint little shop where

she'd been for three years and her ex-boyfriend drained most of her bank account because he'd lost his own job. But Brady wouldn't be interested in all that. No one was interested in hearing a hard-luck story from this particular princess.

"I have to come up with a name for my shop. Got any ideas?"

Brady shrugged and flipped his hair. "No. I guess it won't matter what you call the place. The chicks will love it."

"Chicks?" She pushed at his shoulder. "So are you into chicks?"

"Maybe." He grinned but didn't say anything else.

Cari glanced around at the tourists mingling here and there along the street. She needed to get in on some of this foot traffic. The village was gearing up for the summer festival, which would end with a big Fourth of July celebration in the town square. The crape myrtle lining the long street was blooming in dark pinks and vivid purples. The ancient magnolia trees were bursting with lemon-and-vanilla-scented white blossoms and the hydrangeas lining the park and square were fat with brilliant blue flowers that looked like pudgy sponges. All the merchants on the street had colorful potted plants by their doors and American flags flying in a symmetrical, solid row, giving a rainbow effect as the flags flapped in the breeze and the sun rays shimmered off the asphalt.

"It's good to be home," she said, glancing over at Brady. "A lot has changed since I left."

"Yeah, I'm glad you're back."

Smiling, she thought you couldn't get more Middle America than Knotwood Mountain. She'd always enjoyed the town festivals as a child. It would be so different, being involved as an adult and an actual local merchant. If only she could make this work. First, she'd plant her own container gardens with the cuttings Jolena had given her to root.

Finding roots. That's what she wanted and needed. Her father wasn't here anymore, but his shadow hung over everything she did. And she wanted him to know, to see, that she was trying so hard. She wanted that shadow to become a shield.

Please, Lord, I need Your help. I need guidance and self-control and a lot of patience. A whole lot of patience.

That last plea would certainly come in handy, she thought a few minutes later. After Cari and Brady found a booth by the big window of the diner, a bright white sports car zoomed up to the curb in front of the general store and skidded to a stop.

And out stepped Bridget Stillman, wearing a tight, short floral dress and high-heeled white sandals. Her long blond hair fell in delicate waves down her back as she exited the tiny car, a designer bag strapped around her wrist.

Brady glanced over at Cari then back out the window. "Right on time. She does that just about every afternoon. She's angling for a date with him."

Cari waited a beat then asked, "And does he ever take her up on that?"

Brady shrugged. "I've seen them walk over here

together sometimes and a couple of times they've driven off in her car. Not my problem." He eyed the menu then grinned over at her. "I'm ready for that burger."

Cari nodded, focusing on the special of the day to keep from straining her gaze toward the general store. She'd buy Brady a burger, but her own appetite had disappeared in a puff of white car and shiny chrome, long blond hair and even longer shapely legs. It shouldn't bother her that Bridget was young, gorgeous and apparently living off the fruits of James Duncan's labor. Really it shouldn't bother her at all.

But it did. Which made her even more determined to become a success in the face of Doreen's obvious doubt and scorn. She'd have to work twice as hard to achieve about half as much success. She couldn't let Rick and Jolena down and she refused to let herself down. This would be hard, but it would be worth it. So worth it.

Maybe living well could be her best revenge. And maybe forgetting about how Rick Adams made her smile could be her challenge for the day, or maybe for the rest of her life.

Chapter Six

~

Jolena ambled over to Cari's booth. "Well, look what we have here. It's been many a year since I've seen you two in here together." She glanced across the street at the sports car then rolled her eyes. "Everything okay?"

"Yes," Cari said, shooting Jolena a warning look. "Brady inhaled his burger."

"And what about you?" Jolena asked, eyeing Cari's half-eaten club sandwich. "Not hungry today?"

"I had one of your cinnamon rolls for breakfast," Cari said by way of explanation. "Still full."

"It's nearly dinnertime," Jolena shot back. "You can take the rest of this home for later."

Cari nodded and pushed her plate toward Jolena. "I can't keep taking food from you, Jolena. I have to be a paying customer."

"Are you gonna get on that charity kick again?" Jolena asked, her tone low. "I'll keep a tab for you the way I do with Rick."

Cari looked over at Brady. The boy was absorbed in the last of his French fries. "I appreciate that and I will pay up. We had this conversation on the phone, remember? Right after you swooped in and saved my bacon at the bank the other day. I'd say that's enough, tab or no tab."

Jolena chuckled. "I get it, honey. But I don't mind feeding you either. You're family. It's that simple."

Cari was touched by Jolena's declaration. "Thanks."

After Jolena winked at her then walked away with the remains of her meal, she watched Brady finish his fries. Did she have any family left? Her grandparents were all dead and her father and mother had both been only children. No aunts, uncles or even cousins that she knew of. Maybe Jolena was right. Maybe Cari had to create her own family now that she was alone.

Staring over at Brady, she decided at least she could keep close to him. He didn't seem to mind that she wasn't on his mother's Christmas-card list. Maybe, just like her, he needed a friend, someone to talk to now and then.

"Brady, do you and your sister go to church?" she asked, thinking she needed to do that very thing herself. Her mother had always told her that the church was where you found the community.

He shrugged. "I do sometimes when something cool's going on in Youth. Bridget never goes. She sleeps too late every Sunday."

"And your mom?"

"Oh, she goes. But only to look for clients and to

'network' as she calls it. She sits right up there at the front."

"Of course," Cari replied, hoping the acid in her tone didn't sound too sizzling.

"Do you go?"

"I haven't since I got here last week. Maybe I'll see you there this coming Sunday."

He frowned. "Yeah, whatever."

That attitude didn't bode well, Cari thought. But since she'd had the same attitude for years now, maybe she should sit up and take notice herself. "Well, I enjoyed having this late lunch with you. I hope you'll come by and see me again."

He looked out the window. "I will. I like having stuff to do. I try to stay out of Mom's hair."

"I could use some help fixing up the house," she said. "You saw how big those high-ceilinged rooms are. It's gonna take me at least a week of steady work to get the rooms I want to use for the boutique painted and decorated. But I want to do some of it myself to save money."

"I haven't done much painting but I'm willing to try," he said. "I have some buddies who might want to help out, if that's okay."

"Sure. The more the merrier. Do you have a girl-friend?"

He looked sheepish. "Kinda. Just a good friend."

"That works," she replied, her attention wandering across the street. "Friendship has merit."

And that's when she saw them—Rick and Bridget—emerging from the general store, laughing and talking.

And they were headed right for the diner.

"Oh, it's getting late," she said to Brady. "I guess I'd better get back over to the house."

"Oh, okay." He drained his soda then hopped up. "Thanks for the food."

"Sure. Come by next week and we'll see about training you to paint."

He nodded then turned toward the door, but he took off in the opposite direction of his sister and Rick—not that they even bothered looking up. In fact, a moving truck could have easily come barreling up the street toward them and they wouldn't have noticed.

Cari thought about ducking out the back, but Jolena blocked her where she stood. "Don't go running now. What did your mama teach you about being a lady?"

Cari made a face. "Not to trip up pretty girls in short dresses who've taken advantage of my deceased father's good graces?" Glaring out the window, she eyed Bridget. "Bless her little heart."

"That would be one part of the lesson."

"Oh, all right. I have to face obstacles with my head held high and a sweet smile plastered on my face." She smiled, big and bright. "How's this?"

"As fake as plastic petunias but it's a start." Jolena nodded toward the door. "That girl ain't got nothing on you, baby. You're a Duncan, remember?"

"Yes, ma'am." Cari fluffed her hair and stood firm, her shoulders back. "Bring it on, Blondie."

Jolena let out another chuckle as the bells on the door chimed when it swooshed open. "Rick Adams, did you come back for more of my strawberry pie?"

Rick tore his gaze away from Bridget then glanced at Cari in surprise. "Hello, ladies. Bridget wanted some lemonade."

"So Rick was sweet enough to keep me company," she said, her sights trained on Cari. Giving Cari a dismissive once-over, she said, "I heard you were back."

Cari waited then realized that was all she was going to get. "Yes, I am. And I'm very busy. Just came over for a bite to eat. I saw Brady. He sure has grown."

Bridget twirled her hair and lifted one elegant eyebrow. "That brat. He's whining for a new car, but Mom says he has to wait until he has his for-real driver's license." Then she lifted the other brow. "What was he doing hanging around with you?"

Cari glanced at Rick to see if the same distaste Bridget so obviously had for her had rubbed off on him. He looked embarrassed but his expression went into panic mode, followed by what looked like an I-can-explain mode.

Hoping to protect Brady, she said, "We just ran into each other. No harm done. It was good to see him. And you, too." She moved to leave, hoping she didn't choke on that little fib, but Bridget just stood there, blocking her way. Giving Rick a quick glance, Cari said, "Excuse me."

Rick pulled Bridget out of the way. "See you later, Cari."

Cari didn't answer. Her skin burned with the heat of humiliation as she hurried across the street. She didn't dare look back or hope that Rick would come after her. Why should he? They were just friends, plain and simple if she didn't count the fact that he'd agreed to cosign a loan with her.

While he carried on with her stepsister right in front of her eyes.

What did she expect?

Once she was inside her house, she threw her bag on a nearby chair and walked straight through to the back of the house. She needed privacy and air. And today, she needed to escape, but Rick might find her on the porch. So she headed upstairs, careful to make her way to the turret room. Watching where she stepped, she managed to find a clean spot on the old octagon window seat. And she sat there, looking out through one of the broken windowpanes, wondering why what used to be her sanctuary now felt like her prison. She didn't need to count on anyone for anything, really. She couldn't.

She needed to remember that Rick Adams owed her nothing. Nothing at all. He still was and would always be the blond-haired-long-legged-cheerleader type. Not her type, not even on the radar. Except to hand out favors and make her laugh.

She'd have to accept that Rick was a business acquaintance and a silent partner in a unique business deal. She'd just have to settle for that.

But that would be the only thing she'd settle for.

Rick gave Jolena a pleading look then glanced out the door, watching Cari's retreating figure as she practically ran across the street. Jolena shot him a penetrating, not-so-pleased look but kept her cool. Torn between going after Cari or just minding his own business, he was a man trapped.

And being a typical man, he did nothing to lessen that situation. For now. He'd talk to Cari later. After he managed to get away from Bridget.

"I'll get someone to bring your lemonades," Jolena said, turning so fast her braided hair did a dance around her shoulders.

Bridget seemed oblivious to the undercurrents, Rick noted. But then, Bridget was pretty much oblivious to everyone and everything around her. Shrugging, she giggled. "Cari sure left in a hurry. I think if you'd said 'Boo' she would have fainted. She always was a little skittish around men." Her smile indicated that she, on the other hand, did not have a problem with men.

And why had he let her drag him over here when he had so much to do before closing time in less than an hour?

"Cut her some slack," he said after they'd settled onto bar stools at the counter. Glad there weren't many customers in the diner this time of day, he willed the waitress to hurry with the lemonade. Thankfully, the young girl came right up with two tall plastic cups brimming with sliced lemons and crushed ice. "Cari's had it rough lately."

"So I hear," Bridget said before she slurped her drink. "But, you know, she brought it all on herself. I mean, she always, always caused trouble with her daddy, and he was such a sweet old man—most of the time. Then she went off and got herself all in a mess, money wise. Mama says Cari couldn't manage her money if Ben Franklin himself was sitting right beside her."

Rick watched as Jolena marched toward them, her eyes burning with all the signs to do feminine battle. "I have to get back to work, Bridget. Walk with me."

He grabbed his drink with one hand and her skinny arm with the other. "Thanks, Jolena. Put it on my tab."

"Uh-huh," Jolena said with a grunt. "You'd better pay up on that tab real soon."

Rick knew a threat when he heard one. He was so in hot water. And honestly, he wasn't sure what he'd done to bring this on. Except walk across the street with Bridget, of course. He should have remembered how territorial women could be. And that they never ever let go of a grudge.

Bridget pulled away from him when they were outside. "Hey, I thought we were going to have a nice, quiet talk before you took me out to dinner."

Rick silently counted to ten then prayed for patience. "And I thought we were just getting a quick drink before I got back to work."

She actually stomped her foot. "But dinner, remember? You keep promising and then you always cancel out at the last minute."

How to make her understand? "Bridget, I've never promised you dinner." In fact, he'd never once asked her out to dinner, for that matter. She did the asking and the finagling and tried her level best to manipulate him into a meal. Which he always managed to graciously refuse. Or so he thought. Maybe he was just too nice for his own good. His mother always told him he had a hard time turning away from a pretty, pouting face. And he had the battle scars to prove it, didn't he?

But back to pretty, pouting faces. Bridget had cornered the market on that particular tactic. "Look, I can't go to dinner with you. I have to go out to my ranch and check on the livestock." And find a few quiet hours for himself. No wonder his brother was so reclusive.

Her eyes sparkled with a new plan. "I could go with you. I've never even seen your dusty old ranch. We could go horseback riding then build a campfire."

Rick saw the romantic hope in her baby blues. Trying hard to think of a kind way to extract himself, he said, "My mom's coming with me to visit my brother. And you know Simon doesn't like to be disturbed."

She leaned close, her heavy floral perfume making his nose twitch. "I wouldn't bother your big brother, I promise. I'd focus all of my attention on you."

Once not so long ago, Rick would have been tempted by that flirtatious offer. Once. But he'd changed since then, learned a few things about the female mind-set. And he'd been burned so badly, he was still gun-shy. So why had he allowed Bridget to keep flirting with him and why had he decided getting a cold lemonade with the woman was a good idea, especially when he'd ran smack into Cari and her obvious disapproval in the process?

Because sometimes, in spite of his best intentions, he fell back into the old habits.

Calling out in a silent plea to Heaven, he waited for a few minutes then regained his composure. "Bridget, I can't. I just can't, okay?"

Her sweetness and light turned to anger and darkness in a flutter of overly made-up eyelashes and a twist of tightly held pink lips. "Oh, all right then. Forget it. I've got other plans anyway." And with that, she tossed her still-full lemonade into the nearest trash can and pranced to her convertible. Before Rick could turn around, she was peeling out onto the street in a blur of shining white that caused the crape myrtle to bend in the wind.

That was unpleasant, he thought. He looked around, hoping no one had witnessed that little scene.

And saw a face staring down at him from the turret room of Duncan House. A face full of regret and disapproval. Cari's pretty, perturbed face.

Rick watched as she quickly disappeared from the old, broken window, thinking she really did look a lot like a princess trapped in a castle.

His throat dry, he finished off his lemonade and went back inside to his work, wishing he could figure out women.

And wishing he could explain to one woman in particular that he wasn't as shallow and despicable as she seemed to think he was, in spite of his actions to the contrary.

Chapter Seven

~❧~

A few days later, Cari had just settled down to get some serious paperwork out of the way when a loud knock came at the door. For a small town, this place sure had a lot of foot traffic. That would certainly come in handy when she was open for business. When she opened the door, a petite young woman stood there holding a large crystal vase full of lilies, orchids and tulips.

"Hi, I'm Christie, from Knotwood Florist around the corner. Delivery for Cari Duncan."

"That's me," Cari said, her hands going to her mouth. "What beautiful flowers. Are you sure you got the right address?"

"They're for *you*—Cari Duncan," the girl said, clearly excited. "Look at the colors—I've never seen so many shades of red and pink. And the white lilies—perfect. We rarely get such a big, specific order."

That word *perfect* stuck inside Cari's throbbing

head. She stared at the flowers Christie held with such pride. "Is there a card?"

"Oh, yes," Christie said, clapping her hands. "There. Read it out loud." The girl sure had a lot of enthusiasm for her job.

Cari couldn't help but smile at Christie's glee, but she couldn't share her joy. Instead, a deep shuddering dread centered itself inside her heart as she pulled the tiny card out of the envelope. She should be thrilled about receiving such pretty flowers, but her heart wasn't in it this morning. She'd been too busy trying to salvage her leftover bills. And she had a feeling these were "apologetic" flowers from a man she barely knew. A man she shouldn't be so mad at right now since it really wasn't her business who he shared lemonade with. And yet, her disappointment seemed to be coloring her every mood this morning.

"Read the card," Christie urged, her vested interest in this delivery cute if a bit annoying.

Cari set the flowers down on the window box then opened the card. "'These reminded me of you,'" she read out loud, her hand going to her throat. "'All vibrant and brilliant—and very determined. Welcome home, Cari.'"

The message was signed "Rick."

"Rick Adams," Christie said with a dreamy expression glazing over her eyes. "He came in himself and picked them out. Wow, oh, wow. I wish he'd send me flowers."

"You're too young to wish such things," Cari retorted, then instantly regretted her words. But honestly, was every female in this town in love with the man? "I mean, one day you'll get flowers from a nice man, I'm sure."

Christie looked downright crestfallen. "Yes, a girl can dream, can't she?"

Cari wanted to tell her, no, a girl shouldn't dream. A girl should have a solid, realistic mind-set in both love and business. A girl shouldn't sit around waiting for some prince to come riding up the hill to rescue her. Cari should know since she'd kissed a few frogs. But she didn't have the heart to burst that very big bubble of sheer joy Christie seemed to be floating around in. "Yes, a girl can dream. And the flowers are beautiful."

Christie bobbed her head. "They are." Then she frowned. "I know he's dreamy and all that, but I've never heard of *determined* flowers. What kind of man sends a message like that?"

Grabbing her wallet, Cari handed Christie a tip and gave her a verbal explanation, thinking this question-asking delivery girl wouldn't make it in the aloof, urban big city. "One who's even more determined than these flowers," she replied. "He thinks I'm going to fall for the tried-and-true method, apparently. Thanks for bringing them over."

"No problem," Christie said. Then she pointed a finger toward Cari. "I'll be watching you two."

Cari smiled and waved the girl down the steps then shut the door. "You and about half the town."

After Christie left, Cari let her fingers trail over the fat white lily blossoms. These flowers were a bright spot on a warm summer day. Just what she'd needed after coming face-to-face with both of her stepsiblings the other day. For some reason, she couldn't get seeing Rick with Bridget out of her mind though.

And she knew exactly what Rick's message meant. Tulips and lilies and orchids were no shrinking violets. They forced themselves from the ground into blossoming flowers. Hadn't she done pretty much the same thing when she'd finally found her footing and changed her life? Hadn't she come back home to stand firm against her stepmother? Was she truly blossoming here, or would she wilt back into that passive violet she'd once been?

Maybe Rick was trying to tell her something by giving her a subtle compliment. Or maybe he was just feeling guilty that he'd avoided her over the past couple of days, after he'd been seen hanging out with the enemy.

The enemy? Was that how she saw Doreen and her children? Or was this enemy of her own making? Hadn't she come here seeking revenge? Or would she wind up being miserable herself? How could she be happy if she had to constantly worry about this other family who'd swooped in and messed up her life?

Cari was so confused she couldn't be sure what her own motives were, or what Rick's motives were either, but for some strange reason this mix of flowers did make her smile in spite of her doubts and disappointments.

And that was very unsettling.

Even more unsettling, three hours later he called

and left a message on her cell phone, asking her out to dinner that night. She had to wonder how he'd gotten her number, but then the man always managed to do things that surprised her.

Still, she wasn't going out to dinner with him, no matter how surprising he was.

"I'm not going, of course," Cari told Jolena as they tested paint samples later that day. Holding up a soft green sample card, she said, "I like this one for down here. I want to keep the color authentic to the Victorian era. What do you think?"

"I think you should go," Jolena replied as she squinted at the sample card.

"I was talking about the paint."

"I like the paint. But I love these pretty flowers. I think Rick has a thing for you, suga'."

"No, he has a thing for Bridget. He's just friends with me, and in typical male fashion, he's probably playing both of us."

Jolena tossed down the samples she'd been holding. "Rick is not that kind of man. Bridget throws herself at him and he's just too nice to tell her to back off."

"Too nice? Or too caught up?"

"He might be caught—in a trap. But Rick's too smart to fall for Bridget Duncan, let me tell you. He indulges her because he wants to witness to her. Of course, that girl ain't seen the doors of a church since she was in vacation Bible school as a kid. Rick knows that and he worries about her. That's all."

Cari wasn't convinced. "Are you sure? I mean, he

left Atlanta for a reason. And you said it had to do with a woman. Maybe Bridget reminds him of that woman. She fits the bill. And he didn't seem to be witnessing anything remotely close to a come-to-Jesus talk the other day."

"He's subtle in his witness and ministry. And how do you know the bill?" Jolena countered, shaking her head.

"How do I know?" Cari's chuckle echoed throughout the house. "I remember from high school, for one thing. It just stands to reason that he'd still go after the same type. Bridget is gorgeous. Even I can see that. What chance do I have against that and the fact that she always managed to get the attention of every boy around her, especially the ones I liked. She was too young to notice Rick in high school but she's obviously making up for that now."

Jolena huffed a derisive breath. "She can prance around all she likes. I don't think Rick's gonna fall for that. And you—well, you need to lighten up and just go with things, honey. See what happens."

"I can't go with this, Jolena. I just got back to town and my first week has been full of enough surprises and pitfalls already. I have to be very careful."

Jolena pursed her lips then glanced around. "I've been giving this whole thing some thought and I think it might be a good idea—you and Rick."

Cari's heart did a funny flip. "And why would you think that? Other than you are so obviously trying to fix me up with the man?"

Jolena tapped her leather Mary Jane flats against the

wooden floor. "Well, think about it. According to you, Rick has a certain type of woman he likes. But that type hasn't worked out so great for him. So maybe he needs to try a new type. Such as you. And maybe, just maybe, you need to let go of some of those preconceived notions about the man and try to make nice." She pointed to the flowers centered in the middle of the kitchen table. "The man sent you flowers, Cari. I'd say that's a very good sign."

Cari flipped through the paint samples. "I have to admit, the flowers got to me. They smell so good and they brighten up this old place. It's been a long time since anyone sent me flowers. But I think he sent them out of guilt, not anything anywhere near romantic."

"Then why did he call and ask you to dinner tonight?"

"Maybe because a certain someone gave him my phone number. And you probably demanded he take me to dinner, too. I must be the latest charity case around here."

Jolena put a hand on her hip. "Honey, I'm good but I'm not that good. Rick asked for your number but he called you on his own. I can't tell the man what to do. I can only guide you two toward each other."

"Oh, okay, so he called on his own. And left a message. Why didn't he just walk over here?"

"Maybe because he was afraid you wouldn't open the door?"

"I wouldn't have," she said. "I have things to do tonight." She thought really hard and realized she didn't have much to do except maybe read a book or watch a movie on the tiny television she'd brought with her. Or maybe unpack, clean the whole house for the tenth time and worry about how she was going to make all of this work. In a word, she had nothing going on tonight that couldn't wait.

Jolena figured that out, too. "Yes, like look at sample cards for paint. That's a real fun Friday night. You and Rick should go out and celebrate securing that loan. We did sign the papers this morning."

"Yes, you and I did. But Rick couldn't meet us at the bank. He had to come in later. Or so he said, according to Mr. Phillips. Typical male avoidance tactic."

"He got busy with a shipment and he had several demanding customers wanting to rent rafts and tubes. Not to mention those kayakers—they sure love riding the river." Jolena waved her hands in the air. "The man works day and night in that big old store. He could use a break."

"Or he's too chicken to face me after listening to Bridget trying to knock me down a peg or two."

Jolena nodded on that. "I did give him a little talk about that. Trust me, the man won't ever bring her in for lemonade again when you're on the premises of my diner." Then she continued on, "But if he's chicken, why would he send you flowers and ask you out to dinner?"

"Oh, I don't know," Cari said with a groan. "Maybe to soften me up so he'd have the courage to face me again, or maybe because he just feels sorry for poor little Cari. I don't know and I don't care. I can't do this, Jolena. I just can't."

"You mean you won't do it," Jolena retorted. "You are one stubborn woman. You know something? The only one feeling sorry for Cari around here is Cari."

Cari shook her head, shocked at that suggestion even if it did ring true. "No, like Rick's card said, I'm determined. I have one thing on my mind and that's getting Duncan House back in shape and making a go of my business."

"That's two things," Jolena pointed out.

"You know what I mean."

"Yes, I do," Jolena said, retreating for now. "But I want you to be happy. You could just try with Rick. Just get to know the man. Give him a chance, Cari. You've both been through a lot—bad relationships, the death of loved ones and trying to start over again. You two have so much in common, but you're both tiptoeing around things 'cause y'all think you'll get hurt all over again."

"All in due time," Cari said. "You have a valid case for *friendship*. But I can't go for anything else right now. I won't be ugly to him, but you're right. I don't want to get hurt again. Ever."

Jolena let out a breath. "Okay, then. I gotta go pick up the girls from dance class. You gonna be in church Sunday?"

"I hope to be," Cari replied. "I need to be."

"I hear that," Jolena retorted with a big grin. Then she winked at Cari. "Rick comes every Sunday."

"Of course he does. The man must be a saint."

"Far from it," Jolena said, moving toward the door. "He's just a good man waiting for a good woman."

Cari waved bye, then locked the door behind Jolena, thinking she couldn't be that woman. She was no saint herself and maybe that was the problem.

Maybe she'd never see herself as being good enough for any man. Especially one like Rick who attracted women the way honey attracted bees.

Too much time and energy, that's what he'd require. And Cari didn't have much of either right now.

"Yes, definitely the pale green," she said, concentrating on her paint samples. The color was good for this big open room and the brand was affordable now that she had a line of credit at the bank.

A line of credit Rick had helped her obtain, she reminded herself. Was she being too hard on him? After all, she could tell from seeing Bridget that the girl knew how to operate around the opposite sex. How could she blame Rick for that?

Cari glanced out the window, watching the sun setting over the tip of the mountains peeking behind the buildings. The plump white blossoms of the mountain rhododendrons shimmered like fluffy cotton balls against the breeze. "Lord, am I wrong to judge him when I don't even know him—the real him—and after he's been so kind to me?"

Of course she was wrong. But she couldn't bring herself to call him and tell him that. She just needed some time to think and to sort this out. Deciding if she hurried she could make it to the paint store before it closed, she grabbed her stuff and headed out the door.

She'd start painting tonight. Just some scraping and testing, maybe put a primer on and then try the new color. Her contractor could work around that. Getting a head start would help her to think and it would also make her tired enough to sleep, she hoped. And since she'd set up her small television down here and the cable man had come by earlier to hook up reception, she might find an old movie to watch later. A good solid plan. A lonely, solitary plan, but a good one.

As she hurried out the front door, the scent of lilies drifted through the air, reminding her that she could have had a date tonight. A real date with a real man.

Cari shut the door and got in her car before she had time to change her mind and call Rick back.

Chapter Eight

Cari loved new paint. Something about opening the can and seeing the creamy mix brought her comfort. It represented home and work and creativity, all things she craved and wanted. Once she had these walls painted, she'd refurbish the wainscoting and the window seals and borders. She wanted to scrape away all the layers to get to the real wood underneath, the heart of the house. Same with the staircase. Somewhere underneath the aged off-white paint, there was real mahogany. She remembered it that way and she did have a few pictures from her childhood.

Her contractor, a fatherly man named Rod Green, was just as excited about the renovations as she was. He knew Victorian houses; he'd been working with several other families in Knotwood Mountain to keep their homes intact.

Why hadn't Doreen done the same with this house? It was built around the turn of the century and it was still so beautiful, even now with the last of the sun setting out the front bay windows. Cari would never understand why Doreen had insisted they move from this house in the first place. And Cari had hated the modern cedar house out on the river, even if the surroundings were tranquil and the views stunning.

Or maybe she'd just hated being uprooted and plopped back down in the midst of strangers, her own father changing overnight from loving and concerned to distant and uncaring. Doreen had certainly done a number on him.

Putting those bad memories aside, Cari concentrated instead on the future ahead. The green she'd tested on one small corner of the big wall looked great in the muted light of dusk. She hoped it would be pretty in the early-morning light, too.

Because her budget was tight and the old walls held coats of plain white, she hadn't put on a primer, but she had sanded the rough spots until the old walls looked smooth and ready to get a quick face-lift. Now she'd managed to cover half of one entire wall with the rich green. She stood back and sipped water and nibbled cheese puffs from an open bag, admiring the way the color had cheered up this big open room. It wasn't a major redo but it did make her feel as if she'd accomplished something important.

She was about to get back to painting when someone knocked on the door.

"I need to get a bell," she murmured. She'd had more visitors this week than she'd had in a month back in Atlanta.

For a small town, Knotwood Mountain always had something going on and, with high tourist season beginning, the foot traffic out on the street was picking up. She could hear soulful jazz music coming from the square up by the river park. And every now and then, she'd hear laughter echoing from the river as a group of rafters floated by.

But when she got to the door and saw the man standing underneath the porch light, her heart tripped and sputtered to a stop. All she could hear was the pumping of her pulse inside her head.

Rick Adams.

She hadn't called him about dinner. But apparently, that didn't matter now.

When he knocked again, she called out, "Just a minute." She couldn't hide since he'd probably seen her through the window. Glancing at herself in an old, pockmarked mirror by the door, she groaned. "No makeup and lots of paint smears." And she was wearing cutoff jean shorts, an old UGA T-shirt and her purple fuzzy slippers. Oh, well.

"Cari? I know you're home. And I promised you dinner. So let me in, okay?"

She opened the door, careful to keep the chain lock on. "Rick, I'm not prepared for company. I—"

"But I brought dinner," he said. "Pizza from the Pizza Haus—you remember it? The one that sits right on the river? We all used to hang out there after school and weekends. I ordered the house special, loaded with all that bad stuff that's so good."

Oh, this was so not fair. Had Jolena also told him

about Cari's penchant for junk food? A penchant that had once caused her to put on too many pounds?

Her godmother was even more conniving than she'd realized. In a good way, of course, but still…

He knocked again, softly. "Cari, Jolena is worried about you. I offered to come and check on you."

She gave in and yanked the door open, staring up at him in disbelief. "Jolena forced you to come and check on me?"

"No, not exactly. Technically I offered, since, technically I wanted to take you to dinner tonight. I'll have to practice my powers of persuasion a little more. They don't seem to work on you."

"I'll just reckon…." She groaned as the distinctive smell of deep-dish pizza lifted out to her nose. "I'm not dressed for company."

"You look adorable," he said, shoving his way toward the kitchen. "Oh, you got my flowers. I love the slippers, by the way."

She looked down at her feet. She'd already forgotten about her purple feathery slippers with sequins sprinkled across the feathers—just one of the many feminine items she'd carried in her shop in Atlanta.

Nothing to do about that now, however. "Thanks for the flowers and the pizza, but I didn't say you could come in."

"You didn't slam the door in my face either."

He took a slice of pizza out of the white box and moved it in front of her nose. "Jolena said you don't eat right."

"I wouldn't call *that* eating right," she replied,

pointing to the tempting veggie pizza. "Maybe the veggies, but certainly not the crust."

"She said you skipped lunch today. You need to eat."

"I used to eat, a lot," she said, her resolve dissolving against his endearing smile. "I used food and shopping to make up for my lack of having a family, but I don't want to go back to my old habits." With food or with the wrong man, she reminded herself.

He wasn't buying that excuse. "There's a big difference between eating to survive and stay healthy and starving yourself out of fear."

That made her mad. "So you think I'm starving myself? Out of fear? What kind of fear? Did Jolena also tell you that?"

He put down the pizza slice and crossed his arms, clearly here for the long haul. "She didn't have to. I figured that one out all on my own. Stress does that to a person. You're afraid you'll get fat. Aren't most women afraid of that? It doesn't mean you have to dry up and waste away. And I've watched enough reality television to know it's not about the food. You said it yourself. You were craving something else."

She tried to be flippant in the face of his armchair analysis. "And you would know this because?"

"Because I've been there myself, you know, trying to please everyone else. Trying to live up to a certain expected image, trying to find atonement. But sometimes, you just have to let go and have a pizza-fest, darlin'."

Cari wanted to tell him to leave and take his pizza

with him, but something in his eyes, the same something she'd caught a glimpse of when they'd first reconnected, tugged at her. "So...you couldn't find a date tonight either?"

"I had a date—with you. I wanted to take a very stubborn new-girl-back-in-town out to a fancy dinner, but she refused to allow me that luxury. So here I am, bearing one of your favorite meals out of sheer desperation."

"You've never been desperate a day in your life," she said as she grabbed a wipe rag. "C'mon. I'll find us something to drink. And if you're nice, I might let you help me finish painting that wall over there." Stopping to wash her hands in the old sink, she looked at him over her shoulder. "There's an action movie coming on television later. I guess you could stay and watch that with me, too."

"Deal." He grabbed the pizza and followed her back to the living room.

She motioned toward the window seat where the bay window looked out over the street then went to her new refrigerator to get two soft drinks. When she came back, he had the pizza box open and waiting, his smile triumphant. "So you like action movies?"

Out on the sidewalk, someone walked by, headed to one of the nearby nightspots on the river, their talk and laughter spilling through the open windows of the old house.

"Yes, I do. It's my little secret. I guess it helps me to blow off steam without actually doing harm."

"I've never known such a girly-girl to like manly

movies with shoot-'em-ups and car chases. It's kinda cute, in a very scary way."

Cari didn't know how to explain. "It started after my mother died. I'd spend hours in my room upstairs, watching movies. Sometimes, that was the only thing on and so I got hooked. Of course, we moved out of this house pretty quickly when things changed."

He gave her a sympathetic look. "You mean when Doreen took over."

She nodded, sipped her drink. "Yes. Her idea of family was a bit overblown for my tastes. Doreen always wanted to invite prominent people over for a sit-down dinner, which usually meant I'd be in the kitchen washing up dishes while everyone else was having dessert. She is so not like my mother. My mother knew how to make things perfect. She was a polite, kind woman. I miss that."

"I'm sorry," he said, his eyes holding hers. "I miss my dad. We went through some strained times before he died and I wish we'd had time to really get to know each other. But I have my mom and my brother, Simon. I'll take you out to the ranch to meet him sometime. He'd like you. And I can get you a good deal on a pair of handmade boots."

She liked the way his laugh lines crinkled when he smiled. "You're blessed to be close to both of them. Me, I had this nice little family, in this perfect old Victorian house. But that went away the day my mother died. I think my dad and I could have worked through things if Doreen hadn't come along. That's what I regret the most, that we didn't get a chance to just grieve together and grow stronger by helping each other."

"So you're still rebelling by indulging in action movies now and then?"

"Something like that. But I really do enjoy them."

He grinned and grabbed another slice. Glancing over at the wall, he said, "That looks good. I'll help you finish it so we can get to the movie."

She almost told him, no, never mind. She was supposed to be miffed with him after all. But painting with a buddy was a lot more fun than painting alone. Still, she wanted to offer him a way out. "I was just teasing. You don't have to paint, since you brought dinner."

"I'm here and I want to help," Rick countered. "Can you just let me do that, please?"

He sounded sincere. But she had to torment him a little. "Did Bridget stand you up or something?"

He put down his drink. "I was wondering when we'd get around to that subject." Shrugging, he said, "Look, Bridget is a mixed-up woman who's lonely and confused."

"Oh, I thought that was me."

"You might be mixed up right now, but your heart is in the right place. I can see that. I'm not even sure Bridget has a heart."

She couldn't help but smile at that. "But Bridget seems to think you two have something going on. She sure tried to give me that impression."

"She's wrong." He chewed a piece of crust then leaned forward. "But it's nice to see that you might be a tad jealous. That means you like me a little bit."

Cari threw down her pizza. "This is not jealousy. It's more like shock. Seeing you so friendly with her really threw me, but I don't have any right to be thrown. Let's just drop it, okay."

He studied her face. "I tried to make it up to you."

"Oh, you mean with flowers and food. That usually does the trick for me. So I'd say you've done enough."

"And painting, don't forget that. I am a Picasso with a paintbrush."

She giggled at that. And in spite of her worries, this man did make her laugh. She liked that. A lot.

When he kept watching her, she started to feel self conscious. "What?"

He pushed a napkin toward her cheek. "You have pizza sauce, right there by that lovely mint-green paint smudge." He gently wiped at her face. "There, all gone—the pizza, that is. The paint seems to be dried on good."

Cari had to swallow to hide all the crazy emotions tripping over themselves inside her heart. Fear? She certainly had that. Hope? It was trying to creep back into her soul. Trust? Wasn't so sure about that one yet. But just the brush of the crumpled napkin against her skin made her go all soft and mushy inside.

It had been a very long time since anyone had pampered her or tried to help her. Telling herself she was too needy, taking pleasure in junk food and a man who didn't even know her pain or her flaws, she let the moment slip by. And reminded herself that Rick Adams had his own agenda, flowers and pizza and neediness aside. And she'd be wise to remember that.

* * *

Rick couldn't get this moment out of his mind. His hand holding the stiff white paper napkin against her skin. Her eyes going all wild and wide while she looked at him like a trapped animal needing tender loving care. He'd seen it all there in her eyes, the fear, the need, the distrust and the hope. And he'd felt her pain as clearly as if it had been his own, because he understood her pain so clearly—maybe because it *had* been his own. How to make her see that?

By allowing her to get used to you, came the answer. He couldn't push this, no matter the erratic feelings surging together like river currents inside his soul, and no matter the outcome. He had to give Cari time to adjust, time to realize he wasn't the same person she remembered from high school—even if he did talk to leggy blondes on occasion.

"Let's do some painting," he said, tossing the napkin on the coffee table.

She gave him another confused glance. "Are you sure? I mean, you don't have to babysit me. I'm okay, really. I don't mind spending a Friday night alone. Sometimes, I just need to get away and think, have some quiet time."

"So you want me to leave now, after telling me I could stay, after eating my pizza?"

"No, no, I'm not saying that. I don't want you to feel obligated to stay out of pity."

Rick's heart did a strange little jump. This was different. This was innocent and unassuming and wonderful. This woman didn't care about his status or his bank account, not like the women he'd dated in Atlanta. She only wanted to make sure he wasn't sitting here with her out of some sense of obligation.

If only she knew. He couldn't leave her now, not if his life depended on it. "I want to be here, Cari," he finally said. "And it has nothing to do with feeling sorry for you, okay?"

"Then why did you come?" she asked, clearly shocked.

Which simply endeared her to him even more. "I wanted to see you again," he replied. "That's all."

"But what about—"

He put a finger to her lips. "Not tonight. Tonight let's just enjoy getting to know each other and forget about all the other stuff. Let's paint that wall."

She didn't argue anymore. Instead she got up and found him a paintbrush. For a while, they worked in comfortable silence, the swish, swish of their brushes finding a rhythm that made a nice melody. Then he heard the crunch of cheesy puffs and he looked over to see her wiping cheese powder off her face.

"Here." She offered him the bag. He helped her finish it off.

Finally, Rick asked, "Did you ever think we'd both wind up back here in Knotwood Mountain?"

She stopped painting. "I never wanted to leave, except to go to college. That was my parents' hope for me, so I wanted to get an education then come back here. I've never told anyone this, but I always had a dream of running my little shop right here on First Street. I just never expected to take so many detours to get back here. And I never imagined I'd lose my parents before I saw my dream come true. Or that my little shop would be right here in this house."

He shook his head. "Ironic, huh? I couldn't wait to get away from here. I thought Atlanta was the place where I'd find my fortune and settle down. I found the fortune, but the settling down part didn't go so great." He shrugged. "I wanted certain things—a home and family. And she wanted certain things I couldn't give her—status and a social standing. We parted ways when I realized she wasn't going to marry me because she didn't think I had enough of the 'it' factor. And I'm still not sure what 'it' is."

"Oh, I think you have *it,*" Cari said, laughing. "And bless her heart, it sounds as if she won't be happy with anyone."

"Good point."

Cari dipped her roller then brought it back to the wall. "I had such a crush on you back in high school."

He turned to stare at her. She had paint on her cheek and in her hair. She looked embarrassed. "You did? Why didn't you ever clue me in on that?"

"Yeah, like you would have noticed. You had a girlfriend remember? What was her name? Ginger Cunningham?"

Rick nodded. "Good ol' Ginger. She's married now with three children. Married a farmer. Go figure."

Cari didn't say anything. "You had lots of girl-friends, if I remember correctly."

Rick wondered if he'd done something to hurt her way back then—back when he was so shallow and such a jerk. "I wish we'd been friends in school. I mean that."

She laughed. "No you don't. We can be friends now because we've both changed a lot. But you and me in high school—like oil and water. It's the same old clichéd story. You were the big man on campus. I was a few years behind you—a sophomore when you were a senior—the wallflower who rarely went to any of the fun events. And in the two years after my mother's death, I gained about twenty pounds and became a really bitter person. So no, we couldn't be friends."

He looked sheepish and felt lower than a snake's belly. "I didn't recognize you the other day when you were looking at the red shoes."

She wasn't buying it. "No, you didn't even *remember* me. But that's okay. I wasn't very memorable back then."

He lifted his head to stare at her, trying to convey complete honesty. "Well, you certainly are now."

She looked doubtful, but she nodded again. "Let's finish up and watch the movie."

"Good." After they'd washed their brushes and rollers from the old spigot on the back porch, Rick kicked off his loafers and settled down beside her on the floor.

Using the love seat and fat cushions as a headrest, they sat on the floor in front of the tiny television.

So far so good, he decided, determined to remember everything about her and this night. "Nothing like a good car chase to take your mind off the reality of life."

"That's what I always say," she replied with a grin.

Then she put her feet out in front of her and kicked off her feathery slippers, grinning at Rick with the sweet enticement that seemed to surround her when she was happy.

And right now, this very minute, she seemed very happy.

I'm in serious trouble, he thought. Serious.

But he couldn't stop smiling.

"By the way, really, thank you for the flowers," she murmured as the intro to the movie began. "I love them."

"You're welcome."

He smiled over at her then turned toward the television. And accepted the way all of his protective instincts seemed to merge together while he watched her watching the movie.

Having a spoiled lonely blonde chasing him was interesting and flattering—that was one thing. But to be floored by a sprite of a woman who wore feathered, sequined slippers, ate cheesy puffs and painted walls green was quite another.

Rick felt as if his boring, normal life had just become every bit as exciting as an action movie. And he had a feeling he was in for the ride of his life.

Chapter Nine

Cari woke up and rolled over to find pink and orange ribbons of sunrise lifting out across the mountains.

Glancing around, she stretched and remembered Rick had been here last night, eating pizza, painting and watching a movie with her. They'd talked a bit, laughed some, finished off their food then settled back. Somewhere in there, he'd reached for her hand. About halfway through the good guys chasing the bad guys, she'd gotten drowsy.

She must have drifted off, because next thing she knew, he was nudging her off his shoulder, telling her the movie was over.

"Hey, Sleeping Beauty. Time for me to get home. Go on up to bed and I'll make sure everything's locked up down here."

Cari had nodded, mumbled good-night and quickly went up, washed her face and brushed her teeth then climbed into her bed. And she'd slept like a baby for the first time in weeks.

Because of Rick. He made her feel safe.

She got up and stretched, then got ready for her day. She needed coffee. Padding down the old stairs in her bare feet, she glanced around and saw a note taped to the flower vase. Practically skipping, Cari ran to read it.

"You fell asleep and missed the best part. The good guys won. They always do. I'll call you later. Rick."

Cari held the note in her hands, wondering what was happening to her. Was he one of the good guys? He sure seemed that way. He was a gentleman, kind and chivalrous. He was a shrewd businessman, self-confident and sure. And he was a charmer, no doubt about that. She imagined he helped little old ladies across the street and took in stray animals, too. Definitely hero material.

Not that she was looking.

"What have I done?" she asked as the coffee machine timer kicked on and the dark brew started pouring into the carafe. "What have I done?"

She should have stopped him at the door last night. But instead, she'd let him come in, bearing food and charm, and sit with her, talk to her, laugh with her. And make her feel special. He'd allowed her to fall asleep holding his hand.

"I'm in trouble," she said. And she needed to think about this, a lot more. First, church, lunch with Jolena's family then a Sunday afternoon of painting the rest of the downstairs. That would require a lot of fortitude. And take her mind off Rick, she hoped.

The phone rang, jarring her out of her worries.

Cari saw the caller ID then clicked on the receiver. "Jolena, you are so busted."

"Hush and tell me everything. Did he come by? Did you go out to dinner? Where did you go?"

"Hold on," Cari replied, groaning. "I haven't even had my coffee yet."

"Hurry up. You gotta get ready for church."

"I'll be at church but I just woke up." Cari sighed, inhaled about half a cup of black coffee then cleared her throat. "He came by, thanks to you. And he brought dinner with him."

"Pizza?"

"Yes, since you also told him about that, too. I ate two slices. Thanks very much."

"It won't kill you to indulge now and then."

"I'll have to work it off. I'll have to work off a lot of things."

"So did you two talk? What happened?"

"We talked a bit but he didn't want to discuss any issues or leggy blondes, although he did say he doesn't care about Bridget in that way. He helped me paint a wall and he watched my action movie with me."

"You and those movies, I declare." Jolena's laugh bubbled over the phone. "And then?"

"And then I fell asleep sitting up straight, leaning against the couch—well, actually I think I leaned against his shoulder, too. He woke me and told me he'd let himself out and lock the door for me. I went to bed and fell into a deep stupor. I woke up and found a note on the flowers. He's going to call me later."

"It's a good start. A very good start."

"You know this can't go anywhere, don't you?"

"And why not? And girl, I'm not just talking merger in the sense of a *business* merger. I'm talking merger between two of the cutest people I've ever laid eyes on. You two belong together."

"And how can you know that?"

"I know things, is all," Jolena replied. "Now get on with yourself and get dressed. I'll see you at church. Then we'll go to brunch at my mama's house."

"I can't overeat," Cari said. "But I can't resist your mother's cooking, either."

"Oh, oh. We'll talk at church. Meet me at the doughnut stand in the fellowship hall."

"I'll be there, but no doughnuts for me."

Cari hung up, smiled at Jolena's antics then stared at the flowers bursting forth in front of her eyes.

"This can't happen," she said as she touched one of the fat, lush lilies. "It can't. It's just not possible."

She should make a list of all the reasons why hanging out with Rick Adams wasn't possible, but right now she just wanted more coffee and more time to savor how much she'd enjoyed having him here last night.

"It was worth the extra calories and fat," she decided as she headed toward the bathroom. "And so worth giving up some of my wounded pride."

But taking things further wouldn't be worth the risk of losing her heart, she decided.

Somehow, she'd have to make him see that.

* * *

It didn't help that he was sitting front and center at church and wearing a nice white shirt and a pretty red striped tie. And spiffy black cowboy boots.

It didn't help that she'd dressed extra carefully in a full-skirted vintage green dress she'd found at an antique shop in Conyers, Georgia, or that she'd fluffed her hair and put on mascara and perfume.

And it really didn't help when he turned and caught her looking at him, his smile sure and easy. When he motioned for her to come and sit by him and his mother, she just smiled and shook her head. She needed to stay back in the pew with Jolena. Just so she could take it all in.

As they stood to sing the opening hymn, Cari looked around the old country church. It had been here for over a century and was well maintained and pristine, its walls a pretty stained pine and its high ceiling arched over solid wooden beams. The stained-glass windows glinted like jewels in the sunlight and the old pews felt polished and warm to her touch. Being here renewed her spirit and her commitment to make things work this time around.

I need You, Lord. I need You in my corner.

He had always been there, she knew. But Cari hadn't always turned to God in times of stress or even in times of blessings. She turned to Him now, secure that He would help her through this transition. And maybe, just maybe, He'd help her learn to forgive and forget, too.

When the service was over, her good mood went

south, however. Doreen was going out the door ahead of her, wearing a pink silk dress and bone-colored pumps and smiling up at the minister. "Such a good sermon, Reverend. We could all certainly learn a thing or two about humility around here, don't you think?" She turned and shot Cari a knowing glance then kept moving.

Cari said hello to the minister and caught the sense of disapproval he gave her even while he smiled and welcomed her back. Doreen had struck again with just a word whispered, no doubt.

Cari held up her head and kept moving, the bright sunshine making her squint. When a hand touched her arm, she whirled to find Doreen standing there.

"Good morning," Cari said, trying to move away.

"Hold on," Doreen replied. "I need to have a word with you."

Cari braced herself, wondering what she'd done now. "All right."

"Bridget said she ran into you the other day and you were downright hostile toward her."

Cari had to smile. "We did see each other, but I don't recall—"

Doreen raised a hand. "You listen to me, missy. You might think you can come here and be Miss High-and-Mighty just because you're a Duncan, but that isn't going to change the way people around here view you. We all know the truth. You stayed away when your poor father was deathly ill, while I nursed him and tried to take care of both him and his business. Now you march back in and start trying to take over the town, getting other people to do your dirty work. It won't work, Cari. You'll fail like you always have." She finished in a flurry of breaths. "And another thing, stay away from Brady. I don't need the likes of you influencing my son."

Cari stood there with her mouth open, so shocked she couldn't breathe. "I came home as soon as I heard Daddy was sick. You didn't let me know until it was almost too late." She inhaled and swallowed the lump in her throat. "And I care about Brady. You should know that."

"I only know I don't want you around my children."

Cari lifted her chin. "I won't bother Brady and I certainly don't intend to get chummy with Bridget."

Doreen looked smug. "That's because you can't compete with her. Even if rumor has it you've been buttering up to Rick Adams. You don't stand a chance."

With that, Doreen turned and pranced to her Mercedes.

And Cari stood there, face blazing, while half the town looked on.

Rick hurried over and grabbed Cari by the arm. "Let's get out of here."

She stood frozen, resisting him. "Let me go."

"No, I won't let you go. And I've got a good mind to go after that woman and tell her exactly what I think about her *commands* to you. She's not your boss, Cari. She's not even related to you."

"Thank goodness," Cari said, looking down at the ground. "But I don't want you running interference with Doreen. She'd make your life miserable, too. I just want her to leave me alone."

"You can't let her get to you." He urged her toward his Jeep. "A lot of people in this town have her number and I think you'd be surprised how many of them are glad you're back."

"I doubt that. The minister could barely look me in the eye. She has him in her pocket so why should I expect any better from everyone else?"

"You can expect better from me. Remember that."

"I need to get out of here."

"I'll drive you home."

She held back, the old wall of shame clearly falling around her again. "I'm supposed to go to Jolena's for Sunday brunch. She'll be worried."

He glanced around and spotted Jolena shooing her four daughters toward the car. "Let's go talk to her."

Jolena took one look at Cari's face and grabbed her by the hands. "What on earth?"

"Doreen ambushed her," Rick said, gritting his teeth. Only his mother holding him back had kept him from telling Doreen Duncan what she could do with her superior attitude. The nerve of that woman. "I'm taking her home."

"Why don't you bring her on to Mama's house," Jolena suggested. "And your mama, too. We always have plenty for everybody."

He looked at Cari. "Would you like that?"

She still looked shell-shocked, but she nodded. "Just get me out of here, please."

An hour later, Rick sat with Cari at a picnic table

out underneath an ancient live oak in Mildred Bell's big backyard. The old farmhouse sat whitewashed and looming, right in the middle of a big pasture with mountain vistas all around. A round white gazebo covered with a lush morning glory vine stood, looking like a wedding cake, out near a little pond just past the yard.

"Nice place," he said. "Eat your food."

Cari refused to look at him. "I'm not very hungry."

She'd been quiet on the ride out here. Thankfully, everyone had left her alone. Jolena and his mother had retreated into the kitchen with all the others, intent on getting the potluck dinner set out so the carloads of family and friends could eat.

Trying to make her laugh, he said, "I've never seen a brunch quite like this one. Roast beef and gravy, rice and potatoes, fresh tomatoes and corn, pound cake and coconut cake. I'll have to hang with Jolena and her mom more often."

"They have a large, loving family."

And she didn't.

No wonder she was so close to Jolena.

"So you've known them all a long time?"

"Since I was a baby. Jolena used to work with my mother at the food bank and when I was born, my parents asked her to be my godmother. She'd babysit me every now and then when they traveled. They had been friends since they were little. My mother's family owned the neighboring farm, but they sold out a long time ago. She was the only one left. And now, I guess I'm the only one."

He finally gave up trying to get her to eat. Taking

her hands in his, he said, "But you're not alone, Cari. You know that, don't you?"

She finally looked up at him, her eyes full of a misty misery. "I am alone. I've been alone since my father married Doreen and turned away from me. But I'm used to it. And I need to remember that."

She got up to leave, but he held her back, his hand clutching hers. "Don't be like this. You came back to change all of that. You can't let Doreen's bitterness discourage you. You're better than that."

"Am I?" She whirled on him then, the anger in her eyes like lightning, quick and full of fury. "I came back to find a way to make that woman pay. That's why I really came back. And somehow, I'm going to make her suffer the same way she made me suffer. I won't be humiliated by her again. Ever."

With that, she walked toward the gazebo, her green skirt flaring out around her legs, her head held high. But he watched as she reached up to wipe the tears off her face.

Rick had never seen such anger, such pain. It tore at him, making him realize he'd only thought he knew suffering and despair. But he'd always had a loving family to support him, even when he'd strayed or made big mistakes. And thankfully, he and his father had mended some of their differences long before his father passed away.

What would it be like to become an outcast? To lose a mother to death and a father to another family?

"Everything okay, son?"

He turned to find his mother staring at him with worry in her eyes.

"No, it's not okay. But I hope I can make it better. She just needs a friend, someone to show her how to let go of all that resentment."

"Careful," Gayle warned. "If she's not ready to let go, you might get caught in the cross fire."

"I'm already caught," he admitted. "I can't turn my back on her now."

Gayle shook her head. "This is messy stuff. Doreen won't go down without a fight."

Rick nodded. "You've always told me life can get messy. I just have to deal with it."

Gayle touched a hand to his arm. "Then go out there and talk to her. I'm going to help clean up and catch a ride home with Jolena."

"Thanks, Mom."

"Call me later," she said with a smile.

Rick waved to her then started walking toward the gazebo, his focus on Cari.

She was sitting there, gazing out over the pond, her back to him. And it struck him once again that she looked like a princess trapped in a tower. She was all tangled up in grief and bitterness and so very lost.

She was a princess who really did need to be rescued. From herself.

He just hoped he could be the one to help her, if she'd let him.

Chapter Ten

Rick took Cari back to the church to get her car. Hopping out of the Jeep, he came around to help her down. "Are you gonna be all right?"

She gave him a crooked smile. "I'll be fine. I expected this so I just have to deal with it. She caught me off guard this morning, but this is nothing new, really. Every time I called to speak to my father, every time I tried to send him birthday or Christmas gifts, I was met with this kind of hostility, and my father heard only what Doreen wanted him to hear, I'm sure. Bridget obviously gave her mother a different version of our meeting, coloring me in a bad light, of course. But I can't let it sidetrack me. I just need to keep my nose to the grindstone and stay focused."

"Now you're talking." He wanted to hug her close, to shield her from any more pain but Cari wasn't the kind of girl to fall into a man's arms easily. She was like a wounded bird. She needed a bit of coaxing.

"I'd better go," she said. "I've got lots to do today."

"I could come and help."

"No." She shook her head. "I just need some time alone."

"All right." He pulled a card out of his wallet. "My cell number is on there. Call me if you need me. I'm usually out at my ranch on weekends."

"You mentioned that. I'd like to see it sometime if the offer is still there."

Glad to change the subject, he nodded. "You have an open invitation. It's a few miles north of town near the river. I have horses, if you'd like to ride."

"That might be nice." She glanced away. "I'm glad it's not near Doreen's house." Her father's second wife lived south of town. Not far enough away but good, all the same.

"Maybe next weekend," Rick said.

"Maybe." She didn't sound too excited. "I'd like that."

He took her hand in his, staring down at their joined fingers. Rubbing his other hand across her knuckles, he said, "I'll see you later, then. And I'll follow you back into town."

She put a hand on her car door then stopped. "You go ahead. I need to visit my parents' grave site."

Not wanting to intrude, Rick had no choice but to get in the Jeep and leave. But he stopped at the end of the lane and looked off to the right where the old cemetery lay underneath an outcropping of hills and rocks. His father was buried in that cemetery and he often went to visit the grave site. He understood Cari's need for solitude and privacy but he didn't want to leave her here alone.

The cemetery was well tended and beautiful. Old live oaks formed canopies on each corner of the big lot and crape myrtle and magnolia trees lined the many paths. Stone benches were set here and there, offering rest to the weary and heartbroken. The wind moaned like a sob across the hills and valleys, its song at once soothing and solemn.

Cari walked toward an elaborate memorial stone placed near a towering magnolia tree. She stood for a minute then sank down to her knees, her hands going to her face, her shoulders shaking.

Rick sat there, torn between going to her and giving her some space. He couldn't leave. He turned the Jeep around so he was facing the cemetery and he pulled off the lane and shut down the motor. Then before he could talk himself out of it, he got out of the Jeep and hurried to her.

"Cari?" He sank down beside her. "Cari, I'm here."

She turned to gaze at him, her eyes misty and full of tears. Rick took one look at her face then gathered her into his arms and let her cry.

After a while, she pulled back to wipe at her face then looked down at the two graves. "We had such plans, my mom and I. She was going to take my best friend Tiffany and me on a trip to Europe after we graduated from high school. We started planning it my freshman year." She shrugged and let out a shuddering sob. "She died my sophomore year. And then everything changed. I lost both of them that year. My father just shut down."

Rick swallowed the lump in his throat. "It must have been so hard, dealing with all of that and trying to go to school, too." He wished he'd gone on instincts back then and reached out to her. Well, he was here now and he wasn't about to give up on her.

She nodded, wiped at her eyes again. "I wish we'd had some time alone, you know? I think we could have grown closer. But Doreen didn't allow us that time. She went after him with a vengeance. And she won. She always wins."

Rick didn't know how to help her get past this, so he held her close, hoping his physical presence would be enough for now. And he said a silent prayer, asking God to heal her and ease her pain.

He stayed with her until she got up, then he held her hand as they walked back to her car. She smiled up at him, her lips trembling. "Thank you."

He didn't ask if she'd be okay. He just leaned close and wiped at her damp cheek. "I'll check on you later." Only after he'd watched her drive away did he get back in the Jeep and leave.

And he watched her car through the rearview mirror until she turned off toward town.

Cari had seen Rick's Jeep parked up near the road.

He'd waited for her and then he'd come to her. He was that kind of man, the kind who stayed, the kind who listened and didn't ask questions. The kind of man she'd always dreamed of finding. Maybe she'd been waiting to return here to Rick all this time.

But that scene with Doreen this morning had brought

all her old hurts and insecurities back to the surface. Which meant she had no business dreaming about a relationship with any man right now, let alone a man that Bridget had her eyes on. Even if Rick wasn't interested, Bridget would be territorial and demanding and she'd paint an ugly picture regarding Cari—a picture that some in this town would believe, no matter the truth.

Pulling her car up to the small garage behind the house, Cari wondered if she'd have the strength to finish what she'd started. Had she been wrong to come home?

Maybe Doreen was right. Maybe she should put a For Sale sign on the old house and get out while she still had a chance.

But you just promised your parents you wouldn't do that.

Did they hear me, Lord? Does anyone up there hear me?

She prayed so. She had a few weeks until the big Fourth of July weekend and the crush of tourists who'd pass along these streets. She needed to start setting up her boutique. And that meant putting all of this out of her mind and at least getting the downstairs ready for business.

The paperwork and business permits were in place and she had the loan from the bank. The rest of her inventory was stored at a warehouse in Atlanta, just waiting to be shipped. And once she set up her computer system, she could order more stock online and get back to working on her own designs, too.

She had a perfect room upstairs to use as a workshop

but for now, she could work out of the kitchen if she had to. Feeling better now that she'd had a chance to get back on track, she hurried up the back steps.

And saw that the back door was standing wide open.

Calling out, Cari stepped inside. "Who's there?"

No answer. But she didn't need anyone to shout out why her door was ajar.

She saw the reason right there on the walls. The newly painted walls.

Someone had broken in here and left her a message.

"Go back to Atlanta, loser."

The ugly message, along with a few other choice words, was sprawled in heavy black lettering across the big wall she and Rick had just finished painting. And the rest of her precious green paint was now splattered across the old hardwood floors and all over what little furniture she'd put out.

So much for being determined.

So much for trying to save money by doing some of this work herself. She'd have to get the contractor in immediately to restore the floors.

Cari didn't think she had any tears left to cry after pouring out her heart at the cemetery. So she didn't cry. She just stood there staring, wondering who in the world would break into her house on a beautiful Sunday morning and do this.

Then it hit her and she felt sick to her stomach.

Had this been a random act, teenagers out for a good time?

Or had Doreen and Bridget set out to leave her a definite message?

* * *

Rick reached down to pet the golden retriever he'd adopted from the pound three years ago. "How you doing, Shiloh? Have you been a good boy for Uncle Simon?"

Shiloh danced around his master, his big tongue wagging right along with his fluffy tail.

The door to the big cabin opened and Rick's older brother walked out to stand on the porch. "I'm not that dog's uncle. Now if you want to get married and have some babies, I'll be glad to claim them as my kin."

Rick laughed out loud, used to Simon's bluster. "You love Shiloh and you know it."

"No, I don't." But even as he denied it, Simon whistled to the big dog. Shiloh came running to take one of the treats Simon always kept in his pocket. "What're you doing out here so late on a Sunday anyway?"

Rick wondered that himself. "I didn't feel like going back to my usual Sunday afternoon paperwork. I think I'll go for a nice long ride on Pepper. I'm sure he could use the exercise."

"Uh-huh." Simon settled down on the steps then stared up at his brother, his dark eyes alert and all-knowing. "You must have something heavy weighing on your mind. Nothing ever keeps you away from that store."

Rick took in his brother's old jeans and faded T-shirt. And the boots. It figured that the world-famous boot maker wouldn't bother to make himself a decent pair of shoes. Simon's brown work boots were scuffed and well-worn, but they were still together. A testament to his brother's amazing talent since this had been one of the first pairs he'd ever designed. "You think?"

"I know. You always work. You only come out here and put that stallion through his paces whenever you're fretting over something. Or someone. What's her name?"

"Who said it had anything to do with a woman?"

Simon grinned, his eyes as dark and rich as the river. "Doesn't it always?"

"How would you know? You haven't left this ranch since—"

Simon stopped grinning. "We weren't talking about me."

"Sorry." Rick wanted to kick himself. Simon had lost his wife to cancer when they'd only been married five years. And in the five years since, his brother had become even more of a recluse. Wondering how anyone recovered from that kind of grief, Rick sat down beside Simon and pulled Shiloh close to pet him. "I didn't mean to remind you."

"I'm reminded every day, brother. Let's get back to you."

Rick looked out toward the bluff where the Chattahoochee ran through their property. "Do you remember Cari Duncan? Carinna Duncan?"

Simon squinted. "I know the name, of course."

"She was James and Natalie Duncan's only child."

Simon nodded. "But the old man remarried, right? Some redhead?"

"Yep. A redhead with two children of her own."

"Okay. What's this got to do with you?"

"Cari's back in Knotwood Mountain and she's moved into the old Duncan House, right by our store."

Simon shook his head then looked at Rick. "And you just happen to have noticed this, right?"

Rick inhaled then sputtered out a breath. "Oh, yeah. In fact, I cosigned on a loan for her at the bank. Mom thinks I've lost some marbles."

"And while I don't always agree with our mother, I have to say she might be right on this one. What were you thinking?"

Rick wondered that himself. "I was thinking about helping someone who needed a friend. Cari's solid, Simon. She has a good plan to renovate the place and turn it from an eyesore to a showcase. I'm just a silent investor, her insurance policy."

Simon sat up to stare out into the trees. "You know I don't want any part of running that store, but did it ever occur to you to ask Mom and me about this before you went headlong into it?"

"Well, yes, it did occur to me. But as you just stated, you've pretty much left the business end of things up to me. And Mom never approves of any of the girls I've dated so I thought I'd try something different."

"I'll say. Sure is a risky way to get to a woman's heart. What if she defaults on this loan?"

"Then Jolena Beasley and I will have a nice piece of downtown property to hold and develop or sell for a profit. But she won't default. I know she won't."

Simon got up and brushed off his jeans, his cynical nature evident in his scowl. "You need to get on that horse and go for a good ride, Rick. And clear you head. I can't believe you. I just can't."

Rick got up, too. "I don't need you to believe me. It's a done deal. And I have faith in Cari and her abilities. Even if some people around here don't."

"How well do you know this woman?"

"I went to high school with her."

Simon slapped a hand to his leg. "Well, then, that makes it right as rain." He gave Rick a hard stare. "When I think of some of the people I knew in high school—well, I sure wouldn't cosign a loan with them, let me tell you."

"Cari's not like that," Rick shot back. "She's gonna make this work. You'll see."

"I'm not the one who needs to be worried," Simon said. "I'm going inside for a sandwich then I'm going back to work. Just in case I have to cover you on this crazy plan."

"You've never had to cover me a day in your life and you know it."

"Well, there's a first time for everything."

Rick watched as his brother went inside, slamming the screen door behind him.

"That went pretty good, didn't it, Shiloh?"

The dog barked a response then waited to see what his master was going to do next. Rick headed for the stables, the dog trotting behind him. He quickly saddled his big white Arabian stallion. Pepper snorted and whinnied his approval, his white-and-gray mane fluttering around him, while Shiloh waited impatiently, his tail wagging.

"Ornery. That's what my brother is," Rick said, nudging the horse out into the afternoon sun. "Ornery. And lonely. He needs to get out more."

And...maybe I do need to have my head examined.

But Rick didn't think it would come to that. He wasn't worried about Cari's loan. He was worried about Cari's soul. And right now, she was in the battle of her life.

How could he show her that seeking revenge would only destroy her soul and take away her dignity? How could he show her that she had her heart in the right place, coming home? But she had so many wrong reasons for wanting to make her mark in Knotwood Mountain?

Her mind was too wrapped around her pain and anger to see that. She was so caught up in seeking retribution that she might not see what was right in front of her face.

She could make a difference here. She could stand up to the challenge of forgiveness and win.

Or she could fall flat by holding on to her bitterness and this need to get even.

And *that* could cause her to lose everything.

Chapter Eleven

❧

"Sure is a lot going on next door this morning."

Rick turned from thanking a customer who'd just bought a boxed set of mayhaw jam and some fishing gear to see his mother craning her neck at the front window. "What's the matter?"

"Nothing. Looks like Cari's bringing in the big guns. She's got workers coming and going. Guess she's speeding things up so she can open in time for the big Fourth of July weekend."

After calling to make sure Cari was all right last night, Rick had purposely stayed away, hoping to give her some time to regroup. She'd been so down, but this had turned out to be a busy Monday morning in the general store, so he hadn't had a chance to see her. Business was picking up since the fishermen, rafters and campers were coming up for summer vacations. His entire morning had been all about outfitting people with rafts, tubes and tents, not to mention selling a lot of staples such as rice and beans and his mother's famous jellies, jams and nut mixes.

"I know she hopes to get things going over there as soon as possible." He didn't tell his mother that he'd planned to stop by after work to help Cari paint. "Maybe she decided she couldn't get started on her own, after all."

Or maybe she was pouring herself into work to hide her pain. He'd tried that, still fell back on the old routine every now and then.

"Well, since a certain kindly neighbor helped her secure a big loan, I'd think she's got plenty of money to hire all these people anyway."

Rick ignored the pointed quality of his mother's declaration. "Yes, and that's all the more reason to get started." He eyed the clock. "I'm going to Jolena's for the daily special. Want anything?"

Gayle didn't look fooled. "No, I'll get my own when you're back. I've got some spring dresses to put on clearance. And besides, any food you brought back would be cold."

"Oh, and how's that?"

She pursed her lips. "Oh, because knowing you, you'll stop over at Cari's to see how things are progressing, right?"

"Right." She had him there. "I do have a vested interest in the place."

"You can say that again."

He didn't have time for a retort. Several women came in, chattering and laughing and headed upstairs to see what his mom had on clearance. How did women always know when a sale was about to hit?

Rick left before his mother put him to work bringing more clothes out of the stockroom to show these chirpy early birds. He only had one woman on his mind this morning. And he had a nice pair of red pumps on hold for that woman. Come to think of it, he'd put himself on hold for Cari, too. And that was as surprising to him as it would probably be to Cari if he told her that.

Jolena's was packed with the lunch crowd, but he managed to find a stool at the end of the counter. After waving to Jolena, he told the young waitress he'd have the hamburger steak, fresh field peas and dirty rice, with corn bread on the side.

"Want pie with that?" the waitress asked with a toothy grin.

"Of course. How about apple today?"

"Jolena just baked it fresh. And you know how she likes to slice those apples paper thin."

"Oh, then put a scoop of ice cream on top."

Giggling, the girl ran off to get his food.

He was just finishing up the pie when Jolena managed to get a break. "Hey, Rick. How ya doing today?"

"Okay for a hot, crowded Monday. We've been at it all morning. I can smell those tourist dollars."

"Yeah, we've been steady all morning, too." She leaned close. "Have you checked on our girl today?"

"You mean Cari? No. I called her last night, but I've been busy with customers all morning."

"Uh-huh. I talked to her earlier. She's in a fine pickle, let me tell you."

He drained his coffee. "She was upset yesterday, but I made sure she was okay before I left her. I thought she was okay enough last night, even if she didn't talk much. Maybe I should have checked on her in person."

"Then you don't know?"

His pulse went into overdrive. "Know what?"

"Somebody broke into her place while she was at church. Messed things up good. That's why she's got people over there. She's checking into putting in a security system, and well…they're having to redo the floors and—"

"I'm on my way," he said, jumping up to throw the tip on the table. "Put it on my tab."

"Don't I always?"

He didn't answer. "Throw me some corn bread and vegetables into a to-go box. You know she probably hasn't eaten."

Jolena issued orders and soon he had a bag to take to Cari. "Thanks, Jolena."

"Let me know how she's doing."

Rick hurried out of the diner, his goal of staying away from Cari lifting up with the heat waves moving across the asphalt. He couldn't stay away. Cari needed him. She needed his help and his support. Whether she wanted it or not.

Cari sat out on the back porch steps, hot and sweating, her water bottle held to her throbbing head.

It had been a crazy morning but she was better now. Action meant progress. People milling around meant she was in control.

If only that were true.

"Hi."

She looked up to see Rick standing there, holding a white bag and a big cup full of tea. "Is that from Jolena's?"

"Sure is." He handed her the drink. "Sweet tea with lemon and the vegetable plate with corn bread on the side. And an oatmeal cookie for dessert. And she said to make sure you eat all of it."

Cari took the bag, her mouth watering as the wonderful smells drifted out of the carton. "That won't be a problem. I'm starving."

He sat down beside her. "I had the hamburger steak and gravy with sides. And apple pie."

Her smile was weak. "You are apple pie."

"I'll take that as a compliment."

She didn't say anything for a while. She was too busy breaking her corn bread into the liquid from the creamy peas. Finally, she glanced over at him. "Thank you."

"For what?"

"For looking out for me yesterday after church and calling to check on me last night. I was a mess. And I don't normally fall apart like that."

"You had good reason."

"Did I? I don't know. I'm going to get through it."

Well, at least she sounded calmer today. Or maybe she was just full of a steely resolve. He still wasn't sure about how to read the many moods of Cari Duncan.

"It's hard, losing a parent. I can't imagine losing both of your parents."

She stared out at the honeysuckle vines. "I just wish I'd told my father I loved him when he could actually comprehend what I was trying to say. I should have insisted Doreen let me visit him more. But I didn't want to upset him when he was so sick—and Doreen indicated that I'd do exactly that so I didn't force the issue. I wish I had, though."

"I'm sure he knew your heart."

"But that's just it. I can't be sure. Doreen poisoned him against me to the point that he didn't trust me at all. That hurts more than anything."

"Well, you need to channel all that hurt into your dreams for Duncan House. Once you get this place back in shape, you'll feel better about things. It'll be a real tribute to your folks."

"If I can keep vandals out so I can accomplish that."

He craned his neck toward the open door. "I heard what happened. Did you report it to the police?"

"Oh, yes. But one of the two available officers told me there's very little they can do about it. He filed a report but he didn't seem that concerned. In fact, he was somewhat bothered that I called him away from his Sunday afternoon nap yesterday."

"Did they check for fingerprints? Ask anyone if they'd seen anything?"

She shook her head. "Most of the businesses on the street were closed when it happened. No one was around. It was over before Jolena's weekend manager opened the diner for the Sunday crowd. Which means whoever did this was probably watching my house, waiting for me to leave."

He didn't like that. "Do you have any ideas?"

She finished off a piece of corn bread. "Oh, yes. But I'll look like the bad guy if I accuse them."

Seeing the anger in her eyes, he said, "You don't think—"

"I know," she replied, pushing her food away. "I can't prove it, but I know Bridget had something to do with this. And Doreen probably set her up to it. I think they both want me to stay away from Brady. And you."

"I can't believe that." He didn't want to believe that. "It seems so ridiculous."

"Those two will stoop to anything to get me to leave."

"You didn't tell the cops that, did you? It sounds unbelievable. They can't dictate who you talk to or see."

"No, I didn't accuse them. I figured that would be plain stupid. Doreen probably bullies the police around here just as she does everybody else in this town." She gulped down some ice chips. "It's over and I'm calm now. The floors had to be sanded and buffed anyway. Now they just have to remove what was left of my green paint, too. And that wall we did will have to be redone. They didn't take anything, thank goodness, but they left me a very clear message to leave town." She lifted her shoulders. "But I'm not leaving."

Rick admired her stance. She had changed from yesterday. But that scared him. Even though she'd come back from the ledge she seemed to be hovering over yesterday after church, she sounded even more determined today to prove herself. Or to seek revenge.

"Are you sure you're okay?"

"I'm fine. I had my little meltdown and now I've got things in perspective again. Hissy fit number three over and done with." She got up and tossed her garbage in the big trash bin at the end of the alley. "If they want a fight, I'll give them one. But they are not running me out of town. Not this time."

Rick didn't know whether to cheer her on or beg her to think twice. "That's the spirit. Whoever did this was probably just messing around. The place has been empty awhile. I'm sure some of the local kids think it's a good hangout. And now that someone has moved in, they probably don't like it."

"Several people don't like it," she retorted. "Tough."

"Mind if I have a look inside?"

She waved a hand toward the door. "Go ahead. You need to see where all that loan money is going."

He walked through the kitchen, stepping around drop cords, paint buckets and trays and floor sanders. "Looks like the painting is back on track and the floors will look great once they get buffed out."

She looked over the big wide parlor. "Amazing what a few professional painters can get done. I don't know why I didn't just let them do this in the first place."

"What? And miss out on seeing me try to paint a wall?"

She finally laughed. "We did have a lot of paint all over ourselves, didn't we?"

"Yes. But it was fun. We could work on the upstairs while they fix things down here. So you can at least have some privacy up there. Do you have a plan for your living quarters?"

She looked up the narrow staircase. "Oh, yes. A big sitting room, a nice bedroom off the turret room and a major update on the closets and the other bedrooms and baths. And a small efficiency kitchen. I'll keep the big one down here, too."

"Good plan."

Her gaze swept the cluttered room. "I'll never have this ready by the Fourth, no matter how many people Mr. Green brings in."

"If you let me help you, we can make sure you have things up and running in a hurry. You can have your grand opening the weekend right before the Fourth."

She looked skeptical. "You have a business of your own and you've already done enough."

He didn't want to hear this again. "Cari, can I give you some advice?"

"I guess so."

"You need to learn how to accept help."

She looked confused and surprised. "I thought I was learning. But I also need to learn to do things myself, my way. It's part of what my financial advisor calls 'tough love.'"

Rick wondered when this woman had last received some old-fashioned tender loving care. "Can't we reach a compromise? You want to get your business going and the rest of us want this house to be in good working order—we have an agenda there. It benefits all of us to keep this street clean and fresh for our visitors, right?"

"Right." She crossed her arms and looked down at her sneakers. "I don't know. I guess I can't snap my fingers and make it all pretty. Maybe it would be better to bring in more help."

"Then let me gather some people together, to show you we can do it. And to show Doreen she doesn't own everyone in this town. If we stand up to her together, maybe she'll get the message and back off."

"You'd do that for me?"

The doubt in her eyes and her words undid him. "Of course I would."

She slanted her gaze toward him. "I'll never understand you, Rick."

"Nothing to understand. I just want to help you."

He couldn't tell her that he might want more than that. Much more. He wanted to help a friend; he was sincere in that. But he also wanted to show her that she could trust other people to not only help her, but to hold her up when she felt she was falling. He wanted her to know that God thought she was worth helping.

And he had another reason for reaching out to Cari Duncan. He was beginning to care about her. A lot.

He watched as a whole slew of emotions clouded her eyes. She'd been out there alone in the big world for so long, she'd forgotten what sticking together was all about. Maybe she'd forgotten that once she had been treasured and loved, too. She needed to feel that way again.

As if finally seeing his point, she said, "You know, I've missed this. I'd forgotten about the sense of community that comes with a church family. My father turned against me when I needed him the most. That's a hard lesson to get over. I don't know how to ask for help because I've trained myself not to expect help."

Rick took her hand in his as they stood there with workers buzzing all around. "Then maybe it's time you learned a new lesson. There's no shame in letting others support you along the way. That's how communities are built. That's what holds this town together."

"But not everyone is as kind as you and your family."

"True, but the good far outweighs the bad."

"I hope so. I sure hope so."

A sander cranked up and she motioned him back outside. "Okay, so what did you have in mind?"

Rick pumped his fist in the air. "I'm going to call in some reinforcements to get started on the upstairs. Let me talk to Rod about it, clear things with him and his crew so we don't mess up their work schedule or get in their way. But I think we can make this work and get things moving a whole lot faster for you."

She smiled up at him. "Okay."

For the first time, Rick saw real hope shining in her eyes. And that hope made her look even more beautiful.

Chapter Twelve

Over the next week, Cari felt as if she were on one of the home-improvement shows where they promised to rebuild a house in seven days. Her life was suddenly filled from dawn to dusk with burly workmen and well-meaning friends.

Once Rick had put out the word about helping Cari to renovate Duncan House, people had started showing up, some bringing their own tools, some offering to make sandwiches or run to the hardware store for more supplies, some just there to observe the commotion.

Rick had been careful to work around Mr. Green and the paid contractors, letting them do what they needed to do to bring everything up to code. And that included everything from the electricity to the plumbing.

But the thousand other little odd jobs—Rick and his teams were handling that. The quest to save Duncan House had become the buzzword around here. Jolena even had a sign in the window of the diner, asking for volunteers.

The formidable Mrs. Paula Meadows had deemed the house worthy of the historical society's attention, too. She had the garden club working on landscaping plans while she herself searched for authentic antiques to display in Cari's shop.

"Your mother was a dear lady. *She* had class," Paula had told Cari in a tight whisper. "We're doing this in her honor and we'd love to name the garden after her. When you have your grand opening, we'll do an official dedication ceremony." Then she'd leaned close, her expression bordering on distaste. "That should show certain people what a true Duncan is made of. You're your mother's daughter after all."

Cari had been so touched she could only nod and smile. Her mother would have loved this.

It was so amazing.

"Why are they doing this?" Cari finally asked Jolena one morning after the downstairs gleamed sparkling and new. Everything from the painted walls to the rebuilt kitchen cabinets shimmered and glistened with a fresh new face.

Jolena gave her a cockeyed look then grinned. "You *have* been away too long. This is how we operate here, honey. We stick together."

"Rick told me the same thing." She smiled then hugged her friend. "How could I have forgotten that?"

Jolena patted her back. "You're back now and you've found hope again. That's what matters."

If Cari thought back, she could remember her

parents having just such friends. People who'd show up at the drop of a hat to lend a hand. She'd been so caught up in her resentment and her bitterness, she'd stayed away. And missed out on so much, including much of her father's last days.

Her reasons for staying away still haunted her, however. While Doreen had been quiet over the past week or so, Cari had heard rumors that she was fuming with anger at the way people had rallied around Cari. She fully expected the woman to gather a posse to make Cari cease and desist. She wouldn't be able to relax until she knew Doreen would leave her alone for good.

Today, the youth group from church was upstairs under Rick and Gayle's supervision, putting up new baseboards and drywall in the turret room. They'd made progress earlier today with Rick's guidance and Mr. Green constantly checking on their efforts to make sure the room was renovated to look like the original again. Now they were priming the walls so Cari could paint them later this week.

The old stairs had been reworked and mended all the way up to the second-floor landing. They were now solid and smelled of fresh wood. She planned to stain the banisters once the dust had settled and she had more elbow room. Maybe this weekend.

Heading up them now, she found Brady busy with some other kids upstairs. Rick was showing them how to put the primer on so it wouldn't be too heavy.

"Hi, Brady," she called, waving to him. He'd been here just about every day, quietly doing whatever needed to be done.

He looked embarrassed but waved back.

Cari walked over, admiring the big wall they'd finished in the flat white earlier today. "Good job, kids. I really appreciate this."

Brady looked away. Was he avoiding her?

"How you been?" she asked, playfully slapping him on the arm. "We haven't had much time to talk."

"Good." He turned back to his work on one of the turret room panels.

"Everything okay?"

He nodded but didn't look at her. Cari was about to walk away when he spoke. "I'm not supposed to be here."

Understanding dawned in her mind. "Because of your mother?"

"Yeah. She told me to stay away, but she had to go over to the next town to finish up a deal on a house she sold. She's fit to be tied about all of this."

Cari didn't doubt that. Knowing she was getting to Doreen should bring her a sense of pleasure, but it didn't. Not when she knew Brady could get in trouble for helping.

"And where's Bridget today?"

"In Atlanta, shopping with her friends. She said she hates driving up First Street—too congested these days."

Cari didn't comment on that, but she had to smile. So Bridget, in her infinite wisdom, went into the city just to avoid all of this. The logic was compelling.

Telling herself to take the high road, she turned to Brady. "So they don't know you're here."

"No. I kind of snuck out again. Mom probably hears that I've been helping, but so far she hasn't asked me about it."

Cari admired his fortitude, but she didn't want to get him in any more trouble with those two. "Thanks for coming, but maybe you'd better finish up and get home before they do."

He shrugged. "It's okay. I mean, I don't care what they say. I'm here with the youth group anyway. I like helping. And I like this house."

Some of the other boys snickered. One of them said, "Yeah, he likes it a lot."

"Shut up," Brady snapped, giving the kid a warning glance.

"Hey, cut that out." Rick thumped one of the boys on the head. "Keep at it. We've only got an hour of daylight left."

The boy who'd made the remark shot Rick a harsh glance then gave Brady a fuming look. "Yeah, whatever."

Rick's perturbed expression made the boy go back to work. "They've been at each other all afternoon."

"Why?" Cari asked. "This is a church group, right?"

"Right, but that doesn't mean everyone is sweetness and light. It's Youth Week and we're trying to bring them out of their self-absorbed little worlds to show them how to be responsible. We took them to the food bank yesterday to pack canned goods and deliver them to the area senior citizens. I thought I was going to have a food fight on my hands with that one." He indicated the boy who was still giving both Rick and Brady deep scowls. "Jeff—a hard case."

Cari watched the boy, noticing he kept eyeing Brady. Brady gave the boy several pointed looks in return. What was up with those two? "Maybe it's a girl," she said to Rick.

"Isn't it always?"

His smile made her almost drop her paintbrush. They'd been here like this, working side by side for the past few days, and she was beginning to like it way too much.

She also liked the way they managed to sit and eat together, usually something from Jolena's Diner. His tab had to be sky-high by now, since Rick insisted on feeding the workers most nights.

And he also insisted on staying late after everyone else left. Cari wasn't complaining. She enjoyed having him around.

"It's coming along, isn't it?" he asked now as he stood back to look at the bare canvas of the newly painted walls. "Do you plan to put paint in here, or some wallpaper, too?"

"Maybe wallpaper in the bathroom. But I think here in the bedroom, I want a two-toned effect. The darker blue under the chair railing and the powder blue on the rest. I have a beautiful blue-and-yellow floral quilted throw that'll look good with those colors. And I'll get pillows and bedding to match. Then a nice cushioned seat on the window seat in the turret room. I want it to look like spring in here, all light and airy. Hydrangeas, lots of hydrangeas in the patterns, to match my mother's old bush by the front porch."

She stopped, realizing he'd gone very still beside her. "What is it?"

Rick leaned close, his face inches from hers. "I love hearing you talk about this old place. Your eyes light up and you just get so beautiful."

Cari's blush burned a path down her neck. "I'm happy. Really happy. And I have you to thank for that."

"Me?" He grinned so widely she thought she might fall against the wet wall. "I make you happy?"

Yes, he did. "You've made a lot of this possible, organizing people to work in shifts, bringing everything together. Mr. Green has his crew downstairs and you're doing a lot up here. Teamwork—that's something I'm not that familiar with."

"Oh, so my *teamwork* abilities make you happy?"

"That's part of it, yes." How could she explain to him? And how could she give in to him? Her feelings for Rick scared her more than any confrontation she'd ever had with Doreen. "You've been a real friend, Rick. Amazing considering how we didn't really know each other that well before."

"I knew you," he said, his tone low. "You mentioned you had a crush on me in high school, right?

"Did I mention that? I don't remember."

"Yes, you do. And it's okay. I like knowing that." Before she could protest, he held up a finger. "But there's something I never told you. I never told anyone."

Her heart grew as heavy as her paintbrush. "What?"

"I kind of had a thing for you, too."

Cari shook her head. "No way. You were always with that snobby cheerleader."

"I might have been with her, but every time I'd see you I'd always wonder what was behind that shy smile. And now I know. And I like it."

Cari swallowed, trying to find air. Punching at her chest with a finger, she said, "This me you see right here, this is a whole new me."

"Maybe. We've both grown up a lot, I think. But I believe you were there—the real you—under all that shyness the whole time. And now, you've found your footing and let me tell you, nobody can compete with you. You're one of a kind, Princess."

"One of a kind? That can be good or bad, depending on how you look at things."

He looked down at her, his gaze moving over her face. "Well, from where I'm standing, it's all good. Trust me."

Cari gazed up at him and saw the truth in his eyes. He was being honest with her. "Thank you."

"Thank you? That's all I get?"

"What else do you expect me to say? Thank you for making me feel so happy. Thank you for forcing me to accept help. Thank you for apple pie and sunshine and mountain air."

"You can thank Jolena for the pie and the good Lord for the sunshine and the mountain air. But I appreciate your vote of confidence on my persuasive techniques, I think."

"No, I mean it," she replied. "You're the real deal, Rick."

He glanced around then lowered his head. "I want to kiss you."

Shocked, Cari stole a glance at the kids and Rick's mom on the other side of the room. "That's not going to be easy in this crowd."

"I'll stay to help you clean up," he said, his tone so relaxed and reasonable she had to wonder if he ever lost his cool.

She was sweating bullets here. "Thanks again."

"And when we're alone, really alone, I'll still want to kiss you. But you don't have to thank me for that."

"Is that a warning?"

"No, ma'am, that's a declaration. I've wanted to kiss you for a very long time now." When she didn't say anything, he asked, "Do you want to kiss me?"

Oh, did she ever! She looked down. "Uh, well, yes."

"Good, then let's get the rest of this primer slapped on here and herd these kids out for pizza. We've got plans for later. Big plans."

Cari didn't think she could lift the brush back to the windowsill. Her hands were shaking too much. Rick Adams wanted to kiss her—Cari Duncan.

She was so caught up in that, she forgot time. All she saw was a great pristine white wall that mirrored a fresh new beginning in her own life. All she heard was Rick laughing and talking to his mother and the kids behind them. She managed to finish priming her spot, her eyes seeing white dots because she couldn't look at anyone for fear this was just a dream.

"Miss Cari?"

She pivoted to where a young girl stood smiling

with pride in the arched door to the turret room. Cari stopped and stared, tears welling in her eyes. "It's beautiful. So beautiful."

Her little turret room was once again intact, complete with new windows that looked like the originals. Memories poured through her in the same way the last rays of sun were pouring through the glass. It was whitewashed with primer, clean and pretty, even if it was bare. The little room had been stripped clean, purged and rebuilt. Renewed.

Cari knew that feeling.

"It's perfect," she managed to say.

The girl pointed toward where Brady stood with paint all over him. "Brady said we needed to get this finished today."

Cari walked over to Brady. "Thanks, Brady. Now I can finish painting it and put some furniture in there. It's very pretty."

"It's very pretty, Brady," one of the other boys mimicked.

Jeff—the same boy who'd been picking on Brady before.

Gayle quickly herded them together. "Time to head to the Pizza Haus. C'mon. I have to have all of you back at the church by nine-thirty."

Brady glared at the other kid. "Stop it, Jeff."

Jeff made a face. "You started it."

"Hey," Rick said, getting between them. "Whatever's going on, drop it, right now. We're here to help Cari, not hurl insults at each other."

Jeff waved a hand toward Brady. "But he—"

"Now," Gayle said, pulling Jeff by his old T-shirt. "Downstairs and outside. Leave your brushes in the bucket of water by the back door and leave any other supplies on the back porch."

The boys and girls gathered their things and trooped downstairs, Jeff and Brady still giving each other heavy scowls.

"What in the world is going on with those two?" Cari said to Rick after their footsteps echoed down the steps.

"Hormones?" He shrugged. "Maybe Jeff is teasing Brady because he knows you're kind of his big sister."

"Could be. But they seem so hostile."

"Again, like you said, might be a woman involved."

"But not a girlfriend-type woman," Cari replied. "I wonder if Bridget has been fussing at Brady about me. He told me that she and Doreen don't know he's here tonight."

"He had to sneak here to help you? That is bad."

"That's how those two operate. They aren't kind to anyone who threatens them."

"Are you a threat to them?"

She thought about that. "I'm not purposely trying to be. I just want to get the place ready to open my shop and live my life. As long as they stay clear of me, I'll do the same with them." That old need to get even had died down in the face of so many kind people willing to help her. "I don't think they're worth my time."

"I agree. You can be civil, but you don't have to be around them unless it's necessary."

"I can live with that." She poked at his ribs. "Especially when I'd rather spend time with you."

Rick let out a gasp. "She admitted she likes me. She really likes me."

Cari burst out laughing. "Yes, I like you. There. Are you happy now?"

He pulled her close. "I will be. Now about that kiss?"

She shook her head. "If I'm getting kissed tonight, I want to take a bath and get all gussied up."

"But you look so cute in those baggy cutoff jeans and that Georgia T-shirt."

She pushed at his chest. "A woman has her pride, you know. I don't think you've actually seen me in a dress."

He finished putting lids back on the paint cans. "Oh yes, I have. That pretty green one you wore to church. My favorite. Will you wear it—for our kiss?"

She was sure she was blushing. "I'll be glad to."

"Okay, then it's a date. I'll go get cleaned up and meet you back here. Remember that great little Italian place just outside of town? We could go there for a late dinner?"

"*Is* this a date?"

"I guess it is. If I have to get all cleaned up, might as well make the most of it."

"Good."

"But," he said, and tugged her back into his arms, "how about a peck to hold me until later?"

He didn't give her time to stop him. Instead, he feathered her face with lightweight kisses.

She giggled, her heart hammering a joyful beat. "Go. Now. I want Italian food."

"And I want that kiss."

"I don't think that'll be a problem."

Cari hurried downstairs to thank the last of the workers then waved goodbye to Rick as he passed by, his smile full of promise.

Humming, she hurried to get her things so she could take a shower and put on her green dress. She just might have to pull out a nice pair of shoes, too. She'd saved a few of her favorite ones for special occasions.

Thank You, God, she said as she danced around. *Finally, my life might be coming together.*

This was better than any fairy tale. Way better.

She just hoped reality didn't ruin the whole thing.

Chapter Thirteen

An hour later, Cari heard a knock at the door.

Thinking it was Rick, she hurried from the bathroom to the front of the house and tugged open the door.

But no one was there.

"Rick?"

She thought she heard a noise in the hydrangea bush so she leaned out over the porch railing. And felt something wet and mushy hitting her in the stomach.

Gasping, Cari stepped back and watched as an overripe tomato slid down the front of her dress. "What—?"

The echo of footsteps running away sounded from the street. Sprinting down the steps, Cari saw a shadowy figure heading around the corner. "Wait a minute!"

Did she dare chase after them?

Headlights on the street blinded her. Rick pulled the

Jeep up to the curb and hopped out. "Hey, you must be as anxious as I am…."

He stopped when he saw her dress, his hands grabbing at her arms. "Cari, are you all right?"

She shook her head. "Not really. I have to go change."

Rick guided her up the steps. "What happened?"

She wiped at her soiled dress. "Someone threw a rotten tomato at me."

"You're kidding."

She pointed to the remains of the tomato splattered on the planked floor. "No, I'm very serious. I heard a knock at the door and thought it was you. But when I came out, someone was hiding in the bushes. They threw the tomato then I saw them running away."

He glanced out at the street. "Did you get a good look?"

"No. They were wearing a black hoodie—and whoever it was took off pretty fast." She didn't dare tell him that she'd caught just a glimpse of blond hair falling out from the hoodie the person was wearing.

Rick took her by the hand and ushered her into the house. "I don't get this. Who would do something so stupid and mean?"

But Cari got it. "Like I told you before, I think I know who's doing it. First the spilled paint and the message on the wall. And now, a tomato in my face. Can't you see it has to be Doreen or Bridget?"

Rick looked skeptical. His eyebrows shot up in disbelief. "Cari, this is so juvenile it's laughable. I can't believe two grown women would be so callous."

Heading into the kitchen, she said, "Well, I can." She grabbed a dish towel and wet it then tried to scrub the slimy tomato juice off her dress. "I lived with them for close to two years, Rick. This kind of thing happened to me a lot back then."

Rick shook his head. "You mean they played pranks on you?"

"All the time." Throwing the towel down, she dropped her hands to her sides. She hated the humiliating memories, but he needed to understand. "The worst fight my father and I had was because of those two. Over a pair of shoes, of all things. Bridget wanted to wear my sandals on the same night I wanted to wear them. When I protested, things turned very ugly. My father sided with Doreen and Bridget and I looked like a selfish, spoiled brat for not wanting to share with my sister. She got my shoes and I lost my father."

"I can't believe your dad would turn against you like that—because of a fight over shoes."

"It wasn't about the shoes," she said, the old frustrations coloring her words. "It was about how I was treated—like a stranger in my own home. It was like living in a prison. Bridget paraded her friends around, giggling and poking fun at me. She stole my things then denied everything. And I always came off looking jealous and petty." She hugged her hands to her midsection, the wet stickiness of the tomato making her sick. "And I'll look that way now if they have their say."

He stared at her as if he couldn't comprehend what she was telling him. "I've never heard of that. Whenever a widower remarries, I always think that's a good thing. I wish my mother could find someone, but she seems to like being on her own. I'm sorry your father's second marriage brought you so much heartache. And frankly, I can't understand why anyone would be so shallow and cruel."

Cari dropped her hands to her sides then lowered her head. "It threw me, too. And I didn't handle it very well. So finally, I just gave up and went off to college, hoping things would get better. But they never did. I'd come home on breaks and get the same treatment and it just got worse.

"After one of our famous fights, my father told me not to come back home until I could grow up and behave with a more civil attitude. So I didn't come back until he was too sick to care. After he died, I planned to never return, but here I am."

"And you think they've taken up where they left off?"

"Yes, I do. Doreen warned me to stay away from her children and if she found out Brady was here tonight, well, I guess this is her way of dealing with me." She started up the stairs. "And as for Bridget, she has a major crush on you. I'm a threat to her."

He looked up at her, shocked. "I don't care about Bridget."

"Maybe you should try telling her that."

Running a hand through his hair, he let out a sigh. "It can't be that bad. Maybe you're imagining things because you're still so angry at them."

Cari was in no mood to defend herself, especially

to him. She'd hoped he'd understand, that he truly would be her champion in this. But in spite of all he'd done for her, he didn't get it. Hadn't she learned that she had to stand on her own? She intended to stand up to Doreen this time, no backing down or running away.

And that might cause problems with Rick. His sense of right and wrong didn't provide for such conniving people as Doreen and her daughter.

"I didn't imagine that ugly message suggesting I need to leave. And I didn't imagine this ruined dress. I'm going to change." With that, she hurried upstairs to the small bedroom where her things had been moved during the renovations.

It hurt that Rick doubted her, but then he had no way of knowing the wrath of these people. No one did. They hid it all well, unless Cari was around.

"How can I prove I'm right, Lord?" she asked, hoping for divine guidance. She wasn't sneaky enough to set up a scene where she actually had witnesses. And knowing Doreen and Bridget, they'd be very sure that didn't happen anyway. Rick was right; it was hard to imagine two grown women acting out in such a ridiculous way. But Cari suspected they'd go to any lengths to send her packing. Doreen wanted the property this house sat on and Bridget wanted the man who'd been kind to Cari. End of discussion.

By the time she'd changed into jeans and a clean white button-up shirt, Cari wasn't really in the mood for a romantic dinner. But Rick was waiting for her at the bottom of the stairs.

"I'm sorry," he said, taking her hand. "I loved that dress. Is it salvageable?"

"I'll take it to the cleaners tomorrow," she said, trying to find the happiness they'd shared earlier. "I hope so. It was one of the few I kept when I sold most of my clothes." She didn't tell him that once she would have probably worn the dress a couple of times before sticking it in the back of her closet. Now she treasured it. Just another lesson she'd learned the hard way—to guard her real treasures and appreciate what she had.

"You look great anyway." He held her hand in his then looked up into her eyes. "Can we start over?"

Pushing at her bad mood, Cari nodded. She could tell he was still too shocked to believe her accusations. "I'm not overreacting, Rick. I know they're behind this. They think if they upset me enough, I'll run away like I did before. But this time, I'm not backing down. And if that means a confrontation, then I say bring it on."

His expression turned serious. "What if things get even worse for you? Cari, you could be in real danger living here on First Street. The town is fairly safe, but you're exposed here. There's a lot of late-night foot traffic through here, especially in the tourist seasons of summer and Christmas."

"I'll be fine," she said, touched that he was worried even if he did seem doubtful. "I'm having an alarm system installed for that very reason."

"But that's not until next week," he reminded her. "What if something else happens?"

"I'll deal with it," she said. "I'm okay. Mad about

my dress, yes, and mad that someone would be so stupid in the first place, but I'll be all right."

"My brother keeps my dog out at the ranch. I could bring him to stay with you for a while. Of course, he's just a big old sappy golden retriever."

"I'll be okay. Let's go eat. I'm starving."

"Maybe you should at least report this to the cops."

"And have them laugh at me for getting hit with a tomato? No thanks. They'll just chalk it up to pranksters. They'd never investigate Doreen. She carries a lot of clout in this town."

"Well, so do I," he replied. "I'll go with you."

"No. It's all right." Pushing him toward the door, she said, "Hopefully, this won't happen again. As much as I want to confront them, if I just ignore them maybe they'll take the hint and give up."

But if Doreen was behind these pranks, she'd never give up. Cari didn't think even Doreen would dare try anything completely criminal, but she shivered all the same as she locked the front door.

She noticed Rick had cleaned the tomato off the porch. The man knew the way to a woman's heart. He took care of every detail before she'd even thought about it. But with Rick, it wasn't all about control the way it could be with some men. No, with him, it was just the polite, gentlemanly way to do things. His mama had raised him right, as Jolena would say. And that was why he had a hard time seeing the bad in anyone. His one big flaw, Cari decided.

He opened the Jeep's door and helped her in. "You don't mind the top down, do you?"

"No, not at all." She needed some fresh air. The warm night wind cooled her burning skin.

As the Jeep whirled up the street toward the restaurant, Cari noticed a group standing near a fountain in the main square. "Hey, that was Brady and his friends. I thought they had to go back to the church."

Rick glanced in the rearview mirror. "They might be finished eating pizza. Maybe the chaperones gave them permission to hang out in the square."

"Maybe." Cari wondered again why Brady and Jeff had been so hostile toward each other earlier, since they seemed to be huddled together talking with the others now.

And she wondered why Brady had glanced up to give them a fixed stare as they'd driven by.

Rick's idea of a romantic evening had gone down the tubes as fast as a rafter taking on a spot of rapids. Having a tomato thrown at you could ruin any good mood, he figured. No matter how hard he tried to get back to the good feelings they'd shared earlier, Cari remained quiet and brooding. He hated seeing her this way, especially over two women who, according to her, were as shallow and self-centered as they came.

"Hey, you didn't eat much of your lasagna. I'll get a to-go box."

"No, don't," she said, pushing her plate away. "I'm not very hungry."

Dropping his fork, Rick reached for her hand. "Don't do this. Don't let them win. If Doreen was be-hind what happened and you're letting it get to you this way, then she wins. You know that saying about what angers you controls you? Don't let her control you, Cari."

She glanced up at him, her eyes glistening with pent-up frustration. "She's been in control since the day she pranced into my father's real estate office, pretending to be looking for a job. That's just the way it is."

"Not if you can rise above her shenanigans."

"And how am I supposed to do that? I've asked God to show me the way. I've prayed for strength and patience. I came back here with a hope of finding my home again, but already I'm beginning to regret that decision. I think I came home too late. Way too late."

Rick didn't know how to reach her. "Have you asked God to show you how to forgive? Maybe you've been praying for the wrong things. Maybe you came home for the wrong reasons."

She put a hand to her mouth. "How do I forgive someone who doesn't know the meaning of the word? This woman goes to church each Sunday, but she's evil, Rick. She always twisted the truth to make my father side with her and that tactic caused him to turn on me. How can I justify forgiving that?"

Rick tried again. "Her fate isn't in your hands. If all you say is true, she'll be judged in due time. But don't let her steal your happiness or your chance to be the better person. You have a lot of people supporting you. We're all behind you, Cari. Maybe you should try focusing on that instead of pouring all your energy into this one negative aspect of your life."

She put her head down, her hand on her chin. For a long time, she just sat there looking over at him, her eyes full of a deep hurting pain. Then she finally lifted up, her hands on the table. "You're right. I'm been blessed by all the incredible kindness I've received since I came back. And I don't take that lightly, honestly I don't. But you have to understand, when Doreen married my father, my self-esteem was already low. I'd just lost my mother and my daddy had become distant and depressed. He only married Doreen because he was so distraught about my mother, he didn't grasp what was happening to him. She used his vulnerabilities to take over his life. And once she was inside our home, she took over my life, too. She pitted Bridget against me at every turn. Brady was the only saving grace. He was too young to understand what was going on. And he looked up to me because his sister treated him so badly. We bonded right away, but I can't keep that bond. Doreen will see to that. She'll make sure Brady turns against me, too. She'll keep at it until—"

Rick saw the fear there in her eyes and instantly understood what she was trying to tell him. "You're afraid she'll turn everyone—even me—against you, aren't you?"

Her nod was so brief he almost missed it. But Cari had confirmed her worst fears with that tiny gesture. And like any human being, she didn't want to be alone and isolated again.

Rick's heart opened as he accepted his feelings for her. She'd been a princess once but she'd become an ousted princess, trapped in a tower of loneliness and isolation, banished to a foreign land, away from everyone and everything she loved.

Could he rescue her?

"Cari," he said, pulling her up and into his arms. "I'll never abandon you. God hasn't abandoned you. We're both right here. Do you hear me?" When she didn't answer, he lifted her chin so he could see her face. "Cari, do you believe me?"

She swallowed, her eyes misty and fathomless. "I want to believe you, so much. But you don't owe me anything, Rick. You're just being a good neighbor, a good friend. Because you've become a good man. I only hope I can live up to all that potential you seem to think I have."

He tugged her out of the restaurant, pulling her toward the Jeep. When they reached the vehicle, he turned her around and brought her back into his arms. "I care about you, okay? No matter what, remember that."

The only way he knew to make her see was to show her. So he lifted her chin with his hand and he pulled her toward him, his lips touching hers in a soft, sweet need. That sweet need swept through him like a rushing river, bonding him to her in a purging acceptance.

Cari fell against him, returning the same need, her lips sighing against his. She lifted away but held him close. "I don't deserve you. I'd hate to lose our friendship. You've been so kind to me."

"It's not just about being kind," he said. "It's about

so much more between us." Then he pulled back to stare down at her. "I want to kiss you again, but not like this. I want things between us to be special and I want you to be sure. Just hold on to what we felt tonight. And then, whenever you're ready, you let me know how you feel, okay?"

She bobbed her head then hopped up into the Jeep. They drove the short distance to her house in silence. Rick walked her to the door. "Let me come in and check around."

He didn't wait for her permission. He walked through the old, creaking house, turning on lights and checking locked doors and windows. "Looks okay down here. Let's check upstairs."

She followed him without a word as he turned on lights in each of the rooms upstairs. When they reached the turret room, he flipped on the hanging chandelier, watching as light cascaded across the brilliant whitewashed walls.

And heard Cari's gasp behind him.

He looked back and saw her finger going up in the air toward the turret.

Rick turned and looked at the little octagonal room.

And saw what Cari had seen.

Two of the brand-new windows had been shattered into pieces. Glass covered the window seat and the floor.

And two big rocks lay amid the crushed, broken glass.

Without a word, Cari rushed back down the stairs.

But the echo of her angry steps ricocheted throughout the empty rooms with an eerie cadence that confirmed what she'd believed all along. Someone was definitely trying to send her a message. Rick hoped he could find out who before Cari took matters into her own hands.

Chapter Fourteen

"Yes, I need two new windows installed. Yes, the turret room," Cari explained one more time to Rod Green. "I know, I know. We just finished those two days ago." When she told him what had happened, she had to hold the phone away from her ear. The man didn't like having to repeat the same tasks, especially when it involved vandalism and destruction of property. "I agree, Mr. Green. It's sad and it's not fair, but I need those windows replaced. As soon as possible."

She hung up the phone, drained and discouraged, wondering for the hundredth time if she should leave Knotwood Mountain and never come back.

But what about your father?

The voice inside her head echoed through her tired system. Would she be dishonoring her father if she sold the property and left? What did that matter now, she wondered. She'd dishonored him while he was alive, because she was too hurt and too prideful to come home and fight for him.

Thinking she could have helped him, Cari wished she could change things and turn back the clock to make it right.

Then stay here and fight now.

Did she have the stamina, the strength to do that?

What if Rick got tired of her bitterness and turned on her the way her father had? Cari knew that would break her heart. And right now, her heart was too fragile to take much more.

Remembering how she'd asked him to leave the other night after finding the broken windows, Cari figured Rick had already had enough. She hadn't talked to him in the past couple of days, but the lasting memory of their kiss had stayed with her, reminding her that he cared about her.

Still, she couldn't think about that right now. Now that most of the downstairs had been painted and polished and the alarm system was ready to go, she could finally move the rest of her inventory out of storage and into the shop. Maybe she could lose herself in working on her jewelry designs. That had always brought her joy and working helped to keep her calm and centered. She'd focus on that and put the need to confront Doreen out of her mind.

Grabbing her cup of coffee, Cari walked out onto the big porch, her spirits lifted by the new landscaping. Mrs. Meadows and her formidable team had done a great job of cleaning up the shrubs and weeds. Now the front path leading to the newly painted steps was lined with daylilies and hosta plants. The old crape myrtle by the steps had been pruned and trimmed so that the branches cascaded out like an umbrella offering shade. And the hydrangeas had been shaped and nurtured, their cotton-candy blue and pink blossoms and wide green leaves shining brightly in the morning sun.

She stepped off the porch to admire the new sign that had been delivered yesterday. Hometown Princess. She liked that name for her boutique. It summed her up. And Rick called her a princess all the time, whether she truly was one or not. The wide white sign held deep purple scrolled letters, its border etched with grapevines and flowers. It was dainty and pristine but with a bit of attitude. And she sure needed attitude to pull this off.

Maybe I can learn from the sign, she thought, smiling to herself in spite of her worries.

"It looks good."

Cari whirled to find Brady standing behind her. "Thanks." She motioned him forward. "What are you up to today?"

He shrugged. "Just hanging out. I'm on restriction because—" He stopped, dropped his head.

"Because you came here the other night and helped me with the house?"

Cari knew the answer from his guarded expression. "Mom was pretty hot when she found out. You know how people like to talk around here."

"Yes, I do." Cari sat down on the steps. "I'm sorry you got in trouble. Maybe you shouldn't be seen talking to me."

"I don't care," he said, his tone full of determined pride. "Bridget gets away with everything and…I'm always in trouble."

"I can certainly understand that." Cari didn't dare tell him that his family had made her life miserable. "Sometimes it's hard to just live your life when you've got other people telling you what to do."

He lifted his head. "Yeah, that's it exactly. They're always telling me how to behave, what to wear. Mom worries about what people will think." He shrugged. "She never worries about what I think."

Cari's heart went out to the boy. He was at that delicate cusp between youth and adulthood. That awkward, miserable age. The same age she'd been when Doreen had come into her life. "Wanna come in and have a Danish? Got them fresh from Jolena this morning."

He glanced around. "Sure. Mom won't let me drive since I'm on restriction. I have to walk everywhere even though I have my permit. Might as well hang out with you."

Cari lifted up to put a hand around his shoulder, a disturbing thought crossing her mind. What if some of Brady's friends were harassing her? "You can always hang out with me, okay? Remember that. And I have an ulterior motive. You can help me unpack some of my things for the shop. The shelves are up and ready to display my treasures." Maybe he'd clue her in on the kids he hung out with.

"Cool." He followed her up the steps and into the house, his smile soft with gratitude.

After feeding Brady and giving him a glass of milk, Cari showed him the boxes lining the walls of the small storage room in the back of the house. "Now, be careful with these things," she cautioned. "The jewelry is delicate and we need to hang the necklaces on those old frames I have sitting on the counter. I'll show you how to hook them across the wires."

Brady nodded. "I hope none of my friends come by. They'd rag me for playing with necklaces and bracelets."

Cari tried to sound unconcerned. "Hey, you're helping me out. I'll even pay you for your time. And I might be able to hire a couple of your buddies, too."

He looked surprised, then cautious. "Really? I could use a summer job, but most of my friends are busy."

"Not a good idea to hire everyone, huh?"

He shook his head. "Probably not. And…I'd have to clear it with Mom."

She hadn't considered that. But she did need a stock boy and Brady would be perfect. "I hope she'll agree." Maybe if she begged Doreen. "I can only pay you minimum wage for now and only for a few hours each week. But if it works out and you're interested in working some after school, I might be able to increase that a little bit in the fall."

"That'd be great." He lifted a box and carried it to the front of the building. "So, Mr. Green's all done down here?"

"Yes, thank goodness." She brought another box up front. "They finished the final touches late last night."

Then she made a face. "But…someone broke out two of the turret room windows. He's coming back later today to replace those."

Brady stopped, his hand on a box. "Really? When did that happen?"

Cari pulled out a dainty evening bag that she'd found in a flea market booth. She'd reworked it with rows of costume jewels—sapphires, rubies and emeralds—all marching across the white silk with glittering precision. "The other night, after the youth group was here. And after you all worked so hard on that room. I was so upset I almost gave up." She couldn't voice her suspicions. As much as she resented his mother, she wouldn't talk badly about the woman to her son. "But whoever's messing with me doesn't realize I'm not leaving Knotwood Mountain."

He busied himself with opening another box. "Do you…like…know who did it?"

"No, I don't." At least she couldn't be sure. "Rick said I should report it to the police, but I tried that the first time the place was vandalized and they didn't seem too concerned." She glanced out at the street. Already the tourist traffic had increased. Another week until the big Fourth of July weekend. She hoped she'd be ready for business by then. Turning back to Brady, she said, "I have an alarm system now. I can turn that on whenever I leave. And especially at night. That should stop the vandalism."

He didn't say anything, so she let him go back to unpacking the various items she'd either designed or ordered at market. Soon Cari was immersed in getting her stock in order, the joy of being able to do what she loved overtaking her worries about vandals. Brady worked with her, side by side, his quiet concentration on getting it right making her glad she'd offered him a job.

Two hours later, they'd cleared out most of the boxes from the storage room, but Brady hadn't divulged anything about his friends. Or himself, for that matter. Why did she get the feeling that maybe he did know something about the vandalism? Was he protecting his friends, or his sister?

"This place is beginning to look the way I envisioned it," she said as she offered him a soft drink. "With you helping, I got these things out in half the time it would have taken if I'd done it by myself. I sure do appreciate it."

Brady glanced around, clearly uncomfortable with the frilly blouses and flounce skirts. "Do women really like this stuff?"

"Some women do," she replied, her fingers trailing over a stuffed rack of clothes. "It's all about being unique and different. I try to keep my prices down, though. That way, I can deal in volume and, hopefully, turn a profit."

He took a long swig of his drink. "Yeah, Mom's always talking about making more money. Sometimes, she sits at her desk working on her computer until late at night."

"Your mother always did have a strong work ethic," Cari said. To the point of ignoring her own family, apparently. Then because she needed to know, she asked,

"Does she do okay with her real estate—I mean now that the economy is so bad?"

"I guess," he said, shrugging. "She never talks to me about that stuff. Bridget spends money all the time, though. Mom fusses at her, but Bridget doesn't care."

Of that, Cari had no doubts. But she wondered about other things. "Brady, after I left, was my dad happy? I mean really happy?"

Brady's expression turned cautious and blank. He flipped his bangs and stared out the window, his empty drink can in one hand. "I guess. He…him and me didn't get along so well."

That surprised Cari. "But…he seemed to love all of you so much."

Brady kept staring out the window. "He was sick a lot. Sometimes, he got really nasty with us. He'd scream at Bridget a lot. And he argued with Mom about everything."

Hearing that her father fussed at Doreen should have brought Cari a measure of triumph, but it only left her feeling empty and hollow. Did she really wish her father the same misery she'd suffered? No, she couldn't wish that on anyone. But it hurt her to think he'd become as bitter as she'd been.

"Did he ever mention me?"

Brady turned at her question, his gaze sweeping over her. "Sometimes, after he got really bad off. He'd sleep on the couch in the den and he'd mumble things."

Tears pricked at Cari's eyes. "It's all right. You don't have to talk about it. It's done now. I'm just glad I got to see him before he died."

"He asked for you all the time," Brady said. "That's why Mom finally called you. She didn't want to, but he kept asking."

Cari couldn't stop the tears. "He did?" She wiped at her eyes. "I never knew."

"I didn't mean to make you cry," Brady said, embarrassment coloring his freckled face. "I guess I need to go before Mom sends Bridget out looking for me."

Cari sniffed and wiped her face. "Don't mind me. I get emotional, thinking about my parents."

He went to the kitchen and threw his can in the recycling bin. "I guess it's hard, not having anyone."

Cari could only nod.

"I don't remember my dad. Mom wouldn't talk about him much. She said he was a loser and he wasn't worth discussing."

Ashamed of her own self-centered resentment, Cari had never once given thought to what Brady and Bridget must have gone through with their parents divorcing when they were so young. No wonder they both seemed to have issues. How could she blame them?

Walking with Brady toward the door, she put a hand on his shoulder. "I hope my daddy at least treated you better than that. He was a good father once. I'd like to believe he cared about all of us."

Brady bobbed his head. "I don't know. It's hard to say how he felt." Then he glanced around. "I need to go."

Cari opened the door. "If you want to come by for a couple of hours tomorrow, I could use the help. I'll write you a check at the end of the week."

"Sure."

They walked to the steps. "Thanks again," Cari said.

The sound of a car speeding up the busy street caused her to look up.

Bridget pulled up the short driveway and slammed on the brakes, the convertible skidding to an abrupt stop. "Brady, get in the car, right now. Mom is looking for you. And when I tell her where I found you—" She stopped, her harsh expression moving from Brady to Cari. "You think you can steal my little brother from me, too? Do you, Cari?"

Cari hurried down the steps to face her. "Brady helped me do some unpacking. I'm going to pay him for his time."

"Well, that's funny, considering you had to beg for a bank loan." Smirking at Brady, she said, "Better hurry up and cash that check. Because we all know you don't have a dime to your name. Now get in, Brady. I have a date tonight." She lifted her sunglasses. "With Rick Adams."

Cari's stomach went hot with pain. How could she believe a word coming out of Bridget's mouth? She wouldn't. She couldn't. "Thanks again for helping, Brady."

Brady shot Cari an apologetic look then hopped in the car. Bridget didn't give Cari time to say anything else. She peeled out and took off up the street, her blond locks fanning out behind her head.

But Cari saw the triumphant look Bridget shot her through the rearview mirror.

And she decided she'd had enough. Heading back inside, she grabbed her purse then made sure she set the new alarm.

It was high time she had a one-on-one talk with Doreen. It was time to get everything out in the open, so she could at least start the process of healing. She wanted to stay here and she wanted to get to know Rick better, regardless of how Bridget felt about that. And she wanted to be a good sister to Brady.

Because it was obvious that the kid needed someone in his life who actually cared about him enough to fight for him.

She'd just reached her car when Rick's Jeep pulled up to the curb. And he looked all dressed up and ready for a date.

Chapter Fifteen

Cari wouldn't ask. She refused to stoop to Bridget's level. Never mind that she and Rick had grown closer with each passing day. Never mind that he'd kissed *her*.

Had he kissed Bridget in that same way? The thought twisted her stomach in knots.

"Hi," he said, walking toward her, his smile as sure and steady as always. "I was passing through and saw you coming out of your door. How are you?"

"Fine," she said. "I was just leaving."

"And with such an intense frown on your face, too. Are you going to the banquet?"

Confused, she shook her head. "What banquet?"

He waited for a group of chattering twenty-somethings to pass by out on the sidewalk. "A dinner out at a catfish restaurant on the river south of town. One of the business associations sent me an invitation a couple of weeks ago. I'd almost forgotten about it until—"

"Until Bridget reminded you?" she asked, wishing she could put a muzzle on herself.

"Bridget?" Now he looked confused. "No, my mother reminded me. I would have called you to come with me, but I had to hurry and get cleaned up. I'd really rather not go, but duty calls."

Relief washed through Cari like a warm rain. "I didn't get an invitation, but then I'm not officially open for business yet." And she might not be welcome yet, either. She'd find that out when she finished things up and had her grand opening.

"Won't be long before you'll be just as involved in these things as I am," he said. He looked at his watch. "If you want to come with me…"

She should, just to show Bridget. But the high road beckoned to her. "No, no. I have an errand to run. You go ahead, since you're already dressed and ready." She wondered if Bridget had a seat waiting for him at the banquet. And she wondered if he was being ambushed. Did she dare tell him about Bridget's declaration—that they had a date? No. That would make Cari look like a jealous shrew. Which wouldn't be too far from the truth, come to think of it.

He lingered for a minute then reached up to push a strand of hair off her face. "Hey, are you all right?"

"I'm great. Brady helped me unpack some of my stock this afternoon. Mr. Green has finished most of the tough renovation jobs. The plumbing down here is in better working order now and I have a new refrigerator and stove in the kitchen. I'm going to paint the cabinets later, I think. But as for the front of the place—these two rooms and the hallway—the boutique's coming together. And the alarm system is intact."

"No more trouble since the last time?"

She didn't want to tell him what Bridget had said to her. Or that she was about to go and confront Doreen. "No. All's quiet for now. Maybe it's over."

"I hope so. Only a few days until the Fourth."

"Yep. This summer is going by so fast."

He leaned close. "Well, I guess I'd better get to the restaurant before the fried catfish gets cold." He gave her a quick peck on the cheek. "Do you want to come out to the ranch tomorrow? I'll give you the grand tour and maybe we can go horseback riding?"

Cari thought about turning him down, but her heart told her to go on faith and trust that he didn't actually have a real date with Bridget. And since he'd just kissed her on the cheek, she was pretty sure she had the upper hand for now.

Stop thinking in that way, she told herself. She refused to get into a superficial competition with Bridget. Cari had made a lot of mistakes in her life, but she wasn't as petty and shallow as Bridget Stillman. And she prayed God would guide her to take that high road she was trying so hard to follow. "I'd like that," she said. "But maybe later in the day. I still have a lot to do around here in the morning."

He nodded, his hand touching hers. "I can help you."

"Rick, you have a store to run, remember?"

"Yeah, I guess I do at that. And tomorrow being a

Saturday, we'll be pretty busy. But I have extra staff in place so I can take off early. That way, I can work most of the holiday weekend and give my employees time with their families."

Cari had never known a man like Rick Adams. He was dedicated, devout and thoughtful. He cared about other people and always put others first. Not only could she learn a lesson in business from him, she could also learn a lesson on humanity from him. "Then I guess I'll see you tomorrow afternoon," she said. "Now get going. I don't want you to miss out on your dinner."

"One more kiss," he said, tugging her close. This time, he touched his lips to hers long enough for Cari to sigh and hold him tight.

When he pulled back, she giggled. "We'll be the talk of the town."

"I think we already are," he said through a satisfied grin. "Doesn't bother me one bit."

She believed that. Nothing seemed to bother him.

Another lesson for her.

"Bye," she said, pushing him toward the Jeep. "Don't eat too much."

"They're having cheesecake for dessert," he shouted, hopping into the Jeep. Then he waved, winking at her, before he took off in the late-day traffic.

Cari watched him leave then sank down on the porch steps, all of her self-righteous steam suddenly gone.

What should I do, Lord? She sat there, silent and

still, wondering if she should confront Doreen. Or maybe just talk to the woman about allowing Brady to work for her. What could be the harm in that?

Deciding she couldn't let her temper get the best of her, Cari got up and went back inside to unpack some more. She'd focus on her work here and hope there would be no more vandalism, especially since Mr. Green had done a rush job on fixing the windows in the turret room. And maybe Doreen would slowly come to accept that Cari was here to stay and give Cari a chance to be a friend to Brady.

So she cranked up the music on the local mixed music radio station, poured herself a tall glass of lemonade and became immersed in organizing the boutique, her thoughts centered on having her own date with Rick tomorrow afternoon.

Rick gave Bridget a brittle smile and carefully extracted her arm from his. He'd been set up, plain and simple. Somehow, Bridget and Doreen had managed to get him seated right next to them tonight. And now, only manners kept him from moving to another table. He had to wonder now why Cari had asked him if Bridget reminded him of this dinner. Had Cari known Bridget would be here?

"How's the fish?" Bridget asked, her eyes wide with wonder.

"Good." Rick dropped the direction of his thoughts and looked over at her chicken. He'd ask Cari about her comment tomorrow. "How's your meal?" he asked Bridget, trying to make small talk.

She shrugged, her dangling gold earrings looping around her shoulders. "You know—same old food, same old scene." She leaned close, her perfume stifling him. "We could skip out early. I only came because Mom insisted. And because she told me you'd be seated at our table."

Rick chuckled, sweat beading on his brow. "And I only came because my mother reminded me I'd reserved a seat and paid for my dinner."

Bridget's pout was immediate and completely fake. "And here I thought you came to see me."

"I didn't know you'd be here," he replied, wishing he'd just stayed at Cari's. They could have ordered pizza and unpacked trinkets. "A pleasant surprise," he said, hoping the Good Lord didn't strike him down for fibbing.

Bridget didn't quit. "Well, now that you're here and you see me sitting here, are you glad you came?"

How to answer that? "It's hard to say. These functions are usually boring. But I'm not bored tonight." No, he was too keyed up to be bored.

"Then you are glad to see me," Bridget said, sitting up to lean toward him. "But even though I'm with you, I'm very bored with all these stuffy old people. Let's go for a ride along the river road with the top down."

"You mean in your car?"

"Your car or mine. I don't care. I just want to get out of here before they start handing out the awards." She did a mock yawn. "We can be alone, finally."

Rick looked across the table at Doreen. She'd had

her gaze centered on her daughter and him for most of the night. That is, when she wasn't flirting with the newly divorced car salesman sitting next to her. He was beginning to see Cari's point about these two. They were both a piece of work, smooth operators and definitely always on the prowl.

"Rick?"

He looked back at Bridget. "That sounds nice, really. But it would be rude of me to leave early, Bridget. The people who win these awards have worked hard to help make Knotwood Mountain a better place. We owe them the courtesy of staying here to share in the celebration. I won one myself last year and it was nice to look out over the audience and see the friendly faces."

"Oh, bother," Bridget said, her words exaggerated and harsh. "You sound just like my mother, always thinking about this stupid little town."

"Don't you care about your home?" Rick asked, hoping to sway her. "You know, we have a strong sense of community here. You should come to church sometimes, meet more people your own age. We have a great college-age group. They do all kinds of fun things together."

"Are you kidding me? I'll be twenty-four soon. The kids around here are so lame." She tossed her hair off her shoulder. "I don't do church and I don't hang out with Jesus freaks. And I can't wait to get out of here. Even if I can't go back to school this fall, I'm leaving this place one way or another." Then, her petulance gone for a moment, she smoothed her napkin in her lap. "Unless of course a certain store owner could convince me to stay."

Rick couldn't believe he'd once again gotten caught up in Bridget's little games. So she'd stay if he got involved with her? Like that was gonna happen. He had to extricate himself from this uncomfortable situation, but he refused to leave since she'd only follow him. Looking across the room, he said, "There's the mayor. I need to discuss a few things with her before the awards ceremony starts. Will you excuse me?"

He didn't give Bridget time to answer. Instead he got up and moved through the crowd until he'd made his way to where the mayor stood talking to another woman. After greeting the women and getting into a conversation that lasted a few minutes, he glanced back at the table where he'd been sitting.

Bridget was gone.

Rick hoped she was gone for the night. He breathed a sigh of relief then waited until the last possible moment before heading back to his seat. He shouldn't be so cowardly about this, but he didn't want to hurt Bridget. And he really wanted to be with Cari tonight. That was at the heart of the matter. If he made Bridget angry, she could make things worse for Cari.

Help me, dear Lord.

When he sat down, Doreen looked across at him then got up to come around the table. "She left." She shot him a hostile look. "You need to quit stringing my daughter along, Rick. Make a commitment, one way or another. You can't have both of them."

"What are you talking about?" he asked, his voice low.

Doreen shook her head. "Men are so dense sometimes. You know what I mean. Before Cari came back, you flirted with Bridget all the time. The girl thinks you care about her. And I had hoped…well, never mind what I hoped. I won't have you toying with my daughter's affections, especially since you seem to be over the moon about Cari." She stood to straighten her black dress. "We'll see how that turns out. Cari can be a handful but then you'll just have to see that for yourself. And you will, mark my words. And don't expect Bridget to be waiting in the wings for you when you come to your senses."

Rick stared up at her, shocked and feeling sheepish. Had he been stringing Bridget along? Had she misread his attempts at kindness? "I'm sorry, Doreen. I thought Bridget and I were just friends."

"Well, you thought wrong." She shot him one last frown before returning to the other side of the table with a charming smile for her newest conquest.

Rick listened to the awards being announced, clapping at all the right moments while his mind raced, replaying every encounter he'd had with Bridget over the last few months. For the life of him, he couldn't see past just being polite to the girl but maybe he'd also been blinded to the truth, too. Then he thought again about how Cari had asked him if Bridget was the one who'd reminded him of the banquet tonight. Which meant Bridget had probably paid Cari a visit to purposely let her know they'd be here together tonight.

Great, Rick thought. I've really messed things up now. He should have stayed with Cari, regardless of making appearances and honoring the price of a meal. And it was high time he stood up to Bridget's not-so-subtle overtures toward a romance. He didn't want anything more with Bridget.

This had to stop. He needed to be honest with Bridget once and for all. At least he could agree with Doreen on that point. He'd called himself doing a good deed, trying to tolerate her so he could encourage her to come to church. But that had backfired on him, big-time. It had been easy to flirt with Bridget before, thinking it was harmless and hoping she'd change and find God's grace in the process.

But now, he cared about Cari too much to keep this up.

No, he more than cared about her. He was falling in love with her. And waffling on that wasn't fair to either Bridget or Cari. How could it be that he was always strong and decisive in his business dealings and whenever he dealt with family issues, but when it came to women, he caved like a big old teddy bear?

And that, my friend, is what got you so off track in Atlanta. Was this a pattern that would keep him from ever settling down with one woman? Not if he could help it.

He wanted one woman. He wanted Cari. On that he was sure, at least.

High time Bridget understood the boundaries so she'd stop tormenting Cari. He hoped. He didn't want to make things worse for Cari. Deciding he'd need to handle this situation with a lot of prayer and diplomacy, Rick listened to the rest of the ceremony then left as soon as the dinner was over, his thoughts centered on how to fix the situation he'd gotten himself into without hurting any delicate feminine feelings.

Especially Cari's delicate feminine feelings.

It was after midnight when Cari finished the last of her unpacking then stood back to admire the shelves lined with bold colorful jewelry, sequined and sparkling purses, bright floral scarves, sheer blouses and basic T-shirts. The big round racks centered in the middle of the room held dresses and sweaters, skirts and casual tops and bottoms. And an armoire on the far wall held even more accessories and trinkets, most of them her original designs and her refurbished estate jewelry.

She'd placed pieces of eclectic art around the few open walls to add some whimsy and charm to the furnishings and she'd put the two floral chairs she'd upholstered by the bay windows with an old round wicker table between them. She'd keep fresh flowers on the table as much as possible, maybe by cutting a deal with the florist around the corner.

Soon, she'd have her workshop installed upstairs in the tiny bedroom that had once served as a nursery. If the Lord was willing, she might even one day use that room for its original purpose again—a baby.

That train of thought jarred her. "Wow. First things first. Right now, this business is your baby."

So she changed her thoughts back to the here and now, her daydreams filled with a maternal longing all the same. She could almost picture Rick holding a tiny child.

"Stop that!" Cari whirled to admire the new and improved Duncan House.

Mr. Green and his workers had done an amazing job of cleaning up and renovating the bottom floor of the house. The kitchen still needed a lot of work, but he'd promised Cari he'd finish that part up after-hours and later when the high tourist season had settled down a bit. For now, the plan had been on getting the front hallway and the two main rooms ready for the boutique's opening next week. Now that that task was done, Cari couldn't help but be proud.

"It looks great," she told herself as she tidied up and got ready for bed. Exhausted but elated, Cari headed upstairs with a smile on her face. *Thank You, Lord, for providing me with such a blessing in Mr. Green. And thank You for all the help You sent to me to speed things up.* And Rick was the first one on that list.

She thanked God for Rick and his mother and Jolena and her helpful daughters. For Brady and the youth from the church, for the many well-wishers and neighbors who'd offered help, most of them doing it out of respect for her parents. Thinking she really did have a lot to be thankful for, Cari glanced into the turret room. The moonlight invited her inside the big empty room and since she was naturally drawn toward the round little structure in the corner, she padded over to sit in her favorite spot on the window seat.

The night outside was whitewashed in magnolia-colored moonbeams. The wind lifted the crape myrtle, causing the pink and purple blossoms to fall like lace down to the street below. She could hear the faint sounds of country music coming from the karaoke stage at the Pizza Haus, followed by the laughter of patrons out on the patio overlooking the river. It was nice, sitting here in her home, knowing she'd accomplished a lot over the last month or so. All the hard work was paying off at last.

Cari leaned down, her chin resting on her hands as she stared out into the night, her thoughts on Rick and how much she'd come to care about him. Did he feel the same? His kisses indicated he did.

But he'd spent the evening with Bridget.

Cari sat up, pushing her jealousy aside as she reminded herself Bridget hadn't been honest about their so-called date.

"And I won't fall into her traps," Cari said into the still house. "Never again."

She was turning to head to the small bedroom down the hall when she heard a car zooming up the street below. Glancing down, she watched as the driver of the car threw something into the air. When she heard a thud hitting her front porch, Cari gasped, her hand coming to her throat.

The motion-detector kicked on, lighting up the front yard and her newly installed alarm went off, the sound like a siren shrilling out over the quiet night. As she hurried back downstairs to hit the alarm button, Cari heard the car taking off, tires grinding against asphalt.

And she watched out the bay window as the white convertible sped away into the night.

Chapter Sixteen

❧

Rick could tell something was wrong the minute he knocked on Cari's door the next afternoon. Did she think he'd been with Bridget last night?

You were with Bridget last night, he reminded himself as he took in all the pretty baubles in Cari's shop. But not in the same way he wanted to be with Cari—not in a serious "with her because he really wanted to be there" way. Of course, try telling that to a woman.

"Hi. Are you ready to head to the ranch?"

She nodded then motioned him in, her expression blank and guarded. "I will be in about five minutes."

Trying to gauge her mood, he said, "The place looks fantastic. You're gonna do great business here. Mom doesn't have anything like this in her apparel shop upstairs. We needed something young and hip like this."

"Yes, I think so."

Okay, not exactly the response he was searching for. He tried again. "So how's your morning been?"

She shrugged. "I've had a few phone calls asking when I'll be open and I've had people peering in the windows. The chamber of commerce did a piece in their weekly newsletter for the Sunday paper, so that's brought in some early lookers, too."

"That's a good sign."

She whirled then. "Yes, a very good sign. And speaking of signs, remember the one I had made, the sign that showed the name of my shop? You know, the one I so proudly hung on the front porch a couple of days ago?"

Rick noted the gradual rise in her words with each question she threw out. "Yes, I liked that sign a lot. What about it?"

She waved toward the porch. "Did you happen to notice it's not there today?"

He had not noticed that and now he was thinking probably that was a bad thing, not noticing. "Really? What happened? Did you take it down? Or did it fall? The hooks were solid so they should have held."

"Oh, they would have if someone hadn't come by late last night to purposely throw a brick right into my pretty sign. Knocked it off its hinges and it fell and hit one of my dish gardens and broke the clay pot and destroyed some of my flowers. The sign has a big, ugly gash across the front and one of the chains is broken. I have to have it repaired. And the brick landed on the planked floor and knocked out a hole about four inches wide right by the front door. But you probably didn't notice that either."

He'd have to learn to be more observant. "No, I'm sorry. I didn't."

She stopped to stare at him, took a deep breath, her fingers strumming against a glass countertop. "The vandals have struck again."

"Did you see anything?" Rick asked, concern for her safety overriding any other feelings and his own failings in not noticing.

"Oh, I saw enough."

"Did the alarm work?"

"Yes, the alarm did its job and the motion detector scared them away, thank goodness. The car took off in a hurry."

"But you saw the car?"

She nodded, pushed a hand through her hair. "A white convertible, top down." At his openmouthed surprise, she said, "The driver was wearing a dark hat. Hard to see who it was. But I think we both know who did this."

"Bridget," Rick said, shaking his head. "Are you sure?"

"I saw her car, Rick." Cari started gathering her stuff, then moved to turn off lights and lock doors. "Maybe I should just stay here and guard my property."

"What time did this happen?"

She shrugged. "Around ten-thirty or eleven, maybe."

Bridget had left the dinner at just past eight. Plenty of time for her to fume and go find a brick or two.

"Did the police come?"

"They came and listened to me rant and told me they can't do anything until I have solid proof."

"Did you tell them you thought it was Bridget?"

"Sure did. Even described the car. But they need a license plate number. Since I didn't get that, they can't do a whole lot and they suggested I shouldn't make unfounded accusations. So I'm stuck with having yet another repair to pay for." She sank down onto a round brocade stool. "I'm tired of this. I worked hard yesterday to get everything just right and now this. It's so silly, so ridiculous, even I find it hard to believe. A grown woman resorting to pranks to try and scare me away. She must really have it in for me, or she really has it bad for you." She grabbed her tote bag. "So how *was* dinner with Bridget last night, anyway?"

Rick could see the mad in her eyes, but he also saw a great sadness there, too. He grabbed her and halted her, his hands gentle on her arms. "You want the truth?"

She lifted her chin. "I'd like that, yes."

He stared down at her, wondering how she could infuriate him at the same time she endeared herself to him. "I was miserable at that banquet. Bridget finagled things so I would be at a table with Doreen and her."

"Oh, and I suppose you were just too polite to move to another table, right?"

"Well, yes." It sounded lame to his ears, too. "I got there late and dinner was being served, so I sat down and hoped I could get away."

"But you couldn't?"

This explanation wasn't going very well. "No, not at first. Bridget wanted us to leave, but I told her no."

"That was thoughtful of you. What a sacrifice on your part."

"Look, Cari, I realized last night that I haven't handled things very well with Bridget. But I intend to do something about that."

"Oh, really. Better be careful. She might decide to slash your tires or something."

"That won't happen. Besides, I'm more concerned about what she might do to you. And that's the only reason I didn't talk to her about all of this last night."

"I can handle her," Cari retorted. "Because I've had enough. If I have to stay up all night long and get pictures, I'm going to prove that Bridget is behind this. I don't care how she feels, I'm not leaving town." Her gaze met his, determination in her bright eyes. "And I'm not going to quit seeing you either. That is, if you want to keep seeing me."

"I do want that," he said, glad she felt the same as he did. "That's why I'm going to have to be very clear with Bridget on where we stand."

Cari's expression softened but her tone was firm. "And I intend to do the same thing—tell both Doreen and Bridget how things stand."

Rick sat her down on the window seat. "Don't do anything crazy. I'm going to talk to Bridget and explain that I don't have any feelings other than friendship for her. I was wrong not to tell her that a long time ago."

"You think?" She got up and stomped around amidst the flash of glittery purses and flip-flops, her fingers touching on delicate brooches and earrings as she paced the now-full shop. "It's none of my business how you feel about Bridget or how she thinks she feels about you. But this, Rick, *this* is my business. And I just want to be left alone. I was on my way to talk to Doreen last night when you came by. But once I found out you'd probably be with both of them at dinner, I cooled my jets and decided I'd try to think positive. Well, that's over now. I'm going to sit them both down and explain that if they don't leave me alone I'll be forced to press charges. That is, if I can prove they're doing this."

This wasn't good. Not good at all. "How did you find out Bridget would be at the dinner?"

"Oh, she came by to get Brady and happened to *make sure* I knew you two had a 'date'."

"I'm so sorry. Why didn't you say something? I wouldn't have gone."

"It's not my place to tell you what to do."

No, she wouldn't be that way. Cari wasn't that kind of person. "I wouldn't have gone if I'd known," he repeated.

"No, I'm glad you went. Maybe now you can understand why I have to face them and get this over with."

Rick pulled her around. "Not right now. Right now, I want you to come with me to the ranch and relax. You're too keyed up to make a coherent decision about this. Give it some time and we'll figure out something together."

"I'm running out of time," she said. "They can't keep doing this after I open the shop."

Hoping to make her understand, he held her close. "Cari, are you hearing me? We'll find a way to clear things up. I don't care about Bridget, not the way I'm beginning to care about you. Do you understand what I'm trying to say?"

She looked up at him, her eyes full of doubt. "Do *you* even know what you're trying to say?"

"I think so. It's you, Cari. I care about you. That's all I understand."

"Then yes, you need to clue Bridget in on that. Because if she doesn't back off, I can't be responsible for my actions. I mean it, Rick. I've had it with her. It was bad enough when I lived with this as a teenager, but I was afraid to stand up to them then. I thought if I just took it, my father would defend me and believe me. But that didn't work. Now I have to do what I should have done back then—face them. The only reason I didn't go out to their house last night is because the police warned me to stay away until I had proof. I stayed up half the night trying to figure out how to get proof. But I will confront both of them. I mean it."

Rick believed her. She wasn't the kind to just sit back and take this. Or at least she wasn't that way now. Maybe once, but not now. And that was the scary part.

"Fair enough," he said. "But only after you've cooled off and we can think this through, together. Promise me that?"

She looked down then lifted her head again. "I can't promise you anything. This is something I have to do. It's the only way I can stay here. I have to show them that I'm not a threat to them. No matter what they think about me. And I need to show them that I've changed. I won't be pushed out of my own home again."

At least that statement sounded better than rushing in with bitterness and resentment. "Okay," he said, pulling her into his arms. "I told you, you're not alone anymore. And I've learned a hard lesson dealing with Bridget. I'll stop flirting with her and make sure she understands that I was only trying to be a friend to her. Nothing else. But I won't even attempt that anymore. I'll make it clear to her that she has the wrong impression regarding my feelings for her." Touching his lips to Cari's ear, he whispered, "And I'll show you that my feelings for you are very real."

Cari didn't say anything, but she did relax into his arms. Rick held her there for a long time then helped her lock up and set the alarm. But by the time he'd driven them out to the ranch, she'd settled down into a quiet resolve that worried him more than her anger ever could.

Cari watched as Rick threw a stick so his dog Shiloh could run and fetch it. The dog was adorable, all golden and furry and friendly. And the ranch was beautiful.

Rick had given her the guided tour an hour earlier. The main house was a big, sprawling log-cabin style with a wraparound porch that made it look welcoming and cozy. The furnishings inside were country and quaint but not too chintzy since Rick shared the space with his brother when he didn't have to stay in town in the apartment over the store. His mother had opted to move to a smaller cabin around the bend after their father passed away. It was located near the big cabin but gave each of them their privacy.

And apparently, his brother Simon craved his privacy.

"He stays in his workshop out back day and night," Rick explained. "He was always introverted but since his wife died, well, the man has become more of a hermit than ever. I wish he could find someone to bring him back to life."

Cari's heart hurt for Simon Adams. He'd been deeply in love with his beautiful wife, but cancer had taken her at an early age. Since Cari could relate to that kind of grief after losing her parents, she felt an instant bond with Simon. Even if he did scowl and grunt a lot.

Now Rick ran back up the bank toward her then fell onto the old wooden bench. Below them the Chattahoochee gurgled and flowed, its swift current moving all the way through Georgia to join up with the Flint River and then eventually flow into the Apalachicola River in Florida and the Gulf of Mexico. He'd been right about bringing her here. She felt calmer now, her head clear.

"I love your place," she said, hoping he'd forget her earlier temperamental outburst—hissy fit number four. "Thanks for bringing me here."

He glanced behind them where his horse Pepper grazed with the mare she'd been riding. "I'm glad you came."

"Do you bring all of your girlfriends out here?"

She watched as his expression became wary. "Uh, who wants to know?"

Seeing the amusement in his eyes, she pushed at his arm. "It's a fair question. Answer it."

He laughed then looked out over the river. "You're the first, Princess."

Cari was touched but stunned. "You're serious? You've never brought another woman out here? Not even Bridget?"

He looked at his watch. "Two hours. Pretty good."

"What do you mean by that?"

"I mean her name didn't come up between us for two whole hours."

"Very funny." But she needed to know. "Has she been here?"

"No," he said, taking her hand in his. "She's asked to come, but it just didn't seem right." He shrugged. "This place is special. Simon works here, so he doesn't like gawkers and Mom likes her privacy after dealing with people all day long at the store."

"Then maybe I shouldn't be here."

"No, hear me out. That's not the problem. The thing is—we have this unwritten pact that we only bring special people up to the ranch. It's our getaway. Mom and I work hard at the store all week, so we try to get out here on the weekends at least."

"But you don't always stay out here."

"No. We have an apartment over the store. It's been there since the original owners lived there. We keep it so we can rest on our lunch breaks and I have an office up there. So sometimes Mom or I stay in town."

She grinned. "So I can rest safely some nights knowing you're nearby."

"Yes, ma'am, you certainly can." He pulled her into his arms. "And I'll rest better staying there until you get this vandalism stuff cleared up."

Cari settled her head against his shoulder. "You don't have to do that. I have the alarm now."

"I don't mind. Besides, next week will be crazy with tourists and shoppers. I'll be too beat to drive up here."

Cari thought about the upcoming week. "I'll do a dry run from Monday till Thursday. Then we'll have the grand opening right before the Fourth. That gives us the whole weekend to bring in customers. This will be my first test."

"You're gonna do fine," he said, kissing the top of her head. "It's a great location and you've brought something different and unique to the downtown area. Can't miss."

"I hope you're right." She turned to look up at him. "And I hope whoever is trying to torment me will leave me alone during the holiday weekend. Maybe Bridget will go out of town or something."

"Let's hope so." Then he lifted her chin. "But for now, let's talk about something else."

"Such as?"

"This," he said, lowering his head toward hers.

Cari accepted his kiss with open arms, her joy pushing aside her worries. After the kiss, she lifted her head. "I love the way you change the subject."

He nuzzled her cheek. "I'm good at what I do."

She kissed him again. "You certainly are."

They sat there watching the sun set over the river and the trees, the scent of mountain laurel and his mother's fat, lush daylilies filling the gloaming. Cari wished she could stay right here forever but that was impossible. She'd just have to cherish this sweet memory when the going got tough.

And she had no doubts that this next week would either make or break her chances of being successful in Knotwood Mountain. And possibly successful in loving Rick, too.

Chapter Seventeen

Cari heard the noise even before the floodlights came on. Looking at the clock, she got up and threw on a robe over her cotton pajamas. It was three in the morning and someone was prowling around down on the porch.

Hurrying through the dark house, she wondered what they'd try this time. Would they tear down the red, white and blue bunting she'd so carefully strung across the newly painted porch railings for tomorrow's Independence Day celebration? Would they try to break into her shop and destroy her precious things? Or would they leave another ugly message to scare her?

"Not this time," she said, her flashlight in one hand and a baseball bat in the other. She wouldn't do bodily harm unless she came face-to-face with someone. But she wanted to be armed just in case.

Checking the alarm box by the kitchen door, she

breathed a sigh of relief to see the green light blinking. So far, so good. Maybe the prowler had run away this time.

Then she heard Shiloh's distinctive bark from next door. Rick had brought the dog into town to help Cari protect her property. And sure enough, Shiloh was barking away in the upstairs apartment over the general store.

"Good dog," Cari whispered as she tiptoed down into the shop, careful to stay back in the shadows so she could watch through the big bay windows.

And she saw a shadow hovering there under the lights.

A brave soul, since the yellow glow from the security lights had to be centered on the entire porch and small front yard.

Stepping closer, Cari watched as the figure crept along the wall of the house. Then she saw a hand going up to the wall. The culprit was painting something on her pretty pale yellow house!

"That's it," Cari said, stomping toward the front door. She didn't care if the alarm went off and woke the whole town. She intended to catch this person once and for all.

Yanking open the door, Cari rushed out with the baseball bat held high. Looking down the long porch, she saw the figure stepping backward toward the side railing. "Stop right there. The cops are on the way."

The alarm sounded in the still night. Maybe the police would listen to her now at least. But the shadowy figure, all dressed in black, dropped the can of spray paint and turned and hopped over the porch railing.

Cari ran down the steps and screamed, "Stop, you coward. I mean it. I'm going to press charges."

Rushing around to the alley, she watched as a white convertible cranked and gunned it down the street beside the house, its tires peeling rubber.

"Bridget." She knew it now because she had a partial plate number, one that would be hard to forget. She'd caught a glimpse from the streetlights. But it would be enough. It began with the letters *B-R-I*. And it didn't take much to fill in the rest. Bridget had a vanity plate with her name on it.

"Cari?"

She turned to find Rick and Shiloh running toward her. The dog was barking in a loud candence while the alarm shrilled over and over. "Let me turn off the alarm," she shouted. "I'm okay."

They followed her back to the front and she rushed inside to key in the code. Rick calmed down Shiloh and then the night went silent and still.

But Cari saw the lights from a patrol car outside.

"I saw her this time, Rick," she said. "It was Bridget."

He looked as disgusted as she felt. "You're sure?"

"I saw the car and got a partial plate number, but no, I didn't see her face. She was wearing that black hoodie again. She had a can of spray paint."

Cari hurried to the front porch, her flashlight in her hand. Nodding to the two officers coming up the steps, she said, "The vandal struck again and I got a partial plate. It was Bridget Stillman."

Then she flashed the light up against the wall to find

something written in black: "Closed for Business. Permanently."

"Somebody's trying to shut you down, Ms. Duncan," one of the officers said, shaking his head. "And you're sure it was the Stillman girl?"

"I'm sure it was her car," Cari replied, doubt rearing inside her. She had to be completely sure. She told them about the license plate.

"We'll run it through," the other officer said. "I'll go do that while you give your statement. Then we'll see what happens."

Cari nodded then told the other officer what had happened while Rick stood looking on, his hair tousled, his old T-shirt and gym shorts rumpled.

"Thank you," she said, smiling over at him. Then she reached down to pet Shiloh. "And thank you, too."

She'd just finished her statement when the other officer came rushing back in the open door. "The plates match Bridget Stillman's vehicle, but we've got other problems now."

"What?" Cari asked, surprised at the shocked look on the man's face.

"That vehicle was just in a one-car accident out on the South River road. Ran into a tree. I heard it over the radio. I gotta go."

"Oh, no." Cari turned to grab Rick. "We have to go out there. She might be hurt. Rick?"

"Get dressed," he said. "I'll bring the Jeep around."

She couldn't stop shivering. Cari watched as the paramedics went back into the water where the convertible was partially submerged. They'd had to get the Jaws of Life to bring the unconscious driver out of the mangled vehicle.

And no one would tell her if the driver was Bridget and if the person was dead or alive.

"Rick," she whispered, holding to his shirt. "This is all my fault."

He pulled her into his arms. "You can't say that. You were trying to protect your property. You didn't force her to drive too fast for this curve."

"But I did force the issue. I should have talked to her, asked her to stop."

"It's okay," he replied. Then he shook his head. "I had a talk with Bridget this morning—about everything. I told her the truth—that I had feelings for you. She didn't take it very well. So if this is anyone's fault, it's mine."

Cari put a hand to her mouth. "Surely she wouldn't do anything crazy just because you rejected her."

Rick looked down. "I hope not. Let's pray that she's going to make it."

But Cari knew if something happened to Bridget, it wouldn't be okay. And no matter what Rick had said to Bridget, it *would* be Cari's fault. How could it have come to this? She closed her eyes and prayed over and over for God to help Bridget. She didn't dare ask Him to forgive her. She just wanted Bridget to be alive.

Rick touched her shoulder. "Cari, they're bringing her out."

Cari rushed forward, calling to one of the officers. "Is it Bridget Stillman?"

He turned around to stare at her then shook his head. "No, ma'am."

"What?" Rick stepped forward. "Then who was driving that car?"

The officer's expression looked grave. "Her brother—Brady Stillman. He was behind the wheel. We ID'd him from his driver's permit."

"Brady!" Cari pushed past the officer. "Brady?" She rushed to the gurney, trying to see him. "Is he all right?"

Rick tugged her back, but she kept shouting. "Somebody tell me if he's alive?"

One of the paramedics nodded. "He's alive but he's unconscious. We've got him stabilized. It doesn't look good."

Then Cari saw him. He was wearing a black hoodie, drenched now and torn away from his body by the people who'd worked to save his life. "Brady," she whispered, her hand at her mouth. "Oh, dear God, please let him live."

As the EMT workers lifted him into the ambulance, she turned to the officer standing by her. "Have you called his mother?"

"She's going to meet us at the hospital."

Cari reached for Rick. "I have to go."

"Okay." He guided her toward the Jeep. When he had her safely inside, he stared down at her. "Cari, you understand what this means, don't you?"

Cari numbly bobbed her head, too shocked to do anything more. "Yes. It wasn't Bridget. It was Brady. He's the one who's been vandalizing me. And for the life of me, Rick, I can't understand that." She let out a little sob. "And right now, I don't care. I just want him to be okay."

Dawn poured over the courtyard by the waiting room, the sun's early rays pink and muted as they hit the bubbling fountain just outside the big windows.

Cari glanced over at where Doreen and Bridget sat stiff-backed, their worried expressions colored with fatigue. She'd only spoken to them briefly when they'd rushed into the hospital hours ago.

Doreen had looked at her in surprise. "What are you doing here?"

"I heard about the accident. I had to come."

And no one had questioned her further. They were all too worried about Brady. He was in surgery. Cari tried to remember what the doctors had told Doreen. A ruptured spleen, a collapsed lung, numerous abrasions and contusions. She couldn't remember the technical details. She just knew she wanted Brady to be fixed. She wanted everything to be fixed.

"How did you find out?" Doreen said now, breaking the taut silence surrounding them.

Cari looked up and into Doreen's questioning eyes. Now wasn't the time to tell her the truth.

"Yes, how did you find out?" Bridget's anger hit Cari in the face. Her gaze burned with hostility. "And why are you still here?"

Rick sat up, ready to come to Cari's defense, but she put a hand on his arm. "I care about Brady. You both need to know that."

"We don't need you here," Bridget retorted. "You're not a part of our family anymore."

Her words hurt as badly as a slap in the face, but Cari swallowed her pain. "I understand that, but Brady and I…we were always close. And I saw him a few days ago. He helped me get things ready to open the shop."

"You were trying to turn him against us," Doreen said, the flare of hatred in her eyes overwhelming Cari.

"No, I'd never do that. I wouldn't." She looked over at Rick, saw the reassuring nod he gave her. "I just wanted to be a friend to him."

"He didn't need you," Doreen said, her designer purse held against her stomach like a shield. "You should have stayed away."

One of the officers who'd come to Cari's house walked up the hallway then sat down beside Bridget. "Sorry, Mrs. Duncan, but I have to ask some questions regarding the accident. I won't take long."

Doreen nodded, her focus still centered on Cari. "Make it quick. My head is splitting and I want to make sure I'm available when he comes out of surgery."

The officer nodded. "Why was Brady driving your car tonight, Miss Stillman?"

Bridget frowned over at him. "How would I know? I was on a date when my mom called. He must have sneaked it out of the garage."

"Did you give him permission to take the car, Mrs. Duncan?"

"No," Doreen said. "He was on restriction, so he wasn't allowed to drive even with me in the car. Like my daughter said, he took it without my knowledge."

"And why would he have been seen prowling around Miss Duncan's house on First Street?"

At that question, both Doreen and Bridget looked over at Cari, their expressions blazing with anger and shock.

"What on earth are you talking about?" Doreen asked. Before the officer could answer, she pointed at Cari. "What have you done? What was he doing at your house?"

Cari couldn't speak but Rick held up a hand. "I can explain that, Doreen."

And he told her about the attacks—the painted message on the parlor wall and the porch, the rocks through the turret room windows and the brick thrown into the sign on the front porch.

"We think he was behind all of this. Only we didn't realize it until tonight when Cari caught someone spray painting on her front porch."

Cari sat up, her hands open, palms up. "I saw the car and I thought it was Bridget. I was talking to the police when the call about the accident came over the police radio. I'm so sorry, Doreen. I had no idea."

Doreen stood up, her purse crashing to the floor. "You're sorry? Sorry? You scared my little boy so badly that he drove too fast and crashed his sister's car into a tree and went into the river? You're sorry!"

Rick stood between her and Cari. "Doreen, stop. This is not Cari's fault."

"No," Doreen said, anger making her spit out each word. "Nothing is ever Cari's fault, is it? The way her father changed after she broke his heart and left—that's not her fault, is it? Or me being in debt now because he was too sad and sick to run his business, I suppose that's not Cari's fault either?" She pointed toward Bridget. "Or the way my children were treated, ignored and verbally abused by her father because he was so upset about her, I guess that's not her fault at all. Because of her, he made our lives miserable. Miserable, do you hear? But that's not Cari's fault. Nothing is ever Cari's fault."

She stopped, tears running down her face. "You thought you were the one suffering all these years, didn't you? Well, you have no idea. No idea at all. Your father never loved me or my children the way he loved your mother and you. You won, Cari. You never knew that, but you won. He never got over losing your mother or you. And he made sure I knew that each and every day. And now my son who tried to reach out to you, to make you see, is in there close to death and you're telling me you're sorry, but you think he was trying to mess with you! How dare you!"

Cari sank down in her chair, sobs roiling like a giant undercurrent throughout her body. "Doreen, I had no idea. I never knew."

"Of course you never knew," Doreen shouted. "You never bothered to find out, did you? You never even tried."

Her rage spent, she fell into her chair then broke down, sobbing in Bridget's arms.

"Rick, I think you'd better get her out of here," Bridget said. "And to think I actually wanted you to notice *me*. You two deserve each other." Then she turned to the bewildered officer. "Is that enough of a statement for you?"

Without a word, Rick lifted Cari up and guided her toward the doors to the parking lot and into the Jeep.

Cari sat huddled as he drove through the quiet early-morning streets, her tears silent now as she thought back over everything that had happened since her father died.

Was Doreen right? Had Cari been so blinded by her own pain and grief that she'd failed to see her father's? That she'd failed to try and forgive him? Had he truly treated Doreen so terribly and become so miserable that everything he'd worked so hard for was now gone?

When Rick pulled the Jeep into the alley, he turned to her. "Cari?"

"I'm going in now," she said. "I can't talk about it right now, Rick. I need some time alone."

He came around to help her out of the vehicle. "I'm sorry," he said, his hands running through her hair. "I'm really sorry."

"So am I," she replied, pulling away toward the porch. She didn't look back but she knew this would probably be the last time she saw him. Because she was going inside to pack. She couldn't stay here.

"Cari, don't go," he said. When she didn't turn around, he bounded up the steps and forced her to stop at the door. "You can't run away. You were the one who said you had to face them. And you have. If you leave now, you won't be able to come back again."

"I don't intend to come back again."

Now Rick was the angry one. "And just like that, because you've finally seen the truth, you'll leave everything you have here."

"I don't have anything here."

The minute she said it, she regretted it. And she regretted the horrible hurt she saw in his beautiful eyes.

"Rick—"

"No." He backed away, his head down. "If you can't see what we have together, then you're right. You should go and you should stay away." He pivoted on the bottom step. "Because I can't live with you right next door, knowing that I love you and you can't love me in return. That would never work."

And with that, he walked away, back to his world.

And out of Cari's life.

Cari woke up from a troubled sleep to find it dark outside. And fireworks blasting through the night sky.

The Fourth of July celebration was underway.

But she didn't have a thing to celebrate.

She'd packed some clothes then fell down on her bed and cried her eyes out, finally falling asleep around dusk.

Today was supposed to be her grand opening.

Today was supposed to be the start of her new life here with Rick.

Now it was all over.

Getting up to wash her face, she looked at her cell phone. She'd turned it off, but now she flipped it open and watched it light up. Six messages from Jolena. None from Rick.

After getting a drink of water, she called Jolena.

"You're all right. Thank goodness."

Cari explained what had happened, her throat raw with pain.

"Honey, I know all of that and more," Jolena said. "I'm standing here outside the diner watching the fireworks. Come on out and I'll tell you what I heard."

"I can't," Cari said. "I'll just watch from the turret room, the way I did when I was little."

"Baby, you're gonna be okay," Jolena said. "Brady's gonna make it. He got through surgery and he woke up about an hour ago. Honey, he confessed to the vandalism. He's been asking for you."

Cari thought she couldn't cry anymore. She was wrong. "But why? Why Brady?"

Jolena's voice echoed over the line. "I'll come up and explain."

"Okay. I'll be in the turret room, but I'll unlock the back door for you."

Cari put down the phone and got dressed. She'd get up early tomorrow and go to see Brady. Then she'd leave before she had to face anyone else. But she at least owed Jolena an explanation.

So she sat down on one of the floral cushions she and Jolena had made for the window seat and watched the brilliant sparkling colors shooting through the sky, her heart remembering all she loved about this country and her town, even if that heart was broken. *How can I heal, Lord?*

When she heard footsteps on the stairs, she called out, "Up here, Jolena."

But when she turned to the door, Jolena wasn't standing there.

Rick stood there with a box in one hand and a burning sparkler in the other. "You're missing the show," he said. "So I brought part of it to you."

Tears pricked at Cari's eyes. The lone sparkler spurted in a pure electric white, its brilliance lighting up the whole room. She couldn't speak, couldn't move. Seeing him again hurt her so much, she thought her heart would shatter into pieces right there on the floor.

"What are you doing here?" she asked. "Jolena—"

"Sent me," he replied. "She didn't want to miss the grand finale."

"And what about you? Aren't you missing the highlight of the show?"

"Nope," he said as he watched the sparkler burn out then carefully put the now-blackened stick on the windowsill. "I don't like grand finales. They're just too *final*."

He put the box down then sat beside her. "I like grand openings, however. They're so…promising. But you missed yours."

"I won't be having a grand opening."

"Yes, you will." He tugged her close. "Because I'm here to see that you don't go anywhere. Understand me? I'm here, Cari. Right here."

She saw the need and the sincerity in his eyes. "But

Rick, look what I did. I turned my back on my father because of pride and bitterness. I could have helped him, but I didn't. If I'd only tried, things might be so different now."

"But you did try to make amends when he was dying. And you can do the same thing now, by staying."

"I don't know how to begin."

He kissed her cheek. "Running away won't solve that problem." He touched a hand to her hair. "When we turn from God, He waits for us. And all we have to do is turn around and accept His love and grace. You need to do the same now. You need to accept that I love you and I'm willing to fight for you. But not if you run from me."

"I wasn't running from *you*. I've just made such a mess of things. I didn't think I deserved you."

"I told you, this wasn't your fault. Brady was trying to scare you away so his mom could have this property. He thought he could help her get out of debt, thinking she could buy this cheap from you and then resell it to the highest bidder. Twisted logic, but then he loves her in spite of her flaws. And he heard her telling Bridget about how she'd like to flip the property and make a lot of money to help with the bills."

"But why did he help us with the renovations?"

"The kid was torn between helping you and helping his mom. And his friend Jeff knew about the vandalism, even helped him with some of it. He was holding it over Brady's head and pressuring him to keep doing it. Brady was caught between a rock and a hard place and things got out of hand. But none of that is your fault. You just got caught up in something that was already out of control."

Cari couldn't quite accept that. "So you love me in spite of my flaws?"

"I do." He kissed her lips. "I do. And if you stay, I'll spend the rest of my life trying to show you just how much."

Cari fell into his arms, her tears filled with joy now. He loved her. God loved her. And this time, she wanted to turn toward that saving grace instead of running from it.

She lifted up, her hands around his shoulders. "I love you, too, Rick. And I never want to disappoint you again."

"That won't happen." He kissed her then held her close. "We're gonna work this out, Cari."

She'd have to learn to trust him on that. "What's in the box?"

He grinned then pulled the wrapped box around. "Open it and see."

Cari tore through the bright paper and let out a gasp as she lifted the lid. "My red shoes."

"Your red shoes. I told you I'd save them for a special day." Then he took one out and lifted her foot, knocking her purple fuzzy slippers off. "I think you need to wear these on our wedding day." Placing the other one on her other foot, he said, "That is, if you'll marry me."

"Of course I will, after I take care of a few things." Cari looked down at her feet as the fireworks went into overdrive, blasting away outside the windows of her tiny turret room. "But I'd marry you without the shoes, you know."

"I brought them for leverage, just in case. And besides, Jolena strongly urged me to do it."

"Smart woman, Jolena." Then she touched a hand to his face. "I'll have a long talk with Doreen and make my peace with her and Bridget, and I won't press charges against Brady." She took his hands in hers. "Will you take me to see him?"

He nodded, stroked her hair. "That's a good idea. Time for everyone to heal."

"Yes, time for everyone to heal." She'd make sure of that.

He nuzzled her neck then together they watched the last of the fireworks finale. The night sky lit up with brilliant yellows, reds, blues, whites and greens. Down on the crowded street, cheers went up.

Rick held her tight. "And tomorrow, bright and early, you are going to open your shop. We've already painted over the spot on the porch and your sign is back up. All you have to do is open the doors and let us in."

Cari turned in his arms, her sigh full of contentment. "It took me a while to figure that out, but I'm ready now."

Rick laughed and kissed her, the reflection of happiness from the celebration down on the street centered in his eyes. "Welcome home, Princess."

* * * * *

ORDINARY GIRL
IN A TIARA

JESSICA HART

CHAPTER ONE

To: caro.cartwright@u2.com
From: charlotte@palaisdemontvivennes.net
Subject: Internet dating
Dear Caro
What a shame about the deli folding. I know you loved that job. You must be really fed up, but your email about the personality test on that internet dating site really made me laugh—good to know you haven't lost your sense of humour in spite of everything that skunk George did to you! All I can say is that compared to Grandmère's matchmaking schemes, internet dating sounds the way to go. Perhaps we should swap lives??!
Lotty
xxxxxxxxxxxxxxxxx

To: charlotte@palaisdemontvivennes.net
From: caro.cartwright@u2.com
Subject: Swapping places
What a brilliant idea, Lotty! My life is a giddy whirl at the moment, what with temping at a local insurance company and trying to write profile for new dating site (personality test results too depressing on other one) but if you'd like to try it, you're more than welcome! Of course,

living your life would be tough for me—living in a palace, having (admittedly terrifying) grandmother introducing me to suitable princes and so on—but for you, Lotty, anything! Just let me know where and when and I'll have a stab at being a princess for a change…ooh, that's just given me an idea for my new profile. Who says fantasy isn't good for you???

Yours unregally

Caro XXX

> PRINCESS SEEKS FROG: Curvaceous, fun-loving brunette, 28, looking for that special guy for good times out and in.

'What do you think?' Caro read out her opening line to Stella, who was lying on the sofa and flicking through a copy of *Glitz*.

Stella looked up from the magazine, her expression dubious. 'It doesn't make sense. Princess seeks frog? What's that supposed to mean?'

'It means I'm looking for an ordinary guy, not a Prince Charming in disguise. I thought it was obvious,' said Caro, disappointed.

'No ordinary guy would ever work that out, I can tell you that much,' said Stella. She went back to flicking. 'You don't want to be cryptic or clever. Men hate that.'

'It's all so difficult.' Caro deleted the offending words on the screen, and chewed her bottom lip. 'What about the curvaceous bit? I'm worried it might make me sound fat, but there's not much point in meeting someone who's looking for a slender goddess, is there? He'd just run away screaming the moment he laid eyes on me. Besides, I want to be honest.'

'If you're going to be honest, you'd better take out "fun-loving",' Stella offered. 'It makes it sound as if you're up for anything.'

'That's the whole point. I'm changing. Being sensible didn't get me anywhere with George, so I'm going to be a good time girl from now on.'

She would be like Melanie, all giggles and low cut tops and flirty looks. Melanie, who had sashayed into George's office and knocked Caro's steady, sensible fiancé off his feet.

'I can't say what I'm really like or no one will want to go out with me,' she added glumly.

'Rubbish,' said Stella. 'Say you're kind and generous and a brilliant cook—*that* would be honest.'

'Guys don't want kind, even if they say they do,' Caro said bitterly, remembering George. 'They want sexy and fun-loving.'

'Hmm, well, if you want to be sexy, you'd better do something about your clothes,' said Stella, lowering *Glitz* so that she could inspect her friend's outfit with a critical eye. 'I know you're into the vintage look, but a *crochet top*?'

'It's an original from the Seventies.'

'And it was vile then, too.'

Caro made a face at her. With the top she was wearing a tartan miniskirt from the nineteen-sixties and bright red pumps. She was the first to admit that she couldn't *always* carry off the vintage look successfully, but she had been pleased with this particular outfit until Stella had started shaking her head.

Still, there was no point in arguing. She went back to her profile. 'OK, what about *Keen cook seeks fellow foodie*?'

'You'll just get some guy who wants to tie you to the stove and expect you to have his dinner ready the moment he comes through the door. You've already done that for George, and look where that got you.' Stella caught the flash of pain on her friend's face and her voice softened. 'I know how miserable you've been, Caro, but honestly, you're well out of it. George wasn't the right man for you.'

'I know.' Caro caught herself sighing and squared her shoulders. 'It's OK, Stella. I'm fine now. I'm moving on, aren't I?'

Pressing the backspace key with one finger, she deleted the last sentence. 'It's just so depressing having to sign up to these online dating sites. I don't remember it being this hard before. It's like in the five years I was with George, all the single men round here have disappeared into some kind of Bermuda Triangle!'

'Yeah, it's called marriage,' said Stella. She picked up *Glitz* again and flicked through in search of the page she wanted. 'I don't know why you're looking in Ellerby, though. Why don't you get your friend Lotty to introduce you to some rich, glamorous men who eat in Michelin starred restaurants all the time?'

Caro laughed, remembering Lotty's email. 'I wish! But poor Lotty never gets within spitting distance of an interesting man either. You'd think, being a princess, she'd have a fantastically glamorous time, but her grandmother totally runs her life. Apparently she's trying to fix Lotty up with someone "suitable" right now.' Caro hooked her fingers in the air to emphasise the inverted commas. 'I mean, who wants a man your grandmother approves of? I think I'd rather stick with internet dating!'

'I wouldn't mind if he was anything like the guy Lotty's going out with at the moment,' said Stella. 'I saw a picture of them just a second ago. If he was her grandmother's choice, I'd say she's got good taste and she can fix me up any time!'

'Lotty's actually going out with someone?' Caro swivelled round from the computer and stared at Stella. 'She didn't say that! Who is he?'

'Give me a sec. I'm trying to find that photo of her.' When

the flicking failed, Stella licked her finger and tried turning the pages one by one. 'I can never get over you being friends with a real princess. I wish I'd been to a posh school like yours.'

'You wouldn't have liked it. It was fine if you had a title and your own pony and lots of blonde hair to toss around, but if you were only there because your mum was a teacher and your dad the handyman, they didn't want to know.'

'Lotty wanted to know you,' Stella pointed out, still searching.

'Lotty was different. We started on the same day and we were both the odd ones out, so we stuck together. We were both fat and spotty and had braces, and poor Lotty had a stammer too.'

'She's not fat and spotty now,' said Stella. 'She looked lovely in that picture…ah, here it is!'

Folding back the page, she read out the caption under one of the photographs on the *Party! Party! Party!* page. 'Here we go: *Princess Charlotte of Montluce arriving at the Nightingale Ball—fab dress, by the way—with Prince Philippe.*

'*Philippe, the lost heir to Montluce, has only recently returned to the country,*' she read on. '*The ball was their first public outing as a couple, but behind the scenes friends say they are "inseparable" and royal watchers are expecting them to announce their engagement this summer. Is one of Europe's most eligible bachelors off the market already?*'

'Let me see that!' Caro whipped the magazine out of Stella's hands and frowned down at the shiny page. 'Lotty and *Philippe*? I don't believe it!'

But there was Lotty, looking serene, and there, next to her, was indeed His Serene Highness Prince Philippe Xavier Charles de Montvivennes.

She recognised him instantly. That summer he had been seventeen, just a boy, but with a dark, reckless edge to his glamorous looks that had terrified her at the time. Thirteen years on, he looked taller, broader, but still lean, still dangerous. He had the same coolly arrogant stare for the camera, the same sardonic smile that made Caro feel fifteen again: breathless, awkward, painfully aware that she didn't belong.

Stella sat up excitedly. 'You *know* him?'

'Not really. I spent part of a summer holiday in France with Lotty once, and he was part of a whole crowd that used to hang around the villa. It was just before Dad died and, to be honest, I don't remember much about that time now. I know I felt completely out of place, but I do remember Philippe,' Caro said slowly. 'I was totally intimidated by him.'

She had a picture of Philippe lounging around the spectacular infinity pool, looking utterly cool and faintly disreputable. There had always been some girl wrapped round him, sleek and slender in a minuscule bikini while Caro had skulked in the shade with Lotty, too shy to swim in her dowdy one-piece while they were there.

'He and the others used to go out every night and make trouble,' she told Stella. 'There were always huge rows about it, and one or other of them would be sent home on some private plane in disgrace for a while.'

'God, it sounds so glamorous,' said Stella enviously. 'Did you get to go trouble-making too?'

'Are you kidding?' Caro hooted with laughter. 'Lotty and I would never have had the nerve to go with them. Anyway, I'm quite sure Philippe didn't even realise we were there most of the time. Although, actually, now I think about it, he *was* nice to me when I heard Dad was in hospital,' she remembered. 'He said he was sorry and asked if I wanted to go out with the rest of them that night. I'd forgotten that.'

Caro looked down at the magazine again, trying to fit the angular boy she remembered into the picture of the man. How funny that she should remember that moment of brusque kindness now. She'd been so distressed about her father that she had wiped almost everything else about that time from her mind.

'Did you go?'

'No, I was too worried about Dad and, anyway, I'd have been terrified. They were all wild, that lot. And Philippe was the wildest of them all. He had a terrible reputation then.

'He had this older brother, Etienne, who was supposed to be really nice, and Philippe was the hellraiser everyone shook their heads about. Then Etienne was killed in a freak water-skiing accident, and after that we never heard any more about Philippe. I think Lotty told me he'd cut off all contact with his father and gone off to South America. Nobody knew then that his father would end up as Crown Prince of Montluce, but I'm surprised he hasn't come back before. Probably been too busy hellraising and squandering his trust fund!'

'You've got to admit it sounds more fun than your average blind date in Ellerby,' Stella pointed out. 'You said you wanted to have fun, and he's obviously the kind of guy who knows how to do that. You should get Lotty to fix you up with one of his cool friends.'

Caro rolled her eyes. 'Do you really see me hanging around with the jet set?'

'I see what you mean.' Pursing her lips, Stella studied her friend. 'You'd definitely have to lose the crochet top!'

'Not to mention about six stone,' said Caro.

She tossed the magazine back to Stella. 'Anyway, I can't think of anything worse than going out with someone like Philippe. You'd have to look perfect all the time. And then, when you were doing all those exciting glamorous things, you wouldn't be able to look as if you were enjoying it, because that's not cool. And you'd have to be stick-thin, which would mean you'd never be able to eat. It would be awful!'

'Lotty doesn't look as if she minds,' said Stella with another glance at the photo. 'And I don't blame her!'

'You never know what Lotty's really thinking. She's been trained to always smile, always look as if she's enjoying herself, even if she's bored or sick or fed up. Being a princess doesn't sound any fun to me,' said Caro. 'Lotty's been a good girl all her life, and she's never had the chance to be herself or meet someone who'll bother to get to know her rather than the perfect princess she has to be all the time.'

A faint line between her brows, she turned back to the computer and opened Lotty's last email message. Why hadn't Lotty said anything about Philippe then?

To: charlotte@palaisdemontvivennes.net
From: caro.cartwright@u2.com
Subject: ?????????????
You and Philippe??????????????????????????????????

Lotty's reply came back the next morning.

To: caro.cartwright@u2.com
From: charlotte@palaisdemontvivennes.net
Subject: Re: ?????????????
Grandmère is up to her old tricks again and this time it's serious. I can't tell you what it's like here. I'm getting desperate!

Caro, remember how you said you'd do anything for me when we joked about swapping lives for a while? Well, I've got an idea to put to you, and I'm hoping you weren't joking about the helping bit! I really need to explain in person, but you know how careful I have to be on the phone here, and I can't leave Montluce just yet. Philippe is in London this week, though, so I've given him your number and he's going to get in touch and explain all about it. If my plan works, it could solve our problems for all of us!

Lxxxxxxxxxxxxxxxx

Deeply puzzled, Caro read Lotty's message again. What plan, and what did Philippe have to do with it? She couldn't imagine Philippe de Montvivennes solving any of *her* problems, that was for sure. What could he do? Make George dump Melanie and come crawling back to her on his knees? Persuade the bank that the delicatessen where she'd been working hadn't gone bankrupt after all?

And what problems could *he* possibly have? Too much money in his trust fund? Too many gorgeous women hanging round him?

Philippe will explain. A real live prince, heir to the throne of Montluce, was going to ring her, Caro Cartwright. Caro nibbled her thumbnail and tried to imagine the conversation. *Oh, hi, yeah*, she would say casually when he called. *Lotty mentioned you would ring.*

She wished she knew what Lotty had told him about her. Not the truth, she hoped. Philippe would only sneer if he knew just how quiet and ordinary her life was.

Not that she cared what he thought, Caro reminded herself hastily. She loved living in Ellerby. Her dreams were ordinary ones: a place to belong, a husband to love, a job she enjoyed. A kitchen of her own, a family to feed. Was that too much to ask?

But Philippe had always lived in a different stratosphere. How could he know that she had no interest in a luxury yacht or a designer wardrobe or hobnobbing with superstars, or whatever else he'd been doing with himself for the past five years? She wouldn't mind eating in the Michelin starred restaurants, Caro allowed, but otherwise, no, she was happy with her lot—or she would be if George hadn't dumped her for Melanie and the deli owner hadn't gone bankrupt.

No, Philippe would never be able to understand that. So perhaps she shouldn't be casual after all. She could sound preoccupied instead, a high-powered businesswoman, juggling million pound contracts and persistent lovers, with barely a second to deal with a playboy prince. *I'm a bit busy at the moment*, she could say. *Could I call you back in five minutes?*

Caro rather liked the idea of startling Philippe with her transformation from gawky fifteen-year-old to assured woman of the world, but abandoned it eventually. For one thing, Philippe would never remember Lotty's friend, plump and plain in her one-piece black swimsuit, so the startle effect was likely to be limited. And, for another, she was content with her own life and didn't need to pretend to be anything other than what she was, right?

Right.

So why did the thought of talking to him make her so jittery?

She wished he would ring and get it over with, but the phone remained obstinately silent. Caro kept checking it to see if the battery had run out, or the signal disappeared for some reason. When it did ring, she would leap out of her skin and fumble frantically with it in her hands before she could even check who was calling. Invariably it was Stella, calling to discover if Philippe had rung yet, and Caro got quite snappy with her.

Then she was even crosser with herself for being so twitchy. It was only Philippe, for heaven's sake. Yes, he was a prince, but what had he ever done other than go to parties and look cool? She wasn't impressed by him, Caro told herself, and was mortified whenever she caught herself inspecting her reflection or putting on lipstick, as if he would be able to see what she looked like when he called.

Or as if he would care.

In any case, all the jitteriness was quite wasted because Philippe didn't ring at all. By Saturday night, Caro had decided that there must have been a mistake. Lotty had misunderstood, or, more likely, Philippe couldn't be bothered to do what Lotty had asked him to do. Fine, thought Caro grouchily. See if she cared. Lotty would call when she could and in meantime she would get on with her life.

Or, rather, her lack of life.

A summer Saturday, and she had no money to go out and no one to go out with. Caro sighed. She couldn't even have a glass of wine as she and Stella were both on a diet and had banned alcohol from the house. It was all right for Stella, who had gone to see a film, but Caro was badly in need of distraction.

For want of anything better to do, she opened up her laptop and logged on to right4u.com. Her carefully worded profile, together with the most flattering photo she could find—taken before George had dumped her and she was two sizes thinner—had gone live the day before. Perhaps someone had left her a message, she thought hopefully. Prince Philippe might not be prepared to get in touch, but Mr Right might have fallen madly in love with her picture and be out there, longing for her to reply.

Or not.

Caro had two messages. The first turned out to be from a fifty-six-year-old who claimed to be 'young at heart' and boasted of having his own teeth and hair although, after one look at his photo, Caro didn't think either were much to be proud of.

Quickly, she moved onto the next message, which was from a man who hadn't provided a picture but who had chosen Mr

Sexy as his code name. Call her cynical, but she had a feeling that might be something of a misnomer. According to the website, the likelihood of a potential match between them was a mere seven per cent. *I want you to be my soulmate*, Mr Sexy had written. *Ring me and let's begin the rest of our lives right now.*

Caro thought not.

Depressed, she got up and went into the kitchen. She was starving. That was the trouble with diets. You were bored and hungry the whole time. How was a girl supposed to move on with her life when she only had salad for lunch?

In no time at all she found the biscuits Stella had hidden in with the cake tins, and she was on her third and wondering whether she should hope Stella wouldn't notice or eat them all and buy a new packet when the doorbell rang. Biscuit in hand, Caro looked at the clock on wall. Nearly eight o'clock. An odd time for someone to call, at least in Ellerby. Still, whoever it was, they surely had to be more interesting than trawling through her potential matches on right4u.com.

Stuffing the rest of the biscuit into her mouth, Caro opened the door.

There, on the doorstep, stood Prince Philippe Xavier Charles de Montvivennes, looking as darkly, dangerously handsome and as coolly arrogant as he had in the pages of *Glitz* and so bizarrely out of place in the quiet Ellerby backstreet that Caro choked, coughed and sprayed biscuit all over his immaculate dark blue shirt.

Philippe didn't bat an eyelid. Perhaps his smile slipped a little, but he put it quickly back in place as he picked a crumb off his shirt. 'Caroline Cartwright?' With those dark good looks, he should have had an accent oozing Mediterranean warmth but, like Lotty, he had been sent to school in England and, when he opened that mouth, the voice that came out was instead cool and impeccably English. As cool as the strange silver eyes that were so disconcerting against the olive skin and black hair.

Still spluttering, Caro patted her throat and blinked at him through watering eyes. 'I'm—' It came out as a croak, and she coughed and tried again. 'I'm Caro,' she managed at last.

Dear God, thought Philippe, keeping his smile in place with an effort. *Caro's lovely*, Lotty had said. *She'll be perfect*.

What had Lotty been thinking? There was no way this Caro could carry off what they had in mind. He'd pictured someone coolly elegant, like Lotty, but there was nothing cool and certainly nothing elegant about this girl. Built on Junoesque lines, she'd opened the door like a slap in the face, and then spat biscuit all over him. He'd had an impression of lushness, of untidy warmth. Of dark blue eyes and fierce brows and a lot of messy brown hair falling out of its clips.

And of a perfectly appalling top made of purple cheese-cloth. It might possibly have been fashionable forty years earlier, although it was hard to imagine anyone ever picking it up and thinking it would look nice on. Caro Cartwright must get dressed in the dark.

Philippe was tempted to turn on his heel and get Yan to drive him back to London, but Lotty's face swam into his mind. She had looked so desperate that day she had come to see him. She hadn't cried, but something about the set of her mouth, about the strained look around her eyes had touched the heart Philippe had spent years hardening.

Caro will help, I know she will, she had said. *This is my only chance, Philippe. Please say you'll do it*.

So he'd promised, and now he couldn't go back on his word.

Dammit.

Well, he was here, and now he'd better make the best of it. Philippe forced warmth into his smile, the one that more than one woman had told him was irresistible. 'I'm Lotty's cousin, Ph—' he began, but Caro waved him to silence, still patting her throat.

'I know who you are,' she said squeakily, apparently resisting the smile without any trouble at all. 'What are you doing here?'

Philippe was momentarily nonplussed, which annoyed him. He wasn't used to being taken aback, and he certainly wasn't used to having his presence questioned quite so abruptly. 'Didn't Lotty tell you?'

'She said you would *ring*.'

That was definitely an accusing note in her voice. Philippe looked down his chiselled nose. 'I thought it would be easier to explain face to face,' he said haughtily.

Easier for him, maybe, thought Caro. *He* hadn't been caught unawares with no make-up on and a mouthful of biscuit.

There was something surreal about seeing him standing there, framed against the austere terrace of houses across the road. Ellerby was a quiet northern town on the edge of the moors, while Philippe in his immaculately tailored trousers and the dark blue shirt open at the neck appeared to have stepped straight out of the pages of *Glitz*. He was tall and tanned with that indefinable aura of wealth and glamour, the assurance that took red carpets as its due.

A pampered playboy prince…Caro longed to dismiss him as no more than that, but there was nothing soft about the line of his mouth, or the hard angles of cheek and jaw. Nothing self-indulgent about the lean, hard-muscled body, nothing yielding in those unnervingly light eyes.

Still, no reason for her to go all breathless and silly.

'You should have rung,' she said severely. 'I might have been going out.'

'*Are* you going out?' asked Philippe, and his expression as his gaze swept over her spoke louder than words. Who in

God's name, it seemed to say, would even consider going out in a purple cheesecloth shirt?

Caro lifted her chin. 'As it happens, no.'

'Then perhaps I could come in and tell you what Lotty wants,' he said smoothly. 'Unless you'd like to discuss it on the doorstep?'

Please say you'll help. Caro bit her lip. She had forgotten Lotty for a moment there. 'No, of course not.'

Behind Philippe, a sleek black limousine with tinted windows waited at the kerb, its engine idling. Tinted windows! Curtains would be twitching up and down the street.

No, this wasn't a conversation she wanted to be having in full view of the neighbours. Caro stood back and held the door open, tacitly conceding defeat. 'You'd better come in.'

The hallway was very narrow, and she sucked in her breath to make herself slimmer as Philippe stepped past her. Perhaps that explained why she suddenly felt dizzy and out of breath. It was as if a panther had strolled past her, all sleek, coiled power and dangerous grace. Had Philippe always been that *big*? That solid? That overwhelmingly male?

She gestured him into the sitting room. It was a mess in there, but that was too bad. If he didn't have the courtesy to ring and let her know he was coming, he couldn't expect the red carpet to be rolled out.

Philippe's lips tightened with distaste as he glanced around the room. He couldn't remember ever being anywhere quite so messy before. Tights hung over radiators and there were clothes and shoes and books and God only knew what else in heaps all over the carpet. A laptop stood open on the coffee table, which was equally cluttered with cosmetics, nail polishes, battery chargers, magazines and cups of half drunk coffee.

He should have known as soon as the car drew up outside that Caro wasn't going to be one of Lotty's usual friends, who were all sophisticated and accomplished and perfectly groomed. They lived on family estates or in spacious apartments in the centre of London or Paris or New York, not in poky provincial terraces like this one.

What, in God's name, had Lotty been thinking?

'Would you like some tea?' Caro asked.

Tea? It was eight o'clock in the evening! Who in their right mind drank tea at this hour? Philippe stifled a sigh. He'd need more than tea to get himself through this mess he'd somehow got himself into.

'I don't suppose you've got anything stronger?'

'If I'd known you were coming I would have stocked up on the Krug,' she said sharply. 'As it is, you'll have to make do with herbal tea.'

Philippe liked to think of himself as imperturbable, but he clearly wasn't guarding his expression as well as he normally did, because amusement tugged at the corner of Caroline Cartwright's generous mouth. 'I can offer nettle, gingko, milk thistle…'

The dark blue eyes gleamed. She was making fun of him, Philippe realised.

'Whatever you're having,' he said, irritated by the fact that he sounded stiff and pompous.

He was *never* pompous. He was never stiff either. He was famous for being relaxed, in fact. There was just something about this girl that rubbed him up the wrong way. Philippe felt as if he'd strayed into a different world, where the usual rules didn't apply. He should be at some bar drinking cocktails with a gorgeous woman who knew just how the game should be played, not feeling disgruntled in this tip of a house being offered tea—and herbal tea at that!—by a girl who thought he was *amusing*.

'A mug of dandelion and horny goat weed tea coming up,' she said. 'Sit down, I'll just be a minute.'

Philippe couldn't wait.

With a sigh, he pushed aside the clutter on the sofa and sat down. He'd let Lotty talk him into this, and now he was going to have to go through with it. And it suited him, Philippe remembered. If Caroline Cartwright was half what Lotty said she was, she would be ideal.

She's not pretty, exactly, Lotty had said. *She's more interesting than that.*

Caro certainly wasn't pretty, but she had a mobile face, with a long upper lip and expressive eyes as dark and blue as the ocean. Philippe could see that she might have the potential to be striking if she tidied herself up and put on some decent clothes. Not his type, of course—he liked his women slender and sophisticated, and Caro was neither—but that was all to the good. The whole point was for her to be someone he wouldn't want to get involved with.

And vice versa, of course.

So he was feeling a little more optimistic when Caro came in bearing two mugs of what looked like hot ditchwater.

Philippe eyed his mug dubiously, took a cautious sip and only just refrained from spitting it out.

Caro laughed out loud at his expression. 'Revolting, isn't it?'

'God, how do you drink that stuff?' Philippe grimaced and pushed the mug away. Perhaps he made more of a deal about it than he would normally have done, but he needed the excuse to hide his reaction to her smile. It had caught him unawares, like a step missed in the dark. Her face had lit up, and he'd felt the same dip of the stomach, the same lurch of the heart.

And her laugh…that laugh! Deep and husky and totally unexpected, it was a tangible thing, a seductive caress, the kind that drained all the blood from your head and sent it straight to your groin while it tangled your breathing into knots.

'It's supposed to be good for you,' Caro was saying, examining her own tea without enthusiasm. 'I'm on a diet. No alcohol, no caffeine, no carbohydrates, no dairy products… basically, no anything that I like,' she said glumly.

'It doesn't sound much fun.' Philippe had managed to get his lungs working again, which was a relief. Her laugh had surprised him, that was all, he decided. A momentary aberration. But listen to him now, his voice as steady as a rock. Sort of.

'It isn't.' Caro sighed and blew on her tea.

She had been glad to escape to the kitchen. Philippe's presence seemed to have sucked all the air out of the house. How was it that she had never noticed before how suffocatingly small it was? There was a strange, squeezed feeling inside her, and she fumbled with the mugs, as clumsy and self-conscious as she had been at fifteen.

Philippe's supercilious expression as he looked around the cosy sitting room had stung, Caro admitted, and she had enjoyed his expression when she had offered the tea. Well, they couldn't all spend their lives drinking champagne, and it wouldn't do him any harm to have tea instead for once.

Caro thought about him waiting in the sitting room, looking faintly disgusted and totally out of place. In wealth and looks and glamour, he was so out of her league it was ridiculous. But that was a good thing, she decided, squeezing the teabags with a spoon. It meant there was no point in trying to impress him, even if she had been so inclined. She could just be herself.

'I'm reinventing myself,' she told him now. 'My fiancé left me for someone who's younger and thinner and more fun, and then I lost my job,' she said. 'I had a few months moping around but now I've pulled myself together. At least I'm trying to. No more misery eating. I'm going to get fit, lose weight, change my life, meet a nice man, live happily ever after…you know, realistic, achievable goals like that.'

Philippe raised an eyebrow. 'It's a lot to expect from drinking tea.'

'The tea's a start. I mean, if I can't stick with this, how am I supposed to stick with all the other life-changing stuff?' Caro took a sip to prove her point, but even she couldn't prevent an instinctive wrinkling of the nose. 'But you didn't come here to talk about my diet,' she reminded him. 'You're here about Lotty.'

CHAPTER TWO

'Ah, yes,' said Philippe. 'Lotty.'

Caro put down her mug at his tone. 'Is she OK? I had a very cryptic email from her. She said you would explain about some idea she'd had.'

'She's fine,' he said, 'and yes, I am supposed to be explaining, but it's hard to know where to start. Presumably you know something of the situation in Montluce at the moment?'

'Well, I know Lotty's father died last year.'

The sudden death of Crown Prince Amaury had shocked everyone. He had been a gentle man, completely under the thumb of his formidable mother as far as Caro could tell, and Lotty was his only child. She had taken her dead mother's place at his side as soon as she'd left finishing school, and had never put a foot wrong.

Lotty was the perfect princess, always smiling, always beautiful, endlessly shaking hands and sitting through interminable banquets and never, ever looking bored. There were no unguarded comments from Lotty for the press to seize upon, no photos posted on the internet. No wild parties, no unsuitable relationships, not so much as a whiff of scandal.

'Since then,' Philippe said carefully, 'things have been... rather unsettled.'

'Unsettled' was a bit of an understatement, in Caro's opinion. Montluce was one of the last absolute monarchies in Europe, and had been in the iron grip of the Montvivennes family since Charlemagne. Small as it was, the country was rigidly traditional, and the ruling family even more so. Lotty's grandmother, known as the Dowager Blanche, was only the latest in line of those who made the British royal family's attitude to protocol look slapdash.

Since Lotty's father had died, though, the family had been plunged into a soap opera of one dramatic event after another. A car accident and a heart attack had carried off one heir after another, while one of Lotty's cousins, who should have been in line for the crown, had been disinherited and was currently serving time for cocaine smuggling.

Now, what the tabloids loved to refer to as the 'cursed inheritance' had passed against all the odds to Philippe's father, Honoré. In view of the tragic circumstances, his coronation had been a low-key affair, or so Lotty had told Caro. There had been much speculation in the tabloids about Philippe's absence. None of them could have guessed that the current heir to the throne of Montluce would turn up in Ellerby and be sitting in Stella and Caro's sitting room, pointedly not drinking his horny goat weed tea.

'Amaury was always more interested in ancient Greek history than in running the country,' Philippe went on. 'He was happy to leave the day-to-day business of government in his mother's hands. The Dowager Blanche is used to having things her own way, and now all her plans have gone awry. She's not happy,' he added dryly.

'She doesn't approve of your father?' Caro was puzzled. She'd only ever seen photos of Philippe's father, but he looked tailor-made for the part of Crown Prince. She couldn't imagine why Lotty's grandmother would object to him.

'Oh, he's perfect as far as she's concerned. His sense of duty is quite as strong as hers.' There was an edge to Philippe's voice that Caro didn't understand.

'So what's the problem?' she asked. The truth was that she was having trouble focusing. Part of her was taken up with thinking: there's a *prince* on the sofa! Part was trying not to notice that beneath the casual shirt and trousers, his body was taut and lean.

And another part was so hungry that she couldn't concentrate on any of it properly. She could feel her stomach grumbling. Caro wrapped her arms around her waist and willed it to be quiet. How could she follow Philippe's story when she was worried her stomach might let out an embarrassing growl at any minute?

'Can't you guess?' Philippe smiled but the silver eyes were hard.

Caro forced her mind away from her stomach. 'Oh,' she said slowly. '*You're* the problem?'

'Got it in one,' said Philippe. 'The Dowager thinks I'm idle and feckless and irresponsible and has told me so in no uncertain terms.'

The sardonic smile flashed again. 'She's right, of course. Personally, I've never seen the appeal of duty and commitment. The thought that the future of the Montvivennes dynasty rests with me is almost more than my great-aunt can bear,' he added. 'She's decided that the only way to keep me in line and ensure that I'm not a total disaster for the country is to marry me to Lotty.'

'Lotty said that her grandmother was matchmaking,' said Caro, adding, not very tactfully, 'I'm surprised she'd approve of you, though.'

Philippe acknowledged that with a grim smile. 'She doesn't but, from her point of view, it's the only solution,' he said. 'Once shackled to Lotty, I'll settle down, they think. Lotty's bound to be a good influence on me. She's the perfect princess, after all, and there's no doubt it would be popular in the country. Compared to what the people think, what does it matter what Lotty and I feel?' Bitterness crept into his voice. 'We're royal, and we're expected to do our duty and not complain about it.'

'Poor Lotty! It's so unfair the way she never gets to do what she wants to do.'

'Quite,' said Philippe. He was leaning forward, absently turning his unwanted mug of tea on the coffee table. 'With a new Crown Prince in place, she thought that she would have a chance to get away and make a life of her own at last, but of course my father doesn't have a wife, having been careless enough to let his wife run off with another man, and now Lotty's being manoeuvred into being a consort all over again. I'm fond of Lotty, but I don't want to marry her any more than she wants to marry me.'

'But there must be something you can do about it,' Caro protested. 'I know Lotty finds it hard to resist her grand-mother, but surely you can just say no?'

'I have.' As if irritated by his own fiddling, Philippe pushed the mug away once more and sat back. 'But the Dowager doesn't give up that easily. She's always pushing Lotty and I together and leaking stories to the press.'

'It said in *Glitz* that you were inseparable,' remembered Caro and he nodded grimly.

'That's the Dowager's handiwork. She adores that magazine because they're so pro-royalty. And you've got to admit, it's not a bad strategy. Start a rumour, let everyone in the country whip themselves up into wedding fever and wait for Lotty to cave under the pressure. Montlucians love Lotty, and she'll hate feeling that she's disappointing everyone by being selfish, as the Dowager puts it.'

Caro's mouth turned down as she thought about it. It did seem unfair. 'Why don't you go back to South America?' she suggested. 'Surely the Dowager Blanche would give up on the idea of you and Lotty eventually.'

'That's the trouble. I can't.' Restlessly, Philippe got to his feet. He looked as if he wanted to pace, but the room wasn't big enough for that, so he picked his way through the clutter to the bay window and stood staring unseeingly out to where the limousine waited at the kerb.

'It hasn't been announced yet, but my father is ill,' he said, his back to Caro. 'It's cancer.'

'Oh, no.' Caro remembered how desperate she had felt when her own father had been dying, and wished that she had the courage to get up and lay a sympathetic hand on Philippe's shoulder, but there was a rigid quality to his back that warned her against it. 'I'm so sorry,' she said instead.

Philippe turned back to face her. 'His prognosis isn't too bad, in fact, but the press are going to have a field day with the curse of the House of Montvivennes when it comes out.' His face was carefully expressionless.

'Montluce doesn't have specialised facilities, so he's going to Paris for treatment, and he's been told to rest completely for at least six months. So I've been summoned back to stand in for him. Only nominally, as he and the Dowager keep saying, but they're big on keeping up appearances. I'm taking over his commitments from the start of the month.

'I thought about refusing at first. My father and I don't have what you'd call a close relationship,' he went on with an ironic look, 'and I don't see why they need me to shake a few hands or pin on the occasional medal. If I could have some influence on decisions that are made, it would be different, but my father has never forgiven me for not being a perfect son like my older brother. When I suggested that I have some authority, he was so angry that he actually collapsed.'

Philippe sighed. 'I could insist, but he's ill, and he's my father…I don't want to make him even sicker than he is already. In the end, I said I would do as they asked for six months, but on the understanding that I can go back to South

America as soon as he's well again. There's no point in me hanging around with nothing to do but disappoint him that I'm not Etienne.'

So even royal families weren't averse to laying on the emotional blackmail, thought Caro.

'Meanwhile, you're being thrown together with Lotty at every opportunity?' she said.

'Exactly.' He rolled his shoulders as if to relieve the tension there. 'Then, the other day, Lotty and I were on one of our carefully staged "dates" and we came up with a plan.'

'I wondered when we were going to get to the plan,' said Caro. She made herself take another sip of tea. Philippe was right. It was disgusting. 'What is this great idea of Lotty's?'

'It's a simple one. The problem has been that we're both there, and both single. Of course Lotty's grandmother is going to get ideas. But if I go back to Montluce with a girlfriend and am clearly madly in love with her, even the Dowager Blanche would have to stop pushing Lotty and I together for a while.'

Caro could see where this was going. 'And then Lotty can pretend that it's too awkward for her to see you with another woman and tells her grandmother she needs to go away for a while?'

'Exactly,' said Philippe again.

'I suppose it could work.' She turned the idea over in her mind. 'Where do I come into this? Does Lotty want to come and stay here?'

'No,' said Philippe. 'She wants you to be my girlfriend.'

Caro's heart skidded to a stop, did a funny little flip and then lurched into gear again at the realisation that he was joking. 'Right.' She laughed.

Philippe said nothing.

Her smile faltered. 'You can't be serious?'

'Why not?'

'Well, because…you must have a girlfriend.'

'If I had a serious girlfriend, I wouldn't be in this mess,' he said crisply. 'I'm allergic to relationships. When I meet a woman, I'm clear about that, right from the start. No emotions, no expectations. It just gets messy otherwise.'

Caro sighed. 'Commitment issues…I might have guessed! What is it with guys and relationships?'

'What is it with *women* and relationships?' Philippe countered. 'Why do you always have to spoil things by talking about whether we have a relationship or not and, if we do, where it's going? Why can't we just have a good time?'

Balked of the prowling he so clearly wanted to do, Philippe stepped over to the mantelpiece, put his hands in his pockets and glowered down at his shoes as if it was their fault. 'Six months is about as long as I can stand being in Montluce,' he said. 'It's a suffocating place. Formal, stuffy, and so small there's never any chance to get away.'

He lifted his eyes to Caro's. They ought to be dark brown, she thought inconsequentially, not that clear, light grey that was so startling against his dark skin that it sent a tiny shock through her every time she looked into them.

'I'll be leaving the moment my father is better, and I don't want to complicate matters by getting involved with a woman if there's the slightest risk that she'll start taking things seriously. On the other hand, if she gets so much as a whiff that I'm not in fact serious, the Dowager Blanche will have Lotty back in a flash. For me, that would be a pain, as I'd have to go back to fighting off all the matchmaking attempts, but it would be far, far worse for Lotty. She'd lose the first chance she's ever had to do something for herself. And that's why you'd be perfect,' he said to Caro.

'You're Lotty's friend,' he said. 'I could pretend to be in love with you without worrying that you'd get the wrong idea, because you'd know the score from the start. I'm not going to fall in love with you and you don't want to get involved with me.'

'Well, *that's* certainly true,' said Caro, ruffled nonetheless by the brutal truth. *I'm not going to fall in love with you.*

'But you could pretend to love me, couldn't you?'

'I'm not sure I'm that good an actress,' said Caro tartly.

'Not even for Lotty?'

Caro chewed her lip, thinking of her friend. Lotty was so sweet-natured, so stoical, so good at pleasing everyone but herself. Trapped in a gilded cage of duty and responsibility. From the outside, it was a life of luxury and privilege, but Caro knew how desperately her friend longed to be like everyone else, to be ordinary. Lotty couldn't pop down to the shops for a pint of milk. She couldn't go out and get giggly over a bottle of wine. She could never look less than perfect, never be grumpy, never act on impulse, never relax.

She could never have fun without wondering if someone was going to take her picture and splash it all over the tabloids.

I'm getting desperate, Lotty had said in her email.

'No one would ever believe you would go out with someone like me!' Caro said eventually.

Philippe studied her with dispassionate eyes. 'Not at the moment, perhaps, but with a haircut, some make-up, some decent clothes…you might brush up all right.'

Caro tilted her head on one side as she pretended to consider his reply. 'OK, that's one answer,' she allowed. 'Another might be: why wouldn't anyone believe that I could be in love with you? Don't change a thing; you're beautiful as you are.' She smiled sweetly. 'Just a suggestion, of course!'

'See?' said Philippe. 'That's what makes you perfect. I can be honest with you if you're not a real girlfriend.'

'Stop, you're making me feel all warm and fuzzy inside!'

He smiled at that, and went back to sit on the sofa. 'Look,

just think about it seriously for a moment, Caro. You don't need to come for the whole six months. Two or three would probably be enough for Lotty to get away. We'd both know where we were. There would no expectations, nobody needs to get hurt and, at the end of two months or whatever, we could say goodbye with no hard feelings. I stop my great-aunt hassling me about marriage, you get two months away living in a palace—' the glance he sent around the sitting room made it clear what a change *that* would be '—and Lotty gets a chance to escape and have a life of her own for a while.'

He paused. 'Lotty…Lotty needs this, Caro. You know what she's like. Always restrained, always dignified. She wasn't going to cry or anything, but I could tell how desperate she feels. She's been good all her life, and just when it looks as if a door is opening for her at last, the Dowager and my father are trying to slam it closed again.'

'I know, it's so unfair, but—'

'And you did say you wanted to reinvent yourself,' Philippe reminded her.

Caro winced. She had said that. She clutched at her hair, careless of the way it tumbled out of its clip. 'I just don't know… There's so much to consider, and I can't think when I'm hungry like this!' Uncurling her legs, she put her feet on the floor. 'I'm going to get a biscuit,' she announced.

'I've got a better idea,' said Philippe, checking the Rolex on his wrist. 'Why don't I take you out to dinner? We can talk about the practicalities then, and I could do with a proper drink, not that disgusting stuff,' he said with a revolted glance at his tea. 'Where's the best place to eat around here?'

'The Star and Garter at Littendon,' said Caro automatically, perking up at the prospect of dinner. There was the diet, of course, but she couldn't be expected to make life-changing decisions on a salad and three biscuits, could she? Besides, it was Saturday. It was dinner with a prince, or stay at home with herbal tea and Mr Sexy online.

The prince in question might not be quite as charming as in the fairy tales, but it still wasn't what you'd call a hard choice.

'But you'll never get in on a Saturday,' she added as Philippe took out a super-slim phone and slid it open. 'They get booked up months in advance.'

Ignoring her, Philippe put the phone to his ear. 'Why don't you go and get changed?' was all he said. 'I'm not taking you out in that purple thing.'

The *purple thing* happened to be one of Caro's favourites, and she was still bristling as she pulled it over her head. She hoped the Star and Garter refused him a table and told His Obnoxious Highness that he'd have to wait three months like everyone else.

On the other *hand*, she reminded herself, the food was reputed to be fabulous. Way out of her price range, but no doubt peanuts to Philippe. It wouldn't be *so* bad if he got a table after all.

Now, what to wear? The Star and Garter—if that was where they were going, and Caro had the feeling that Philippe usually got what he wanted—deserved one of her best dresses. Caro ran her eye over her collection of vintage clothes and picked a pale blue cocktail dress made of flocked chiffon. Perhaps the neckline was a *little* low, but she loved the way the pleated skirt swished around her legs when she sashayed her hips.

Sucking in her breath to do up the side zip, Caro tugged up the neckline as far as she could and sauntered back downstairs with a confidence she was far from feeling. Philippe was still on the sofa, looking utterly incongruous. Unaware of her arrival—she could have spared herself the sauntering—he was leaning forward, reading something on the laptop she had abandoned earlier when she had gone in search of biscuits.

Her laptop! Too late, Caro remembered what she had been doing when depression had sent her to the kitchen. Shooting across the room, she banged the laptop closed, narrowing missing Philippe's fingers.

'What are you *doing*?'

Not at all perturbed, Philippe sat back and looked up at her.

'You know, I'm not sure Mr Sexy is the right guy for you.'

'You shouldn't look at other people's computers.' Caro was mortified that he had witnessed how she had been spending her Saturday night. She glared at him. 'It's very rude.'

'It was open on the table,' Philippe pointed out, unfazed. 'I couldn't help but see what you'd been doing. It was quite an eye-opener, I must say. I've never looked at a dating site before.'

Well, there was a surprise. Young, rich, handsome, a prince, and he'd never had to resort to internet dating. Incredible, thought Caro.

'I don't see you finding Mr Right amongst that lot, though,' he said. 'They're not exactly oozing charisma, are they?'

'They can't all be princes,' snapped Caro, pushing him out of the way so she could shut the computer down. 'That's not what I'm looking for either. I just want an ordinary life with an ordinary guy, which is not something *you'd* be able to understand.'

Philippe shook his head. 'You know, I don't think you've been entirely honest in your profile,' he said, nodding at the computer. 'You didn't say anything about how prickly you are.'

'You read my profile?'

'Of course,' he said. 'It's called research. If we're going

to be spending time together, I need to know what I'm going to be dealing with. I must say, I don't think that picture does you justice,' he went on.

He eyed Caro's dress, unimpressed. 'You might want to warn any prospective matches about your odd taste in clothes before you meet,' he added with unnecessary provocation. 'What are you wearing *now*?'

'I'll have you know this is one of my best dresses,' she said, too cross with him to care what he thought about her clothes. 'It's an original cocktail dress from the Fifties. I had to save up to buy it online.'

'You mean you handed over money for that?' Philippe unfolded himself from the sofa. 'Extraordinary.'

'I love vintage clothes,' said Caro. She held out the skirts and twirled. 'I wonder who bought this dress when it was new. Did she buy it for a special occasion? Was she excited? Did she meet someone when she was wearing it? A dress like this has a history. I like that.'

Philippe blinked at the swirl of chiffon and the tantalising glimpse of a really excellent pair of legs. The dress was an improvement on the purple cheesecloth, there was no doubt about that, but he wished that she had put on something a little less…eccentric. A little less *provoking*. Only Caroline Cartwright would choose to wear a sixty-year-old dress!

Maybe it did suit those luscious curves, but it still looked odd to Philippe, and he scowled as he sat in the back of the limousine next to Caro. He had decided to ignore—loftily— her fashion faux pas, and was annoyed to discover that the wretched dress kept snagging at his attention anyway. He blamed Caro, who kept tugging surreptitiously at the neckline, which only drew his eyes to the deep cleavage. Or she was crossing those legs so that the chiffon skirt slithered over her thighs. Philippe shifted uneasily, adjusting his seat belt. He was sure he could hear the material whispering silkily against her bare skin. She had twisted up the mass of nut-brown hair and fixed it with a clip so obviously casually shoved in that he expected any moment that it would all tumble free.

It was very distracting.

Caro wasn't supposed to be distracting. She was supposed to be convenient. That was all.

'I can't believe you got a table!' Caro looked as if she couldn't decide whether to be delighted or aggrieved when the limousine pulled up outside the Star and Garter.

'I didn't. Yan did.' Philippe nodded at an impassive giant who sat next to the driver in the front seat.

Caro lowered her voice and leant closer, giving Philippe a whiff of a clean fresh scent. 'Is he your bodyguard?'

'He prefers to be known as my personal protection officer,' said Philippe. 'He's a very handy man to have around, especially when it comes to getting tables.'

'Everyone else has to wait months. I suppose he dropped your title?' she said disapprovingly.

'I'm sure he did. What else is it for?'

'We can go somewhere else if you object to Yan pulling rank,' he said, but Caro shook her head quickly, so that more strands escaped from the clip. She smoothed them from her face.

'I've always wanted to eat here,' she confessed. 'It's horrendously expensive and most people only come for special occasions. I wanted to come with George when we got engaged, but he didn't think it was worth the money.' She sighed a little and the generous mouth curved downwards. 'We had pizza instead.'

To Philippe, who had eaten at some of the world's top restaurants, there was nothing special about the Star and Garter. It was pleasant enough, he allowed, simply decorated with subtle lighting and enough tables for the place to feel lively without being so close together you were forced to listen to anyone else's conversation.

He was used to the way the buzz of conversation paused when he walked into a restaurant, used to ignoring it while the manager came to greet him personally, used to exchanging pleasantries on automatic pilot, but all the time he could *feel* Caro beside him as clearly as if she were touching him. He kept his eyes courteously on the manager, but he didn't need to look at Caro to know that she was looking eagerly around her, practically humming with anticipation, careless of the fact that her fashion sense was fifty years out of date. Her eyes would be bright, that wretched, tantalising hair escaping from its clip.

And then, abruptly, he felt her stiffen and inhale sharply, and he broke off in mid-sentence to glance at her. She was rigid, her face white and frozen. Philippe followed her stricken gaze across the restaurant to where a couple were staring incredulously back at her.

It wasn't his problem, Philippe told himself, but somehow his arm went round Caro and he pulled her into his side in a possessive gesture. 'I hope you're hungry, *chérie*?' he said, trying not to notice how the dress slipped over her skin beneath his hand.

Caro looked blindly up at him. 'Wh…What?'

'Do you want to go straight to the table or would you rather have a drink at the bar first?' He kept a firm hold on her until the blankness faded from her eyes and understanding dawned.

'Oh.' She moistened her lips. 'Let's go to the table.'

'Excellent.' Philippe turned to the manager. 'We'll have a bottle of your best champagne.'

'Certainly, Your Highness.'

Caro was tense within the circle of his arm as they followed the waiter to their table. She didn't look again at the couple, but her lips were pressed tightly together in distress or anger, Philippe couldn't tell.

'All right?' he asked, when the waiter had gone.

'Yes, I…yes.' Caro shook out her napkin and smoothed it on her lap with hands that were not quite steady. 'It was just a shock to see them here.'

'That was your ex, I take it?'

'George, yes, and his new fiancée.' Her voice vibrated with suppressed anger. 'I can't *believe* he brought Melanie here. She doesn't even *eat*! That's how she looks like a stick insect.'

Philippe glanced over at the table. As far as he could see, Melanie was slim and pretty and blonde, but she would look muted next to Caro.

'I wonder if they're celebrating their engagement?' Caro went on, but he was glad to see the colour back in her face. Shock, it seemed, had been superseded by fury. 'Clearly, Melanie's too good for *pizza*!' She practically spat out the word.

'Maybe she'll wish that they'd gone for pizza instead now that you've arrived,' said Philippe, picking up the menu. 'It can't be much fun trying to celebrate your engagement when your fiancé's ex is on the other side of the room and he can't take his eyes off her.'

'Oh, he's not looking at *me*,' said Caro bitterly. 'He's looking at *you* and wondering what on earth a guy like you is doing with a boring frump like me!'

Philippe's dark brows shot up. 'Boring? *You?*'

His surprise was some consolation, Caro supposed. She opened the menu and pretended to read it, but the words were a blur and all she saw instead was George's face the day he'd told her it was over. He'd waited until she came back from the supermarket, and told her while she was unpacking the bags. Now Caro couldn't look at a carton of orange juice without feeling queasy.

'George thinks I'm boring.' She pressed her lips together against the jab of memory. 'He always said that he wanted to marry someone like me, but then he fell in love with Melanie because she was sexy and fun and everything I'm not, apparently.'

Turning a page unseeingly, she went on, 'There's a certain irony in that. I spent five years being careful and dressing conventionally, and deliberately *not* being fun or obvious, just so that I would fit into his world. I'd have done anything for him.'

Whenever she thought about how much she had loved George, her voice would crack like that. It was mortifying because she was over him now. Pretty much.

'Lotty said you'd been engaged, but that it was over,' Philippe said in that cool, couldn't-give-a-damn voice. 'It's one of the reasons she thought you might like to come to Montluce. A chance to get away for a while.'

'It *would* be nice.' Caro hadn't thought of that aspect of things before. She'd been too busy thinking what it would be like to spend two months with Philippe, who was sitting opposite her looking remote and gorgeous and totally out of reach in spite of being only a matter of inches away.

'Ellerby's a small town,' she said, 'and I spend a lot of time dreading that I'm going to bump into George, like just now.'

Although this time it hadn't been so bad, after all, she realised. There'd been that horrible moment when she'd seen George there with Melanie, and she'd been gripped by that old mixture of misery and rage and humiliation. They were a cosy twosome and she was left alone…and then, suddenly, she hadn't been on her own. Philippe had put his arm around her and made it look as if they were a couple, and she'd seen the astonishment flash in George's face.

Caro looked at Philippe. The dark brows were drawn together as he studied the menu and, with those piercing eyes shielded for once, she could let her gaze travel down his straight nose to the cool set of his mouth, where it snagged in spite of her efforts to tear her eyes away. Looking at it made her feel quite…funny.

He hadn't hesitated to step in and rescue her, while she had been floundering.

'Thank you for earlier,' she said.

'Earlier?'

'You know, making George think we were a couple.' He'd been so quick, seeing instantly what was needed, before she'd even thought about how to react. 'They always see me looking lonely and miserable and pathetic,' she said, laying down the menu so that he could see how grateful she was. 'I don't look like that when I'm with you.'

CHAPTER THREE

'ARE you still in love with him?' Philippe asked and then looked as if the question had caught him unawares. 'I mean, it would be difficult for you to act as my girlfriend if you were,' he added.

'No.' She didn't sound quite as sure as she should have done, Caro realised. 'No,' she said again. 'I adored George. When he broke off our engagement, it broke my heart. For a long time I told myself that I wanted him back, that I still loved him, but now…now I think maybe I love the idea of him more than the reality.'

She saw Philippe flick a brief, uncomprehending glance at George. No, he wouldn't understand.

'I know he's not particularly good-looking or glamorous, but he was everything I've ever wanted. He belongs.'

Philippe looked mystified.

'I never belonged anywhere,' she tried to explain. 'My dad was a mechanical engineer, and when I was small we moved around from project to project overseas. Then he got ill, and we moved to St Wulfrida's.'

'That was Lotty's school,' he remembered, and Caro nodded.

'That's where we met. My mother got a teaching post there, Dad applied to be the handyman so they could be together, and I got a free education as part of the deal. Except I was never going to belong in a school like that, where all the other girls had titles or triple-barrelled names. I wasn't nearly posh enough for them. Lotty was my only friend, and I wouldn't have got through it without her.'

'Funny,' said Philippe, 'that's what she said about you.'

Caro smiled. 'We got each other through, I think. Neither of us could wait to leave. St Wulfrida's doesn't exactly excel in academic achievement, so after GCSEs Lotty went to finishing school, and I went to the local college to do A levels. I thought that would be better, but of course I didn't fit in there either. I was *too* posh for them!'

'What's the big deal about belonging, anyway?' asked Philippe. 'You're lucky. You can go wherever you like, do what you like. That's what most of us want.'

'I don't,' said Caro. 'Dad died when I was fifteen, and my mother five years later, so I don't have any family left.'

She smiled wistfully. 'I suppose I've been looking for a home ever since. When I came to Ellerby and met George, I really thought I'd found a place to belong at last,' she went on. 'George's family have been here for generations. He's the third generation of solicitors, and he's *part* of Ellerby.' Caro searched her mind for an example. 'He's on the committee at the golf club.'

Philippe raised his brows.

'I know,' she said, even though he hadn't said a word, 'it doesn't sound very exciting. But being with George made me feel safe. He had a house, and it felt like being part of the community. I think that's what I miss more than anything else.'

The wine waiter arrived with the bottle of champagne just then, and they went through the whole palaver of showing Philippe the label, opening the bottle with a flourish, pouring the glasses.

Caro concentrated on the menu while all that was going on, a little embarrassed by how much she'd blurted out to

Philippe. He was surprisingly easy to talk to, she realised. Perhaps it was because he so clearly didn't care. Or maybe it was knowing that he was so far out of her league she didn't even need to try and impress him with her coolness or her success. She wasn't here to be clever or witty or interesting. It didn't matter what he thought of George, or of her.

The realisation was strangely exhilarating.

When they'd ordered, Philippe picked up his glass and chinked it against hers. 'Shall we drink to our plan?'

Anything for you, Lotty, she had said once. Still in the grip of that odd sense of liberation, Caro touched his glass back with the air of one making an irrevocable decision. 'To our plan,' she agreed. 'And to Lotty's escape.'

Philippe sat back in his chair and eyed her thoughtfully across the table. 'You're good friends, aren't you?'

'Lotty was wonderful to me when my father died.' Caro turned the stem of her champagne glass between her thumb and fingers. 'He'd been ill for months, and there was no question of us going on holiday, so Lotty asked me if I wanted to spend part of the summer with her, in her family villa in the south of France.'

She lifted her eyes and met Philippe's cool ones. 'You were there.'

'Lotty said that we'd met once,' he said. 'I vaguely remember that she had a friend who was around and then suddenly gone. Was that you?'

'Yes. I hung around with Lotty until my mother rang to say that Dad had had a relapse and was in hospital again. She said there was nothing I could do, and that I should stay in France and enjoy myself. She said that was what Dad wanted, but I couldn't bear it. I was desperate to see him.'

The glass winked in the candlelight as Caro turned it round, round, round.

'I didn't have any money, and Mum was too worried

about Dad to think of changing my ticket,' she went on after a moment. 'Lotty was only fifteen too, and she was so shy that she still stammered when she was anxious, but she didn't even hesitate. She knew I needed to go home. She talked to people she would normally be too nervous to talk to, and she sorted everything out for me. She made sure I was booked onto a flight the next day. I've no idea how she did it, but she arranged for someone to pick me up at the airport in London and take me straight to the hospital.

'Dad died the next day.' Caro swallowed. Even after all that time, the thought of her beloved father made her throat tight. 'If it hadn't been for Lotty, I'd never have seen him again.' She lifted her eyes to Philippe's again. 'I'll always be grateful to her for that. I've often wished there was something I could do for her in return, and now I can. If spending two months pretending to be in love with you helps her escape, even if just for a little while, then I'll do that.'

'It must have been a hard time for you,' said Philippe after a moment. 'I know how I felt when my brother died. I wanted everything to just…stop. And I wasn't a child, like you.'

He set his glass carefully on the table. 'Lotty was good to me then, too. Everyone understood how tragic it was for my father to lose his perfect son, but Lotty was the only one who thought about what it might be like for me to lose a brother. She's a very special person,' he said. 'She deserves a chance to live life on her own terms for a change. I know this is a mad plan,' he went on, deliberately lightening the tone, 'but it's worth a shot, don't you think?'

'I do.' Caro was happy to follow his lead. 'If nothing else, it will convince George and Melanie that I've moved on to much bigger and better things!'

She shot George a victorious look, but Philippe shook his head. 'Stop that,' he said.

'Stop what?'

'Stop looking at him.' He tutted. 'When I take a girl out to dinner, I don't expect her to spend her whole time thinking about another man!'

'I'm not!'

'You're supposed to be thinking about *me*,' said Philippe, ignoring her protest. 'George is never going to believe we're having a wild and passionate affair if he sees you sneaking glances at him.'

'He's never going to believe we're having a wild and passionate affair anyway,' said Caro, ruffled. 'He thinks I'm too boring for that.'

'Then why don't you show him just how wrong he is?' Philippe leant forward over the table and fixed Caro with his silver gaze. He really had extraordinary eyes, she found herself thinking irrelevantly. Wolf's eyes, their lightness accentuated by the darkness of his features and the fringe of black lashes. It was easier to think about that than about the way her heart was thudding in her throat at his nearness.

'How do you suggest I do that?' she said, struggling to hold on to her composure. 'We can hardly get down and dirty under the table!'

A faint contemptuous smile curled the corners of Philippe's mouth. 'Well, that would certainly make the point, but I was thinking of rather subtle ways of suggesting that we can't keep our hands off each other. For a start, you could keep your attention fixed on me, rather than on him! If we were really sleeping together, we'd be absorbed in each other.'

'It doesn't always have to be about you, you know,' grumbled Caro. 'Anyway, I *am* looking at you.' She fixed her eyes at him. 'There. Satisfied?'

'You could make it look as if you adore me and can't wait for me to drag you back to bed.'

'Oh, that's easy.' Caro summoned a suitably besotted expression and batted her lashes at him.

'What's the matter?' asked Philippe.

'Nothing's the matter! I'm looking adoring!'

'You look constipated,' he said frankly. 'Come on, you must be able to do better than that.'

'You're the expert on seduction,' said Caro, sulking. 'You do it.'

'OK.' Philippe reached across the table for her hand, turned it over and lifted it. 'Watch and learn,' he said, pressing a kiss into her palm.

Caro sucked in a breath as a current of warmth shot up her arm and washed through her. Her scalp was actually tingling with it. Bad sign. Willing the heat to fade, she struggled to keep her voice even.

'Oh, that old chestnut,' she said as lightly as she could. 'I would have done the hand-kissing thing, but I thought it would be too boring.'

'Kissing's never boring,' said Philippe. Now he was playing with her fingers, looking straight into her eyes, brushing his lips across her knuckles until she squirmed in her seat. 'Not the way we do it, anyway. Or that's what we want it to look like. We want everyone to think that we've just fallen out of bed, don't we? They ought to be looking at us and seeing that we can't keep our hands off each other. That we can't wait until we get home and I can undress you, very, very slowly, until you beg me to make love to you again.'

The sound of his voice and the tantalising caress of his fingers were doing alarming things to Caro. Heat was uncoiling in the pit of her belly and her mouth was dry. She had to get herself back under control.

'I never beg,' she said, but not nearly as steadily as she would have liked.

Philippe looked into her eyes and smiled. 'You do when you're with me.'

'I don't think so,' said Caro, but his smile only deepened.

She could see the candlelight flickering in the silver eyes, and her heart was thumping so loudly she was afraid the other diners would turn round and complain about the noise.

'Yes, you do, because I'm the only one who knows that behind closed doors you're a wild, passionate woman.' His voice was a tangible thing, velvet smoothing seductively over her skin. It would be so easy to succumb to it, to the warm, sure hands and the wickedly attractive smile, and Caro had to physically brace herself against it.

'Gosh, do women really fall for this stuff?' she asked.

'It's working, isn't it?'

For one horrible moment, Caro wondered if he could see her toes curling. 'Working?'

'You haven't been looking at what's-his-name at all.' It was true. She had completely forgotten about George for a while there. 'But he's been looking at you,' Philippe went on in the same disturbingly arousing voice, 'and he's very much afraid that you've found yourself a much, much better lover.'

Caro's eyes flickered to George, who was looking as if he'd been stuffed. Maybe there was something in this technique of Philippe's after all.

Philippe sat back smugly. 'And that's how it's done,' he said. 'Now you have a go.'

Her hand was throbbing where his lips had grazed her skin. Flustered by Philippe's abrupt transition from lover to teacher, Caro tucked the stray strands of hair behind her ears and assumed a nonchalance she wasn't feeling.

'Well, I *would*, but the food will be arriving any second and I don't want to spoil your appetite.'

'Coward,' he said softly. 'Besides, it's good practice for you. You're going to have to do better than screwing up your face if you're going to convince the Dowager Blanche that we're mad about each other.'

'Oh, all right.' Caro took a fortifying sip of her champagne and moistened her lips nervously while she thought, and saw Philippe's gaze fix on her mouth. She hadn't even started yet! Surely it couldn't be as easy as that?

Leaning forward, she rested her arms on the table, hugged them together and tried a seductive smile. She felt a fool, but Philippe's eyes dropped to her cleavage, and his eyes darkened unmistakably.

Encouraged, Caro felt around with her foot and managed to hook the toe of her shoe around his ankle. With a little manoeuvring, she could rub her foot tantalisingly up and down his calf. It felt awkward but it seemed to be working.

She waited for Philippe to burst out laughing, but he didn't. There was just the suspicion of a smile around his mouth as the light gaze returned to her face.

'How am I doing?' she asked.

'I think you may be a natural.'

Was he being sarcastic? Caro eyed him suspiciously but it was impossible to tell what he was really thinking.

It was a relief when their starters arrived and she could sit back. Funny, she had forgotten about how hungry she was while Philippe had been kissing her fingers. Now she picked up her fork to dig into her wild mushroom risotto and discovered that for possibly the only time in her life, her appetite had deserted her.

But Caro wasn't going to waste her one and only opportunity to eat at the Star and Garter. She made herself savour the food and refused to let herself think about Philippe sitting opposite her with his warm hands and his warm mouth.

'That was delicious,' she said, putting her fork down at last.

'Yes, it wasn't bad,' said Philippe indifferently. Michelin starred restaurants would be two a penny to him, of course. He held out his hand. 'Come on, back to looking besotted.'

'Must I?' sighed Caro, but she took his hand and, at the feel of his strong fingers curling around hers, a shiver of pleasure snaked through her.

Clearing her throat, she said, 'We ought to talk about practicalities.'

'Practicalities?'

To her consternation, Philippe turned her hand over so that the soft skin of her forearm was exposed. Now he was rubbing his thumb softly over her wrist, where her vein pulsed with awareness.

Caro swallowed hard and soldiered on. 'What's going to happen next?'

He would go back to Montluce in the next couple of days, Philippe told her. He would break the news about their supposed relationship to the Dowager Blanche and give Lotty a chance to make her own plans to leave. Then he would escort his father to Paris for his treatment.

'He won't want me, but he ought to have someone other than servants there for the operation,' he said. 'Once he's through that, I'll come and pick you up, and we'll go back to Montluce together. Will ten days or so be enough time for you to get ready?'

She nodded, desperately trying to ignore that stroking thumb, which was playing havoc with her breathing. 'I'm only temping,' she said unevenly. 'I just need to give a week's notice.'

'Once we're there, you won't have to do much,' Philippe said. 'Hang around with me. Convince my great-aunt that you adore me. Hold my hand like this. The usual stuff.'

'It doesn't sound very interesting,' said Caro austerely to cover the booming of her pulse.

'No, but it shouldn't be hard either.'

'Where—' She stopped, mortified by how high her voice sounded, and coughed. 'Where will I stay?' That was better, huskier, almost normal.

'With me,' said Philippe. 'We're not going to convince anyone that it's a serious relationship if we're not living together. I've got apartments in the palace in Montvivennes. Not where I'd choose to live, but it's comfortable enough.'

Apartments, plural? That sounded big. Caro was reassured. 'Plenty of space for both of us, then?'

'Oh, yes.' His eyes met hers, clearly knowing exactly the way her mind was going. 'Of course, we'll have to sleep together,' he said.

'That won't be necessary, surely?' Caro stiffened and tried to pull her hand away, but he held her tight. 'No one need know where I'm sleeping as long as I'm staying with you.'

'That's what you think.' Philippe's voice was crisp. 'There are servants in and out of the apartments all the time, and it would be a miracle if they didn't talk to each other. They'll wonder just what kind of relationship we have if we're not sleeping together, and word will get back. My great-aunt knows everything that goes on in the palace. She's got a spy network that would put the CIA to shame.'

'Couldn't we tell her you respect me too much to sleep with me before marriage?'

He offered her a sardonic smile in return. 'Yes, she'll believe that!'

Caro managed to tug her hand away at last. It was all very well for Philippe to sound coolly amused about the whole business, but he must have slept with millions of beautiful women. He was probably used to sleeping with strangers. The thought of sleeping with her clearly hadn't left *him* with an unnerving fluttering underneath his skin and in the pit of his stomach. *He* hadn't been misery-eating, so he didn't have to worry about what she would think when he took his clothes off.

Philippe naked…Caro's mind veered off track momentarily to imagine him pulling off his shirt with a grin. She could picture the lean, hard planes of his body with startling ease: the flex of his muscles under his skin, the broad chest, the flat stomach. The power and the grace and the sheer, sinful sexiness of him.

Her cheeks burned at the thought. She *really* didn't want her imagination to start running wild like that, especially not when taking off her own shirt would reveal all those extra pounds she had put on since George dumped her...and it wasn't as if she had been sylphlike to start with. No, there would be no undressing going on, under any circumstances.

'We can put a pillow down the middle, if you like,' said Philippe, apparently reading her mind without difficulty.

Without being aware of what she was doing, Caro cupped the wrist where he had stroked her with her free hand as if to calm the soft skin there, which was quivering still from his touch.

'You don't sound bothered one way or the other,' she said, unable to keep the snippiness from her voice.

He shrugged. 'I'm not. It's entirely up to you, Caro. I'm more than capable of keeping my hands to myself, so there's no need to panic.'

'I'm not panicking,' she said crossly. 'I'm just trying to think how it would work.'

She took her hand from her wrist and sat straighter. It was time to be sensible. 'If you say that we need to share a bed, then that's what we'll do. I'm not going to be silly about it. But I think sex would just confuse the issue,' she said, rather proud of her coolness this time. 'I think it would be easier if we agreed that we would be just friends while we're together.'

'Friends?' he repeated, expressionless.

'Yes, you know, when you have a good time but don't want to sleep together.'

'I've got friends,' he said. 'They're just not usually women.'

'There's nothing usual about our relationship, though, is

there, Philippe? You're a prince, I'm an ordinary girl with no
interest in anything other than an ordinary life. You're wealthy
by any standard, and I'm temping to pay my rent. You go out
with beautiful, glamorous women, and I'm neither,' Caro said.
'We've got absolutely nothing in common apart from Lotty,
but just for two months we're going to be together. I'm not
interested in you, and I think it's pretty clear you're not going
to be interested in me, so it makes sense that we should agree
to be friends at least, don't you think?'

Why not? Philippe asked himself. Caro was right. It would
be much easier this way. The last thing he wanted was to get
involved with someone who would fall in love with him. That
would complicate matters and it would all get very messy.
There would be tears and scenes and demands for commitment and stormings off. Philippe had been there before, and
he couldn't afford anything similar this time if he didn't want
to be left at the mercy of the Dowager Blanche's matchmaking
plans again.

So it was just as well Caro had made it clear that she wasn't
interested in him. There was no need to feel nettled. It wasn't
as if she was *his* type either. Caro was right: she wasn't beautiful, she wasn't stylish. She was untidy and distracting, that
was all.

It was just that he couldn't shake the feel of her. When he'd
put his arm around her to cross the restaurant, he'd rested his
hand on the flare of her hip and felt the silky material of her
dress shift over her skin with a shock of awareness. He'd held
her wrist and felt the blood beating in her veins, and that, too,
had been like a current thrilling through him. He looked away
from her mouth.

'Fine by me,' he said, as carelessly as he could. 'Friends it
is, and we'll get that pillow out as soon as we get there.'

Philippe was used to eating with women who automatically chose the least fattening meal on the menu and it was a

revelation to watch Caro oohing and aahing over her choice. Philippe himself was largely indifferent to food—he reserved his passion for the wine list—but it was impossible not to enjoy eating with someone who took so much pleasure in it. Caro would close her eyes blissfully while she savoured every taste and texture. She loaded up forkfuls from her dish and insisted he try it, and reached over to help herself to a taste of his, until he suggested that they simply swap plates.

He was being sarcastic, but Caro was delighted at the suggestion and promptly handed over her plate. 'George always refused to share like this,' she confided. 'He said it was embarrassing to pass plates over the table and that everyone would look at us.'

'And this was a guy who accused *you* of not being any fun?'

'He probably swaps plates with Melanie,' she said with a sigh.

'You should have tried leaning over the table so that he could fall down your cleavage,' Philippe said. 'I'm sure he'd have swapped anything you wanted then.'

'Do you really think so?' The blue eyes rested wistfully on George and Philippe was conscious of a quite irrational stab of jealousy.

He was used to being the centre of attention. His dinner companions were invariably beautiful, just as Caro had said. They flirted and sparkled and charmed and laughed at all his jokes. It was a salutary experience to be with Caro, who was far more interested in her ex-fiancé than in him. She was more interested in the *food* than in him, come to that.

Philippe told himself that he was amused, but the truth was that he was just a little piqued by her indifference. Here was he, a prince famous for his charm and his wit and his sexual prowess, having to work to keep the attention of a woman who wasn't even really pretty, and who didn't feel the least need to keep him entertained. Not that he wanted to be entertained, of course, but still…

It was annoying to find that his leg was tingling where she had rubbed her shoe so tantalisingly, and that his eyes kept snagging on that mouth, or drifting to that luscious cleavage. Philippe suspected that Caro had no idea how she looked, with that provocative mouth and that wickedly lush body, so at odds with the combative glint in her blue eyes and the sharpness of her tongue.

I'm not interested in you, she had said.

Just as well.

For the first time in her life, Caro refused pudding. Finally, she'd made it to the Star and Garter, and she wasn't hungry! Life could be so unfair sometimes.

'Ready to go?' asked Philippe. 'Let's make sure we make an exit.' Very casually, he rested a hand at the nape of her neck as they passed George's table. It was a perfect proprietorial gesture, and it felt disturbingly intimate to Caro. The warmth from his fingers snaked down her spine, making her shiver.

'They'll be leaving any minute themselves,' Philippe murmured as he opened the door for her. 'Do you want to kiss me?'

'What?' Caro stopped dead and stared at him. 'No, of course not!'

'Sure? Because here's an opportunity to convince George that you're having a passionate affair, if you want to,' he said, all reasonableness. 'He *might* have been convinced by all the hand-holding, but it was all a bit tame, wasn't it? Whereas if he sees you enjoying a steamy kiss, there's not going to be much doubt in his mind that you're a passionate, exciting woman having a better time without him, is there?'

Caro hesitated. The idea of making George believe that she was in the throes of a wild affair was deeply appealing, she had to admit. For too long, she'd felt dull and repressed next to bubbly Melanie, and hated that deadly feeling that they both felt sorry for her.

But this was His Serene Highness Prince Philippe of Montluce... Did she really have the nerve to kiss him? On the other hand, they *had* agreed to be friends, hadn't they? 'Are you sure you wouldn't mind?' she asked doubtfully.

In reply, Philippe spread his arms. 'What are friends for? Besides, it'll be good practice for us. We're going to have to kiss in Montluce, so we might as well get used to it.'

True. Good point. Caro took a deep breath. 'Well...okay, then.'

'Come over here.' Philippe took her hand and led her over to the limousine, which waited in the glow of a single street light immediately opposite the door. 'There's no point if George can't see us, is there? They won't be able to miss us here.' He turned and leant back against the limousine. 'Off you go, then.'

'Where's Yan?'

'Don't worry about Yan. He's used to looking the other way.'

'Right.' Above them, the sky was a dark, dark blue, and the cool night air brimmed with the scents of a northern summer. A little current of excitement ran under Caro's skin. Moistening her lips, she stepped towards him, then hesitated.

'I feel silly.'

'That's because you're too far away. You'll find it easier if you get a bit closer.'

Caro took another step. It brought her up against him. She could smell his cologne—subtle, expensive—and, when she rested her palms against his chest, she felt the hard solidity of him through the fine material of his shirt.

The street lamp cast a surreal orange glow over everything, but at the same time Caro could see exactly what she was doing. It was like being on stage, and now she had to perform.

Gripped by shyness, she stared fixedly at Philippe's collar while her hands pressed against his chest and the warmth of his skin seemed to pulse through her, slow and steady like his heartbeat.

'I don't want to hurry you, but they'll be out soon,' said Philippe and his voice reverberated through her hands.

'Right,' she said again, and swallowed. Passionate, exciting…she could do it.

Forcing her eyes up from his collar, she let them drift up the strong column of his throat. She could see the faint prickle of stubble and, without giving herself time to think, she touched her lips to the pulse beating there.

Philippe inhaled slowly. His hands hung loosely by his sides, but she felt the tension in his body, and she smiled. Maybe he wasn't quite as cool as he made out.

Her heart was thudding painfully, *bang, bang, bang* against her ribs. She kissed the pulse again, then drifted soft kisses up to his jaw. It felt deliciously rough beneath her lips and she slid her hands to his shoulders.

'I think you'd better get on with it,' said Philippe, but a smile rippled through the words.

'Stop talking,' she mumbled, making her way along his chin. 'You're putting me off.'

'I'm just saying. George will be out any second.'

Caro pulled away, exasperated. 'I can't do it if you're going to do a running commentary!'

'Then make me stop talking,' he challenged her.

'Fine.' Defiantly, she stepped back up to him and put her hands on his shoulders once more. Then she leant into him, angling her face up and pressing her mouth against his. His lips were warm and firm and relaxed and curved into the faintest of smiles.

Was he laughing at her? Caro kissed him again, nibbling little kisses at the edge of his mouth where his smile dented, teasing his lips open so that their tongues could twine together, and it felt so warm, so right, that she forgot everything else. She forgot George and Melanie. She forgot the plan. She forgot about just being friends. There was only the taste of him and the feel of him and the astonishing sweetness spilling through her.

Then Philippe's arms closed round her at last and he pulled her hard against him, and the sweetness was swept away by a surge of heat. It was wild and dark and fierce, a current that swirled around them, sucking them down, pulling them off their feet. Caro was lost, tumbling in the frantic wash of desire. She linked her arms around his neck to anchor herself, murmuring low in her throat, something inarticulate that might have been protest, or might have been longing.

Somehow Philippe had found the clip in her hair and pulled it free. It fell, unnoticed, to the ground while he slid his fingers through the silky mass, twisting, twining, holding her head still so that he could kiss her back, and he was good, oh, he was good…Caro thrilled at the sureness of his lips, the hard insistence of his hands that slid down her spine to cup her bottom and lift her against him.

She could feel his arousal, and she pulled her mouth from his so that she could gasp for breath.

'Philippe…'

She wasn't even sure what she meant to say, but Philippe, who was kissing her throat and making her shiver with delight at the heat and the hunger of it, stilled as if she had whacked him across the head.

Caro felt him draw a ragged breath, then another. 'Good God,' he said, sounding shaken, and let her go. 'Maybe that's enough practice for now.'

Practice? Desperately, Caro tried to bring her scattered senses back under control. She needed a decompression chamber, somewhere to learn to breathe again, a staging post between heady pleasure and the slap of reality where there was no touch, no taste, no feel, no giddy swing of the senses but only the chill of standing alone on a summer's night remembering that none of it had been real.

CHAPTER FOUR

MONTLUCE was such a tiny country that it didn't even have its own airport, so they were to fly to France and drive the rest of the way. In Caro's experience, flying meant a lot of queuing, a lot of delays, a lot of shuffling onto a crowded plane and shifting impatiently for the inevitable passenger who blocked the aisle for long minutes while he fussed about stashing away his duty-free in the overhead lockers.

Flying with Philippe was very different. The limousine he'd sent to pick her up in Ellerby that morning bypassed the terminal and deposited her right by the plane on the tarmac. Her bags were whisked away while Caro climbed out and stood looking dubiously up at the private jet. It looked very small. The wind was whipping tendrils of hair around her face and plastering them against her lips as fast as she could pull them free.

She was very nervous.

And cross with herself for feeling that way. Everything was going ahead exactly as they'd planned. Lotty was ecstatically grateful and would be gone before Caro and Philippe arrived. Once in Montluce, there would just be the two of them.

Which would be *fine*, Caro told herself. They had agreed to be friends, hadn't they? If it hadn't been for that stupid kiss…

But she wasn't supposed to be thinking about that. It had

been a mistake, they'd agreed afterwards. Both of them had been carried away by the pretence, but pretence was all it had been. It wasn't as if it had been a real kiss.

The trouble was that it had *felt* real. The firm curve of his mouth, his breath against her skin, the insistence of the sure hands cupping her buttocks and pulling her into him…oh, yes, it had felt real, all right. She could still feel the glittery rush, the heat. Philippe had been so hard, so surprisingly solid, so *male*. Every time Caro thought about him, her muscles would clench and a disturbing sensation, half shiver, half shudder, would snake its way down her spine.

Not that she would make the mistake of believing it had meant anything to Philippe. Just because she could admit he was attractive didn't mean that she was going to lose her mind. Caro might be many things, but she wasn't a fool.

After announcing their relationship to a relieved Lotty and a furious Dowager Blanche, Philippe had escorted his equally disappointed father to Paris to start his treatment, but for the last three or four days he'd been in London. Caro knew this because she'd seen his picture in *Glitz*. He'd been snapped coming out of a nightclub with Francesca Allen. Usually referred to as 'Britain's favourite actress', Francesca was famously beautiful, famously intelligent, famously nice— and famously married. The tabloids were having a field day speculating about what they were doing together.

It was a stupid thing to have done, given everything Philippe had had to say about convincing the Dowager Blanche that he was serious about *her*, Caro thought, and told herself that was the only reason she was feeling monumentally miffed. She wasn't silly enough to be jealous. *I'm more than capable of keeping my hands to myself*, Philippe had said, and Caro had no problem believing him, kiss or no kiss. A man like Philippe, used to hanging around with beautiful women the likes of Francesca Allen, was hardly likely to be tempted by an ordinary, overweight, eccentrically dressed Caroline Cartwright, was he?

No, being friends was the only way to get through the next few weeks. As a friend, she wouldn't have to worry about what she looked like, and there would be no need to feel twitchy about other, far more beautiful, women prowling around him. She could relax and enjoy herself with a friend.

Caro had barely reminded herself of that when Philippe appeared, ducking out of the cabin, long and lean and tautly muscled in a pale yellow polo shirt and chinos, and the breath whooshed out of her. He looked the same, and yet different, more *immediate* somehow: the cool mouth, the winged brows, the crisp line of his jaw, the startling contrast between the icy eyes and the darkness of his hair.

It must be something to do with the brightness of the light, the freshness of the breeze. Why else would the sight of him sharpen her senses and make her feel as if every cell in her body was alert and tingling?

At the top of the steps, Philippe looked down at Caro and was startled by how pleased he was to see her.

Of course, it would have been horribly awkward if she'd changed her mind, Philippe told himself. His announcement that he was bringing a girlfriend no one had ever heard of back to Montluce hadn't gone down well, to say the least, and he'd been subjected to endless harangues on the subject from his great-aunt, while his father had retreated into bitter disappointment as usual. Only Lotty, hugging him with a speaking look of gratitude, had stopped him from telling them what they could all do with their duty and responsibility and booking himself on the first plane back to Buenos Aires.

Philippe had been glad to escape to London and enjoy his last few days of freedom for a while. He'd met up with friends, played polo at the Guards Club, been to parties and dinners and renewed his acquaintance with the beautiful Francesca

Allen. He wasn't looking forward to the next six months, and couldn't decide whether this mad pretence with Caro Cartwright was going to make things better or worse. She was so different from the other women he knew. Not beautiful, not glamorous. Just ordinary. And yet Philippe had been surprised at how vividly he remembered her.

How vividly he remembered that kiss.

He'd been prepared for awkwardness, not for sweetness. Not for softness a man could lose himself in if he wasn't careful.

The memory made Philippe uncomfortable. He didn't do losing himself. But he'd been taken unawares by the way the dress slipped over her skin. The heat shooting through him had sucked the air from his brain, and the message to step back and keep his cool hadn't reached his hands.

Or his mouth.

Or the rest of him.

Philippe didn't understand it. Caro Cartwright ought to be the last woman to have that kind of effect on him. She wasn't even pretty, and as for her clothes…! Today she wore jeans and boots, with a plain white T-shirt, which wouldn't have looked too bad if she hadn't spoiled it by wearing an oversize man's dinner jacket over the top, its sleeves rolled up to show a brilliant scarlet lining. At least she was tall enough to carry it off with a certain panache, he allowed grudgingly.

No, Caro wasn't his type at all.

And yet there she stood, blue eyes wary and all that hair blowing around her face, and his heart unmistakably lifted.

Odd.

'There you are,' he said, pushing the discomfited feeling aside. It was too late to change his mind now. He went down the steps to greet her. 'I was beginning to wonder if you'd changed your mind.'

'I did think about it,' Caro confessed. 'But then I heard

from mutual friends that George is worried I might be going off the rails. He's obviously found out who you were, and he thinks you've got a bad reputation,' she said cheerfully. 'Now he's afraid that I'm going to do something stupid and get hurt—and, as we all know, he's the only one allowed to hurt me! So I thought I'd come after all, and send lots of messages home to make sure he knows what a glamorous time I'm having while Melanie is going to the supermarket and making George his tea the way he likes it. Then we'll see who's having the most fun, fun, fun!'

'Excellent,' said Philippe. 'In that case, you'd better come aboard.'

Caro was deeply impressed by the inside of the plane, which was fitted out with six plush leather seats, wall-to-wall carpeting and a lot of polished wood. Yan was already there, sitting in the cockpit.

'Take a seat,' Philippe said. 'Now you're here, we're ready to go.'

Caro looked around. 'Where's the pilot?'

'You're looking at him.'

'You're not a pilot!'

'I'm not? Then we're going to be in trouble because there's no one else to fly the plane.'

'I'm serious,' said Caro uneasily as she sat down in the seat nearest the front. 'Are you sure you know how to fly?'

Philippe settled himself in the cockpit and began flicking switches. 'Sure. I did a five-minute course a few years ago.'

'Really?'

'No, of course not really!' he said, exasperated. 'You don't think they let you in the air unless you're properly qualified, do you?'

'They might if you can stick Prince in front of your name,' said Caro with a dark look, although she was reassured to see Yan beside him. Surely he wouldn't let Philippe fly unless he knew what he was doing? 'The rules don't usually apply to people like you.'

'Well, in this case they do,' said Philippe. 'I've got a licence, I assure you. What do you think I've been doing for the past few years?'

'I don't know. Playing polo?'

'Pah! Who wants to get on a horse when you can fly a plane?'

'What, you mean you just get in your plane and fly around in the sky?' It seemed a bit pointless to Caro.

'No, I fly to places,' he said, his hands busy checking dials and switches. Caro just hoped he knew what he was doing.

'What places?' she asked suspiciously.

'I go wherever a plane is needed. I've got a friend who organises logistics for a number of aid organisations. They might need a development worker transported in a remote village, or tents dropped after an earthquake…if you haven't got the time or the money to get through the bureaucratic red tape, I'm your man.'

Philippe glanced over his shoulder at Caro. 'It gives me something to do when I'm bored,' he said, as if he feared he might have given too much of himself away. 'And it's more fun than polo! Now, fasten your seat belt while we finish the pre-flight check here.'

He turned back to the controls. 'Er, what's this red button again?' he pretended to ask Yan. 'Oh, right, the eject seat. Oops, better avoid that one! So the start button must be…oh, yes, I remember now. All right in the back there?' he called over his shoulder to Caro.

'Ha, ha, ha,' she said in a monotone. 'That's a fake laugh, by the way!'

'Relax,' he said. 'I hardly ever crash. Besides, I thought you'd decided to have fun, fun, fun, and what could be more fun than flying around in a private jet?'

'It won't be much fun when the plane crashes,' she grumbled.

The plane didn't crash, of course, but it felt as if something even more disastrous was happening inside her as she watched Philippe push the throttle remorselessly forwards. His long hands were absolutely steady as they shot along the runway, and Caro's stomach dropped away as the plane lifted into the air.

She was more impressed than she wanted to admit. Why had she assumed that he had been living an idle trust fund existence? She should have realised that a man like Philippe would be bored with nothing to do but party all day. There was that reckless edge to him that she had noticed even as a boy. It was all too easy to imagine him flying planes into war zones, dodging bullets or volcanic ash or pot-holed runways. He would thrive on the danger.

Philippe had been very quick to dismiss what he did, Caro had noticed. *Something to do when I'm bored*, he had said. There must be plenty of other jaded rich people out there, but how many of them would risk their lives for others the way he did? Philippe could get his thrills racing cars or helicopter skiing or doing any of the other extreme sports that catered to the very rich and very bored, but instead he flew his plane where it was needed. No doubt he did enjoy it, but Caro thought it was more than possible that he would go anyway.

She liked that about him, and she liked the fact that he clearly didn't publicise what he was doing. He wasn't like so many other celebrities, using charity work to raise their own profiles. Caro wondered if even Lotty knew.

From where she sat, she could see the hard edge of Philippe's jaw, the flash of his smile as he turned to speak to Yan beside him. Caro could see one powerfully muscled arm. Her eyes drifted from the dark, flat hairs on his forearm to the broad, strong wrist, and on to the firm fingers holding the joystick, and a disquieting ache stirred low in her belly.

She made herself look away, out of the window. The seat was pressing into the small of her back as they climbed up through great blowsy drifts of clouds, up into the blue. There was no going back to real life now. Instead, she would spend the next two months as Philippe's girlfriend. Caro's eyes slid back to his profile, etched now against the bright sky. She could see the creases at the edge of his eye, the corner of his mouth, and remembering how warm and sure it had felt against her own made her stomach tilt anew.

Two months beside him. Two months trying not to notice the cool set of his mouth or remember the feel of his hands.

The squirmy feeling in Caro's belly intensified. Nerves, she decided at first, but when she looked out at the clouds and felt the plane soaring upwards and thought about the weeks ahead she finally recognised the feeling for what it was.

Excitement.

'Oh, what a beautiful car!' Caro gasped when she saw the Aston Martin waiting for them at the quiet airfield where they landed. Philippe watched her practically fall down the steps in her eagerness to get at it.

Unless it was her eagerness to get out of the plane, of course.

'Oh, you beauty!' she said, running a hand lovingly over the bonnet. 'A DB9! I've never seen one before.' She looked up at him, her eyes shining. 'Is it yours?'

'It is.' She was so vivid standing there in the sunlight, her face alight with enthusiasm, that Philippe's breath hitched in a new and disturbing way, and for a moment he couldn't remember how to be.

'This isn't like you.' Ah, yes, that was better. Cool, indifferent. That was him. 'You know the car's not second-hand, don't you? And you can't eat it? I wouldn't have thought it was your kind of thing at all.'

'I make an exception for cars.' Caro let her hand smooth over the bodywork in a way that made Philippe's throat dry ridiculously. He fought for a casual expression, but all he could think, bizarrely, was: *lucky car.*

'Can I drive?' she asked, with a speculative look from under her lashes, trying it on.

'Absolutely not,' he said firmly.

'Oh, please! I'll behave very, very nicely.'

'No.'

'You're supposed to be in love with me,' she pointed out as she straightened.

'I'd have to be besotted before I let you drive my car,' he said, and opened the passenger door for her. 'Most girls would be happy to be driven.'

'I'm not most girls,' said Caro, but she got in anyway and he closed the door after her with a satisfying clunk.

'You can say that again,' said Philippe, walking round to get in behind the wheel. Now she was stroking the seat and the wooden trim, leaning forward to gaze at the dashboard, wriggling back into her seat with a sigh of pleasure. It was practically pornographic! Not enough oxygen was getting to his brain and he had to take a breath, horrified to find that the hands he laid on the steering wheel weren't entirely steady.

The clear glass starter button glowed invitingly red, reminding him that he was in control. Philippe pressed it and the engine purred into life.

'What about Yan and the luggage?' Caro dragged her attention back from the car for a moment.

'He'll follow in the other car,' said Philippe, nodding back to a black SUV with tinted windows.

'Isn't he supposed to be protecting you?'

'He'll be right behind.' Philippe put the car into gear. 'But for now it's just you and me.'

'Oh,' was all Caro said, but a little thrill shivered through her all the same.

Just you and me.

It wouldn't be just the two of them, of course. Lotty had told her about the palace servants, and there would always be Yan or a member of the public wanting their hand shaken. Just as well, Caro told herself firmly. It would be much easier to be friends when there were other people around.

'Where did you learn about cars?' Philippe asked as they turned onto the main road.

'From my father.' The road was clear ahead, and Philippe put his foot down. The car responded instantly, surging forward. Caro felt the pressure in the small of her back and settled into it with a shiver of pleasure. 'He loved cars. He always had some banger up on the blocks and he'd spend hours tinkering with it. When I was little I'd squat beside him and be allowed to hand him a spanner or an oily rag. Even now the smell of oil makes me think of Dad.'

Caro smiled unevenly, remembering. 'Driving an Aston Martin was his dream. He'd be so thrilled if he could see me now!' She stroked the leather on either side of her thighs. 'And envious!'

Distracted by the stroking, Philippe forced his attention back to the road. 'It sounds like you had a good relationship with your father.'

'I adored him.' She touched the lapels of the jacket she wore. 'This is Dad's dinner jacket. He wore it for a school dance once, and no one recognised him. It was as if none of them had ever looked at him when he was wearing his handyman overalls, but put on a smart jacket and suddenly he was a real person, someone they could talk to because he was dressed like them.'

Caro fingered the sleeve where she'd rolled it up to show the scarlet lining. 'I remember Dad saying that some people are like this jacket, conventional on the outside, but with a bright, beautiful lining like this. He said we shouldn't judge what's on the outside, it's what's inside that really matters. I think of him every time I put this jacket on,' she said.

'My father thinks the exact opposite,' said Philippe. 'For him, it's *all* about appearances. No wonder I'm such a disappointment to him.' He was careful to keep his tone light, but Caro looked at him, a crease between her brows.

'He can't be that disappointed if he trusts you to stand in for him while he's sick.'

'Only because it wouldn't look right if he didn't make his only surviving son regent in his absence, would it? What would people *think*?'

In spite of himself, Philippe could hear the bitterness threading his voice, and he summoned a smile instead. 'Besides, it's not a question of trust. It's not as if they're going to let me loose on government. My father thinks it'll be good for me to experience meetings and red boxes and the whole dreary business of governing, but all that's just for show too. There's a council of ministers, but the Dowager Blanche will be keeping a firm hold of the reins. I'm trusted to shake hands and host a few banquets, but that's about it.'

'You could take more responsibility if you wanted, couldn't you?'

'They won't let me.' Caro could hear the frustration in his voice, and she felt for him. It couldn't be easy knowing that any attempt to assert himself would be met by his father's collapse. 'And I daren't risk insisting any more,' Philippe said. 'Not when he's so sick, anyway. My father and I may not get on, but I don't want him to die.'

'Why doesn't he trust you?' Caro asked, swivelling in her seat so that she could look at him. 'I know you were wild when you were younger, but that was years ago.'

'It's hard to change the way your family looks at you.'

Philippe glanced in the mirror and pulled out to overtake a lumbering truck in a flash. 'Etienne was always the dutiful, responsible son, and I was difficult. That's just the way it was.

'Etienne was a golden boy—clever, hard-working, responsible, handsome, charming, kind. I could never live up to him, so I never tried. I was only ever "the spare" in my father's eyes, anyway,' he said. 'I didn't even have the good sense to look like him, the way Etienne did. Instead, I take after my mother. Every time my father looks at me, he's reminded of the way she humiliated him. I sometimes wonder if he suspects I'm not even his son.'

Philippe hoped that he sounded detached and ironic, but suspected it didn't fool Caro, who was watching him with those warm blue eyes. He could feel her gaze on his profile as surely as if she had reached out to lay her palm against his cheek.

'I never heard anything about your mother,' she said. 'What did she do?'

'Oh, the usual. She was far too young and frivolous to have been married to my father. It's a miracle their marriage lasted as long as it did. She ran away from him eventually and went to live with an Italian racing driver.'

He thought he had the tone better there. Careless. Cynical. Just a touch of amusement.

'Do you remember her?'

'Not much,' he said. 'Her perfume when she came to kiss me goodnight. Her laughter. I was only four, and left with a nanny a lot of the time anyway, so I don't suppose it made much difference to me really when she left. It was worse for Etienne. He was eleven, so he must have had more memories of her.'

Philippe paused. 'He would have been devastated, but he

used to come and play with me for hours so that I wouldn't miss her. That was the kind of boy he was.'

'I didn't realise you were so close to him.'

Caro's throat was aching for the little boy Philippe had been. Her father had been right. You could never tell what someone was like from the face they put on to the world. All she'd ever seen of Philippe had been the jacket of cool arrogance. It had never occurred to her to wonder whether he used it to deflect, to stop anyone realising that he had once been a small boy, abandoned by his mother and rejected by his father.

'He was a great brother,' said Philippe. 'A great person. You can't blame my father for being bitter that Etienne was the one who died, and that he was left with me. You can't blame him for wishing that I'd been the one who died.'

'That's…that's a terrible thing to say,' said Caro, shocked.

'It's true.' He glanced at her and then away. 'It was my fault Etienne died.'

'No.' Caro put out an instinctive hand. 'No, it was an accident. Lotty told me.'

'Oh, yes, it was an accident, but if it hadn't been for me, he'd never have been on the lake that day.' The bleak set to Philippe's mouth tore at her heart. 'Lotty's father was Crown Prince, and his brother still alive, with his two sons,' he went on after a moment. 'There was no reason to believe we'd ever inherit. My father had a vineyard, and Etienne was going up to look at the accounts or something equally tedious. He envied me, he said. To him it seemed that I was the one always having a good time. He said he wished he could do the same, but he was afraid that he didn't have the courage.'

He overtook a car, and then another and another, the sleek power of the Aston Martin controlled utterly in his strong hands.

'"Come water skiing with me", I said,' he remembered

bitterly. '"For once in your life, do what *you* want to do instead of what our father wants you to do." So he did, and he died.'

'It wasn't your fault,' said Caro.

'My father thinks it was.'

'It wasn't.' Without thinking, she put her hand on his shoulder. Through the yellow polo shirt, she could feel his muscles corded with tension. 'It was Etienne's choice to go. You didn't make him fall, and you didn't kill him. It was an accident.'

'That was what Lotty said. She was the only one who stood by me then,' said Philippe. 'If it had been up to my father, I wouldn't even have been allowed to go to the funeral. "If it wasn't for you, Etienne would still be alive," he said. The Dowager Blanche persuaded him to let me go in the end, for *appearance's sake*.' His voice was laced with pain.

'As soon as it was over, I left for South America. I didn't care where I went, as long as it was a long way from Montluce, and my father felt exactly the same. If it hadn't been for inheriting the throne, he'd have been happy never to see me again, I think, but when he became Crown Prince, he didn't have much choice but to be in touch. He'll never be able to forgive me, though, for the fact that Etienne didn't have time to get married and secure the succession.

'There's a certain irony in that,' Philippe said with a sidelong glance at Caro. 'Etienne was gay. He was very, very discreet, and my father never found out.'

'You didn't tell him?'

'How could I? It would have destroyed him all over again. All he's got left is his image of Etienne as his perfect son. I'm not going to spoil that for him. It wouldn't bring Etienne back and, anyway, he *was* perfect and, clearly, I'm not.'

'But why don't you tell him that you've changed?'

'Who says that I have?'

'The old Philippe wouldn't have flown in emergency supplies,' said Caro, and he lifted a shoulder.

'It would take more than a few flights to change my father's view of me,' he said. 'My father isn't a bad man, and if it's easier for him to keep thinking of me as difficult, why should I insist that he changes his mind? He's had enough grief without me demanding his attention and approval. I'm not a child,' said Philippe.

'I think it's unfair,' said Caro stoutly. 'I think if they're going to make you regent, they should give you the responsibility to act too.'

'Lots of people live with unfairness, Caro. I've seen people struggling to get by without food or shelter or a stable government. They haven't got schools or hospitals. There's no running water. *That's* unfair,' he said. 'Compared to that, I think I can bear a few months of not being allowed to make decisions. I'll use the time to familiarise myself with how the government works and then, when I'm in a position to make a difference, I will. Until then, I can live with a few pointless rituals.'

Caro was still looking dubious. 'It's not going to be much fun for you, is it?'

'No,' said Philippe, 'but we're not there yet.' Leaning across, he turned up the volume on the sound system and slanted a smile at her. 'We've got about an hour until we hit the border. Let's make the most of being able to behave badly while we can, shall we?'

Caro never forgot that drive. The poplars on either side of the road barred the way with shadows, so that the sunlight flickered exhilaratingly as the car shot beneath them with a throaty roar, effortlessly gobbling up the miles and sliding around the bends as if it were part of the road.

The sky was a hot, high blue. Cocooned in comfort, enveloped in the smell of new leather and luxury, she leant back in her seat and smiled. The windscreen protected her from the worst of the wind, but a heady breeze stirred her hair and she could feel the sun striping her face while the insistent beat of the music pounded through her and made her feel wild and excited and *alive*.

She was preternaturally aware of Philippe driving, of the flex of his thigh when he pressed the clutch, the line of his jaw, the alertness of his eyes checking between the road and the mirror. He changed gear with an assurance that was almost erotic, and she had to force herself to look away.

Caro could have driven on for ever that morning, her face flushed with wind and sun and Philippe beside her, with that long, lean, powerful body, his smile flashing, his hands rock-steady on the wheel, but all too soon he was slowing and reaching out to turn the music off.

'Time to behave, I'm afraid,' he said. 'This is it.'

Tucked away in the mountains, Montluce was one of Europe's forgotten back waters, cut off from the great traffic routes where borders flashed past in the blink of an eye. Not only was there a real border with a barrier across the road, but there were two guards in braided uniforms. Caro began to dig around in her bag for her passport as Philippe slowed down.

'You won't need that,' said Philippe. 'This is my border, remember?'

The guards came sharply to attention when they recognised Philippe, who stopped long enough to exchange a few words in French with them. Caro watched the men relax. There was some laughter before they saluted smartly and, at a word from the officer, the junior guard leapt to open the barrier.

Philippe acknowledged his salute as he drove through. 'What?' he said, feeling Caro staring at him.

'That's the first time I've realised that you're royal,' she said. 'I mean, I knew you were, of course, but I hadn't *seen* it. Those men were *saluting* you!'

'You'd better get used to it,' Philippe said. 'Montluce is big on formality. A lot of bowing and curtseying and saluting goes on.'

'But you knew what to do.' Caro didn't know how to explain what a revelation it had been to see the assurance with which Philippe had received the salutes, how clearly he had been able to put the guards at their ease without losing his authority. Even casually dressed, there was no mistaking the prince. That was when it had struck her.

He was a prince.

CHAPTER FIVE

PHILIPPE might say Montluce didn't mean much to him, but a subtle change came over him as they drove up into the hills. Caro puzzled over what it was, until she realised that he looked at home. Perhaps it had been hearing him speak French. His English was so flawless that it was easy to forget that he wasn't British, but here he looked more Gallic than usual, his gestures more Continental.

It was a beautiful country, with wooded hills soaring into mountains whose bare tops glared in the sun. The smell of pines filled the drowsy air as they drove through picturesque villages, past rushing rivers and up winding roads dappled with the light through the trees. Caro felt as if she were driving into a magical kingdom, and she was sure of it when they came over the range and saw the valley spread out below them. A large lake gleamed silver between the mountains and the city of Montvivennes on the other. Caro could see the palace, a fairy tale confection with turrets and terraces made of pale elegant stone, and she couldn't prevent a gasp.

From a distance, it could have been made of spun sugar, mirrored serenely in the lake. She wouldn't have been at all surprised to see princesses leaning out of the towers, goblins guarding the gate and princes hacking their way through rose thickets. There would be wicked stepmothers and fairy godmothers, pumpkins that turned into coaches, wolves that climbed into bed and licked their lips when Little Red Riding Hood knocked at the door.

'Please tell me there's a tame dragon,' she said.

'Well, there's my great-aunt,' Philippe said, 'but I wouldn't call her tame.'

Montvivennes was an attractive city with the same timeless air as the palace. It seemed almost drowsy in the sunshine, the only jarring note being a group of protestors with placards clustered beside the main road that led up to the palace.

Caro tried to read the placards as they passed. 'What are they protesting about?'

'There's a proposal to put a gas line through Montluce,' said Philippe. 'They're worried about the environmental impact.'

A few moments later, they drove through the palace gates to more saluting and presenting of arms and came to a halt with a satisfying crunch of gravel in a huge courtyard.

'Wow,' said Caro.

Close to, the palace was less whimsical but much more impressive. The imposing front opened onto a square with plane trees. Behind, long windows opened onto terraces and formal gardens leading down to the lake, beyond which the hills piled up in the distance to the mountains.

Philippe switched off the engine and there was a moment of utter stillness. Caro saw two ornately dressed footmen standing rigidly at the top of the steps. It all felt unreal. Any minute now she was going to wake up. She wasn't really here with a prince, about to walk into his palace.

And then the footmen were coming down the steps, opening the car doors, and somehow Caro found herself standing on the gravel looking up at the elaborate doorway.

'Ready?' Philippe muttered out of the corner of his mouth as he came round to take her arm.

'Oh, my God.' Caro was frozen by a sudden surge of panic. 'Do you think we can really do this?'

Philippe put a smile on his face and urged her towards the steps. 'We're about to find out,' he said.

It wasn't your usual homecoming, that was for sure. No family members hurried out to greet them with a hug. Instead, they passed through serried ranks of servants, all dressed in knee breeches and coats with vast quantities of gold braid. Caro was all for vintage clothes, but that was ridiculous.

Philippe greeted all of them easily, not at all daunted by the formality. Caro's French wasn't up to much, but she caught her name and it was obvious that he was introducing her, so she smiled brightly and tried to look as if she might conceivably be the kind of girl Philippe would fall madly in love with.

She trotted along behind Philippe as they were led ceremonially to his apartments, trying hard not to be intimidated by the palace. It was decorated with the extravagant splendour which, like the footmen's livery, had been all the rage in the eighteenth century. There were sweeping staircases, vast glittering chandeliers, marble floors, massive oil paintings and lot of gilded and uncomfortable-looking Baroque furniture.

There were an awful lot of long corridors, too. 'It's like being in an airport,' Caro whispered to Philippe, 'and having to walk miles to the gate. You should think about having one of those moving walkways put in.'

Of course, airports didn't have footmen placed outside every room, presumably so that no member of the royal family would have to go to the effort of opening a door for themselves. As Philippe appeared, they would get to their feet and stand to attention, only to sink back onto their chairs when he had passed with a nod of acknowledgement. It was like a very slow Mexican wave.

Philippe's apartments were on the second floor of one of the palace wings. They were airy, gracious rooms, most with views out over the lake to the mountains beyond, but impersonally decorated.

'Home, sweet temporary home,' said Philippe, looking around him without enthusiasm.

'It's not exactly cosy, is it?' Caro was wandering around the room, touching things and feeling ridiculously self-conscious. The rooms were huge, but knowing that there were all those servants outside the door made it feel as if she and Philippe had been shut away together.

Just you and me.

They certainly weren't going to be cramped. There was a large sitting room, a dining room with a beautifully equipped but untouched kitchen behind a breakfast bar, a study and three bedrooms, each with a luxurious en suite bathroom.

'And this is our love nest,' said Philippe and opened the last door with a mock flourish.

'Oh.' Caro made an effort of unconcern but all she could see was the huge bed. The bed where she was going to sleep with Philippe tonight. The fluttering started again in the pit of her stomach.

'Plenty of pillows, as you can see.' Philippe's voice was Martini dry. 'And the bed is wide enough to put one down the middle if you're feeling twitchy.'

She was, but no power on earth would have made her admit it.

I'm more than capable of keeping my hands to myself.

'You said yourself that won't be necessary,' she managed. 'I'm sure you have more experience than I do of these situations.'

'I don't know about that. The pillow question hasn't come up very often before, I must admit.'

No, because the women Philippe took to bed would be sexy, sophisticated and size six at the most. They wouldn't have to worry about holding in their tummies. Their legs would always be waxed, their nail polish unchipped, their skin perfect. Caro was prepared to bet they never, ever dribbled into their pillows or woke up with mascara rings under their eyes.

'But then, you don't usually sleep with someone like me, do you?'

'No,' he said slowly. 'That's true.'

It was odd seeing her here, in her father's old jacket. She was completely out of place in all the baroque splendour, but her eyes were a deep blue and the sun through the window cast a halo of gold around the cloud of hair that tumbled to her shoulders. The formal apartments were warmer and more welcoming with Caro in them.

Philippe remembered quite clearly dismissing the idea that he might want to sleep with Caro. But that was before he'd kissed her. It didn't seem nearly so unlikely now.

She had wandered over to the window and stood there looking out, hugging the jacket around her so that he could see the flare of her hips. Her legs were strong and straight in the jeans. There was nothing special about her, not really. Other girls had blue eyes and creamy skin and hair that felt like silk when he slid his fingers through it. Caro was lusher than most, warmer than most, more vibrant than most, but she was still just an ordinary girl, Philippe reminded himself. Not the sort of girl he desired at all.

'I won't lay a finger on you unless you ask me to,' he said. 'So you can relax.'

'Oh, sure,' said Caro, turning from the window. 'Great idea. Relax. After all, I'm in a strange country, living in a palace and I'll be going to bed with a prince tonight. What on earth have I got to be nervous about?'

Philippe rolled his eyes at her sarcasm. 'Nothing,' he said. 'We're friends, remember?'

He could see her remembering that had been her idea. 'Yes,' she conceded reluctantly at last.

'And friends trust each other, don't they?'

'Ye…es.'

'So you're going to have to trust me when I say you've got nothing to worry about.'

Caro stood there, chewing her lip. 'You're right,' she said after a moment. 'I'm sorry.'

'Well, now we've got that sorted, we can get on,' said Philippe briskly. 'We've been summoned to an audience with the Dowager Blanche at four o'clock. Sadly, saying we're busy is not an option. At some time I need to see my father's equerry, too, but what would you like to do until then?'

Caro looked hopeful. 'Have lunch?' she said.

To: charlotte@palaisdemontvivennes.net
From: caro.cartwright@u2.com
Subject: I'm here…where are you?

Dear Lotty

I was going to ask where you are, but then it might be better if you didn't tell me, as I might not be able to withstand your grandmother's interrogation. She's pretty scary, isn't she?

Philippe took me to meet her today—oh, no, that's right, I didn't meet her, I was presented. And I had to learn how to curtsey! Philippe gave me a whole lesson on etiquette before we went. I suppose you take it all for granted, but I was completely bamboozled by everything I had to remember. I was really nervous, and I think Philippe was too. He had that aloof look on his face, the one that doesn't give anything away, but I noticed that on the way there (a five mile trek along the palace corridors, or that's what it felt like) he kept shooting his cuffs and running his finger around his collar as if it was too tight. He'd changed into a suit for the Dowager Blanche, and I must say he looked pretty good, although I didn't give him the satisfaction of saying that, of course. Philippe knows perfectly well how attractive he is, without me puffing him up any more.

Caro lifted her fingers from the keyboard and flexed them as she reread what she had written. Was there too much about Philippe in there? She didn't want Lotty getting the wrong idea. But how could she not mention him? She'd better make it clear that they had a strictly platonic relationship.

We've decided to be friends, which is great because it means we don't have to be polite to each other. He's certainly not polite about me. I put on my best dress in honour of the occasion (you know, the apple-green tea dress I bought last year) and he was beastly about it. I won't repeat what he said, but it was very rude. And I won't repeat what I said to him in return, because that was even ruder!

There, that sounded suitably casual and friendly, didn't it? Caro started typing again.

Anyway, back to the Dowager. She doesn't exactly operate an open door policy, does she? When we finally made it to her apartments, we had to go through endless antechambers, each one bigger than the last, and naturally we never had to do anything demeaning like opening a door ourselves. Instead, there was a whole army of footmen whose sole job seems to be to fling open doors. Weird. (Or maybe it seems perfectly natural to you???)

We eventually found ourselves facing your grandmother across acres of polished parquet. Philippe didn't tell me about that, and I'd worn my pink shoes, the ones with the kitten heels. BIG mistake! The floor was so slippy the best I could manage was a teeter and we'd just about made it when my foot skidded out beneath me. I would have fallen splat on my face if Philippe hadn't grabbed my arm. He's pretty quick when he wants to be, isn't he? I was mortified, but then I looked at Philippe and I saw that he was trying not to laugh, and of course that set me off, and I got the giggles.

Caro felt her lips tugging at the memory, although it hadn't been that funny at the time. There was nothing worse than trying not to laugh when you knew that you absolutely, definitely mustn't. With the Dowager Blanche's glacial eyes on her, she had had to bite down hard on the inside of her cheeks, and at one point she had been convinced that her eyeballs had been about to pop with the pressure of keeping the giggles in.

Still, I managed a curtsey, which I thought was pretty good under the circumstances but Philippe told me afterwards I looked as if I was laying an egg.

I wouldn't say your grandmother gave me the warmest welcome I've ever had. In fact, a midwinter swim in the Antarctic would probably have seemed balmy in comparison, but it was obvious she blamed me for you leaving. Don't worry, I played along and Philippe was brilliant! He lifted my hand to his lips and kissed my knuckles and told your grandmother that he was in love with me and that he would only stay if he had my support, so he expected me to be treated with respect!!!! He almost had me fooled.

She had better not tell Lotty that her hand had tingled all evening from the impression of his fingers, or that she could still feel the graze of his lips against her knuckles.

I could tell your grandmother didn't like it, but at least she didn't seem to realise it was just an act, so that's something. I had to sit through an icy interrogation about my family, friends, utter lack of connections (or job, come to that), but don't worry, I only gave her my name, rank and serial number. Actually, Lotty, I felt a bit sorry for her. I think that beneath all the guff about duty and responsibility and behaving like a princess, she's really worried about you. Can you get a message to her to say that you're all right at least? Don't say where you are, though, as she's ready to send in the entire Montlucian army to bring you back if necessary! But I think she needs to know you're safe—and I do too!

I suspect the grilling Philippe got was even worse, but it was in French so I didn't understand it. But when our audience was finally at an end we were both very relieved to get out of there. I had to hang on to Philippe as we walked backwards (!!!!!!) across that floor, and he kept hold of me when we were allowed to turn our backs at last and escape. We started off walking sedately through the anterooms, but the further down the corridor we got, the faster we walked, and by the time we reached the staircase we were running and laughing. It was such a relief to be able to let all the giggles out, and somehow it didn't seem so bad knowing that Philippe had had to grit his teeth to get through it too.

Caro paused, remembering how the two of them had run down the grand staircase, laughing. The steps were shallow and carpeted in red, and they swept round and down to the magnificent marble hall where an array of footmen watched impassively.

Philippe had let go of her hand by then, but his eyes had been warm and alight with laughter and that dark, sardonic look had disappeared altogether. Caro's heart had stumbled for a moment when they'd reached the bottom of the stairs and she'd looked into his face. It had been like looking at an entirely different man, one whose brother hadn't died, one whose father didn't blame him.

Shaking the memory away, she went back to her email.

So, I've survived my first encounter with the Dowager Blanche. It wasn't a complete disaster. For some reason her little pug—Apollo?—took a shine to me. He sure is one ugly dog! Difficult to know which end of him is less attractive. I was worried he was about to have a heart attack with all that wheezing, but he came to sit on my foot while your grandmother was lecturing Philippe in French about something, and I made the mistake of patting him. After that, he wouldn't leave me alone. I said I'd take him for a walk sometimes, which Philippe thought was heroic of me, but he was quite cute really, I suppose, and besides, what else am I going to do with myself? Philippe seems to be lined up for royal duties, but there isn't a lot for me to do except sit on the balcony and look at that beautiful lake (which isn't such a bad plan, now I come to think of it.)

It's beautiful here, Lotty. I don't think I'll ever find my way round the palace or get to grips with all the formality, but the setting is magical. Like being in a fairy tale kingdom, where nothing feels quite real.

I'd better stop. Philippe had to go to some reception for financiers, so I've had the evening to myself, and I thought it would be a good chance to drop you a line—or quite a few lines, as it's turned out. It's all so new to me, and there's so much I'd love to talk to you about. Can't wait to catch up properly when all this is over and compare notes!

Hope you're having a fab time out there in reality, Lotty. Let me know, OK?

Lots +++++++++ of love

Caro

When Philippe came back later that night, Caro was already in bed. She was sitting up against the pillows, a book in her hands and a pair of glasses on her nose. Her face was scrubbed, the cloud of chestnut hair tucked behind her ears, and she was buttoned up to the throat in a pair of old-fashioned pyjamas, patterned with sprigged rosebuds so faded they were almost invisible.

No sheer negligees for Caro, Philippe realised. No wispy lace or dainty straps designed to slide seductively over a shoulder. He ought to be glad that she had so little interest in attracting him, so why did the sight of her make him feel so grouchy?

'Don't tell me, they're vintage pyjamas?' he said, loosening his tie and trying to roll the irritation from his shoulders.

'As a matter of fact, I bought them when they were new.'

'What, when you were twelve?'

'I've had them a long time,' she admitted with a defiant look over her glasses. 'They're comfortable.'

'There couldn't be any other reason for wearing them,' said Philippe sardonically. She certainly hadn't bought them with seduction in mind!

So it was annoying to realise how appealing she looked, there in bed. The modest pyjamas only drew attention to her lush curves, and the glow from the bedside lamp picked out golden lights in her hair. Seduction was clearly the last thing on Caro's mind, but she looked warm and soft and inexplicably inviting all the same.

Philippe jerked his tie free from his collar with unnecessary force.

'How was your evening?' Caro asked.

'Tedious. I shook hands, smiled, pretended to listen intelligently to someone droning on about financial forecasts. Welcome to the exciting world of royalty.'

Sitting on the edge of the bed, he tugged off first one shoe, then the other and tossed them aside. 'And that was just one evening! I'm not sure I can stand the thought of another six months of this. I'm going to expire of boredom by the end of the week!'

'Lots of people have to put up with boring jobs,' Caro pointed out as his socks followed the shoes.

'Very true. But give me a night flight through a thunderstorm any day!' Philippe swung his legs up onto the bed and made himself comfortable against the pillows, linking his arms behind his head.

Coming home to someone felt strange. Not as uncomfortable as he'd thought it would be. In fact, he'd even found his steps quickening as he said goodnight to Yan and approached the apartments, and he'd been glad to see the light on in the bedroom and to know that Caro was still awake.

He'd been surprised at how pleased he was to have her

with him that afternoon too. Grimly enduring his great aunt's tongue-lashing, he'd watched her tussling with that stupid dog and felt a smile quivering at the corners of his mouth. Once or twice she had met his eyes with a speaking look, or the tiniest roll of her eyes.

Funny how the Dowager's lecture hadn't seemed nearly so bad when there was someone there to sympathise, to be an ally. To escape with and run laughing down the great palace staircases.

Philippe rolled onto his side to face Caro and propped himself up on one elbow. 'What about you? What have you been doing?'

'I emailed Lotty.' Abandoning the pretence of reading, she put her book on the bedside table and took off her glasses. 'I'd feel better if I knew she was OK. Wherever she is, it's going to be very different from here.'

'She'll be all right. Lotty's tougher than she looks.'

Philippe stretched, yawned and rubbed the back of his head. It felt surprisingly comfortable to be lying here, chatting to Caro at the end of a long day. He'd never done this with a woman before. They'd been lovers, or he'd been leaving. They'd never been friends.

'Did you have anything to eat?' he asked her.

Caro laughed, that husky, faintly suggestive laugh that crisped every nerve and sinew in Philippe's body. 'Have you ever heard that expression involving bears and woods?' she said. 'Of course I did! I felt really lazy ringing the kitchen and asking them to send something up the way you told me. I can't get used to not doing everything myself.

'It's weird with all these servants around,' she said, pulling up her knees and shifting a little so that she could look at Philippe. 'You must have half the population of Montluce working here!'

'Hardly that.' Aware of the swing of her breasts, her

scent, Philippe was horrified to hear that his voice sounded hoarse.

'They asked me what I wanted to eat, so I said could they let me try some Montlucian specialities? They sent up these amazing quenelles of trout from the lake, and the most wonderful tart made with apricots.'

Caro chattered on about food, and Philippe kept his gaze firmly fixed on her face so that he wouldn't think about how close she was, or how it might feel to undo the buttons on her pyjama top very, very slowly, to slide his hands beneath the soft material, to roll her beneath him and press his lips to her throat and let them drift lower and lower until she stopped talking about food and what the head chef said and—

'What?' He sat up, tuning in belatedly. 'You went to the *kitchens*?'

'That's what I'm telling you. I took the tray back so that I could ask the chef for the tart recipe and he was *so* nice. Jean-Michel…do you know him?'

'No,' said Philippe, who had never been to the kitchens in his life.

'He wrote it out for me, but it's in French, of course. I might have to get you to translate it. I can get the gist of it, I think, but—'

'Caro,' he interrupted her, clutching his hair, 'what were you doing wandering around in the kitchens? The footman is supposed to take the tray away.'

'Laurent?' she said knowledgeably. 'He did offer, but I said I'd rather go myself. I'm glad I did. I had much more fun down there.'

Philippe pinched the bridge of his nose between thumb and forefinger. 'It didn't occur to you that it might be inappropriate for you to be sloping off to the kitchens and being on first name terms with the staff? Everyone's watching to see if you're going to be a suitable princess, and fraternising with the servants makes it look as if you don't know how to behave.'

'One, there's no question of me being a princess, so it doesn't matter how I behave,' said Caro, 'and two, it's an absurd attitude in any case. This is the twenty-first century.'

'This is also Montluce, which is an absurd place.'

Philippe sat up and began undoing the top buttons of his stiff dress shirt and Caro looked at him sharply.

'What are you doing?'

'What does it look like I'm doing? I'm getting ready for bed.' His voice was muffled as he took hold of his collar and pulled the shirt over his head.

'Aren't you going to use the bathroom?'

Philippe's hands paused at the top of his zip. Caro was sitting straight up, the colour running high in her cheeks. 'You don't need to look,' he said. 'We're stuck with each other for the next few weeks. Don't you think we should at least get used to being comfortable together?'

'There's nothing comfortable about watching you strip off in front of me,' she snapped. 'I bet you don't even have a pair of pyjamas!'

'I can't rival yours for style, I agree, but I've got these.' He waved a pair of dark silk pyjama bottoms at her. 'I've had to get used to wearing them in this damn place. People are wandering in and out the whole time.'

Alarmed, Caro pulled the sheet up to her chin. 'Not in here?'

'Not unless there's a constitutional crisis, but you never know, so don't worry, I'll be decent,' said Philippe. 'But I'll get changed in the bathroom if that makes you feel better.'

When he came out, Caro was lying under the cover, holding it tight under her nose. A pillow was wedged firmly down the middle of the bed.

'I know what you said about having no trouble keeping your hands off me,' she said, seeing his expression. 'It's just to stop me rolling against you in the night by mistake. I think we'll both sleep better having it there.'

Philippe threw back the cover on his side of the bed and got in. 'If you say so,' he said.

To: caro.cartwright@u2.com
From: charlotte@palaisdemontvivennes.net
Subject: Re: I'm here...where are you?

I'm here, and loving it! Thank you so much for being there, Caro. Without you and Philippe, I'm not sure I would ever have had the courage to go. I won't tell you where I am, but it's wild and beautiful, and I've got a job!!! I'm doing all sorts of things I've never done before—peeling potatoes, answering the phone, writing a shopping list, making a pot of tea—and it's fun! I know you'll roll your eyes, but it's exciting for me. By the time I go to bed, though, I'm exhausted, so I'd better be quick. Just so you know that I'm fine, and yes, I've sent a message to Grandmère as well.

I know she can be daunting, but her bark is really worse than her bite. And if Apollo liked you, that will be a big thing. Grandmère might not let on, but she adores that dog. He's her only weakness, so I'm sure she'll be impressed that he's taken to you, as he hates everyone else and is always biting people.

I'm really glad you and Philippe are getting on so well. How well, exactly????? Should I be reading anything between the lines??? Tell me all!

Grosses bises

Lxxxxxxxxxxxxx

Caro was smiling as she read Lotty's message—only Lotty would be excited at peeling potatoes!—but her smile faded when she got to the end. How had Lotty got the idea that there might be anything between her and Philippe? She thought she'd been so careful to make it clear that they were just friends!

Not that there had been much friendliness that morning. Philippe had been crabby from the moment he woke up, and had stomped off to a meeting with the First Minister in a thoroughly bad mood. When Caro had told him she planned to take Apollo for a walk, he'd just grunted at her and told her to stick to the grounds—as if she'd risk taking the Dowager Blanche's dog out into the city. She wasn't *stupid*.

The truth was that Caro was feeling scratchy and out-of-sorts too. She hadn't slept well. How could she be expected to sleep when Philippe was lying next to her half naked?

Yes, he'd had those low-slung pyjama bottoms on, but that had left his chest bare. Solid, brown, tautly muscled, it taunted Caro from the other side of the bed. Her hands had twitched and throbbed with the longing to reach out and touch him, to feel the flex of muscles beneath the smooth skin. She'd tried not to look, but it had been impossible not to notice the powerful shoulders, the fine dark hairs arrowing downwards.

Heart racing, blood pounding, Caro lay and imagined sliding her fingers through those hairs. His body would be hard, solid, *warm*. He was so close, too. It would be so easy to roll over and reach for him.

And that would have been a big mistake.

Thank God for that pillow.

She'd been too hot in her pyjamas, but she didn't want to thrash around in case she woke Philippe. As far as she could tell from her side of the pillow, he was sleeping peacefully, quite unbothered by her presence in the bed with him. She might as well be a *bolster*, Caro decided vengefully.

Eventually irritation had subsided into glumness, swiftly followed by brisk practicality. What did she think? That Philippe would take a look at her in her pyjamas and rip them off her? She *looked* like a bolster, and if she knew what was good for her she would behave like a bolster too.

Otherwise it was going to be a very long two months.

Well, there was no point in sitting around feeling cross. Caro finished the *pain au chocolat* that the palace kitchen had sent up for breakfast along with a perfect cup of coffee—she was going to be the size of a house, if not a palace, by the time she left—and pushed back her chair.

From the kitchen window she could look down at the courtyard at the front of the palace. Outside the railings, tourists milled around, pointing and taking photographs.

She belonged down there with the ordinary people, Caro thought, not up here in a palace, like a Cinderella in reverse, having her breakfast brought up by soft-footed servants. She belonged with an ordinary man, not a prince.

It wouldn't do to forget that.

The *pain au chocolat* had been delicious, but she wanted to make her own breakfast. Philippe was in meetings most of the day, so she could amuse herself. She would go back to the real world where she belonged, Caro decided, washing up her breakfast dishes without thinking in the kitchen. Grabbing her bag, she thrust her feet into comfortable walking sandals and set off for the great sweeping staircase that led down to the palace entrance.

She would go and explore.

CHAPTER SIX

INSTINCT led Caro away from the smart part of town and into the old quarter, with its crooked lanes and balconies strung with washing. Even at that hour of the morning it was warm, but the tall buildings cast the narrow streets into shadow and Caro was content to wander in the shade until she found herself on the edge of the market square, dazzled and blinking at the sudden flood of sunlight.

Settling her sunglasses on her nose, Caro took one look at the stalls selling a spectacular range of local produce and drew a long breath of appreciation. There were glossy aubergines, and artichokes and great piles of onions, stalls selling great hams and salamis or piled high with bread, or enormous wheels of cheese. Her bad mood quite forgotten, Caro drifted along, sniffing peaches, squeezing avocados, tasting tiny bits of cheese and hams that the stallholders passed over for her to try.

Her French was rusty, to say the least, but when it came to food Caro had never had any problems communicating. She pantomimed swooning with pleasure, which seemed so much more appropriate than the only words she knew: *c'est très bon*, which didn't seem at all adequate. It went down well with the stallholder, anyway, who laughed and offered her a different cheese to try.

Before she knew what had happened, she was being plied

with different cheeses and urged to try every one. Everyone was so friendly, Caro thought, delighted. They were all having a very jolly time. She learnt what all the fruit and vegetables were called, and the stallholders or her fellow shoppers corrected her pronunciation with much laughter and nods of encouragement. This was much more fun than sitting in the palace feeling cross about Philippe.

She would get some cheese and bread for lunch, Caro decided, and some of those tomatoes that looked so much more delicious than the perfectly uniform, perfectly red, perfectly tasteless ones they sold in the supermarkets in Ellerby. It was only then that she remembered that she hadn't had an opportunity to change any money yet. All she had was some sterling, which was no help at all when you wanted to buy a few tomatoes.

Caro was in the middle of another pantomime to explain her predicament when the stallholder stopped laughing and stared over her shoulder. At the same time she became aware of a stir in the market behind her and she turned, curious to see what everyone was so interested in.

There, striding towards her between the stalls, was Philippe, and at the sight of him her heart slammed into her throat, blocking off her air and leaving her breathless and light-headed.

Philippe was smiling, but Caro could tell from the tightness of his jaw that he was furious. Behind those designer shades, the silver eyes would be icy. Yan was at his shoulder, expressionless as ever.

The market fell silent, watching Philippe. It was difficult to tell quite what the mood was. Wariness and surprise, Caro thought, as she disentangled her breathing and forced her heart back into place. She could relate to that. It was what she felt too. Not that she had any intention of letting Philippe know that.

'Oh, hello,' she said, determinedly casual. 'What are you doing here?'

'No, that's my question,' snapped Philippe, who was gripped with a quite irrational rage at finding Caro safe.

Lefebvre, the First Minister, had spent the morning droning on about the increased threat from environmental activists who were protesting about some pipeline, although why he was telling him Philippe couldn't imagine. The Dowager Blanche had no doubt already decided what would be done.

He'd found his mind drifting to Caro. He'd been short with her that morning, but it wasn't actually her fault that he hadn't been able to sleep. Philippe couldn't get the image of her in those shabby pyjamas out of his mind. He'd imagined unbuttoning the pyjama top very slowly, slipping his hands beneath it to smooth over silky skin. Imagined hooking his thumbs over the waistband to slide the bottoms down over the warm curve of her hips and down those legs she insisted on hiding away.

This was ridiculous, Philippe had told himself, shifting restlessly. He liked women in silk and sheer, slithery lingerie, nightclothes that were feminine and flirty and fun. He was in a bad way when he was getting turned on by a pair of frumpy pyjamas.

The fact that he needed that damned pillow stuffed between them had left Philippe feeling edgy and irritable and he'd woken in a thoroughly bad mood.

When Lefebvre had finally left, Philippe had gone back to apologise to Caro, only to find the apartments empty. Mademoiselle Cartwright had gone out, the dolt of a butler had informed him when Philippe had established that she wasn't in the gardens either.

'She said that she wanted to explore the city. Mademoiselle Cartwright was charming,' he had added.

Mademoiselle Cartwright was a damned nuisance, Philippe

had corrected him, Lefebvre's warnings running cold through his veins. What if someone had seen Caro strolling out from the palace? She would be an easy target.

Yan had made him stop and work out where Caro was most likely to be. Anywhere there was food, Philippe realised, and they had headed straight for the market. It was that or trawling through every café and restaurant in town.

And now here she was, quite safe and obviously having a wonderful time, and Philippe was perversely furious, with her and with himself, for having, for those few minutes, been so ridiculously worried.

'I thought I told you to stay in the palace grounds?' he said, smiling through clenched teeth. Even though they were talking in English, he couldn't have the row he really wanted in front of all these people, which made him even crosser.

Caro looked taken aback. 'I thought you just meant if I was taking Apollo out.'

'What do I care about the dog? It's you I'm worried about! I told you that there's been unrest recently. I *told* you that's why Yan goes everywhere with me, but you, you toddle off on your own without a thought for security!'

'You also told me the situation wasn't likely to affect me.' Caro actually had the nerve to roll her eyes at him. 'So let me get this right…I'm not allowed to go to the kitchens, and I'm not allowed to go outside the palace either?'

'Welcome to my world,' gritted Philippe, still smiling ferociously. 'Anyone could have got to you without protection.'

'Oh, rubbish,' said Caro. 'Nobody's the slightest bit interested in me. Or at least they weren't until you appeared. If you hadn't come rushing down here, nobody would have had a clue I had anything to do with you at all.'

This was so patently true that Philippe could only grind his teeth and glare at her.

'Anyway, I'm glad you've come, actually,' she went on

breezily. 'I wanted to buy some of this cheese, and I was trying to explain that I didn't have any money.' Completely ignoring Philippe, who was still trying to make her understand the reality of the security situation, she smiled at the stallholder and mimed trying the cheese. He nodded, delighted, and cut off a generous piece, which she handed to Philippe, who was trying to talk about security threats.

'Now, try this,' she said. 'Tell me if that's not the best cheese you've ever tasted!'

Philippe felt the flavour burst on his tongue and he was gripped by a strange heightened awareness, as if all his senses were on full alert. He could smell the bread on a nearby stall, hear the murmurs of the people watching. And then there was Caro, her face bright, head tilted slightly to one side, blue eyes fixed on his face to see what he thought of the cheese.

Cheese! That was all she cared about! *She* wasn't knotted up about the night before. And he shouldn't be either, Philippe reminded himself, irritated. How could he be knotted up about a woman who dressed the way Caro did?

Today's outfit was evidently based on a Fifties theme. Some kind of red top and a turquoise circle skirt with appliquéd tropical fruits. Ye Gods! Only Caro could stand there covered in bananas and pineapples and look so right in them. She ought to look ridiculous, but actually she looked bright and vivid and fresh, and pretty in a quirky way that was just her own.

'Well?' she demanded.

Philippe swallowed the last of the cheese. If she could be relaxed, so could he.

'Very good,' he said, and repeated it in French for the stall-holder, who puffed out his substantial chest and beamed.

'Can we buy some? I haven't got any cash.'

'I haven't either,' he had to admit.

They turned as one to look at Yan, who didn't miss a beat,

producing a wallet and handing it over to Philippe without expression while his eyes checked the crowd continuously.

'Thanks,' said Philippe as he flipped it open in search of cash. 'I'll sort it out with you later.'

Caro craned her neck to see inside the wallet. 'Fantastic,' she said. 'How much have we got to spend?'

She was very close, close enough for her hair to tickle his chin, and Philippe could smell her shampoo, something fresh and tangy. Verbena, perhaps, or mint.

They bought the cheese, and then Caro insisted on dragging him onto the next stall, and then the next. She made him taste hams and olives and tarts and grapes, made him translate for her and talk to people, while Yan followed, his eyes ever vigilant.

For Philippe, it all was new. Nobody had ever told him how to behave on a walkabout—the Dowager Blanche and his father were great believers in preserving the mystique of royalty by keeping their distance—but, with Caro by his side, chatting away and laughing as they all corrected her French and made her practice saying the words correctly, it wasn't hard to relax. People seemed surprised but genuinely delighted to see their prince among them, and he found himself warmed by their welcome as he shook hands and promised to pass on their good wishes to his father in hospital.

Montluce had always felt oppressive to Philippe before. He associated the country with rigid protocol and fusty traditions perpetuated for their own sake and not because they meant anything. The country itself was an anomaly, a tiny wedge of hills and lakes that survived largely because of its powerful banking system and the tax haven it offered to the seriously rich. Until now, the people had only ever seemed to Philippe bit part actors in the elaborate costume drama that was Montluce. For the first time, he found himself thinking about them as individuals with everyday concerns, people who shopped and cooked and looked after their families, and looked to *his* family to keep their country secure.

He'd never been to the market before, had never needed to, and suddenly he was in the heart of its noise and chatter, surrounded by colour and scents and tastes. And always there, in the middle of it all, Caro. Caro, alight with enthusiasm, that husky, faintly dirty laugh infecting everyone around her with the need to smile and laugh too.

'What are you planning to do with all this stuff?' he asked, peering into the bag of tomatoes and peppers and red onions and God only knew what else that she handed him.

'I thought I'd make a salad for lunch.'

'The kitchens will send up a salad if that's what you want,' he pointed out, exasperated, but Caro only set her chin stubbornly in the way he was coming to recognise.

'I want to make it myself.'

By the time Philippe finally managed to drag her away from all her new friends at the market, both he and Yan were laden with bags. He hoped the Dowager Blanche didn't get wind of the fact that he'd been seen walking through the streets with handfuls of carrier bags or he would never hear the end of it.

'You know, it would be quicker and easier to order lunch from the kitchens,' he said to Caro as she unloaded the bags in the kitchen.

'That's not the point.' She ran the tomatoes under the tap and rummaged around for a colander. 'I like cooking. Ah, here it is!' She straightened triumphantly, colander in hand. 'I worked in a delicatessen before it went bust, and I loved doing that.

'That's my dream, to have a deli and coffee shop of my own one day,' she confided, her hands busy setting out anchovies and bread and peppers and garlic, while Philippe watched, half fascinated, half frustrated.

'I thought your dream was to belong in Ellerby with the pillar of the community?'

'George.' Caro paused, a head of celery in her hand. 'Funny, I haven't thought about him at all since I've been here…' She shook her head as if to clear George's image from her mind. 'No, not with George,' she said, upending the last bag, 'but with someone else, maybe. The deli would be part of that. I'd know everyone. I'd know how they took their coffee, what cheeses they liked.'

She stopped, evidently reading Philippe's expression. 'At least I've *got* a dream,' she said. 'All *you* want is to avoid getting sucked into a relationship in case some woman asks you to do more than stay five minutes!'

'We don't all have your burning desire for a rut,' said Philippe. 'I've got plenty of dreams. Freedom. Independence. Getting into a plane and flying wherever I want. Seeing you wear clothes bought in this millennium.'

Caro stuck out her tongue at him. 'You can give up on that one,' she said, peering at the high-tech oven. 'I suppose there's no use asking you how this works?'

'I've never been in here before,' he said, but he eased her out of the way and studied the dials. If he could fly a plane, he could turn on an oven, surely?

'Brilliant!' Caro bestowed a grateful smile on him as the grill sprang to life, and Philippe felt that strange light-headed sensation again, as if there wasn't quite enough oxygen in the air. She was very close, and his eyes rested on the sweet curve of her cheek, the intentness of her expression as she adjusted the temperature.

Caro had her sights fixed firmly on her return to England, that was clear. Well, that was fine, Philippe told himself. He had his own plans. As soon as Caro had gone, he would invite Francesca Allen to stay, he decided. Her divorce should have been finalised by then, and they could embark on a discreet affair to see him through the last stultifying months of boredom here in Montluce. Francesca was always elegantly dressed, and she knew the rules. She had a successful career and the last thing she'd want right now would be to settle down. If Philippe had read the signs right, she was looking to enjoy being single again. She'd be perfect.

The trouble was that he couldn't quite remember what Francesca looked like. Beautiful, yes, he remembered that, but nothing specific. He didn't know the exact curve of her mouth, the way he knew Caro's, for instance, or the precise tilt of her lashes. He didn't remember her scent, or the warmth of her skin, or the tiny laughter lines fanning her eyes.

'If you're going to stand around, you might as well help,' said Caro, shoving a couple of ripe tomatoes into his hands. 'Even you can manage to chop up those!'

So Philippe found himself cutting up tomatoes, and then onions and celery, while Caro moved purposefully around the kitchen.

'How did your meeting this morning go?' she asked him as she watched the skins of red and yellow peppers blister under the grill.

'Pointless. Lefebvre is clearly under instruction to tell me everything but stop me from interfering in anything. Apparently, I'm to go out and "meet the people". It's clearly a ruse to get me out of the way so that he and the Dowager Blanche can get on with running things,' said Philippe, pushing the chopped celery into a neat pile with his knife. 'I'm supposed to be getting the country on the government's side about this new gas pipeline they're trying to put in but that's just my token little job.'

Caro turned from the grill. 'What pipeline?'

'It's taking gas from Russia down to southern Europe.' He pulled an onion towards him and turned it in his hand, trying to work out the best way to peel it. 'The easiest and most convenient route is through Montluce, and the government here has been in discussions with the major energy companies across Europe. We—as in my father and the Dowager Blanche—are keen for it to go ahead as it will allegedly bring in money and jobs.'

'So what's the problem?'

'That's what I asked Lefebvre but he was evasive and, when I pressed him, he said that my father had made the decision and did I feel it was important enough to challenge him when he was so sick. So I don't know. People need jobs, and they need energy. On the face of it, the gas line makes sense to me.'

When the salad was ready, Caro tossed it with her hands in a bowl and carried it out to the balcony overlooking the lake. They ate at the table in the shade, and Philippe poured a glass of wine, surprised at how comfortable it felt.

'I forgot to tell you,' he said, leaning over to top up Caro's glass, 'we're dining with the First Minister and his wife tonight.'

Caro sat up in consternation. 'But I thought I wasn't going to any official events!'

'It's not a state occasion.' Philippe didn't think that he would tell her that he had made it clear to Lefebvre that he would like her invited. Even now, Madame Lefebvre would be tearing up her seating plans. He wouldn't be popular.

Caro was looking dubious. 'Will it be very smart?'

'Very,' said Philippe firmly. 'Is it too much to ask you to wear a dress made this century?'

'I can't afford to buy new clothes.'

'*I'll* buy them,' he said, exasperated. 'I don't care what it costs.'

'Absolutely not, said Caro stubbornly. 'I'm not going to do some kind of Cinderella makeover for you! That wasn't part of our deal and, anyway, I don't want any new clothes. I've got a perfectly adequate wardrobe.'

Although that might not be *strictly* true, Caro conceded later as she contemplated the meagre collection of clothes spread out on the bed. She had two evening dresses, one midnight-blue and the other a pale moss colour subtly patterned with a darker green. She was fairly sure Philippe would hate both of them, but Caro thought they were quite elegant.

After a brief eeny-meeny-miny-mo, Caro picked up the moss-green and wriggled into it. It was cut on the bias so that the slippery silk hung beautifully and flattered those pesky curves. She smoothed it over her hips, eyeing her reflection critically. She didn't think she looked too bad.

The dress had a long zip at the back, and she couldn't quite reach the fiddly fastening at the top. Clicking her tongue in exasperation, she braced herself for his reaction and went to find Philippe.

He was waiting on the balcony, watching the lake, with his hands thrust in his pockets. He'd changed earlier into a dinner jacket and black tie, and he looked so devastating that Caro's mouth dried and her nerve failed abruptly. She stopped, overwhelmed by shyness. How could she ever walk into a room and expect anyone to think that she could attract a man like this?

Then he turned and the familiar exasperation swept across his face. 'Good God,' he said. 'Where do you *find* these clothes?'

Perversely, that made Caro feel much better and she stepped out onto the balcony. 'Online, mostly,' she said, 'although there are some wonderful vintage shops around. Do you like it?' she added provocatively.

'I'm not going to say anything.'

Caro laughed. She could cope with Philippe when he was being rude or cross. She could deal with him as a friend. It was only when she let herself think about that lean, hard body that she ran into strife. When she let herself notice the easy way he moved or those startling silver eyes.

The heart-clenching line of his jaw.

His mouth. Oh, God, his *mouth*.

No, she couldn't afford to notice any of it.

Friends, Caro reminded herself. That was what they were.

'Can you do me up?' she asked, glad of the excuse to turn her back to him. She had left her hair loose, and now she piled it on top of her head with her hand so that he could pull the zip up the last half inch and fasten the hook and eye at the nape of her neck.

Philippe didn't move for a moment, but then he took his hands out of his pockets and stepped towards her. His first impression had been exasperation that Caro was wearing yet another frumpy dress, but the closer he got, the less dowdy it seemed. She was standing, quite unconsciously, in a shaft of evening sunlight that made her look as if she had been dipped in gold. It warmed the creamy skin and burnished her hair, turning it to the colour of aged brandy.

He set one hand to the small of her back to hold the base of the zip still, and took hold of the zip with fingers that felt suddenly clumsy. Her neck was arched gracefully forward and he could see the fine, soft hairs at the nape of her neck. She smelt wonderful, with that elusive fragrance that was part spice, part citrus, part something that was just Caro.

Very slowly, *very* slowly, Philippe drew the zip upwards. He saw those tiny hairs on her neck stiffen as his fingers brushed her skin, and he smiled. Caro wasn't quite as indifferent as she pretended. That was good.

On an impulse, he bent and pressed his lips to the curve of her throat where it swept up from her shoulder, and she inhaled sharply.

No, definitely not indifferent.

'Th…thank you,' she managed and would have stepped away, but he put his hands lightly on her hips. Beneath his fingers, the silk shifted and slithered over her skin and every cell in his body seemed to tighten. So small a detail and yet so erotic, he marvelled. It was only an old green dress, it was only Caro, and yet…

And yet…

Philippe wasn't looking forward to the evening ahead. Lefebvre and the other members of the government would go through the motions with him, but their contempt for the Crown Prince's feckless son was thinly veiled. You had to earn respect. Philippe was OK with that, but it would be nice to be given a chance.

But he could forget all that with Caro between his hands. As he turned her, she let her hair fall and put out her own hands to capture his wrists. Her eyes were wide, the deep, dark blue that made him think of the ocean surging out beyond the reef.

'I don't think this is a good idea,' she said.

'What isn't?'

'Whatever you've got in mind.' A flash of the old Caro there, and Philippe smiled.

'I'm tense,' he said. 'I need to relax, and what could be more relaxing than kissing a beautiful woman?'

Faint colour flushed her cheekbones. 'It's just me. You don't need to bother bringing out all the old lines.'

'Maybe it's not a line,' he said. 'Maybe I mean it. Maybe you are beautiful.'

'I'm a friend,' Caro said with difficulty, but her eyes were snared in his and they were darkening with desire, Philippe could tell.

'A beautiful friend,' he agreed.

Dipping his head, he put his mouth to hers, softly at first, but when she parted her lips on a soft sigh, he deepened the kiss, startled by the jolt of lust. His fingers tightened at her hips, but the material just slipped over her skin and he couldn't get a good grip of her.

Almost reluctantly, Caro's hands were sliding up his sleeves to his shoulders, and with something like a groan he gathered her closer. There was a kind of desperation to his kiss as he fisted the dress over her bottom, then let it go in frustration when he realised he was holding silk and not her.

Caro was mumbling 'I'm not…I don't…oh…' but she was kissing him back, warm, generous kisses, and his head reeled with the rightness of it and the sweetness and the hunger.

The ordeal of the dinner ahead forgotten, he eased the zip back down and was backing through the doors and towards the bedroom when a throat was cleared somewhere in the room.

'The car is waiting, *Altesse.*'

Philippe sucked in an unsteady breath as he lifted his head. That was the trouble with having servants. They were always there, ready to remind you that you had somewhere to go, someone to see, something to do. They could never just *leave you alone…*

Squeezing his eyes shut, he fought for control. 'We'll be there in a minute,' he grated.

'Altesse.' The door closed softly behind the footman.

Philippe dragged a hand through his hair and looked ruefully down at Caro, who was flushed and trembling, mouth soft and swollen. 'I'm sorry,' he sighed. 'We're going to have to go.'

Somehow she managed a smile. 'Perhaps it's just as well. I told you it wasn't a good idea,' she added, which sounded more like her.

'I thought it was a very good idea. Didn't you enjoy it?'

Her eyes slid from his and she stepped back, away from him. 'That's not the point. We agreed to be friends.'

'Friends can kiss, can't they?'

'Not like that,' said Caro. 'I don't think we should do it again.'

They were going to have an argument about that, thought Philippe, and it was an argument he was determined to win.

'We'll talk about it later,' he said, taking her arm. 'Right now, we've got to go.'

Dinner was preceded by a drinks reception to which the great and good of Montluce had been invited to meet Philippe. Caro stood beside him, smiling and shaking hands. If she was feeling intimidated by the ferociously smart women whose gazes flickered over her dress, she didn't show it. Amongst all those elegant little black dresses, Caro looked gloriously different.

Philippe was proud of her. She *wasn't* beautiful, but he was having trouble keeping his eyes off her all the same. How was he supposed to concentrate on being a prince when his body was still humming with that kiss? When all he could think about was the creaminess of her skin, her warmth, the delicious softness shot through with excitement? When every time her mouth curled in a smile the blood drained from his head?

And when she was murmuring comments out of the side of her mouth that made him want to laugh and strangle her and carry her off to bed all at the same time?

The Foreign Affairs Minister came up to be presented. 'Look, Apollo's here,' Caro whispered in his ear, and Philippe found himself looking at bulbous brown eyes, a stubby nose and mournful jowls that gave Marc Autan an expression so exactly like his great-aunt's pug that it was all Philippe could do not to burst out laughing. Out of the corner of his eye, he could see Caro biting down hard on the inside of her cheeks. Shaking Monsieur Autan's hand and making small talk with a straight face was one of the hardest things Philippe had ever done.

'Behave yourself,' he said out of the side of his mouth when Monsieur Autan had at last moved on. 'You're going to get me cut out of the succession.'

Still, he missed her at the dinner, which was just as pompous and tedious as he had expected. They sat at a long table so laden with candelabras and silverware that he could only converse with the person on either side of him.

Caro had been put at the other end of the table, no doubt on Dowager Blanche's instructions. Her lack of French didn't seem to be stopping her having a good time. He kept hearing that laugh, the laugh that whispered over his skin and made his blood throb.

Philippe gripped his glass and glared down the table at the men on either side of Caro, who were so clearly enjoying her company. This wasn't the way it was supposed to be at all. He was the jaded one, the one who was always in control. The one who left before things got out of hand. He wasn't the one who sat there and longed desperately for her to notice him.

And then Caro did look up and their eyes met. She didn't smile, and nothing was said, but Philippe looked back at her and the awful pressure in his chest eased at last.

They were silent in the back of the limousine that took them back to the palace. Still silent, not touching, they walked along the quiet corridors and up the double staircase. Only when the last footman had bowed and closed the last door did Caro break the silence.

'I don't think we should do this,' she said as if they were in the middle of a conversation, which perhaps they were. Her voice trembled with nerves. 'I think we should stick to what we agreed.'

'You want to leave the pillow in the middle of the bed?'

'Yes.' She swallowed, knowing that she was doing the right thing but unable to remember why. 'You said you'd wait until I asked,' she reminded him. It was hard to keep her words steady when her throat was tight with desire and the air struggled to reach her lungs. 'You said you wouldn't sleep with me if I didn't want to.'

Philippe reached out and twisted a lock of her hair around his finger almost casually. *'Are* you sure you don't want to?'

'No…yes…I don't know,' she said with a kind of desperation, and he dropped his hand and stood back.

'All right.'

Her heart cracked to see the guarded look back on his face. 'Philippe—'

'It's OK.' He smiled, but it didn't reach his eyes. 'You go and put that pillow in place. I'll be out on the balcony.'

Caro sat on the edge of the bed and looked down at her shaking hands. Who was she trying to kid? Of course she wanted him.

And she could have him, she knew that.

She should be sensible. Philippe was never going to want to settle down and if he did, it wouldn't be with her. There was no point in dreaming about a future with him, but tonight Caro didn't care about the future. She only cared about now, and right then she wasn't sure she could bear to lie there in her pyjamas and know that he was on the other side of that pillow.

The boom and thump of her pulse reminded her of the pounding music as they drove through France towards the border with Montluce. *Let's make the most of being able to behave badly while we can*, Philippe had said as he'd turned up the volume.

Caro's head knew that she ought to behave sensibly, but

her body wanted to behave very badly indeed and, in the end, her body won.

And she couldn't undo the zip on her own.

Philippe was sitting on the balcony, beyond the block of lamplight from the open French windows. His feet were up on the railings, his face in shadow. He had taken off his jacket and tie and the white shirt gleamed against his throat. In silence he watched Caro as she paused in the doorway.

'I can't reach the zip,' she said.

He got slowly to his feet. 'Come here, then.'

Deliberately, Caro stepped out of the rectangle of light into the shadows.

'Turn around.'

She turned and lifted her hair as she had done earlier. Philippe took the zip and eased it slowly downwards.

The night air was cool against her skin. Caro drew an unsteady breath and let her hair fall without turning.

There was a long pause, and then Philippe gently brushed her hair aside to blow softly on the hollow of her neck. Caro shivered, so snarled in longing that she couldn't have moved if she had tried. She was taut, desperate for his touch, and when his arms slid round her to pull her back against him, she nearly wept with relief.

'You know no one's going to interrupt this time, don't you?' he said as he pressed kisses down the side of her throat.

Caro tipped her head to one side and closed her eyes with pleasure. 'Yes.' Her voice was barely a thread.

He cupped her breasts, his long fingers warm through the silk, then slid them lower, burning her bones to liquid, her blood to fire. His mouth was so wickedly exciting, his hands so insistent. Caro leant back into him, helpless against the hungry thud of desire.

'Shall I stop?' Philippe murmured against her ear.

'No,' she whispered. 'Don't stop.'

'I have to wait until you ask me,' he reminded her wickedly, and she could feel his mouth curving on her skin.

An answering smile curled the corners of Caro's mouth. 'Please,' she said. 'Please don't stop. Please make love to me.'

Philippe eased the dress from her shoulders. It fell in a puddle of silk and Caro turned to face him, her skin luminous in the dim light. Putting his hands to her waist, her drew her back against him. 'It will be my pleasure,' he said.

CHAPTER SEVEN

SHE had known it would be a mistake. Her head had known, anyway. Her body still thought it had been a great decision.

Caro lay on her side and looked at Philippe, who was sprawled next to her, his face buried in a pillow. She could hear him breathing, deep and slow. She wanted to lay her hand on his warm flank and feel it rise and fall, wanted to press her lips to the nape of his neck and kiss her way down his spine, vertebra by vertebra, wanted to wrap her arms around him and press into him, to lose herself in his sleek strength.

But then she would wake him, and she couldn't think clearly with those silver eyes on her. Caro tucked her hands under the pillow, out of temptation's way.

She needed to think, to get a grip on herself.

She hadn't known it could be like *that*.

Caro had liked making love with George. She'd liked the intimacy of it, liked the cosiness and the familiarity, liked lying next to him and feeling reassured that he wanted her.

There had been nothing cosy last night with Philippe. It had been harder, fiercer, more urgent. It had been hot and wild, and once slow and sweet. It had been terrifying and thrilling and extraordinary. Every cell in Caro's body was still reeling, drunken with amazed delight.

For her, the night had been a revelation. Philippe had made

her feel sexy exciting, *powerful*. Caro knew that she would never be the same again.

But she was no different from all the other women Philippe had made love to. Caro knew that too. She would be a fool if she thought that she could be. If all those sophisticated beauties hadn't been able to hold Philippe's interest, it was hardly likely that ordinary Caroline Cartwright would be able to, was it?

Her eyes roamed over him, lingering on the curve of his shoulder, the sheen of muscles in his back, the lean lines of hip and thigh. He was all sleekness and leashed power, like a big cat at rest.

How could a girl like her ever hold on to a man like Philippe?

She couldn't.

The pale light of early morning was sneaking through a crack in the curtains. It was time to start being sensible. Caro would have liked to have been the kind of woman who could enjoy a passionate affair without getting emotionally involved, but she had a feeling that it would be a lot harder in practice than in theory.

She was more than half in love with Philippe already, she acknowledged to herself in the half light, with her body humming with satisfaction from his touch. It wasn't surprising. She was only human, after all, and he was gorgeous and intelligent and funny and an incredible lover and a friend. What was not to love?

The fact that he would leave. The fact that he wouldn't, and maybe couldn't, love her in return. And even if Philippe were to think himself in love, it would only ever be on a temporary basis. Nothing in his experience had led him to accept that love could last. Abandoned by his mother, dismissed by his father…it wasn't surprising Philippe didn't believe in happy-ever-afters.

But that was what *she* wanted. Glow fading, Caro rolled onto her back and looked at the ceiling. She did want that happy-ever-after. She wanted to be with a man she could love unreservedly, who would love her back and let her stay and who would always be there for her. A man she could build a life with. A man she could be happy with.

That man would never be Philippe.

If she had any sense, she would tell Philippe it mustn't happen again. She would say that she wanted to go back to being just friends. She would put her pyjamas back on tonight and shove that pillow back down the middle of the bed.

Caro's body rebelled at the thought. How stupid for two single, healthy adults to lie side by side for two months without touching, without exploring the dark, delicious pleasure of making love, without giving into the passion that could burn so high between them. It would be a sinful waste.

Why *not* make the most of these next few weeks? Time enough to be sensible after that, Caro told herself. Here in Montluce, she was living a fairy tale. Living in a palace, with a prince, with a man like Philippe…how could it be real? One of these days, she was going to wake up and discover that she was a frog again, but it wasn't time to go back to the real world just yet.

She would have the next two months, Caro decided. Two months with Philippe, two months to learn about loving and living in the moment. She could allow herself that, surely?

As long as she never forgot that it would only be for those two months. The dream would end and she would go back to the real world, and that meant that she had to be careful. Somehow she would have to find a way of not getting any more involved than she already was. It would be easier for Philippe if she didn't spoil things by getting clingy and needy, and it would be better for her, too, to put up some defences before it was too late.

Beside her, Philippe stirred and rolled over, throwing an arm over her in his sleep and pulling her back into the hard curve of his body. Caro felt the weight of his arm and allowed herself to stroke it up from the wrist, loving its strength and solidity and the silkiness of the fine, flat hairs.

She just hoped it wasn't too late already.

By the time Philippe woke, Caro had showered, was dressed and had herself well under control. She hoped.

Yawning and rubbing his hair, he wandered out onto the balcony where Caro was sitting with her feet up on the railings. For once she looked positively normal, in capri pants and a sleeveless shirt.

In fact, Philippe realised, she looked more than normal. She looked fresh and pretty and glowing, and he smiled, liking the feeling that he was the one who had made her glow like that. He had a feeling that he was glowing himself. Last night had been unexpected. Incredible. Who would have thought it?

'There you are! Good morning…' He put a hand on top of Caro's head and tipped it back so that he could kiss her mouth but, although she smiled, she turned her head at the last moment and his lips touched her cheek instead.

Taken aback by her reaction, Philippe looked down into her face with raised brows. 'What?' he said. 'You didn't mind kissing me last night!'

Caro flushed. 'That was last night. It's morning now.'

'Yes, and it's early morning too. Let's go back to bed.' His hand slid down her hair moved slid beneath it to caress her neck. 'I missed you when I woke up,' he told her, his voice deep and caressing. 'What are you doing out here?'

'Thinking,' said Caro.

'It's too early to think,' said Philippe, but he pulled out a chair to sit down and put his feet up on the railings beside hers. 'What are you thinking about?' he asked after a moment. 'Last night?'

'Yes,' she said. 'And you.'

He slanted a look at her face, hoping to coax a smile. 'I hope you're thinking good things?'

'I'm thinking sensible things,' said Caro firmly. 'I'm not going to pretend last night wasn't fantastic, because it was. You know that. And I hope…well, I'd like to do it again—if you wanted to, of course,' she added quickly.

More relieved than he wanted to admit, Philippe grinned and reached for her hand. 'I think I could bear it. In fact, let's do it again right now!'

'I haven't got to the sensible bit yet.' Caro tugged her hand free with some difficulty. 'In the bedroom, at night, we can do whatever we want, but during the day, I think we should go back to being just friends.'

'What, so I can't kiss you or hold your hand?' Philippe tried for sarcastic but only succeeded in sounding put out. 'What, in God's name, is the point of that?'

'It would help us keep things separate.'

'Separate? What for?' He scowled. 'What are you talking about?'

Caro got up, hugging her arms together the way she did when she was uncertain. 'Philippe, I'm going home in a few weeks,' she said. 'I want to meet someone else then and have a real relationship. I don't want to be hung up on you. Can't you see that if we kiss each other like you wanted to do just now, it'll be so much harder to remember that we're only pretending?'

Philippe's expression hardened. 'I wasn't pretending last night. Were you?'

'We're pretending that we're in love, and we both know that's not going to happen.' Caro turned to look at the lake, picking her words with care. 'I don't want to fall in love with you, Philippe.'

'There's no danger of that, is there? You're always telling me I'm not your type,' he said.

'You're not, but who's to say what madness I'll take into my head if there are more nights like last one and if the nights turn into days? If you're…affectionate…I might forget myself and do something silly.' She mustered a smile as she glanced over her shoulder at him. 'You know how women get ideas in their heads!'

That was true, Philippe thought. Spend two consecutive nights with a woman and suddenly it was all about a 'relationship' and what he wasn't doing right. It was the reason he avoided intimate situations. So why was he getting all grouchy because Caro was suggesting exactly what he wanted?

'I've had my heart broken,' Caro was saying. 'I don't want to go through that again. I'd rather keep things in separate compartments.'

She drew a breath. 'Sometimes…with George…I was trying too hard to be what he wanted. With you, I didn't need to worry about being right for you because I know I'm not, and you're not right for me. I know I'm never going to have a proper relationship with you and it's…liberating, I suppose.'

Unable to meet his eyes, she stared fixedly at his collarbone. 'But one day I'd like to find someone who *is* right for me and, when I do, I want it to be really special. I don't want to be so hung up on you I can't give myself completely to him.'

Philippe scowled. 'What are you trying to say here, Caro? I'm just a fling before you settle down with Mr Perfect?'

'No…well, sort of, I suppose.' Caro stepped back out of his grasp. 'I just want to enjoy myself,' she said. 'I want to have fun and not feel inhibited, but at the same time I don't want to get so involved that I lose sight of the fact that I'll be going back to Ellerby in a couple of months and then it will all be over.

'No strings, no commitment,' she said, her blue eyes direct. 'Strictly temporary. I'd have thought it would be your dream scenario,' she added with a touch of her old asperity.

It was. Philippe knew that he ought to be delighted.

'We're not going to convince many people of our supposed love affair if I'm not allowed to touch you,' he found himself grumbling.

Caro had thought of that, too. 'Obviously, I'll do whatever's needed to give the right impression, but when we're on our own, well, I'd prefer to keep any intimacy for the bedroom.'

Philippe eyed her almost resentfully. For someone so warm, she could be a very cool customer.

'So I'm to keep my hands to myself until the bedroom door is closed, is that right?'

'I think it would be easier for both of us,' she said. 'You don't want me complicating matters by falling in love with you, do you?'

Of course he didn't. Why would he want that? He'd spent his whole life running away from precisely that situation.

Philippe glared out at the lake.

'You do see that it makes sense, don't you?' said Caro after a moment.

'Oh, yes, yes, I suppose so,' he said irritably.

But it wasn't how he had planned to start the morning.

'Have you seen the papers today?'

The Dowager Blanche picked up a sheaf of newspapers and dropped them back on the table as if she couldn't bear to touch them.

'I haven't had a chance yet,' said Philippe, wishing he were down in the gardens with Caro, who had taken Apollo the pug for a walk.

'Your father gets up at five o'clock every morning to familiarise himself with the news before breakfast.'

Philippe set his teeth. He towered over his great-aunt, but she always made him feel like a grubby schoolboy. 'What are the papers saying?'

For answer, the Dowager Blanche picked up the paper on top of the pile and tossed it across to him. Philippe caught it and turned it round. The front page was dominated by a huge headline: *THE NEXT PRINCESS?* Below was a photo of the market, filling half the page. The camera had caught Caro popping a piece of cheese in his mouth. Her sunglasses were perched on her head and they were both smiling.

It was a good picture of Caro. Her expressive face was alight with laughter and fortunately the head and shoulders shot cut off most of her eccentric outfit. Philippe thought she looked vivid and engaging, and he…he looked *happy*, he realised with something of a shock.

'I could hardly believe my ears when I heard that you had been wandering around the *market*.' The Dowager Blanche's voice was like a lash.

Once she had been a great beauty. You could still see it in her bone structure and her famous elegance, but her expression was one of icy hauteur. She could hardly have been more different from Caro.

'What were you thinking?' she went on. 'We are not one of those populist monarchies, thank God. Your father keeps his distance, and the people are respectful. If you start behaving like the people, you will be treated like one of the people, and you will lose your throne before you have even sat on it!

'This…this *Caroline* is totally unsuitable.' She cast a glance of dislike at the newspapers. 'They're saying you're besotted with her.'

'Perhaps I am,' said Philippe, dropping the paper back onto the table and clasping his hands behind his back once more.

'How can you want her and not Charlotte?' The Dowager's

expression was uncomprehending. 'She's clumsy and badly groomed and she has no idea how to behave.'

'She's warm and friendly,' said Philippe. 'What better way is there to behave? And she may not be classically elegant, but she has her own style. She's…unusual.'

'She looks like a scarecrow,' said the Dowager, unimpressed. 'She's not even beautiful!'

'She is to me,' he found himself saying.

'Then you must be in love! How vulgar.'

Contempt dripped through her voice. Philippe inclined his head in courteous agreement, but inside he felt jarred, as if he had walked smack into a wall.

Love? He didn't do love. Lust, yes, he did that. And that was *all* he felt. He might want to smile at the thought of Caro. He might want to touch her and already be thinking about how he would tell her about this interview. Sometimes meeting her eyes might make him want to laugh, but that wasn't being *in love*.

His great-aunt was watching his expression and her eyes narrowed. 'You can't marry her,' she said.

Philippe turned abruptly and went over to stand by one of the long windows that looked out over the gardens. Below, he could see Caro, who was trying to teach Apollo to run after a stick.

She waggled the stick in front of the pug's nose, and then threw it onto the lawn. Apollo sat on his rump and looked at her blankly. Caro pointed at the stick, then demonstrated by galloping onto the grass to fetch it. She brought it back and dropped it in front of Apollo, who regarded it without interest.

Watching her, Philippe felt some of his frustration ease and the corner of his mouth twitched.

'Why can't I marry her?' he asked.

'I'd have thought it was obvious! You will be Crown Prince

one day,' the Dowager said. 'You owe it to your father to find a suitable bride. We don't want Montluce to become the laughing stock of Europe.'

'Several heirs to thrones around Europe have married commoners,' Philippe pointed out. 'It hasn't done those countries any harm.'

'Those brides at least look the part.' The Dowager joined him at the window. 'Can you say the same of Caroline Cartwright?'

She gestured down at Caro, who had repeated her demonstration with the stick and had stopped to catch her breath. Her face was pink, her shirt creased and her hair tumbled messily to her shoulders.

No, she didn't look like a princess.

Unaware of their gaze, Caro pulled a clip from her pocket and put her hair up in an untidy twist before fixing it into place and smoothing the stray hairs from her face. The shirt strained across her breasts as she lifted her arms, and Philippe felt the sharp stir of desire.

'Everyone likes her,' he told his great-aunt.

'The staff.' She waved a dismissive hand. 'I heard she's been hobnobbing with the footmen and distracting the kitchen staff. Tell her to stop it.'

'It's not just the staff.' Philippe crossed back to pick up the paper she'd shown him earlier. 'The people like her too.' He tapped the article. 'It says so here.'

A lesser woman would have snatched. As it was, there was a definite crispness in the way his great-aunt took the paper from him and reread the enthusiastic piece with an expression of distaste.

'*Everyone was charmed,*' she read, not sounding in the least charmed. 'Hmm.' Her expression grew thoughtful. Philippe could see her clever mind calculating.

'This English girl isn't for you, Philippe,' she said at last.

'You know that yourself. Perhaps you're jaded and she's a fresh taste for a while, but I don't expect it to last and, if you were honest, you'd know that too. As it is, you'll be bored in a month or so and then you'll be ready for someone more sophisticated again.'

And then I'll find Charlotte and bring her home, Philippe could practically hear her thinking.

'In the meantime, if you insist on keeping Mademoiselle Cartwright with you, we might as well capitalise on her popularity. She's new and different, so of course the people are enthused.' She shrugged elegantly. 'Take her with you when you go out on official visits. Perhaps she'll draw some attention away from all these pipeline protests.'

'It might be a better idea to talk to the protestors and settle the issue,' Philippe suggested and his great-aunt stiffened.

'Your father has already made a decision about the pipeline. These people have no business making a fuss about things they know nothing about. Camping on the streets!' She snorted. 'Ridiculous!'

'Perhaps they have legitimate concerns.'

But the Dowager Blanche was having none of it. 'That's not how things are done in Montluce. It is not for you to interfere.'

'One day it *will* be for me to interfere,' he pointed out.

'Fortunately, that day has not yet come,' she flashed back. 'I suggest you stick to what you agreed to do, unless you are hoping to drive your father to his death. He has already suffered enough from your recklessness and irresponsibility.'

She launched into a scathing lecture about his attitude, behaviour and prospects while Philippe gritted his teeth and reminded himself that she was an old lady who had lost both her sons.

'Leave the government to Lefebvre,' she said, winding down at last. 'If you want to make yourself useful, encourage your more famous—and sober—friends to come to my annual ball. It's in aid of an international medical charity, so it's a good cause, and some celebrity guests might lend a certain cachet to the proceedings. That's something you *can* do.'

Philippe thought about the flights he had funded, the planes he had flown into disaster areas, the boxes of tools and tents and water purification tablets that had helped people survive.

'Certainly, *Altesse*.'

When at last the Dowager let him go, Philippe went straight down to the garden to find Caro. She was sitting on the steps from the terrace with Apollo, both of them puffing, in spite of the fact that Caro had had about ten times as much exercise as the pug.

Philippe was aware of his tension loosening at the sight of her. 'It's like a soundtrack to a porn film out here with all this heavy breathing.'

Caro swung round, her heart lurching unmistakably at the sight of him, tall and dark and devastating in the suit he had to wear to meet his great-aunt every day. Every fibre of her sang and cheered in recognition. This was the man who had loved her last night, the man whose hands had taken her to mindless delight. Whose body she had explored, inch by inch. Whose mouth…

Stop it! Caro told herself fiercely.

It was too early to be thinking like that, but once that bed-room door closed tonight… She shivered in anticipation.

'I'm exhausted,' she said. 'Apollo doesn't seem to have the least idea of how to be a dog. He doesn't do walking or running after sticks or anything.' She fondled the dog's ears all the same. 'Do you, dog?'

Philippe's face was set in grim lines as he sat down on the steps beside her, hooking two fingers inside his collar to loosen it. He was looking forbidding, and Caro leaned against his shoulder, bumping it in greeting.

'How did today's ticking off go?' she asked, wanting to see him smile, wanting to see the tension leak from his shoulders.

'Oh, you know. I'm a disappointment to everyone. No sense of duty. Why couldn't I just marry Lotty, blah, blah, blah. The usual.' Philippe spoke lightly, but she sensed it was with an effort.

'Oh, dear, she's not warming to me, is she? After I walked Apollo, too!'

'She's hoping my passion for you will burn out before your wardrobe brings the entire state of Montluce into disrepute. Our little trip to the market didn't go down well,' he told her. 'You're on the front of all the papers.'

Caro sat bolt upright. '*I* am?'

'You're a celebrity now,' said Philippe, 'and now the Dowager Blanche is going to use you. You're to accompany me on the various visits I've got to do. The idea is that everyone will be so excited about what you're wearing that they won't be interested in the gas line protests. She's counting on a media frenzy.'

'A media frenzy? About *me*?' Caro stared at him in disbelief.

'Hard to believe, I know,' he said. 'Especially given your propensity for jumble sale cast-offs. You can start tomorrow. I'm opening a new wing at the hospital in the afternoon, so you can come to that.'

'But won't it look a bit official?' Caro pulled a face. 'Everyone will think we're about to announce our engagement if I start tagging along like that. I wouldn't have thought the Dowager Blanche would have wanted to encourage that idea.'

'She doesn't, but I managed to convince her that I am utterly besotted by you.'

Caro leant so that their shoulders were touching once more. It was amazingly comforting. 'She's still worried about Lotty, and she's fretting about us,' she said. 'Maybe we should tell her that you've no intention of marrying me. That would make it easier for her. You could say you're just obsessed with my body.'

'I could, but I'm not going to. Let her fret,' said Philippe. 'In fact,' he went on, smoothing her hair behind her ear and fixing his eyes on her mouth, 'let her fret right now.'

It was pathetic. The merest graze of his fingers and she went to pieces. Caro swallowed. 'I thought we agreed no touching when we're alone?'

'But we're not alone,' he said. 'My great-aunt is certainly glaring down at us from the window up there, and who knows who else is watching? There'll be some footman who might like to earn a little more by leaking how in love we are to the press. I don't think we should deny him his perk, do you?'

His hand slid underneath her hair and he tugged her gently towards him and, as he put his mouth to hers, Caro closed her eyes at the jolt of wicked pleasure. She ought to push him away, she thought hazily. This was a mistake.

But it didn't feel like a mistake with the sunlight spilling around them on the steps. It felt right, it felt perfect. Parting her lips with a little sigh, she abandoned herself to the sweetness that surged through her, and the current that ran like wildfire under her skin.

One hand rested on the stone step, the other crept up to Philippe's arm and she sank into him, giving back kiss for kiss until Apollo decided that he needed her attention. He started to bark and scrabble at Philippe until they broke reluctantly apart.

'Get out of here, dog,' said Philippe, telling himself to keep it light, not wanting Caro to guess how shaken he was.

'He's defending me,' said Caro, giving Apollo a pat with a hand that was still trembling. 'He thinks you're hurting me.'

'I'm not hurting her, mutt.' Philippe pretended to glare at Apollo and reached for her again, but Caro evaded him and got to her feet, brushing herself down.

'Not yet,' she said under her breath.

To: charlotte@palaisdemontvivennes.net
From: caroline.cartwright@u2.com
Subject: Waving and shaking
Isn't it amazing how quickly you can get used to things? I feel as if I've been living in a palace and hanging out with royalty for ever! It's only been a month, but already I'm an old hand at waving and shaking hands, and my curtsey is coming on a treat.

I'm not sure why, but your grandmother decreed that I should accompany Philippe on official visits—maybe she thinks I'll embarrass him so much he'll dump me in favour of someone more suitable, i.e. you? But you're safe for now. Philippe still can't accept that vintage is a style choice and is invariably rude about what I'm wearing, but otherwise we're getting on fine.

Caro stopped typing. *Getting on fine.* It sounded so bland, but she couldn't tell Lotty the truth. She couldn't tell her how Philippe closed the bedroom door every night and looked at her with that smile that made her blood zing. How they made love with an abandon that made Caro burn just to think about it. How the touch of Philippe's lips or Philippe's hands quivered over her body all day. Sometimes she would look at him and the knowledge of how the muscles in his back flexed at her touch would thrill through her, and she would long for night to come so that she could hold him again.

No, that was between her and Philippe. It was their secret, their other life, the one she struggled to keep separate the moment they stepped through the bedroom door.

Philippe has a punishing schedule, arranged by Lefebvre and your grandmother to keep him out of mischief, he thinks. Over the past month we've visited hospitals, inspected factories, attended receptions, sat through endless concerts and admired some really impressive charity projects. I guess you're used to all of this, but it's all new for Philippe as well as for me. I think he's really good at it, actually. He always rolls his eyes when he sees what's on the schedule for the day, but I've noticed that he's got a real knack for seeming charming and interested without losing that glamour that makes people feel special for having the opportunity to meet him in the first place. It's charisma, I suppose.

I tag along in the background. Philippe always tells me I'm going to be bored, and sometimes when I hear what's in store, my heart sinks a bit, but you know what? I always end up enjoying myself. I've been overwhelmed by the welcome we get. I know it's for Philippe, but sometimes people call out to me and want to shake my hand too! Little girls are always thrusting posies at me, and by the time I get home—

Caro broke off. She shouldn't think of the palace as home. It was a place she was staying for a couple of months and she had better not forget it. Ellerby was *home*. She deleted 'home'. She typed instead:

By the time I get back to the palace I'm laden with flowers. My French is improving by leaps and bounds, but I still need Philippe to interpret most of the time. I'm not sure he always translates correctly, because there always seems to be a lot of laughter, and I have a funny feeling it's all at my expense! But he swears blind he's not taking liberties.

So basically, Lotty, I'm having a great time! Even on the most tedious of visits, I can always catch Philippe's eye, which makes it easier to sit through some symphony of squeaky chairs or an earnest explanation of the difference between pre-stressed and reinforced concrete (bet you're sorry you missed that one!) It's hard not to enjoy yourself when everyone is so kind and friendly and nice to you all the time! Maybe I would get sick of it after a while, and I don't need to tell you how sore your hand is at the end of the day after it's been shaken a million times, but for now it's good fun. I've got the rest of my life to be just one in a crowd, after all!

Caro

xx

Not every day was taken up with visits. Sometimes Philippe had meetings with ministers or senior officials and, of course, he had to check in daily with the Dowager. Every morning a red box of government papers would arrive, which he would have to read and discuss with his great-aunt. Caro knew how much he loathed those meetings, and how torn he was between wanting to make some real changes and a reluctance to distress his father.

In spite of the difficult relationship between Philippe and the Dowager Blanche, Caro suspected that he didn't want to hurt her either, so he swallowed his frustration and talked about going back to South America, where he could fly and do something more useful than shake hands. Caro thought it was a shame. He had the potential to be a thoughtful and progressive ruler, if only his family would accept him for how he was.

It was hard now to remember how dismissive she had been about Philippe at first. She had seen him as a two-dimensional figure, a cardboard cut-out of a playboy prince, and he played up to that, as if he didn't want anyone to guess that beneath the glamour and the good looks, beneath that dazzling surface gloss, was a man of integrity and intelligence, who chafed at the restrictions of royal life, while yearning—Caro was sure—for his father's approval?

She fell into the habit of walking Apollo in the gardens whenever Philippe met with the Dowager Blanche so that she could be there for him when he came out. He was always rigid with frustration, and it took a little while to coax him back into good humour, but Caro made him stroll with her by the lake and, between the tranquil water and the mountains and Philippe gradually unwinding beside her, that soon became one of her favourite parts of the day.

By and large, they were sticking to their agreement, although Philippe cheated whenever they were in public. It gave him the perfect excuse to touch Caro: a hand in the small of her back to move her along, an arm around her waist, fingers tucking stray tendrils of hair behind her ears, a knuckle grazing her cheek in a brief caress.

'Just annoying the Dowager Blanche,' said Philippe, holding up his hands innocently whenever Caro tried to protest.

'Stop it,' she would mutter, but she didn't mean it. Ignoring the strict instructions of her brain, her body clamoured for his touch, however brief. She only had to watch him turn his head and smile at the crowd, or bend down to shake an old lady's hand, and Caro's treacherous body would clench with longing for the night to come.

She didn't tell Lotty that either.

CHAPTER EIGHT

To: caro.cartwright@u2.com
From: charlotte@palaisdemontvivennes.net
Subject: Style icon
Caro, you're in Glitz!!!! There was a whole piece about
how you've revolutionized fashion in Montluce. I understand a vintage dinner jacket is now the must-have item
in every Montlucian woman's wardrobe! I was drinking a
cup of tea (I LOVE tea!) when I opened the magazine and
nearly spat it everywhere when I saw your picture. Then I
couldn't explain what was so funny to Corran and had to
make up some lame excuse about thinking that I recognised you. I hardly did! You look like you'd be a fabulous
princess. Why didn't we swap places before? Why don't
you and Philippe think about making it permanent? It
says in Glitz that he adores you…is there anything I need
to know?????
Xxx Lotty

To: charlotte@palaisdemontvivennes.net
From: caro.cartwright@u2.com
Subject: Re: Style icon
Who's Corran?????
Cxxxxxxxxx

Caro didn't want to lie to Lotty, and it was too complicated to explain the arrangement she and Philippe had made, so she left it at that.

In her inbox at the same time was a message from Stella, who had also seen the *Glitz* article and had made a point of showing it to George and Melanie. George looked sick as a pig, she reported gleefully, and Melanie wasn't looking nearly as perky now.

Caro closed Stella's email without replying immediately. George and Ellerby seemed so distant now. It was hard now to remember how desperately she had loved George, how hurt she had been when he had left her for Melanie.

She was glad that Stella had emailed. It would be too easy to start thinking that this life with Philippe could last for ever, too easy to forget that it was all nothing but an elaborate pretence.

It was time to get a grip on reality again, Caro decided. Already a month had passed. Only another four weeks, and she would be back in Ellerby. Back to where she could find the life she had always wanted: settled, secure, in the heart of a community.

A life without Philippe

She was going to miss him. Caro made herself realise it every day, so that she never forgot that it was going to happen. Because what alternative was there? Philippe wasn't in love with her and, even if he were, she didn't have what it took to be a princess. Her face wasn't right, her clothes weren't right and, however friendly the welcome she'd had at Philippe's side, *she* wasn't right either.

Anyway, she didn't want to be a royal, Caro reminded herself. She would go wild, hanging around with nothing to do but cook the occasional meal. No, she needed to go home and get on with her life. She had been thinking a lot about her deli, and how she could borrow enough money to set it up.

She wanted to stock some of Montluce's specialities. She had learned to make quenelles and the famous *tarte aux abricots* from Jean-Michel, the palace chef, who had given her his secret recipe when he recognised a kindred obsession with flavour. So she concentrated on that, and not on how much would miss laughing in bed with Philippe.

Philippe lay stretched out on one of the sofas and reached down to pull a sheaf of documents from the red box on the floor beside him. 'You wouldn't believe a country this small would generate quite so much paperwork, would you?' he grumbled, flicking through them. 'Report and accounts from the potato growers of Montluce… Waste management solutions for the city of Montvivennes… Forests have been felled to print these reports and who's interested in them? Nobody!'

'The potato farmers might be,' Caro suggested.

'Show me a farmer who wants to read a report!' Philippe looked up at Caro, who was sitting at the table, laptop open in front of her. Her lips were pursed, the fierce brows drawn together. 'What are you doing?'

'Checking my account at right4u.com… Can you believe it? I've only had *one* message in a month, and that's from Mr Sexy so it doesn't count.'

Philippe sat up. 'What are you checking dating sites for?' he demanded, outraged. 'You're with me.'

'Only temporarily,' Caro pointed out, cucumber-cool. 'I wouldn't want to miss out on someone perfect. The good guys get snapped up straight away.'

'You couldn't do any snapping up, anyway,' said Philippe crossly. 'You may only be a temporary girlfriend, but you've still got a good month to go.'

To his annoyance, Caro clicked on a link, and he got up to see what interested her so much. 'I wouldn't arrange to meet him or anything,' she said. 'I could just make contact and see if we've got anything in common. A sort of cyber flirtation. You don't want me to miss out on Mr Right, do you?'

Philippe was standing at her shoulder, glaring at the profiles on the screen. 'Which one is Mr Right?'

'I was wondering about this one.' She pointed at a photograph of someone who had called himself Homebody. He was a serious-looking man who described himself as loyal, trustworthy and affectionate.

Her hair was tumbling down from its clip as usual. He wanted to tidy it up, clip it neatly so that it wasn't so…distracting. Or did he want to pull the clip out completely to let the silky mass tumble to her shoulders? Did he want to push his fingers through it and tilt her face up to his?

Philippe scowled. That wouldn't be *allowed*, or at least not according to Caro's rules. He couldn't believe he had agreed to them. She was supposed to be his girlfriend. He ought to be able to put his hands on her shoulders, or kiss the side of her throat. He ought to be able to cajole her away from that stupid site and over to the sofa so that he could kiss her properly.

But they were outside the bedroom and there was nobody else around, which meant that he wasn't allowed to touch her at all. And he had given his word.

'Affectionate?' he jeered, taking out his bad temper on Homebody instead. 'You might as well get yourself a dog!'

'I think he sounds nice,' said Caro defiantly. She scrolled through Homebody's profile. 'Look, he's a teacher.'

'Why's that a good thing?'

'He'll be sensible, and reliable, and good with kids.'

'Not if he's anything like any of the teachers I ever had!'

She ignored that, and read on. 'He likes eating out and staying in—just like me.'

'Everybody likes eating out sometimes and staying in

sometimes,' said Philippe, determined to dismiss Homebody. 'That doesn't tell you anything.'

'You don't,' said Caro. 'When do you ever have a cosy night in?'

'We've stayed in a couple of evenings.' Philippe had been surprised how much he'd enjoyed both of them, in fact. He'd never done the whole lying-on-a-sofa-watching-a-DVD thing before. With a glass of wine and Caro commenting all the way through it, he had been able to see the appeal, definitely.

'Only because you're here in Montluce. You wouldn't do that normally, would you?'

Philippe couldn't remember what normal was any more. There was only this life, with Caro. Coming home from some tedious meeting and finding her humming in the kitchen. Enduring his great aunt's lectures, knowing that she would be able to make him laugh afterwards. Watching her engage with everyone she met, watching her smile, taking every opportunity to touch her.

Lying in bed with her, talking, laughing, making love.

Waking up with her in the morning.

That was normal now.

Sometimes he would sit on the stool at the counter and watch her moving around the kitchen while he told her about his meetings, and she listened to what he said, unlike the First Minister or the Dowager Blanche. She'd listen and ask questions and challenge him, and Philippe had a horrible feeling he was going to miss all that when she went.

Because she would go. She was always talking about her plans for the delicatessen she wanted to open when she got back to Ellerby. Philippe wanted to tell her to stop it, but how could he? It wasn't as if he wanted her to stay for ever. There was no question of that. He was only here until his father came home, and then he would go back to South America. He could fly when he wanted, party when he wanted. He could date sophisticated women who wouldn't know where the kitchen was. There would be risk and challenge and uncomplicated relationships. That would be much more fun than red boxes and watching Caro cook.

Wouldn't it?

'This Homebody guy sounds catastrophically dull,' he decided. 'You'd be bored witless at the end of one of those cosy nights in.'

'You don't know that,' said Caro, obviously perversely determined to see Homebody as the perfect man for her. 'Look, he says he's got a good sense of humour.'

Philippe was unimpressed. 'Everyone's going to say *that*,' he said. 'He's hardly going to admit that he's dullness personified, is he?'

'We've got lots in common,' Caro insisted. 'He ticks all my boxes: steady, decent, ordinary. A guy like that isn't looking for a glamourpuss or a sex kitten. He wants someone steady and decent and ordinary—like me.'

'I don't know why you persist in thinking of yourself as ordinary,' said Philippe, throwing himself back down onto the sofa.

He felt edgy and restless at the idea of Caro with another man. What if Homebody *was* the one for her? He would be the one coming home to find Caro pottering around in the kitchen. *He* would be able to reach for her in bed and have all that warmth and passion to himself.

Was everything he was showing Caro really going to benefit a man who could describe himself as Homebody?

'Ordinary girls don't dress out of a jumble sale catalogue, for a start,' he said, forgetting that he'd come to appreciate her quirky style. No matter how eccentric the clothes, Caro wore them with flair. Not that he was going to tell her that. It would be no fun if he couldn't give her a hard time about her wardrobe, would it? 'They don't spend their whole time in the kitchen or hobnobbing with the staff.'

As far as Philippe could tell, Caro was on first name terms with every footman and maid in the palace. She knew everyone in the kitchen, and had met all the gardeners on her walks with Apollo. She was always telling him about Yvette's worry about her elderly mother, or the fact that Michel rode a motorbike on his days off, that Gaston grew wonderful tomatoes or that Marie-Madeleine had a crush on the head butler, which no one, including Philippe, could understand.

'Ordinary girls don't have servants to hobnob *with*,' Caro pointed out dryly. 'I'm just being myself.'

'I still don't think you should waste your time on Homebody,' said Philippe, disgruntled. 'He looks shifty to me. What if he's a serial killer?' he asked, raising another objection. 'He's not going to put that in his profile, is he? It could all be a ruse to lure someone ridiculously trusting like you back to his lair.'

Caro rolled her eyes. 'I'd meet him somewhere public at first and, anyway, I've got to do *something* if I want to find someone to have a serious relationship with.'

'I don't know why you're bothering. I wouldn't waste my time on online dating sites.'

'You don't have to. I'm sure the women will all be queuing up to console you the moment I've gone!'

She could at least sound upset at the prospect, thought Philippe darkly. Scowling, he went back to the red box. 'Don't be ridiculous!'

'Is Francesca Allen coming to the Dowager's ball?'

Philippe looked up, eyes narrowing at the apparent non sequitur. 'She's invited, yes. Why?'

'I remember reading in *Glitz* that you and she had a bit of a thing going,' said Caro casually.

'Oh, well, if you read it in a magazine, it must be true!'

'Is it?'

Philippe opened the first file. 'More exploring the possibilities of a thing,' he found himself admitting. 'She's a beautiful woman,' he said, to punish Caro for talking about going home. 'I hope she will come to the ball. It's only a week or so before you leave, so it would be a good time to catch up with her again.'

He remembered being bowled over by Francesca's beauty when he'd met her. Maybe he would be again. Someone like Francesca Allen would be just what he needed once Caro had gone. They could amuse each other until he could go back to South America. Francesca wouldn't be interested for longer than that, anyway. Yes, she would suit him fine.

'She'd make a good princess,' Caro said in a neutral voice.

'If I ever think about marrying, I'll bear her in mind,' he said with a sarcastic look that successfully disguised, he hoped, the way the thought of her going pressed on his chest like a small but leaden weight.

Silence fell. Philippe forced his attention back to the contents of the red box. He skimmed through the first two files, dropping them onto the carpet when he'd finished.

'Now what?' he sighed as he pulled out yet another sheaf of papers. 'Good grief, a report on integrated weed management! Who writes this stuff?'

He took the first page and made it into a paper plane, which he sent sailing over to land on Caro's keyboard.

She threw it back. 'That could have a state secret on it. You should be careful.'

'Yes, I'm sure that intelligence agencies around the world are in competition to see who can find out how Montluce manages its weeds!' Philippe flicked through it. 'I don't know why they think I need to read this stuff, anyway. It's not as if anyone is interested in my opinion. That weasel Lefebvre just sneaks round to see the Dowager Blanche and does what she tells him to do.'

The weed management report tossed aside, he picked up the next file and pulled out a piece of paper to make another paper plane.

'Stop that,' said Caro, as it came sailing her way. She batted it aside. 'You won't be able to throw paper planes at Francesca Allen.'

'I'm bored. I hope you're not sending a message to Dullbody—' Philippe broke off in the middle of folding another plane. 'Hang on...'

'What is it?'

Frowning, he smoothed out the page once more. 'This is about the pipeline,' he said slowly.

'The one all the protests are about?'

He nodded as he read on. 'It's an estimate of costs. It looks as if the construction company are lobbying to build the pipeline overground, which would obviously be much cheaper for them. That's a little detail they haven't mentioned to anyone yet!'

'What's the betting Lefebvre slipped this in amongst all these boring documents in the hope that I wouldn't notice?' His jaw tightened. 'They've spent a few weeks making sure I'm not expecting anything remotely interesting and now they're banking on the fact that I'll just scrawl my signature without reading this properly. Here, let me have that plane back, will you, Caro?' he said. 'I think I'd better see what that says too.'

Caro retrieved the page from the floor and sent it back to Philippe, who unfolded it carefully and put the report back together. Sitting up, his brows drawn together in concentration, he read it from beginning to end, so absorbed that he barely noticed when Caro got up to make some coffee.

There were footmen waiting outside, but she couldn't get

used to the idea of asking someone to go along to the servants' galley and boil water for her when she had access to a perfectly adequate kitchen to use herself. The Dowager Blanche, she had heard, insisted on a tray of coffee at exactly the same time every day. Everything had to be set out precisely, and woe betide the maid or footman who put the sugar in the wrong place, or piled the biscuits haphazardly on the plate instead of setting them out in a neat circle. Caro had heard that there was a plan of the tray pinned up in the servants' galley but she thought this was probably a myth.

Philippe was looking very grim by the time he had finished reading He gathered the papers together neatly and put them back in the file. 'I think it's time I had a little chat with the Dowager Blanche,' he said.

Philippe was preoccupied as he made his way back to his apartments. The footman—Guillaume?—leapt to open the door, and he nodded absently in thanks.

As the door closed behind him, he looked around, struck by how homely the apartments felt now. It was hard to put a finger on just why they were more welcoming. It could have been something to do with the recipe book face down on the coffee table, the cardigan tossed over the arm of the sofa.

Or maybe it was the smells drifting out from the kitchen. He usually found Caro there, her face intent as she chopped and stirred. For someone so messy, she was extraordinarily calm and organised when she was cooking and she produced mouth-watering delicacies, pâtés and little tarts and savoury pastries which she brought out for him to taste. He would need to start taking some exercise or he'd put on weight, Philippe thought.

She appeared now, wooden spoon in one hand. 'How did you get on with the Dowager?'

'Pretty much as you'd expect.' Philippe yanked at his tie

to loosen it and unbuttoned his collar. There was no question of popping in on his great-aunt. He'd had to wait until the next day, and put on a suit before he could see her. 'I'm not to interfere. Montluce has a delicate relationship with its powerful neighbours, and we can't jeopardise the little influence we have. My father made his wishes known, and I'm to sign the agreement on his behalf and stop asking questions. Et cetera, et cetera, et cetera.'

'What are you going to do now?' asked Caro.

'I don't know.' Philippe paced restlessly, rolling his shoulders in frustration. 'Let's get out of here, for a start,' he decided abruptly.

They drove up into the mountains, Yan shadowing as always in the black SUV. Philippe drove in silence and Caro let him think without interruption. The sun flickered through the trees and the air was heady with the scent of the pines that lined the winding road.

Away from Montvivennes, the roads were quiet and when they dropped at last into a valley and stopped beside a broad, shallow river it was hard to believe that they were only an hour from the bustling city.

'Let's walk for a bit,' said Philippe.

Yan waited with the cars and they followed the riverbank until the water split around a cluster of boulders deposited by a long-vanished glacier, forming deep green pools. It was very quiet, just the sound of the river and an insect droning somewhere. Caro sat on the smooth rock and took off her sandals so that she could dangle her feet in the water.

'It's so peaceful here.' Leaning back on her hands, she drew a deep breath of pine-scented air. Beside her in the dappled sunlight, Philippe had rolled up his trousers and his feet hung next to hers in the clear, clear water. 'I'm glad we came out.'

She glanced at Philippe. 'You've been here before?'

'This was Etienne's favourite place,' he said slowly, look-ing around as if comparing it to his memories. 'Our father would bring us up here sometimes, until Etienne grew out of splashing around in rock pools.'

He didn't need to add that his father hadn't thought to bring his younger son on his own.

Deep in thought, Philippe looked down at their feet dan-gling together in the water, and Caro let her gaze rest hungrily on the uncompromising planes and angles of his face. She knew him so well now. She knew exactly how his hair grew at his temples, how the laughter lines fanned his eyes. She knew the texture of his skin and the precise line of his jaw and his mouth…that mouth that made her heart turn over every time she looked at it.

'This is where the pipeline will go.' Philippe lifted his head and looked around at the peaceful scene. 'It's going to rip through this valley, with no effort made to disguise it, and then they'll blast through those hills there, and push it through into the valley beyond. This river will never be the same.'

Caro was dismayed. 'How can they even think about it?'

'There are only a few villages in this valley. Yes, it's beauti-ful, but what is one valley compared to the energy needs of millions of people? It's not as if Europe is short of beautiful valleys either, they'll say. And who cares about Montluce, anyway?'

'You do,' said Caro, and he turned his head to meet her eyes for a long moment.

'I can refuse to sign the agreement,' he said. 'I can say that the plan is unacceptable as it stands at the moment, and that construction and energy companies are exploiting our need for international support. I can say that the environmental cost is too high. But, if I do, my father will take it as a direct rejection of his authority. He's over his operation, so that's something, but what if the stress affects him the way they say it might? I don't want to be responsible for my father's death as well as my brother's,' he finished bitterly.

'He won't die,' said Caro. 'He's just using his illness to manipulate you, and it's not fair. You can't threaten to collapse every time your will is crossed!'

'You're probably right,' he said after a moment. 'The best case scenario is that he loses his temper with no side effects. I can live with that, but he won't forgive me.'

Behind the matter-of-factness, Caro could sense what a difficult decision it was for Philippe and her heart ached for him. He might say that he was resigned to his family's contempt, but deep down she knew that he yearned for his father to accept him, to approve of him, to forgive him for living when his brother died. It wasn't too much to ask, surely?

Philippe was watching the mountains. 'But it's not just about me and my father, I know that,' he said after a moment. 'I've been thinking about all the people I've met over last few weeks. Decent, ordinary people, who have trusted my family for centuries to do the right thing for the country. Montluce is theirs. They don't want it ripped up and exploited unnecessarily, and if I'm in a position to make sure that doesn't happen, I can't let them down. I can do what's right for them, or for my father, but not both.'

Caro didn't answer immediately. She was trying to find an answer that would make the decision easy for Philippe, but she couldn't do it. 'Your father trusts you to do the right thing, or he'd never have made you regent,' she said gently, but Philippe shook his head.

'He'll never trust me.'

The bleakness in his face made Caro put out a hand without thinking. 'Give him a reason to trust you now,' she said, twining her fingers with his. '*I* trust you.'

Philippe looked down at their linked hands. 'You're touching me,' he said.

'I know.'

'There's no one around to see us.'

A smile trembled on her lips. 'I know.'

He smiled too, then, and leant towards her, and Caro met him halfway for a kiss that made her senses reel with its sweetness. Disentangling their hands, she slid her arms around his neck and pressed into him, and when Philippe kissed her again something unlocked inside her and she abandoned herself to the rush of pleasure. The sunlight poured around them, in them, spilling through Caro, and there was nothing but Philippe, the taste of him and the feel of him and the rightness of being in his arms.

'We'd better go back,' Philippe sighed against her hair a long time later, and Caro didn't resist when he took her hand as they walked back to the car.

Fishing the car key out of his pocket, he held it out to Caro. 'Do you want to drive?'

Caro's mouth dropped open. 'You'd let me drive?'

'If you want to.'

She took the key slowly. 'I thought you'd have to be besotted to let a woman drive your car?'

'Maybe I am,' said Philippe.

There was uproar when Philippe announced that he was refusing permission for the pipeline to go ahead under the existing agreement. The Dowager Blanche was incandescent, and there were worried reports about the Crown Prince's condition from the doctors in Paris. Lefebvre and the Montlucian government quailed before the might of the great energy companies and all those invested in them.

But the people cheered. On the way back from the river, Caro had dropped Philippe at the protestors' camp and he'd walked calmly into the middle of the angry mob. 'I'll listen,' he had said. 'Let's see if we can work something out.'

Dismissing Lefebvre's spluttering objections, Philippe re-negotiated the pipeline deal over the course of a long and bruising session, at the end of which it was agreed that the pipeline would be laid underground, not just in Montluce but along the entire route. Jobs would still be created, energy still supplied, but Philippe had won a package of concessions on the environment that the protestors had put forward.

The public response was astonishing. Philippe's stand made headlines across Europe. *Plucky little Montluce takes on energy giants* trumpeted the headlines. Suddenly every-body wanted to know about the country and visitors poured in, to the delight of the fledgling tourist trade.

Philippe himself missed most of the excitement. He went to Paris to tell his father in person about the agreement he had made on his behalf. 'He may refuse to see me,' he told Caro, 'but I have to try. Will you be all right here on your own for a couple of days?'

'Of course,' she said. 'Don't worry about me. I hope your father's proud of you, Philippe,' she added. 'I am.'

Barely had Philippe left the palace before Caro was sum-moned to see the Dowager Blanche.

It was soon clear who the Dowager blamed for Philippe's rebellion. Caro had never been subject to the full force of the Dowager's anger before, and she was more daunted than she wanted to admit, but she thought of how often Philippe had endured tongue-lashings from his great-aunt and gritted her teeth. Arguing would only make things worse, she knew, but when the Dowager started on Philippe, she could hold her tongue no longer.

'He is *not* spoilt!' she said furiously. 'How could he be spoilt when nobody in his family apart from his brother has ever given him any attention or credit for anything he does? And he's not selfish, either! A selfish man would have left the father who had ignored him for years to deal with his cancer by himself. Philippe didn't do that. He gave up his life and came back, and he's had nothing but contempt from you and everyone else as a result.'

The Dowager was outraged. 'How dare you speak to me like that?'

'I dare because no one else will speak up for Philippe, and the truth is that he cares for you too much to tell you this himself. But you should look around you, *Altesse*. The people outside the gates don't despise him. They think he's going to be a bold, innovative prince who will take this country into the twenty-first century a decade after the rest of the world. They like him. He's not stuffy or aloof. He's warm and accessible and he listens. He is a good man who's just discovering what he can do with his position.'

'He's gone directly against his father's wishes and my wishes and the wishes of the government in the matter of this pipeline,' said the Dowager, her voice icy with fury.

'He hasn't done it lightly, but he knows it's the right thing to do. Philippe isn't thinking about what's easy for himself, or even what's easy for you. He's thinking about what's right for Montluce.'

'*We* will decide what's right for this country!'

'No,' said Caro. 'The people will decide.'

Philippe returned two days later to a rapturous welcome that moved him more than he wanted to admit. People lined the streets, cheering as the cavalcade from the border swept past and outside the palace, they thronged around the roundabout.

He wished Caro was with him to share it.

She was waiting for him in the apartments, and Philippe's heart contracted at the sight of her smile. The footman closed the door behind him and she threw herself at him with a squeal of excitement. 'You're a hero!' she said as he swung her round. 'Have you seen the papers?'

'Some of them.' Philippe grinned, pleased by her reaction. 'But I wouldn't have been able to do it without you, Caro.'

'Me? I didn't do anything!'

'I wouldn't have had the courage to stick to my guns without you,' he said seriously. 'I'm not sure I would have cared enough.'

'But you care now.' Belatedly, Caro realised that she was still clinging to him and disentangled herself. 'This is your place, Philippe. You can make a difference here.'

'Perhaps.'

He told her about his father, who had been on the point of disinheriting him before it became clear just how popular Philippe's stand had been. 'He bawled me out for not following orders, of course, but in the end he acknowledged that it hadn't been a bad decision. Coming from him, that's high praise!'

'That's good,' said Caro, pleased. Personally, she thought the Crown Prince should have gone down on his knees and thanked Philippe for single-handedly transforming Montluce's standing in the world, but 'not a bad decision' was progress of sorts.

Philippe picked up a book Caro had been reading and made a show of looking at it. 'He asked if I would stay on after he gets back,' he said abruptly, dropping the book back on the table. 'He thinks he'll find it more tiring now, and I could take on some of his duties.'

'What did you say?'

'I said I would as long as I could continue to take some decisions.'

'Well…' Caro's smile seemed forced. 'That's great.'

CHAPTER NINE

THERE was a long pause. Philippe could practically see the excitement draining out of the air.

Caro hugged her arms together. 'This changes things, doesn't it?' she said at last.

'In what way?'

'Well, now you're ready to be here permanently, you really need the right kind of woman by your side,' she said with difficulty. 'Maybe the Dowager was right about that, at least. You should be looking for a princess.'

Philippe stiffened, instinctively resisting the suggestion. 'I don't have to think about that yet.'

'Why wait? There's no point in us pretending much longer if you're going to stay anyway. I'm just a distraction, Philippe,' said Caro. 'It's been fun, but I think it's time I went home.'

A cold feeling settled in the pit of Philippe's belly. 'You said you'd stay two months.'

'That's only a week or so away. I'm ready to go back,' she said. 'I want to be ordinary again.' She smiled brightly at him. 'All of this…it's been amazing, and I'll never forget this time we've spent together, but none of it's been real, has it?'

It had felt real to Philippe. Smoothing his hands over her skin, listening to her breathe, watching her sleep. The taste of her, the smell of her. That had all been real.

Caro moistened her lips as if unnerved by his silence. 'I've had enough of the fairy tale. I'm not what you need, Philippe, and you can't give me what I really want. I need to go home and meet someone I can build a real relationship with. A real life.'

You can't give me what I really want.

Philippe's face was shuttered. It was true. Caro deserved to be loved in a way he never could. She deserved commitment and security and a belief in happy-ever-afters that he just couldn't give her.

'Very well,' he said, his voice tight.

Caro had done exactly what she had promised to do. She had enjoyed herself, but she had never forgotten that it was all a pretence, and now she had had enough of pretending. It had just been *fun* for her.

The cold feeling solidified into a stone lodged deep inside him. He wasn't going to show her how hurt he was. He *wasn't.*

'If that's how you feel,' he said, 'I'll make arrangements for you to fly home tomorrow.'

The Dowager Blanche, however, had other ideas. Before Philippe had a chance to arrange anything, they were both summoned to see her.

'I think she's going to have my head chopped off for insubordination,' said Caro nervously. 'We had a bit of a row last time.'

'You *argued* with the Dowager? You're a brave woman!'

The Dowager looked coldly at Caro when she curtsied before her but, instead of whipping out the blindfold, she gestured them both to the sofa opposite. This was possibly the most uncomfortable piece of furniture Caro had ever sat on. Designed for elaborate hooped skirts, there were no cushions so you had to sit bolt upright, and its gilt legs were so spindly that Caro was afraid the whole thing would collapse when Philippe sat beside her.

There was a frigid silence, broken by Apollo's wheezing as he recognised Caro. He waddled over to wag his bottom at her, and she patted his head.

'Good boy,' she said. He was never going to be the most beautiful dog in the world, and he had steadfastly refused to compromise his dignity by running after a stick, but she was quite fond of him now.

The Dowager was sitting very erect on the facing sofa. 'Well, I see you have been putting Montluce on the map,' she said to Philippe with a true aristocrat's disdain for popularity. 'I was disappointed that you directly disobeyed your father, I admit, but it seems that the decision is not *quite* the disaster we feared it would be. Indeed, your father tells me that you will be staying on to share his duties with him. I am pleased to hear it. You have learnt responsibility, it seems.'

Philippe manufactured a smile and kept his reflections to himself. 'I hope so.'

'I am getting old,' she said, not looking in the least old with her gimlet eyes and rigidly elegant posture. 'Hosting the ball this year will be too much for me. It is time to hand on responsibility to the next generation, so I would like you two to host it on my behalf.'

She ignored the aghast look that Philippe and Caro exchanged. 'Mademoiselle Cartwright tells me that you are much more competent than I give you credit for,' she added to Philippe in her crisp tones. 'I trust that, between you, you can manage a ball without creating the kind of furore we've seen over the last few days?'

'You can't go now,' Philippe muttered to Caro when the Dowager finally let them go. 'I'm not hosting that ball on my own!'

'I've never even *been* to a ball,' objected Caro. 'I haven't got a clue what to do.'

'You just have to stand there and greet people when they

come in. Look as if you're enjoying yourself, and I know you can do that.' He stopped halfway down the great sweeping staircase. 'I know you want to go, Caro,' he said, 'but please stay until after that.'

Caro bit her lip. The ball would be the first time the Dowager had trusted Philippe with anything, and it was an important test. She couldn't leave him to do it on his own, apparently abandoned by his girlfriend only days before.

'All right,' she said. 'I'll stay for the ball, but then I'll go.'

This was one last thing she could do for Philippe. She would stand by his side and help him show the Dowager Blanche what a great prince he could be if given the chance.

And that meant looking the part for once, Caro decided. This was one occasion her vintage clothes just wouldn't do.

There was an extra buzz of excitement about the preparations for the ball that year. Montluce wasn't used to being in the news, and it suddenly found itself at the top of the cool destinations list. Two days before the ball, Philippe's A-list friends began to arrive, exclaiming at the quaintness of the country. The jet set were enchanted to discover that this was one place they couldn't jet to, and that made it all the more charming.

Philippe was torn between pride in his country and a sense of dislocation. These were his friends. He had partied with them, danced with them, skied with them, dined with them... they shouldn't feel like strangers, but they did. Only Jack, fellow black sheep and hellraising companion for many years was the same.

'I like Caro,' he said to Philippe. 'She's not your usual type.'

'No,' said Philippe shortly. He was trying not to think about Caro.

They were having dinner, about twenty of them, and in one

of her mad vintage outfits, Caro was outshone by everyone. She was wearing the same dress she had worn to that dinner with the First Minister, the one she had worn the night they'd first made love, and Philippe's body clenched at the thought of easing that zip down once more.

Beside him, Francesca Allen had an incandescent beauty. She was witty and intelligent and charming, and everything he could want in a princess. He should have been dazzled by her.

But it was Caro who kept catching at the edge of his vision: her smile, the way she waved her hands around, the hair falling out of its clip as usual. She'd said she would be intimidated by his friends, by their confidence and glamour, but Philippe thought she was the most confident of all. She was just herself. Caro didn't have to put on a front because she didn't care. She was going back to Ellerby.

'She's been a refreshing change,' he said to Jack, deliberately careless. 'But she's going home soon. It's been fun,' he said, using Caro's line, 'but it's run its course.'

He shrugged. If Caro was desperate to leave, he wasn't going to beg her to stay. He was a Montvivennes prince, after all, and he had his pride. 'And, let's face it, she's not exactly princess material. I was wondering if Francesca might need consoling after her recent divorce...' Philippe let his voice trail away suggestively.

'Good idea,' said Jack. 'Francesca would put Montluce on the map. She's got that whole Grace Kelly thing going on.' He eyed Francesca critically. 'High maintenance, but worth it if you're in the market for a princess. She'd be perfect, in fact.' His eyes strayed down the table to where Caro was laughing. 'And you won't mind if I chat Caro up then, will you?'

Yes, Philippe *did* mind, but he couldn't say so. He had to watch jealously as Jack manoeuvred himself into a seat next to Caro and set about entertaining her. Jack was all wrong for her, Philippe thought vengefully. He just hoped Caro had the wit to see through him. Jack could be charm itself when he chose.

From the other end of the table, Caro tried not to notice how beautiful Francesca was, or how Philippe rested his arm on the back of her chair, how he smiled at her and leant close to murmur in her ear. There was no point in being jealous. She was the one who'd insisted he'd be good with Francesca, after all.

But it hurt all the same.

Get through the dinner, Caro told herself. Get through the ball. Then she could go home to Ellerby and remember what was really important.

Philippe and his friends were going sailing on the lake the next day. Caro had excused herself, saying vaguely that she had things to do.

It was all very well deciding to ditch her vintage look for something more elegant, but it was so long since she'd bought anything new that Caro didn't know where to start. In the end, she had enlisted the help of Agnès, the most stylish of the maids, who made even the uniform they had to wear look chic. 'I need a dress,' she told Agnès, whose eyes lit up at the challenge of transforming Caro.

Off the peg wouldn't do, Caro gathered. She needed a *real* dress, and Agnès had a cousin whose sister-in-law—or perhaps it was the other way round, Caro got a bit lost in the rapid French—was a Paris-trained designer just striking out on her own.

Ziggi turned out to have bright blue hair, and for a while Caro wondered if she'd made a terrible mistake in putting herself in her hands, but Ziggi made the dress in record time, and when Caro saw herself she was astounded.

'You like?'

'I don't know what to say...' Caro gaped at her reflection.

Somehow those extra pounds had gone, and she looked svelte and stylish.

Agnès beamed. 'You are like a *princesse*!'

'Oh, no,' said Caro involuntarily, backing away from her reflection. She wasn't supposed to be looking like a princess. She was supposed to be looking smart enough not to embarrass Philippe, that was all.

But it was too late now. Ziggi had made the dress for her, and was confidently awaiting a flood of commissions after Caro wore it to the ball.

'It just needs the hair,' said Agnès firmly.

'I'm ready.'

At the sound of Caro's voice, Philippe turned sharply from the window. He'd been pacing around the apartments while she was closeted with one of the maids, getting dressed for the ball. The two of them were starting the evening with a glass of champagne in the Dowager Blanche's apartments, and there would be hell to pay if they were late.

But that wasn't why he was on edge.

It should have been a perfect day. He'd left the red boxes behind and been sailing with his friends. For those few hours, he'd been Philippe again, not a prince. The sun had shone, the company was good. Everyone had had fun. Only he had spent the entire time wondering where Caro was and what she was doing. She'd been evasive when he'd asked her what her plans were. He pictured her at her laptop, planning her return to Ellerby, maybe even arranging to meet Homebody, and he was seized by an irrational fear that she would be gone by the time he got back.

He'd made some excuse to turn the boat back to the palace earlier than planned, only to find the apartment empty. All the wooden-faced footman at the door could tell him was that Caro had gone out with one of the maids and a protection officer. It sounded safe enough, but Philippe couldn't relax until she came back.

Then she'd come in and all the breath had leaked out of him. She'd had her hair cut, and it bounced chic and shiny around her face. The new look flattered the shape of her jaw, Philippe could see that, emphasising her cheekbones and making the navy-blue eyes look huge. She looked slimmer, sexier, infinitely more stylish.

She looked wonderful.

He hated it. He wanted the old Caro back, Caro with the messy hair that irritated him. He wanted to be able to pull the clip from her hair himself and twist his hands in the silky mass. He didn't want this stunning stranger with Caro's eyes and Caro's voice.

'What do you think?' she asked nervously.

Somehow Philippe found his voice. 'I thought you didn't believe in makeovers?'

'The Dowager Blanche is always going on about my hair,' said Caro. 'I thought I'd save myself another lecture.'

She had done it for him, Philippe knew. Now he turned, braced for another new look, and was astounded to find himself hoping against hope that she would be wearing one of her crazy vintage outfits so that he could go back to being exasperated.

He was out of luck. And out of breath.

The last scrap of air in his lungs evaporated at the sight of Caro standing in the doorway. Her dress, cunningly ruched at the bodice to flatter her figure, was red, a rich ruby colour that fell in elegant folds to the floor. Above the striking neckline, her shoulders rose, lush and glowing. She looked stunning.

Philippe cleared his throat. 'You didn't get that at a jumble sale.'

'No.' She moistened her lips. 'I've never worn a dress like this before. Agnès has done my make-up for me, too. I feel...odd.'

'You don't look odd—for once,' Philippe couldn't resist adding.

That sounded more like him. Caro had been feeling stiff and awkward, like a little girl in her mother's shoes. She couldn't interpret the look in Philippe's eyes, but her pulse was thudding and thumping. She was glad to hear the acerbic note in his voice. It made her feel more herself, too, and she relaxed into a smile until Philippe spoiled it by stepping close to her and tilting her chin with one hand.

'You look beautiful,' he said, stroking his thumb along her jaw line, and Caro's smile faded at his expression.

'So do you,' she said unevenly. It was true. He was magnificent in a formal uniform of a dress coat, with gold epaulettes and a sash.

'We're a pair, then,' said Philippe and held out his arm before Caro could reply. 'Shall we go?'

The Dowager's sharp eyes swept over Caro critically as she negotiated a curtsey in her long dress. 'I see you're wearing a decent dress for once,' she said. 'Simple but very effective. Hmm.' Lifting a hand, she summoned her lady-in-waiting. 'Hélène, can you bring me the Hapsburg set?'

Caro glanced at Philippe, who had gone very still. 'What's a set?' she mouthed, but Hélène was already back from the next room and handing the Dowager a flat leather box.

'Ah, yes…' The Dowager Blanche gave a hiss of satisfaction as she lifted out a diamond necklace that made Caro gasp. 'I wore this at my engagement ball. I think it would be appropriate.'

'Oh, no,' stammered Caro. 'I couldn't…'

'Nonsense,' snapped the Dowager, with a return to her old form. 'You'll look naked in a dress like that without any jewellery, and clearly Philippe hasn't bought you anything appropriate. An oversight,' she said, and Caro saw Philippe wince.

'It's far too valuable,' she tried to protest, but the Dowager stopped her with a disdainful look.

'It's just for tonight.' She held out the necklace to Philippe. 'My fingers are stiff. You put it on her.'

'Avec plaisir.'

The diamonds flashed as he draped the necklace around Caro's neck and fastened it with deft fingers. His hands were warm as they lingered on her shoulders.

'Now the earrings.'

Caro put those in herself. She was trembling. It felt all wrong to be wearing these incredible jewels. She wasn't a princess. But the loan of the necklace was a symbol of the Dowager Blanche's approval, another step towards accepting Philippe. How could she possibly say no?

'There.' The Dowager stood back at last. 'You both look most acceptable for once.'

A select group of guests were invited to a formal dinner before the ball. It was served in the state dining room, at a huge table laden with glittering dishes. Caro was relieved to be sitting next to Philippe's friend, Jack, who had twinkling eyes and a merry smile. He oozed charm and flirted as naturally as breathing, but somehow it was impossible to take him seriously.

But then, that was how she had used to think of Philippe, Caro realised.

'Philippe's changed,' said Jack as if reading her mind. 'He's not as restless. Before he'd take off at a moment's notice and the more dangerous the situation, the more he liked it. Just hearing about some of those aid flights made my hair stand on end, I can tell you. It was like he was driven to risk himself as much and as often as he could, and then he'd come back and party, cool as you please.'

He paused at Caro's expression. 'You *do* know about the flights?'

'Yes,' said Caro, 'I know.'

'Thank God for that,' said Jack, relieved. 'He gets very haughty if I mention it sometimes, and just brushes it aside. A lot of celebrities use charity work to raise their own profiles, but Philippe just gets out of his plane and slips away before anyone can thank him.

'I've never spoken to him about it, but a field director for one of the agencies he helps told me once that he finances a lot of the operations he flies too,' Jack confided. 'Of course, the rest of the time he spends amusing himself—skiing, sailing, partying. People think that's all there is to him.'

They both looked up the long table to where Philippe sat, charming Francesca on one side and a haughty countess on the other, and looking every inch the idle aristocrat, as if a thought beyond amusing himself and others had never crossed his mind.

'It's easy to underestimate Philippe,' said Jack.

Caro's eyes rested on Philippe's face, searching for the man she knew was there behind the playboy mask. The man who was teasing and tender, the man who had risked his relationship with his father to do what he thought was right. The man whose smile as he closed the bedroom door made her bones dissolve.

'Yes,' she agreed, 'it is.'

Philippe watched Caro with her head close to Jack's and made himself unclench his fingers from the stem of his glass before he snapped it. They were getting on well.

Too well.

He couldn't blame Jack. Caro was like a flame in that red dress. Warm, vibrant, mesmerising. Philippe was still reeling from the sight of her. Fastening the necklace around her neck,

it had been all he could do to stop himself dragging her back
to his apartments and kissing her senseless.

You can't give me what I really want.

It hasn't been real.

I want to go home and have a real life.

Philippe repeated Caro's words to himself like a mantra.
She was right. He couldn't ask her to live like this all the time.
She would hate it. Tonight she might look the part, but this
wasn't what Caro really wanted. An ordinary life, she'd said.
An ordinary man who would love her and stay with her and
be able to give himself completely.

He couldn't be that man. He couldn't let down his father
and give up his inheritance to live in Ellerby with Caro. What
would he do there? He didn't know how to be ordinary.

And Caro didn't want to be here, although you would never
guess it to watch her chatting to the starry guests in the same
way that she talked to the staff and the stallholders in the
market.

Philippe saw her smile at one of the footmen and hold up a
thumb and finger in a message of approval to the chef, Jean-
Michel. She had spent much of the previous week in the kitchens, discussing the menu with him. Philippe suspected that,
given the choice, Caro would rather be down there in an apron
than up here in the state dining room dripping diamonds.

But she knew instinctively how to circulate amongst the
guests when the ball opened. Between them, they tried to talk
to everybody and make them all feel welcome. The muscles
in Philippe's cheeks ached with smiling as he danced with as
many women as possible.

Just once did he succumb to temptation and dance with
Caro. Holding her close, he thought about how right she felt
in his arms. She fitted him perfectly. Her hair was soft against
his cheek, and he could breathe in her scent.

When had she become so familiar to him? Her face was

hidden against his throat, but he didn't need to see her to picture the precise bold sweep of her brows, the exact curve of her mouth, the stubborn set of her chin.

How was he going to manage without her? In one blinding moment, Philippe knew that he couldn't.

'Don't go back to Ellerby, Caro.' The words came out in a rush, unbidden. 'Stay here with me. Please.'

Caro pulled back slightly to look up into his face. 'Philippe, I can't,' she said, her eyes anguished. 'I don't belong here.'

'You do! Look at you! There isn't a person here who wouldn't believe you were born a princess.'

She smiled shakily at that. 'This is make-believe. Perhaps I can look the part in this dress and your great-aunt's diamonds, but what about tomorrow when I hand back the necklace and am wearing my vintage clothes again? Nobody would be fooled then.'

'The truth is you don't want to belong.' Philippe couldn't keep the bitterness from his voice.

'I *do*.' Caro's throat was tight. 'I want to belong more than anything, but not here.'

The ball was a huge success, everyone said so, but it felt like a nightmare to Caro. Her face felt rigid with smiling as she moved through a blur of colour and chatter and music. She could feel the weight of the necklace around her neck and she touched it constantly, alarmed by the dazzling glitter of it that kept catching at the corner of her eye. It felt all wrong to be wearing something so magnificent. Caro smiled and smiled and felt wretched. Every now and then she would get a glimpse of Philippe through the crowds, tall and strong, effortlessly the centre of attention, and every time her heart would flip over and land with a sickening thud.

There was a prince who had finally found his place.

There was a man who flew through gunfire and tropical storms if help was needed.

There was Philippe, who held her every night and whose body she knew almost as well as her own.

She loved all of them, but none could give her the home and family she craved.

'I'm never going to belong in a royal palace, Philippe, and you know that as well as I do.' Caro could hear her voice beginning to crack, and she swallowed. 'Please don't say any more. It'll only make it harder than it already is.' She drew a steadying breath. 'I'm leaving tomorrow.'

All around them, people danced and laughed. The chandeliers sparkled and the band swung into a new number to cheers.

'So tonight is our last night?' said Philippe.

Caro's throat was so constricted she could barely speak. 'Yes,' she managed. 'This will be the last time.'

Caro woke first the next morning. She lay with her arm over Philippe, feeling it rise and fall in time with his steady breathing. Her face was pressed into the back of his neck, and she could smell the clean, male scent of his skin. She loved him, and her heart was breaking because she knew she had to leave him. It would be better for him and better for her, she knew that. But it hurt so much, she couldn't breathe.

It had been nearly three in the morning before they were able to leave the ball. Together they had walked in silence, not touching, up the sweeping staircase and along the corridor to Philippe's apartments. Even at that time of the night, there was a footman on duty outside to open the door.

Philippe had barely waited until they were inside before he reached for Caro, and she had gone willingly, fiercely. Late as it was, they had made love in a desperate silence. There were no more words to say.

Philippe stirred and rolled over to face Caro. He smiled at her, and her heart contracted. This was the man she would remember always, the man with blurry eyes and rumpled hair and early morning stubble, not the magnificent prince of the night before.

'We need to talk,' she said, and his smile faded as memory returned.

With a sigh, he rolled back to stare up at the ceiling. 'Now?'

'We ought to decide what we're going to tell everyone.' Caro pulled herself up against the pillows, taking the sheet with her. She had to be matter-of-fact about this. It wouldn't help Philippe if she started howling the way she wanted to.

'We can say that you met Francesca at the ball and we've had a big row because I'm jealous,' she suggested. 'You can tell everyone I've stomped off in a huff, if you like.'

Philippe scowled. 'I don't like. No one would believe it, anyway. You're not the stomping type.'

'All right, if anyone asks, we'll just say that we've decided we're incompatible,' said Caro. 'At least it has the advantage of being true, in a way.'

Philippe fixed his eyes on the ceiling. He had woken to find Caro beside him and, for one wonderful moment, everything had felt right. And then she had reminded him that she was leaving and the rawness was back. This was why he had never let a woman close before. He had known that she would just abandon him in the end, the way his mother had done.

Intellectually, Philippe knew that wasn't fair. Intellectually, he knew that if it ever came to choosing a wife, he needed one who was prepared to let him keep his distance. He knew that Caro would be happy in Ellerby. Oh, yes, intellectually, he knew quite well that she was right about everything.

But it still felt all wrong.

'How are you going to get home?' he asked later, when they were up and dressed and sharing an awkward breakfast.

'I booked a flight from Paris yesterday,' Caro told him. 'I'll get a taxi to take me across the border, and then I can get a train.'

'Don't be ridiculous,' Philippe said irritably. 'Yan will take you to Paris. When do you want to go?'

'When I've said my goodbyes,' she said. She got up to wash her coffee mug and plate, a habit she had never been able to shake. 'I'd better take the necklace and earrings back to the Dowager, too,' she said, determinedly bright. 'At least I can make her happy. That's one person who'll be glad to see me go!'

But her audience with the Dowager Blanche didn't go at all as expected. When Caro explained that she would be going home that day, the Dowager stared at her unnervingly.

'For good?'

Caro stretched her mouth into a wide smile. 'Yes.'

'Why?'

'I thought you'd be pleased,' she said involuntarily.

'I asked you why,' said the Dowager in freezing accents and Caro jumped in spite of herself.

'Philippe and I have decided that our relationship isn't going to work.'

'Nonsense!'

'It's not nonsense!' said Caro, forgetting that she wasn't allowed to argue back.

The Dowager actually harrumphed. Caro had never heard anyone do that before in real life. 'I was under the impression that you loved my great-nephew?'

'I do,' said Caro in a low voice, her momentary amusement fading. 'I love him very much but, as you keep reminding me, he's a prince and I'm just a very ordinary girl. It's been fun, but it's time for him to get serious now and find a serious woman who'll be a worthy princess for Montluce. But that won't be Lotty,' she thought she had better add, just in case the Dowager got her hopes up.

'No,' said the Dowager, to Caro's surprise. 'I see that now. Not that Charlotte appears to be in any hurry to come home from wherever she is,' she added querulously, suddenly no different from any other confused and irritable elderly lady.

'She'll be back,' Caro said, trying to comfort her.

She bent to fondle Apollo's ears, feeling ridiculously choked up at the thought of never seeing him again. 'Be a good dog,' she said. 'Work on the stick chasing.'

Straightening, she faced the Dowager, who was looking haughtier than ever, her lips were pressed together in a very thin, very straight line. But her eyes were suspiciously bright and, on an impulse, Caro leant forward and kissed her cheek. 'Goodbye, *Altesse*,' she said.

There were other goodbyes to say. Down in the kitchens, there was a gloomy atmosphere and every maid and footman wanted to shake her hand and say how sorry they were that she was leaving. Agnès cried a little, and Jean-Michel presented her with a collection of his recipes.

And then came the last, and hardest, goodbye.

CHAPTER TEN

'So, you're really going?' said Philippe. Caro's bag was waiting by the door, and she was shrugging on her father's jacket and trying not to cry.

'Yes.' She summoned a smile and squared her shoulders, determined to make it a good farewell. 'This has been one of the best times of my life, Philippe. Thank you for everything, and I…I hope we'll always be friends.'

'I'm going to miss you,' he said as if the words had been wrung out of him.

'I'll miss you too,' said Caro, her voice cracking, and when Philippe opened his arms she went straight into them. He held her very tightly, not speaking, for a long, long moment and Caro's throat was painfully tight. She couldn't have spoken if she had tried.

Eventually, Philippe let out a long breath and let her go. 'Goodbye, Caro,' he said.

'Goodbye.' Eyes blurring with tears, Caro turned for the door, lifted her chin and from somewhere found a smile so that she could leave with her head high.

For the last time, she walked down the sweeping staircase and out past the palace servants who had gathered to wave farewell, keeping her smile in place all the way. Yan was waiting with the black SUV, and he held open the door so that Caro could get into the back. Only then, hidden behind the tinted windows, could she let herself cry at last.

It felt as if she were being torn away like a snail from its shell as Yan drove her back over the hills to the border, and then on the fast road to Paris. When they got to the airport, he drove her right up to the entrance, opened the door and got out her bag for her. She was going to have to get used to opening her own doors from now on, Caro reflected.

She turned to hold out her hand to Yan and thank him. Expecting his usually impassive nod, she was astounded when he shook her hand warmly. 'If there is ever anything I can do for you, *mademoiselle*, you have only to ask,' he said.

It was the first time she had heard him speak.

Caro smiled shakily. 'Just make sure Philippe is safe,' she said.

'I will,' said Yan, and then he got into the car and drove away, back to Montluce, leaving Caro alone outside the terminal building with her tatty bag at her feet, just an ordinary girl once more.

To: caro.cartwright@u2.com
From: charlotte@palaisdemontvivennes.net
Subject: What happened???

Caro, I'm worried. What happened?? I've just rung Grandmère, and she said you'd gone. She's cross with you and cross with Philippe. Then I rang Philippe, and he shut me out. He was talking, but it was like after Etienne died. He was very cool and very polite and somehow not there at all. He just said everything was 'fine', which it obviously isn't. I thought everything was going so well? I thought you and Philippe were friends, but he sounds so distant now, and you're not there. Tell me you're OK, at least.

Lotty xxxxxxxxxxxxxxxxxxxxxx

To: charlotte@palaisdemontvivennes.net
From: caro.cartwright@u2.com
Subject: Re: What happened???
Hi, Lotty

Yes, I'm OK. I've been home a couple of weeks, and I'm starting to remember what real life is like. I'm sorry you've been worried, but Philippe is right, things are fine. I suppose you've guessed by now that we were more than friends. I can tell you that now, but we ended it by mutual agreement. Right from the start, we always knew it couldn't last.

Caro stared at the screen. Her eyes were tight with unshed tears and her throat felt as if a great stone had been lodged in it since that awful day she had said goodbye to Philippe. It had been so easy to tell herself that she understood it was temporary and that she was just making the most of their time together. She *had* known it couldn't last, but how did you stop yourself falling in love?

She had tried so hard to keep those nights separate from the time when she and Philippe were just friends, but it hadn't made any difference. Of course she had fallen in love with him. How could she not?

She missed him. She missed her friend. She missed her lover. She missed the way he smiled at her and the way he rolled his eyes whenever he saw what she was wearing. She missed moving around the kitchen, listening to him talk. She missed lying next to him in the early morning, curled into the hard curve of his body.

Caro went back to her email. She owed Lotty the truth now.

When things aren't so painful, I hope Philippe and I can be friends again, but I don't know. I don't know if I could bear to see him with someone else. He's such a special person, he deserves someone perfect. The thing is, I can't talk about him to anyone except you. To everyone else, he's just a prince from some tiny country nobody had ever heard of until the fuss about the pipeline. They can't see beyond the fairy tale to the man he is, and I can't explain. I guess that goes with the territory when you're royal.

I miss Montluce, Lotty. I miss the people and the lake and the mountains. I even miss your grandmother and Apollo! I miss Philippe most of all. Things may be difficult for him at the moment, but he's found his place in Montluce, and that means more to him than he realises right now. When his father comes home, I think Philippe will be able to build a relationship with him at last, and that's what he needs most of all. I don't fit in with Philippe's life now, and he wouldn't fit in with mine, that's for sure, so I know I've made the right decision, even if it hurts right now.

Caro's mouth trembled. Funny how knowing that you'd made the right decision was no comfort at all. Why did everyone pretend that it helped? It didn't. Nothing helped.

Please don't worry about me, Lotty. I'll be fine. I'm thinking of setting up my own deli and café at last, specialising in produce from Montluce, and have even been to the bank to talk about a business loan. That will be exciting when I can get it up and running. Right now I'm temping again, and there's too much time to think, and to remember. Fortunately my 'celebrity status' was very short-lived and limited to those who read Glitz (not that many in Ellerby, thank goodness!) so I haven't had too many people recognise me. My life in Montluce seems so far away now, anyway. It's taken me a little while to adjust to normal life, but I'm nearly there. I know I need to start meeting men, so I've been looking on right4u.com again. To be honest, I can't imagine falling in love with anyone else right now, but I know I have to get back into it. I'm not expecting to meet someone right away, but I can at least show willing.

Caro stopped typing again. It was hard to explain to Lotty the depression that gripped her every time she looked at her potential matches on the site. They were all perfectly decent men, but none of them were Philippe.

I'm glad you've been in contact with the Dowager Blanche, I think she misses you more than she can say.

The way she missed Philippe. But she wasn't supposed to be thinking about Philippe, Caro reminded herself. Hadn't she decided enough was enough? She was tired of this constant ache for him, the constant looking for him and remembering that he wasn't there.

He wasn't there when someone said something ridiculous, or when she turned to catch his eye, knowing that he would share the joke.

He wasn't there to roll his eyes at her clothes or be rude about her cooking.

He wasn't there when she lay wretched at night, longing and longing to be able to turn and reach for him.

Two weeks passed, then three, and it didn't get any easier, whatever Caro told Lotty. She tortured herself imagining Philippe with Francesca Allen. Was Francesca sitting on the balcony with her feet up on the railings beside Philippe's? Was she waving and accepting posies? Did she spend long, sweet nights in Philippe's bed?

The thought of it was a knife twisting inside Caro, and she flinched at the pain of it. The temptation to email Philippe or to look up events in Montluce on the internet was huge, but she wouldn't let herself give in. She couldn't bear to see pictures of Francesca beside him. Knowing would be worse than imagining, Caro decided.

No, she had to get on with her own life. One evening when Stella was out with a new boyfriend, Caro took a deep breath and logged onto right4u.com. Just to look, she told herself. She would never find the perfect man sitting at home. Her mind veered to Philippe, but she yanked it back. She needed Mr Right, not Prince Right.

She hadn't logged on for a while, so she wasn't expecting any messages, but there were two. Mr Sexy was still hopeful, and there was a new message from Ordinary Guy. Well, that sounded promising.

Ignoring the ache in her heart, Caro clicked on his profile. No photo, but that wasn't unusual. He certainly sounded like a perfect match—over ninety per cent. So she ought to be excited, right? This guy was everything she'd ever wanted: steady job, own house, interested in the same things as her. He'd spent a lot of time overseas, he said, but now he wanted to settle down with the right woman. After years of resisting the idea, he was ready for marriage and a family.

He could even punctuate. His message was brief. *You sound like someone I'd like to get to know. What about meeting up for a drink some time?*

So he didn't sound that romantic or glamorous or exciting, but that was fine by Caro. She had done romance and glamour. This time she needed sensible and ordinary.

Stella frowned when she heard that Caro had agreed to meet him. 'Are you sure you're ready for this?'

'No,' said Caro. 'I'm not sure, but I've got to start some time, Stella. I'm not expecting this guy to be the one, but he sounds nice enough. I'm thinking of this as a practice run.'

But it felt as if there was a great weight on her heart as she got ready to go out that night. On the screen, Ordinary Guy was perfect. She should be more excited at the idea of meeting him, Caro knew, but how could she be excited when he wasn't Philippe, when he wouldn't have Philippe's hands and Philippe's mouth and Philippe's body? When he wouldn't click his tongue against his teeth in exasperation, or draw her to him with a smile that promised deliciously sinful pleasure?

How could he do that, when he was just an ordinary man?

Perhaps it was unfair to waste his time, Caro thought guiltily, but she couldn't spend the rest of her life pining for something that could never be. No, she decided. She would go, she would smile and she would be pleasant. She could always come home after one drink.

It was difficult to care what she looked like. Caro rifled through her wardrobe without interest and finally put on the dress she had worn that first night with Philippe when he had taken her to the Star and Garter. She had been wearing this dress the first time he'd kissed her, Caro remembered. How desperate she had been about George then. Perhaps one day she would be able to look back and marvel that she had felt this wretched about Philippe too.

The steps outside the Town Hall were empty when Caro arrived. She looked at her watch. Seven o'clock, as promised. She would wait ten minutes, she decided, and then she would go.

Hugging the light cardigan around her shoulders, Caro sat

on the top step in the last of the evening sun and let herself miss Philippe. Only for five minutes, she promised herself. Five minutes of remembering the taste of him, the feel of his body, the wicked pleasure of his hands. The laughter in his eyes. How easy it was to be with him, how comfortable to lean against his shoulder and feel that everything was all right as long as he was there.

There was a tight prickling behind Caro's eyes and she squeezed them shut, willing the tears away. Just what she needed on a first date: to be caught crying for another man. She shouldn't do this, shouldn't let the bittersweet memories in. It only made things worse.

Oh, God, someone was coming… Caro heard the footsteps and hastily knuckled the tears from under her eyes. Please, please, please don't let this be Ordinary Guy, she prayed.

'Waiting for someone?'

Caro's eyes flew open at the familiar voice. 'Philippe!'

Her heart was hammering high in her throat as she stared at him, longing to believe that he was real, but hardly daring to. He *looked* real. The saturnine features, the lean, powerfully muscled body, his mouth, his hands…yes, they were all as she remembered. Only the anxiety in the silver eyes was unfamiliar.

'What are you doing here?' she asked rudely, too startled to remember her manners or the fact that he was a prince.

'I've got a date,' said Philippe, sitting down beside her on the step.

'A *date*? In *Ellerby*?' Caro couldn't take it in. It was too incredible to have him there, close enough to touch. She wanted to pat him all over to check that he was real. She wanted to burrow into him and press her face into his throat and hold on to him for ever and ever.

'I'm meeting a princess,' he said. 'Who's expecting a frog.'

Understanding dawned through Caro's haze. 'It was *you*?'

'Meet Ordinary Guy,' said His Serene Highness Prince Philippe Xavier Charles de Montvivennes.

Caro couldn't decide whether to laugh or cry. 'You're not ordinary,' she said. 'You're a prince. That whole profile you wrote was one big fib!'

'It said we were a ninety per cent match for each other,' Philippe reminded her. 'And it wasn't a fib. Every word of that profile was true.'

'The steady job?'

'Well, no job's secure for life nowadays,' he conceded, 'but, barring revolution, being prince in Montluce should be safe enough. My father is back in his own apartments, but he's still resting. We've agreed that I'll take over more of his duties on a permanent basis, so I'd call that a job. And I've got somewhere to live, just like I said on the profile.'

'A palace!'

'Hey, it's a roof over my head.' Philippe's smile faded. 'But that's all it is without you, Caro. It isn't a home. It hasn't been since you left that day. That damn palace, stuffed with paintings and antiques and footmen and it's just been…empty. I hate it without you, Caro,' he said. 'Please come back.'

Caro had begun to tremble. 'Philippe…'

'I know what you're going to say,' he interrupted her before she could go on. 'You want an ordinary life, an ordinary man to share it with. I know that. That's why I let you go.'

He still hadn't made any move to touch her, but sat, like her, with his feet drawn up on the step below and his arms resting on his knees. 'I told myself that you were right, that you would only be happy if you came back here, and that I should look around for someone else, who was comfortable with life in a palace.

'I did try, Caro.' Philippe turned his head to look at her and his silver eyes were so warm Caro marvelled that she could ever have thought of them as cold. 'I took Francesca out to dinner, and tried to imagine her as a princess. And I could do it, no problem. She'd make a great princess…but I couldn't imagine her with *me*.

'That's when I realised that under all the trappings, I *am* just an ordinary guy. I'm like everyone else: muddled, insecure, blaming my parents for my own failures. I'm going to stop doing that now, Caro. I'm grown up, and I can make my own choices and live with the consequences.'

He looked away, across the square, squinting a little in the slanting evening sun.

'I've spent so many years afraid to commit myself to anyone in case they left and I had to *feel* something, and then you did leave, and it did hurt, but I survived. If I hadn't known you, hadn't loved you, I wouldn't have been hurting, sure, but I wouldn't have given up that time for anything, Caro.'

Caro found her voice at last. 'You *love* me?'

'Of course I love you.' Philippe sounded almost impatient as he looked back into her eyes. 'I just didn't dare admit it to myself, or to you.' He took Caro's hand at last. 'You must have known.'

'I thought it was just lust.' Caro's pulse was pounding so hard she was sure the steps must be shaking with it.

'There was a lot of lust,' he agreed.

'Or friendship.'

'That too,' said Philippe, lifting her hand to brush a kiss on her knuckles. 'I missed that, Caro. I've never had a friend like you before. I've never had anyone I could just be myself with. I don't think I knew who "myself" was until you kissed me and turned me into a frog.'

He smiled at her. 'You made me realise that I'd been a frog all along. I didn't lie in that profile. Maybe I do live in a palace and maybe I am a prince, but those are just trappings. Underneath, I want the same things all ordinary guys do. I want someone to come home to at the end of the day. Someone I can talk to, laugh with. Someone I can hold and who'll hold me through bad times and the good. That's ordinary, isn't it?'

Caro's heart was so full it was pressing painfully against her ribs and swelling up to block her throat. 'It's…amazing,' she managed while her fingers twined around his as if they had a mind of their own.

'I want *you*, Caro,' said Philippe, his voice deep and urgent. 'Not just someone. You. I need you there, with me.'

'But what about your father? He'll be so angry. And the Dowager Blanche…they won't let you be ordinary, Philippe.' Caro was struggling to be sensible. In her head, she had been through this so many times. 'It's incredible that you love me,' she made herself say, 'but it doesn't change who I am, and it doesn't change who you are. You're still a prince and I'm never going to make a princess.'

Tenderly, Philippe pushed a curl back from her face. 'You're the only one who thinks so.'

'The Dowager Blanche certainly doesn't think so!'

'Oh, yes, she does. She might not show it, but she likes you. She liked the way you stood up to her. Apollo might have put in a good word too, because she told me that I was a great dolt for letting you go.'

Caro's jaw dropped. *'Really?'*

'Really,' said Philippe with a smile. 'The Montlucians think you'd make a great princess, too. There's an entire country waiting for you to come back, Caro! As for my father, he's just pleased that I'm ready to settle down. Even Yan opened his mouth and wished me luck.'

Caro shook her head to clear her spinning mind, but Philippe misinterpreted the gesture. 'Don't say no!' he said, grabbing her other hand and pulling her round to face him. 'I know how you've always dreamed of an ordinary life, Caro, but why settle for ordinary when what we've got could be *extraordinary*?

'And I don't mean where and how we live,' he went on with an edge of desperation. 'I mean being together, being friends, loving each other and trusting each other and being there for each other. We're so lucky to have found someone we can have that with. *That's* what's extraordinary.'

Caro stared at him. Philippe was right. Was she holding onto one dream because she was scared to reach for a bigger and better one?

'Ordinary Guy sounded so perfect,' she said slowly. 'Exactly the man I'd always wanted.'

'He is perfect,' said Philippe. 'I made damn sure he would be when I wrote that profile. I didn't want to risk you not agreeing to meet me.'

'I still don't understand why you didn't just ring. It would have been much easier.'

'But then you'd have just come out with all that you're-a-prince-I'm-unsuitable stuff and refused to meet me,' he pointed out. 'It was the only way I could think of to talk to you and make you see me not as a prince, but as the ordinary guy you've wanted all along.'

Caro pulled her hand from his to lay her palm against his cheek. 'You did it very well,' she told him. 'I was convinced that I would never find anyone more suitable for me, and yet when I walked down here I was more depressed than I've ever been in my life.'

'*Depressed?*'

A smile trembled on her lips. 'Because I knew that however perfect Ordinary Guy was on paper, I'd already met the perfect man for me, and he wasn't ordinary at all.'

Philippe let out a long breath. 'He wouldn't happen to be a prince, would he?' he asked hopefully, turning his face so that he could press a kiss into her palm.

'He would,' said Caro. 'When you came just now, I was crying. I'd just realised that even though he was nothing like the kind of man I thought I wanted, only he would do.' The blue eyes filled with tears. 'And now you're here, and I'm so happy, I can't believe it...' Her voice broke.

'Caro.' Philippe reached for her then, pushing his hands into her hair and pulling her into him for a long, long, sweet kiss. 'Caro, say you love me,' he mumbled against her temple when he lifted his head at last.

'I love you...I love you...I do,' she stammered, incoherent with happiness.

'Say you'll marry me and be my princess.'

She stilled at that, knowing that this was her last chance to grasp at being sensible. Placing the flat of her hands against his chest, she held herself away from him. 'Are you sure, Philippe?' she said doubtfully. 'I do love you, but we're so different. It won't be easy.'

'No, it won't be,' said Philippe. 'But who wants easy when they can have incredible? Yes, we'll have to work through some tough bits, but won't that be worth it when we see what an amazing life we can build together?'

He drew her back against him. 'Come on, Caro, stop looking for difficulties. Just kiss me again and tell me you'll marry me.'

Caro's eyes were starry with happiness as she wound her arms around his neck. 'All right,' she said obediently. 'I will.'

'Ready?' Lotty smiled as she twitched Caro's train into place. 'How do you feel?'

'I can't believe this is really happening,' Caro confessed. Outside, she could hear the church bells ringing across the wintry city in great, joyous peals. 'I keep thinking I must be dreaming.'

'Then I'm in the same dream,' said Stella, peeking out of the window. 'Have you *seen* how many people there are out there? The entire population of Montluce has come to see you married, Caro!'

'No pressure, then!'

'You'll be fine,' Lotty soothed. 'And you look incredible.'

'Thanks to your grandmother.' Caro smoothed down her dress with unsteady hands. Soon after she'd returned to Montluce, the Dowager had taken her aside and stiffly offered her the dress that she had worn for her own wedding fifty-five years earlier.

'I've observed that you don't wear new clothes,' she had said. 'But of course, if you would prefer a new designer dress, that is entirely up to you.'

But Caro had been thrilled with the dress. It was a dress fit for a princess, with full skirts, a fitted bodice and a spectacular train. Lace covered her arms and the ivory satin was sewn with seed pearls that gleamed and shimmered as she moved. It had had to be let out in places, that was true, but it felt very special to be getting married in the Dowager's dress. Lotty's grandmother had lent her diamond drop earrings, too, and the antique corsage tiara that held the gossamer fine veil in place.

Now it was time to go. Caro was shaking with nerves as she lifted her skirts to walk carefully down the great staircase. Philippe's father was waiting for her at the bottom. He was an austere man, still thin from his treatment, but growing stronger every day. Caro had been pleased to see the wary relationship that was growing between father and son. As she had no father and no close male relatives, the Crown Prince had offered to give her away himself, and now he smiled at the sight of her.

'My son is a lucky man,' he said. 'Come, let us go.'

A big, low limousine with wide windows waited in the courtyard, where what seemed like the entire palace staff had turned out to wish her well for her wedding. They cheered as Caro was helped into the car by a footman, and the train was piled in after her. Then Philippe's father got in beside her.

As the car came out of the gates, another huge cheer went up from the waiting crowds. The flag at the front of the car fluttered as they drove along streets lined with smiling, waving people and the frosty air rang with bells. Caro's throat thickened with nervousness and emotion and she gripped the bouquet of white roses so tightly her knuckles showed white.

A feeling of unreality had her in its grip, and her smile felt as if it had been fixed on her face. This couldn't be real. This couldn't be her, Caro Cartwright, being driven through cheering crowds to marry a prince. Any minute now, she would wake up and find that she had been dreaming.

Then they were at the cathedral, and Lotty and Stella were there to help her out of the car and pull out the train onto the red carpet. The cheers were even louder there. Caro's smile felt more wooden than ever. She wasn't nervous, she realised. She was terrified.

The Crown Prince offered his arm. As they entered the cathedral, the big wooden doors swung shut behind them and the trumpeters in the clerestory struck up.

Caro had an impression of a mass of people, all smiling, all staring at her. She could feel the train dragging behind her, the weight of the tiara on her head, the heavy satin skirts. The aisle seemed to go on for ever, while the music swelled. It had to be a dream.

And then she saw Philippe waiting at the altar. He was dressed in full regalia, with golden epaulettes, medals and a sash across his chest and a sword at his side, but Caro didn't see the uniform. She saw the smile that was just for her and, all at once, the dreamlike feeling vanished, and she forgot the television cameras and the watching congregation. There was just Philippe, waiting for her, and it was real after all.

Theirs might be an extraordinary wedding, but the vows they were making were the same that every couple made, and they were real too.

When it was over, Philippe kissed her there in front of everybody, and they made their way back down the aisle. The bells were pealing and the sun glittered on the snowy rooftops as they emerged from the cathedral to cheers and whistles.

A carriage drawn by six white horses with nodding plumes waited at the bottom of the steps. Philippe and Caro smiled and waved, and then the train had to be negotiated into another vehicle, but at last they were in and they set off through the city streets lined with crowds. Caro's arm was already aching from all the waving.

'You've still got the balcony to go,' murmured Philippe, 'but let's give them something else to cheer about.' And he kissed her thoroughly, to the delight of the cheering, flag-waving crowd.

Caro was flushed and laughing when they got back to the palace. They paused for a moment to wave to the crowds once more before stepping into the cool of the marbled hall out of sight of the cameras. Even then there was no opportunity to be alone. The hall was lined with palace servants, and Caro had her first taste of how her life had changed when she was greeted with smiling bows and curtseys. Laughing, she hooked her train over her arm, and together she and Philippe climbed the staircase she had descended so nervously earlier.

The reception was to be held in the state ballroom. 'Quick,' said Philippe, opening a door to one of the side rooms. 'Before the others get here!' And he pulled Caro inside and kissed her against the door until they heard the unmistakable sounds of everyone else arriving.

'I suppose we can't skip out on our own wedding,' he said regretfully, letting her go at last.

'Careful of the Dowager's dress!' Blushing, Caro patted her hair and wondered if it was going to be obvious to everyone what they'd been doing. She hadn't put up much of a protest. 'Now I need to redo my make-up. Agnès will kill me!'

'She can't be cross with you now. You're a princess,' said Philippe. 'Besides, you look beautiful.' He studied her critically for a moment before straightening her tiara. 'There, you're ready to go again.'

He stayed by her side as they moved through the throng of guests. Caro smiled and kissed endless cheeks, but all the time she was acutely aware of Philippe, of his touch on her back, his hand on hers, his arm at her waist.

Outside, she was vaguely aware of chanting, but it was only when the doors were thrown open and she and Philippe stepped out onto the balcony to a roar of approval that Caro realised how many people were gathered outside waiting to see them. The sheer number and noise of the crowd made her gasp.

The view down over the mass of fluttering Montluce flags was dizzying.

'Philippe,' she said, turning to him with her heart in her eyes. 'I've just had a revelation.'

'I hope that it's how much you love me?' said Philippe, waving at the crowds.

Caro slid her hand into his. 'All those years I longed for a place to belong, and I never dreamt I would feel that I did on a palace balcony! But it isn't about a place,' she realised wonderingly. 'It's about being with you.'

'Quite right.' Philippe grinned and pulled her into him for a kiss while the crowd roared and cheered and whistled and waved flags below. '*This* is where you belong, Caro. Right here in my arms.'

'I've found my frog at last,' she sighed happily.

Philippe watched her turn to wave and smile at her new subjects, and he held her hand tight in his. 'And I've found my princess,' he said.

THE PRINCE'S
CINDERELLA BRIDE

CHRISTINE RIMMER

For MSR, always

Chapter One

Maximilian Bravo-Calabretti, heir to the Montedoran throne, stepped out from behind a low cluster of fan palms and directly into the path of the woman who'd hardly spoken to him since New Year's.

Lani Vasquez let out a small squeak of surprise and jumped back. She almost dropped the book she was carrying. "Your Highness." She shot him a glare. "You scared me."

The high garden path that wove along the cliffside was deserted. It was just the two of them at the moment. But anyone might come wandering toward them—one of the gardeners looking for a hedge to trim, or a palace guest out for a brisk early-morning stroll. Max wanted privacy for this. He grabbed her hand, which caused her to let out another sharp cry.

"Come with me," he commanded and pulled her forward on the path. "This way."

She dug in her heels. "No, Max. Really."

He turned to face her. She flashed him a look of defiance. Still, he refused to let go of her soft little hand. Her sweet face was flushed, her thick midnight hair loose on her shoulders, tangled by the wind off the sea far below.

He wanted to haul her close and kiss her. But he needed to get her to talk to him first. "You've been avoiding me."

Her mouth quivered in the most tempting way. "Yes, I have. Let go of my hand."

"We have to talk."

"No, we don't."

"We do."

"It was a mistake," she insisted in a ragged little whisper.

"Don't say that."

"But it's the truth. It was a mistake and there's no point in going into it. I don't want to talk about it."

And he didn't want to hear that. "Just come with me, that's all I'm asking."

"I'm expected at the villa." She worked as a nanny for his brother Rule and his wife. They owned a villa in the nearby ward of Fontebleu. "I have to go now."

"This won't take long." He turned and started forward again.

She let out a low, unhappy sound, and for a moment, he was certain she would simply refuse to budge.

But then she gave in and followed. He kept hold of her hand and pulled her along. Not glancing back, he cut off the overlook path and onto the rocky hillside, finding a second path that twisted up and around, through a copse of olive trees and on to where the land flattened out to a more cultivated formal garden.

High, green hedges surrounded them, and they walked on thick grass. The grass gave way to a rose garden. Now, in February, the buds were only just forming on the thorny stems. Beyond the budding roses, he took a curving stone path beneath a series of trellises. Still she followed, saying nothing, occasionally dragging her feet a little to let him know she was far from willing.

They came to a gate in a stone wall. He pushed through

the gate and held it for her, with his free hand, going through after her and then closing it behind them.

Across another swath of lawn, between a pair of silk floss trees, the stone cottage waited. He led her on, across the grass, along the stepping-stones that stopped at the rough wood trellis twined with bare, twisted grapevines. The trellis shaded the rough wood door.

He pushed the door open, let go of her hand and ushered her in first. With a quick, suspicious glance at him, she went.

Two windows let in enough light to see by. Sheets covered the plain furniture. It took him only a moment to whip off the coverings and drop them to the rough wooden floor, revealing a scarred table with four chairs, a sofa, a couple of side tables and two floral-patterned wing chairs. The rudimentary kitchen took up one wall. Stairs climbed another wall to the sleeping area above.

"Have a seat," he offered.

She pressed her lips together, shook her head and remained standing by the door, clutching her book tightly between her two hands. "What is this place?"

"It's just a gardener's cottage. No one's using it now. Sit down."

She still refused to budge. "What *are* you doing, Your High—?"

"Certainly we're past that."

For a moment, she said nothing, only stared at him, her dark eyes huge in the soft oval of her face. He wanted to reach out and gather her close and soothe all her troubles away. But everything about her warned, *Don't touch me.*

She let out a breath and her slim shoulders drooped. "Max. Really. Can't you just admit it? We both know it was a mistake."

"Wrong." He moved a step closer. She stiffened a little,

but she didn't back away. He whispered, "It was beautiful. Perfect. At the time, you thought so, too—or so you said."

"Oh, Max. Why can't I get through to you?" She turned from him and went to one of the windows.

He stared at her back, at her hair curling, black as a crow's wing, on her shoulders. And he remembered…

It was New Year's Eve. At the Sovereign's New Year's Ball.

He asked her to dance and as soon as he had her in his arms, he only wanted to keep her there. So he did. When the first dance ended, he held her lightly until the music started up again. He kept her with him through five dances. Each dance went by in the blink of an eye. He would have gone on dancing with her, every dance, until the band stopped playing. But people noticed and she didn't like it.

By the fifth dance she was gazing up at him much too solemnly. And when that dance ended, she said, "I think it's time for me to say good-night."

He'd watched her leave the ballroom and couldn't bear to see her go. So he followed her. They'd shared their first kiss in the shadows of the long gallery outside the ballroom, beneath the frescoes depicting martyred saints and muscular angels. She'd pulled away sharply, dark fire in her eyes.

So he kissed her again.

And a third time, as well. By some heady miracle, with those kisses, he'd secured her surrender. Lani led him up to her small room in the deserted apartment of his brother Rule's family. When he left her hours later, she was smiling and tender and she'd kissed him good-night.

But ever since then, for five endless weeks, she'd barely spoken to him.

"Lani. Look at me.…"

She whirled and faced him again. Her mouth had softened and so had her eyes. Had she been remembering that night, too? For a moment, he almost dared to hope she would melt into his arms.

But then she drew herself up again. "It was a mistake," she insisted for the fourth time. "And this is impossible. I have to go." She headed for the door.

He accused, "Coward."

The single word seemed to hit her between the shoulder blades. She let go of the doorknob, dropped her book to the rough entry table and turned once more to meet his waiting eyes. "Please. It was just one of those things that happen even though it shouldn't have. We got carried away...."

Carried away? Maybe. "I have no regrets. Not a one." He was *glad* it had happened, and on New Year's Eve, too. To him it had seemed the ideal way to ring in a whole new year—and right then, a dangerous thought occurred to him. God. Was there a baby? If so, he needed to know. "We should have been more careful, though. You're right. Is that why you keep running away from me? Are you—?"

"No," she cut in before he could even get the question out. "We were lucky. You can stop worrying."

"I miss you," he said, before she could start in again about how she had to go. "I miss our discussions, our talks in the library. Lani, we have so much in common. We've been good friends."

"Oh, please," she scoffed. But there was real pain in her eyes, in the tightness of her mouth. "You and I were never friends." All at once, her eyes were too bright. She blinked away tears.

He wanted only to comfort her. "Lani..." He took a step toward her.

But she put up a hand and he stopped in midstride. "We've been *friendly*," she corrected. "But to be more is beyond inappropriate. I work for your brother and sister-in-law. I'm the *nanny*. I'm supposed to set an example and show good judgment." She swallowed. Hard. "I never should have let it happen."

"*Will* you stop saying that it shouldn't have happened?"

"But it *shouldn't* have."

"Excuse me. We are two single adults and we have every right to—"

"Stop." She backed a step toward the door. "I want you to listen, Max. It can't happen again. I won't let it." Her eyes were dry now. And way too determined.

He opened his mouth to insist that *it* most certainly *would* happen again. But where would such insistence get him? Except to send her whirling, flinging the door wide, racing off down the walk and out the gate.

He didn't want that. And arguing with her over whether that unforgettable night should or should not have happened was getting him nowhere, anyway. They didn't need arguing. They needed to reestablish their earlier ease with each other.

So in the end he answered mildly, "Of course you're right. It won't happen again."

She blinked in surprise. "I don't... What are you saying?"

"I'll make an agreement with you."

She narrowed her eyes and peered at him sideways. "I don't want to bargain about this."

"How can you know that? You haven't heard my offer yet."

"Offer?" She sneered the word. He held his silence as she nibbled her lower lip in indecision. Finally, she threw up both hands. "Oh, all right. *What,* then? What is your offer?"

"I'll promise not to try to seduce you," he suggested with what he hoped was just the right touch of wry humor, "and you'll stop avoiding me. We can be..." He hesitated, remembering how she'd scoffed when he'd called them friends. "...what we used to be."

She aimed a put-upon look at the single beam in the rough-textured ceiling. "Oh, come on. Seriously? That never works."

"I disagree." Light. Reasonable. Yes, just the right tone. "And it's unfair to generalize. I think it can work. We can *make* it work." Until she admitted that being what they used to be wasn't nearly enough. Then they could make it work in much more satisfying ways.

She hovered there in front of the door, staring at him, unblinking. He stared right back, trying to look calm and reasonable and completely relaxed when in reality his gut was clenched tight and he'd begun to lose hope he would ever get through to her.

But then, at last, she dropped her gaze. She went to the rustic dinner table, where she ran her finger along the back of one of the plain straight chairs. He watched her, remembering the cool, thrilling wonder of her fingers on his naked skin.

Finally, she slanted him a look. "I love Montedoro. I came here with Sydney thinking I would stay for six months or a year, just for the life experience." Sydney was his brother Rule's wife and Lani's closest friend. "Two years later, I'm still here. I have this feeling, and it's such a pow-erful feeling, that Montedoro is my real home and I was only waiting to come here, to find the place I was meant to be. I want to write a hundred novels, all of them set right here. I never want to leave."

"I know. And no one wants you to leave."

"Oh, Max. What I'm trying to say is, as much as I love it here, as much as I want to stay forever, if you or any of your family wanted me gone, my visa would be revoked in a heartbeat."

"How many times do I have to tell you? No one wants you to go."

"Don't pretend you don't get it. Love affairs end. And when they end, things can get awkward. You're a good man, a kind man. But you're also the heir to the throne. I'm the help. It's...well, it's hardly a relationship of equals."

Why did she insist on seeing trouble where there was none? "You're wrong. We *are* equals in all the ways that really matter."

She made a humphing sound. "Thanks for that, Your Highness."

He wanted to grab her and shake her. But somehow he managed to remain still, to speak with calm reproach. "You know me better than that."

She shook her head. "Don't you get it? We went too far. We need to back off and let it go."

Let it go—let *her* go? Never. "Listen. I'm going to say it again. This time I'm hopeful you'll actually hear me. I would never expect you to leave Montedoro, no matter what happened. You have my sworn word on that. The last thing I would ever want is to make things difficult for you."

Heat flared in her eyes again. "But that's exactly what you've done—what you *are* doing right now."

"Forgive me." He said it evenly, holding her dark gaze.

Another silence ensued. An endless one.

And then, at last, she spoke again, her head drooping, her shining, softly curling hair swinging out to hide her flushed cheeks. "I hate this."

"So do I."

She lifted her head and stared at him, emotions chasing themselves across her sweet face: misery, exasperation, frustration, sorrow. After a moment she confessed, "All right. It's true that I miss...having you to talk to."

Progress. His heart slammed against his rib cage.

She added, "And I adore Nick and Constance." His son, Nicholas, was eight. Connie was six. Lani was good friends with Gerta, Nick and Connie's nanny. Rule's children and his often played together. "I..." She peered at him so closely, her expression disbelieving. "Do you honestly think we could do that, be...friendly again?"

"I know we could."

"Just that and only that." Doubt shadowed her eyes. "Friendly. Nothing more."

"Only that," he vowed, silently adding, *Until you realize you want more as much as I do.*

She sighed. "I... Well, I *would* like to be on good terms with you."

Light, he reminded himself as his pulse ratcheted higher. *Keep it light.* "All right, then. We are...as we were." He dared to hold out his hand to her.

She frowned. He waited, arm outstretched, arching a brow, trying to appear hopeful and harmless. Her gaze darted from his face to his offered hand, and back to his face again. Just when he was certain he would have to drop his hand, she left the table and came and took it. His fingers closed over hers. He reveled in the thrill that shivered up his arm at her touch.

Too soon, she eased her hand free and snatched up her book. "Now, will you let me go?"

No. He cast about for a way to keep her there. If she wouldn't let him kiss her or hold her or smooth her shining hair, all right. He accepted that. But couldn't they at least talk for a while the way they used to do?

"Max?" A slight frown creased her brow.

He was fresh out of new tactics and had no clue how to get her to let down her guard. Plus he had a very strong feeling that he'd pushed her as far as she would go for now. This was looking to be an extended campaign. He didn't like that, but if it was the only way to finally reach her, so be it. "I'll be seeing you in the library—where you will no longer scuttle away every time I get near you."

A hint of the old humor flashed in her eyes. "I never scuttle."

"Scamper? Dart? Dash?"

"Stop it." Her mouth twitched. A good sign, he told himself.

"Promise me you won't run off the next time we meet."

The spark of humor winked out. "I just don't like this."

"You've already said that. I'm going to show you there's nothing to be afraid of. Do we have an understanding?"

"Oh, Max…"

"Say yes."

And finally, she gave in and said the words he needed to hear. "Yes. I'll, um, look forward to seeing you."

He didn't believe her. How could he believe her when she sounded so grim, when that mouth he wanted beneath his own was twisted with resignation? He didn't believe her, and he almost wished he could give her what she said she wanted, let her go, say goodbye. He almost wished he could *not* care.

But he'd had years of not caring—long, empty years when he'd told himself that not caring was for the best.

And then the small, dark-haired woman in front of him changed everything.

She turned for the door.

He was out of ways to keep her there, and he needed to accept that. "Lani, wait…"

She stopped, shoulders tensing, head slightly bowed. "What now?" But she didn't turn back to him.

"Let me." He eased around her and pulled the door wide. She nodded, barely glancing at him, and went through, passing beneath the rough-hewn trellis into the cool winter sunlight. He lingered in the open doorway, watching her as she walked away from him.

Chapter Two

"What is going on in that head of yours?" Sydney O'Shea Bravo-Calabretti, formerly kick-ass corporate lawyer and currently Princess of Montedoro, demanded. "Something's bugging you." The women sat in kid-size chairs at the round table in the playroom of the villa Sydney and Rule had bought and remodeled shortly after their marriage two years before.

Lani, holding Sydney's one-year-old, Ellie, kissed the little one's silky strawberry curls and lied without shame. "Nothing's bugging me. Not a thing."

"Yes, there is. You've got this weird, worried, faraway look in your eye."

Okay, yeah. Yesterday's confrontation with Max in the little stone house had seriously unnerved her. She'd thought about little else since then. She'd told no one what had happened on New Year's, not even Sydney. And she never would. But she had to give Syd *something,* some reason she might be distracted—anything but the truth that, while Sydney and Rule and the kids were here at the family's villa, Lani had led His Highness up to her room at the palace and done any number of un-nannylike things to his magnificent body.

Limply, she offered, "Well, the current book is giving me

fits." That should fly. She was in the middle of writing the final book in a trilogy of historical novels set in Montedoro. Syd had been her best friend for seven years and knew that she could get pretty stressed out while struggling with the middle of a book where the story had a tendency to drag.

Syd was so not buying. "The current book is *always* giving you fits. There's something else."

Crap. Lani frowned and pretended to think it over for a minute. "No, really. It's the book. That's all. There's nothing else."

"Yolanda Vasquez, you are lying through your teeth."

So much for the sagging-middle excuse. What to try next?

No way was Lani busting herself. Syd had her back, always. But it was just too tacky to get into, the nanny-slash-wannabe-writer getting naked at New Year's with the widowed heir to the throne—whom the whole world knew was still hopelessly in love with his lost wife. *"Lying through your teeth,"* she echoed brightly. "What does that mean, really? Some expressions are not only overused, they make no real sense. I mean, everything we say, we say through our teeth, right? I mean, unless we *have* no teeth."

Syd didn't even crack a smile. "You think you're distracting me from asking what's up with you. You're not."

"Nani, Nani…" Ellie squirmed around until she was facing Lani. Then she reached up her plump right hand and tried to stick her fingers into Lani's mouth.

Lani gummed them. "Mmm. Yummy, tasty little fingers…" Ellie giggled and bounced up and down. Lani kissed her again, that time on her button of a nose, after which she started squirming again and Lani hoisted her high. Ellie laughed in delight as Lani swung her to the floor.

The little sweetheart was only thirteen months and already walking. For a moment, she wobbled, steadying herself on her fat little feet. And then she toddled to her brother's open toy box and started rooting around in it.

Syd's phone chirped. A text. She took it out and read the message. "Rule. He won't be home till after seven." She started composing a reply. Lani breathed a cautious sigh of relief that the subject of what could be bothering her was closed.

Over at the toy box, Ellie pulled out a soft green rubber turtle, which she carried across the playroom to four-year-old Trevor, who sat quietly building a slightly tilted Lego tower.

"Turt," she said, beaming proudly, and held it out to him as Syd chuckled and texted.

Trev gave Ellie his usual so-patient big-brother look, took the toy from her and set it down on his other side. Ellie frowned and toddled carefully around to reach the turtle again. She bent with great concentration and picked it up. "Tev," she said.

Trevor went on building his tower.

Sydney put her phone down. "So you're *not* going to tell me?"

Resigned to continued denials, Lani dished out yet another lame evasion. "Syd, I promise you, there's nothing to tell." Were her pants on fire? They ought to be.

And right then, before Sydney could say anything else, Ellie cheerfully bopped Trev on the head with the rubber turtle—not hard enough to hurt, but hard enough to get his full attention.

Trev scowled. "No hitting," he said, and gave her a light shove.

She let out a cry as her baby legs collapsed and she landed, plop, on her butt. The impact caused Trevor's shaky tower to collapse to the playroom floor.

Trev protested, "Lani! Mom! Ellie is being *rude!*"

Ellie promptly burst into tears.

Both women got up and went over to sort out the conflict. There were hugs and kisses for Ellie and a reminder to Trev that his sister was only one year old and he should be gentle with her.

Trev apologized. "I'm sorry, Ellie."

And Ellie sniffed. "Tev. Sor-sor." She sighed and laid her bright head on Sydney's shoulder.

Then Sydney's phone rang. She passed Ellie to Lani and took the call, after which she had to go and attend a meeting of one of her international legal aid groups. Lani was left to put the kids down for their nap.

She felt guilty and grateful simultaneously. Once again, she'd escaped having to tell Sydney that she'd had sex with Max on New Year's Eve.

At the muffled creak of one of the tall, carved library doors, Lani glanced up from her laptop.

Max.

He wore a soft white crewneck sweater and gray slacks, and his wonderfully unruly hair shone chestnut brown in the glow from the milk-glass chandeliers above. His iron-blue eyes were on her, and her heart was galloping so fast she could hardly catch her breath.

He'd said he wanted them to be as they used to be.

Impossible. Who did he think he was kidding? There was no going back to the way it had been before. And the more she thought about it—which was all the time since their conversation in the gardener's cottage—the more she was certain he knew that they couldn't go back.

And she would bet that was fine with him. Because he didn't *want* to go back. He wanted to be her lover, wanted more of the heat and wonder of New Year's Eve.

And okay, she wanted that, too. And she knew it would

be fabulous, perfect, beautiful. For as long as it lasted. Until things went wrong.

Because, as she'd tried so very hard to get him to see, love affairs ended. And there were too many ways it all could go bad, too large of a likelihood she'd be put on a plane back to Texas. Yes, all right. It might end amicably. But it also might not. And she wasn't willing to risk finding out which of the two it would be.

She stared in those beautiful eyes of his and thought that she ought to confront him for being a big, fat liar, for saying how he missed her friendship when he really only wanted to get back in bed with her.

But then, who was she to get all up in anyone's face about lying? She'd yet to tell Syd the truth. And she wanted to be Max's lover as much as he wanted to be hers.

However, she wanted the life she had planned for herself more. Risking all of her dreams on a love affair? She'd tried that once. It hadn't ended well.

He gave her a slow nod. "Lani." A shiver went through her—just from the sound of her name in his mouth.

"Hi, Max," she chirped way too brightly.

"Go on, do your work. I'm not here to distract you."

Liar. "Great." She flashed him a smile as bright and fake as her tone and turned her gaze back to her laptop.

He walked by her table on his way to the stairs that led to the upper level. She stared a hole in her laptop screen and saw him pass as a blur of movement, his footfalls hushed on the inlaid floor. He mounted the stairs, his back to her. The temptation was too great. She watched him go up.

At the top, he disappeared from sight and she heard another door open, no doubt to one of the locked rooms, the vaults where the rarest books and documents were kept. She wasn't allowed into any of those special rooms without the watchful company of the ancient scholar who acted as palace librarian or one of his two dedicated assistants.

In fact, she wouldn't be allowed into the library at all at eight o'clock at night if it wasn't for Max.

A year ago, he'd presented her with her own key to the ornate, book-lined, two-story main room. To her, it was a gift beyond price. Now, whenever she wanted to go there, anytime of day or night, she could let herself in and be surrounded by beautiful old books, by a stunning array of original materials for her research.

Library hours were limited and pretty much coincided with the hours when she needed to be with Trev and Ellie. However, most days from about 5:00 p.m. on, Rule and Sydney enjoyed time alone with each other and their children—usually at their villa. They welcomed Lani as part of the family if she wanted to stay on in the evening, but they had no problem if she took most nights off to work on her latest book.

With the key, she could spend as many evening hours as she pleased at the library. And later, at bedtime, her room in the family's palace apartment was right there waiting. Then, early in the morning, it was only a brisk walk along landscaped garden paths down Cap Royale, the rocky hill on which the palace stood, to Fontebleu and the villa.

Pure heaven: the laws, culture and history of Montedoro at her fingertips in the lovely, silent library with its enormous mahogany reading tables and carved, velvet-upholstered chairs. Yes, there were some language issues for her. Much of the original material was in French or Spanish. The French, she managed all right with the aid of her rusty college French and a couple of French/English dictionaries. She knew a little Spanish, but not as much as she probably should, given her Latino heritage. Max, however, spoke and read Spanish fluently and was always happy to translate for her, so the Spanish texts were completely accessible to her, too. Until New Year's, anyway.

It had worked out so perfectly. Lani stayed at the palace several nights a week. She took her laptop and worked for hours. No one disturbed her in the library, not in the evening.

No one but Max—though he didn't really disturb her. He came to the library at night to work, too. An internationally respected scholar and expert on all things Montedoran, he'd written a book about the special, centuries-long relationship between Montedoro and her "big sister," France. He'd also penned any number of articles on various points of Montedoran law and history. And he traveled several times a year to speak at colleges, events and consortia around the world.

Before New Year's, when he would join her in the library, they would sit in companionable silence as she wrote and he checked his sources or typed notes for an upcoming paper or speech. He'd always shown respect for her writing time, and she appreciated his thoughtfulness.

Sometimes, alone together in the quiet, they would put their work aside and talk. And not only in the library. Often when they met in the gardens or at some event or other, they might talk for hours. They had the same interests— writing and history and anything to do with Montedoro.

They'd shared a special kind of friendship.

Until New Year's. Until she finally had to admit that she'd done it again: gotten in too deep with the wrong guy when she needed to be concentrating on the goals she'd set for herself, the goals that she never quite seemed to reach, no matter how hard she worked.

Right now, she should get up and leave—and she would, if only she hadn't foolishly agreed that they could go back to the way they were before.

Right. As if that was even possible.

But still. She'd said she would try. And the hopeless romantic idiot within her wanted at the very least to remain friendly with him, to *be* his friend, which she had been before New Year's, in spite of her denials the other day.

So she stayed in her seat, laptop open in front of her.

A full ten minutes passed before he reappeared on the stairs—ten minutes during which she did nothing but stare at the cursor on her screen and listen for the sound of his footsteps above and call herself five thousand kinds of stupid. When he finally did come down, he was carrying a stack of folders and books.

She waited for him to engage her in some way, her teeth hurting she was clenching them so hard. But he only took a chair across and down from her, gave her another perfectly easy, friendly nod and bent his gorgeous head over the old books and papers.

Well, okay. Apparently, he *was* just there to work.

Which was great. Fabulous. She put her hands on her keyboard and her focus on the screen.

Nothing happened. Her mind was a sloppy soup, a hot mess of annoyance, frustration and forbidden longing. She yearned to jump up and get out of there.

But something—her pride or her promise to him yesterday, maybe—kept her sitting there, staring blankly at her own words, which right then might have been hieroglyphics for all the sense they made to her.

Eventually, she managed to type a sentence. And then another. The writing felt stiff and unnatural. But sometimes you had to write through a distraction. Even a really big distraction, like a certain six-foot-plus hunk of regal manliness sitting across and down from you.

For two full hours, she sat there. So did he, tapping away on a tablet computer, poring over the materials he'd brought down from upstairs. She sat there and she wrote.

It was all just garbage she'd end up deleting, but so what? They were being as they used to be, sitting in silence, working in the library.

Except that it was nothing like it used to be. Not to her, anyway. To her, the air felt electrically charged. Her tummy was one big knot, and the words she was writing made no sense at all.

At ten after ten, she decided she'd sat there writing meaningless drivel and pretending there was nothing wrong for long enough. She closed her laptop, gathered up her stuff and rose.

He glanced up then. "Leaving?"

She hit him with another big, fake smile. "Yeah." She hooked her purse on her shoulder and picked up her laptop. "Good night."

"Good night, Lani." He bent his head to his notes again.

And somehow, she couldn't move. She stood there like a complete fool, staring at his shining, thick hair, at his impossibly broad shoulders to which his soft white sweater clung so lovingly. She wanted to drop back into her chair and ask him about his day, to tell him the real truth—that she missed him in the deepest, most elemental part of herself. That she wished things were different, but she was not a good choice for him as a friend or a lover or anything else, and he ought to know that....

He glanced up a second time. "What is it?" he asked. Gently. Coaxingly.

"Nothing," she lied yet again.

He began closing books and stacking papers. "I need to take everything back upstairs. Only a minute, and I'll walk you out."

"No, really. It's fine, I—"

He stopped and pinned her with a look. "Wait. Please."

The problem was, in spite of everything—all she could

lose, all the ways it wasn't going to work—she *wanted* to wait for him. She *wanted* to be his friend again.

And more. So much more...

"Fine," she said tightly.

He tipped his head sideways. "You won't run out on me?"

She pressed her lips together and shook her head while a frantic voice in her mind screamed, *You idiot, what's wrong with you? Get out and get out now.* "I'll be right here."

He gathered the materials into his big arms and turned for the stairs. She stood rooted to the spot as he went up, knowing she ought to just duck out while he wasn't looking—but somehow unable to budge.

He came back down again and picked up his tablet. "All right. Let's go."

A few minutes later, along a wide, marble-floored corridor on the way to Rule and Sydney's apartment, he stopped at a gilt-trimmed blue door.

She frowned at him. "What's this?"

He clasped the ornate gold latch and pushed the door inward. On the other side, dimly, she saw a sitting room. "An empty suite," he said. "Come inside with me."

She moved back a step. "Bad idea."

He held her gaze, levelly. "A few private minutes together in a neutral setting. We'll talk, that's all."

"Talk." She said the word with complete disbelief.

"And *only* talk," he insisted. He sounded sincere.

And she was tired of resisting, fighting not only him, but also herself. She *wanted* to go in that room with him. It was hopeless. Every minute she was near him only made her want to steal one minute more.

She let him usher her in.

He turned on a lamp. She sat on a velvet sofa and he took a floral-patterned armchair.

"All right," she said. "Talk about what?"

"Why making love with me on New Year's Eve has upset you so much. To me, it was exactly right, a natural step. The *next* step for us. I don't understand why you can't see that."

She stared at him and said nothing. The truth was too dangerous.

He watched her face as though memorizing it. "I miss those black-rimmed glasses you used to wear. They made you look so serious and studious."

She'd had laser surgery six months before. "Life is easier without them in a whole lot of ways."

"Still, they were charming."

She almost messed up and gave him a real smile. But not quite. "You dragged me in here to talk about how you miss my glasses?"

He set his tablet on the low table between them. "Put down your laptop."

She had it clutched to her chest with both hands. It was comforting, actually. Like a shield against doing what she really wanted and getting too close to him. But fine. She set it down—and felt suddenly naked. "This is ridiculous."

"I've been thinking it over," he said as though she hadn't spoken, a thoughtful frown carving twin lines between his straight, thick brows.

"Max. Why are we doing this? There's just no point."

He shrugged. "Of course there's a point. You. Me. That something special between us."

"You still love your wife," she accused. And yeah, it was a cheap shot, the kind of thing a jealous girlfriend looking for promises of forever might be worried about. Lani was not looking for promises of any kind, no way.

He answered without heat. "My wife is gone. It's almost four years now. This is about you and me."

"See?" she taunted, childishly. Jealously. "You're not denying that you're still in love with her. She's still the one who's in your heart."

Something happened in his wonderful face then. Some kind of withdrawal. But then, in an instant, he was fully engaged again. "This is not about Sophia. And we both know that. You're just blowing smoke."

Busted. "Can't you just...? I mean, there have to be any number of women you could have sex with, be *friends* with, any number of women who would jump at the chance to get something going with you."

His mouth twitched. What? He thought this was funny? "Any number of women simply won't do. I want only one, Lani. I want only you."

Okay. Crap. That sounded good. Really, really good. She made herself glare at him. "You're working me. I know what you're doing."

He sat there so calmly, looking every inch the prince he was, all square-jawed and achingly handsome and good-hearted and pulled-together. And sincere and fair. And way, way too hot. "If working you is telling you the truth, then yes. I am shamelessly working you. I waited five endless weeks for you to come to me again, to tell me whatever it is that's keeping you away from me. It was too long. So I took action. I'm not giving up. I'm not. And if you could only be honest, I think you would admit that you don't *want* me to give up."

Why did he have to know that? It wasn't fair. And she needed, desperately, to get out of there. She grabbed her laptop and popped to her feet. "I need to go."

He shifted, but he didn't rise. He stared up the length of

her and straight into her eyes. "No, Lani. You need to stay. You need to *talk* to me."

Talk to him. Oh, no. Talking to him seemed only to get her in deeper, which was not what she wanted.

Except for when it was *exactly* what she wanted.

He arched a brow and asked so calmly, "Won't you please sit back down?"

She shut her eyes tight, drew in a slow, painful breath—and sat. "I'm not…ready for any of this with you, Max."

He reached out and took her laptop from her and carefully set it back on the low table. "Not ready, how?"

Her arms felt too empty. She wrapped them around herself. "It's all too much, too…consuming, you know? Too overwhelming. And what about the children?" she demanded.

He only asked, "What about them?"

"They have a right to a nanny who isn't doing their daddy."

"And they have just such a nanny. Her name is Gerta—and in any case, you're *not* doing me, not anymore."

She let out a hard, frustrated breath. "I'm just saying it's impossible. It's too much."

He kept right on pushing her. "What you feel for me, you mean?"

She nodded, frantically. "Yes. That. Exactly that."

"So…I'm too much?" His voice poured through her, deep and sweet and way too tempting. It wasn't *fair,* that he should be able to do this to her. It made keeping her distance from him way too hard.

She bobbed her head some more and babbled, "Yes. That's right. Too much."

"*I'm* too much and Michael Cort wasn't enough?"

Michael. Oh, *why* had she told him about Michael? She'd dated the software designer until she saw Sydney with Rule and realized that what she had with Michael was…exactly what Max had just said it was: not enough. "You and Michael are two different things," she insisted, and hated how wimpy and weak she sounded.

"But we're the same in the sense that Michael Cort and I are both men you decided not to see anymore."

"Uh-uh. No. I was with Michael for over a year—and yes, I then decided to break it off. But you and me? We're friends who slept together. Once."

His eyes gleamed. "So then, we *are* friends?"

She threw up both hands. "All right. Have it your way. We're friends."

"Thank you, I will—and about Michael Cort…"

"There is nothing more to say about Michael."

"Except that I'm not in the same league with him vis-à-vis you, correct?" He waited for her to answer. When she didn't, he mildly remarked, "Ouch."

God. Did he have to be so calm and reasonable on top of all the hotness and being so easy to talk to and having the same interests as she did? He was a quadruple threat. At least. "Can we just not talk about Michael?"

"All right. Tell me why you find this thing between us… how did you put it? 'Overwhelming' and 'consuming' and 'too much.'"

"Isn't that self-evident?"

"Tell me anyway."

Against her better judgment, she went ahead and tried. "Well, I just…I don't have time to be consumed with, er, passion, now. There are only so many hours in a day and I…" Dear Lord. Not enough time to be consumed with passion? Had she really said that?

"Tell me the rest," he prompted evenly.

She groaned. "It's only that, well, my dad's a wonderful teacher, the head of the English department at Beaufort State College in Beaufort, Texas, which is west of Fort Worth..." He was frowning, no doubt wondering what any of that had to do with the subject at hand—and why wouldn't he wonder? For a person who hoped someday to write for a living, she was doing a terrible job of keeping to the point and making herself understood.

"You told me months ago that your father's a teacher," he reminded her patiently.

"My father is successful. He's head of his department. My mother's a pediatrician. And my big brother, Carlos, owns five restaurants. Carlos got married last year to a gorgeous, brilliant woman who runs her own dancing school. In my family, we figure out what we want to do and we get out there and do it. Okay, we don't rule principalities or anything. But we contribute to our community. We find work we love and we excel at it."

"You have no problem then. You have work you love and you're very good at it."

"Yes, I'm good with children, and I love taking care of Trev and Ellie."

"You're an excellent nanny, I know. But that isn't the work you love, really, is it?"

She folded her hands in her lap and stared down at them—and wandered off topic some more. "My dad wanted me to follow in his footsteps and be a teacher. From the first, I knew I wanted to write. He said I could do both. Of course, he was right. But I didn't want to do it his way, didn't want to teach. We argued a lot. And the truth is I wasn't dedicated to my writing, not at first. I had some... difficulties. And I took my sweet time getting through college."

"Difficulties?"

Why had she even hinted at any of that? "Just difficulties, that's all."

"You're not going to tell me, are you?"

She shook her head tightly and went on with her story. "My parents would have paid for my education, even though they weren't happy with my choices. But I was proud. I wanted to make it on my own."

"You *were* proud?" he teased.

She felt her cheeks grow warm. "Okay, yeah. I *am* proud. I met Syd and we were like sisters from the first. I went to work for her, became her live-in housekeeper before she had Trev, to help put myself through school. And then once I got my degree, I stayed on with her, working for her, but with plenty of time to write. I worked hard at the writing, but it never took off for me. I lacked focus. Until I came here, until I knew the stories I wanted to write. And now I do know, Max. Now I've got the focus and the drive that I need, plus the stories I want to tell."

Max was sitting forward in the chair, his gray-blue gaze intense. "Have I somehow given you the idea that I think you should stop writing and spend every spare moment in bed with me?"

"Uh, no. No, of course you haven't. It's just that I have goals and I need to meet them. I need, you know, to *make* something of myself. I really do, Max."

He went on leaning forward in the chair, watching her. And she had that feeling she sometimes got around him, the feeling that used to make her all warm and fuzzy inside, because he *knew* her, he understood her. Too bad that lately, since New Year's, that feeling made her worry that he knew too *much* about her, and that he would use what he knew to push her to do things his way. He said, "You want your parents to be proud of you—and you don't feel that they are right now."

Her mouth went dry. She licked her lips. "I didn't say that."

He went further. "You're embarrassed that it bothers you, what your parents think. Because you're twenty-nine years old and you believe you should be beyond trying to live up to their ideals. But you're not beyond it, Lani. You're afraid that it will somehow get out that we've been lovers and that your mother and father will read about it in the tabloids, tacky stories of the nanny shagging the prince. You're afraid they'll judge you in all the ways you're judging yourself. You're afraid they'll think less of you, and you already feel they look down on you as it is."

"No. Really, they're good people. They *don't* look down on me, and I love them very much."

"Plus, you're clinging to a completely unfounded idea that I'll grow tired of you and have you banished from Montedoro in shame."

She groaned. "Okay, it really sounds silly when you put it that way."

"Good. Because it *is* silly. I've given you my word that it's never going to happen. And I never break my word." He was frowning again, holding her gaze as though he could look right through her eyes into her mind. "There's more, isn't there? Something deeper, something you haven't told me yet. Something to do with those 'difficulties' you had that you wouldn't explain to me."

Uh-uh. No. Not going there. *Never* going there. "It doesn't matter."

"Yes, it does."

It was long in the past. She'd survived and moved on, and she didn't want to get into it with him now—or ever. She lifted her chin to a defiant angle and kept her mouth firmly shut.

Without warning, he stood. She gasped and stared up at him, a breathless weakness stealing through her at the sheer masculine beauty of him. And then he held down his hand to her. "Take it," he said with such command and composure that it never occurred to her to do anything else.

She put her fingers in his. A dart of hungry fire flew up her arm, across her chest and downward, straight into the secret core of her. She should tell him to let go. But she didn't. She only rose on shaky feet to stand with him and then stared up at him dazedly as hot, sweet memories of New Year's Eve flashed through her brain.

He said gruffly, "There's nothing wrong with wanting your mother and father to be proud of you. It gets dangerous only when you let your need for their approval run your life."

She managed to muster a little attitude. "Do you have any idea how patronizing you sound?"

He only smiled. "Hit a nerve, did I? Also, you should know that very few authors can write a decent book before the age of thirty. Good writing requires life experience."

"Do you think you're reassuring me? Because you're not."

"I'm praising you. You've written five books and you're not thirty yet. One is okay, two are quite good and the most recent two are amazing."

"Five and a *half* books." She was currently stuck in the middle of number six. "And how do you know how good they all are? You've only read the last two." He'd actually offered to read them. And she'd been grateful for his helpful ideas on how to make them better. That was before New Year's, of course.

He added, "*And* you're published."

Yes, she was. In ebook. Just that past December, as a Christmas present to herself, she'd self-published the three women's fiction novels she'd written before she moved to Montedoro. So far, unfortunately, her e-book sales gave a whole new meaning to the word *unimpressive*. She was holding off on self-pubbing the new trilogy, hoping to sell them as a package to a traditional publisher.

And suddenly she got what he was hinting at. "You downloaded the three books I e-pubbed, didn't you?"

One big shoulder lifted in a half shrug. "Isn't that what you put them on sale for—so that people will buy them?"

Her heart kind of melted about then. How could she help but melt? He not only made her want to rip off her clothes and climb him like a tree, but he was a very good man. He was constantly finding new ways to show her that he really did care about her and the things that mattered to her. It wasn't his fault that she had trouble trusting her own emotions.

Her throat burned with all the difficult stuff she didn't know how to tell him. "Max, I…" She had no idea where to go from there.

And then it didn't matter what she might have said. He wiped her mind free of all thought by the simple act of lifting her chin lightly with his free hand and lowering his lips to hers.

Chapter Three

Max knew he was out of line to kiss her.

He'd made a bargain with her to keep his hands to himself, and yet here he was with one hand tipping up her soft chin and the other wrapped firmly around her trembling fingers. It was not playing fair.

Too bad. He wanted to kiss her, and at the moment she was going to let him do it.

So he did. Lightly, gently, so as not to startle her or have her jerking away, he settled his mouth on hers.

Pleasure stole through him. Warm velvet, those lips of hers. They trembled like her hand. He made no attempt to deepen the kiss, only drew in the haunting scent of her perfume: gardenias, vanilla and a hint of oranges all tangled up with that special, indefinable something that belonged only to her skin.

Lani. Yolanda Ynez. Her name in his mind like a promise. Her warmth and softness so close, calling to him, making him burn as he hadn't burned in years.

Making him *feel* as he'd never thought to feel again.

She made things difficult when they didn't have to be.

And yet, there was, simply, something about her. Some combination of mind and spirit, heart and scent and skin and bone that worked for him, that spoke to him. There was something in the core of her that called to him. Something within her that recognized him in a way he'd despaired long ago of ever being known.

He'd been asleep for almost four years, walking through his life like a ghost of himself, a dutiful creature, half-alive.

No more. Now his eyes were open, his mind and body one, whole, fully engaged.

Whatever it took, whatever he had to do to keep feeling this way, he would do it. He refused to go back to being half-alive again.

"Max." She breathed his name against his mouth.

He wanted to continue kissing her for the next century or two. But she wasn't ready for a century of kisses. Not yet. He lifted his head. "Not giving up on you," he vowed.

For once, she didn't argue, only stepped away and snatched up her laptop. He got his tablet and ushered her ahead of him out the door.

"Nicholas!" Gerta Bauer called sharply as the eight-year-old aimed his N-Strike Elite Retaliator Blaster Nerf gun at the back of his unsuspecting sister's head.

Nick sent his nanny a rebellious glance. Gerta narrowed her eyes at him and stared him down. Nick glared some more, but he did turn the toy gun away from Connie's head. He shot the trunk of a rubber tree instead, letting out a "Hoo-rah!" of triumph as the soft dart hit the target, wiggled in place for a moment and then dropped to the ground.

Connie, totally unaware she'd almost been Nerfed, continued carefully combing the long, straight black-and-white hair of her Frankie Stein doll. Meanwhile, Nick grabbed the fallen dart and forged off into a clump of bushes in search of new prey.

Trev, armed with his Supergalactic Laser Light Blaster, charged after him. "Nicky! Wait for me!" He pulled the trigger. The gun lit up and a volley of blasting sounds filled the air.

Gerta chuckled and tipped her head up to the afternoon sun. "Did I tell you that Nicholas is all grown up? He's too old for his nanny. He told me so this morning before school. 'Only babies have nannies,' he said."

Lani, on the garden bench beside her with Ellie in her lap, caught the butterfly rattle the toddler had dropped before it hit the ground. "He's exercising his independence."

"Me!" Ellie demanded, exercising a little independence of her own.

Lani kissed the top of her head and gave her back the rattle, which she gleefully began shaking again. "Is he still throwing fits when it's time to do his homework?"

Gerta's broad, ruddy face wore a self-satisfied expression. "For the past week, he's been getting right to it and getting it done. I took your advice and had his father talk to him about it."

Lani's pulse accelerated at the mere mention of Max. Honestly, she was hopeless, telling him no over and over— and then kissing him last night.

She needed a large dose of therapy. Or a backbone. Or both.

Gerta was watching her. "What's the matter?"

"Not a thing," Lani answered too quickly. Gerta frowned but didn't press her. And Lani asked, "So the homework is getting done?"

Gerta turned her head up to the sky again. "Yes, the homework is getting done."

Ellie giggled and said, "Uh-oh. Poopy."

She definitely had.

Gerta laughed, waved her freckled hand in front of her face at the smell and offered, "You could change her right here on the bench…."

But Lani was already shouldering the baby bag and lifting Ellie into her arms as she stood. "No. It's a little chilly out here." Ellie dropped the rattle again. Lani caught it as it fell and tucked it in the bag. "Plus I doubt a few baby wipes are going to cut it."

Ellie giggled some more and pecked a baby kiss on Lani's chin. "Nani, Nani…" The weak winter sunlight made her hair shine like polished copper. Even with a loaded diaper, she was the sweetest thing. Lani felt the old familiar ache inside as she gently freed her hair from the perfect, plump little fist. It was an ache of love for this particular child, Syd's baby girl, all mixed up with a bone-deep sorrow for what might have been, if only she'd been a little wiser and not nearly so selfish way back when.

Gerta held up a key. "Use our apartment. It's much closer." She meant the palace apartment she lived in with Nick and Connie. And Max.

Lani's thoroughly shameless heart thumped faster. Would Max be there?

Not that it mattered. It didn't, not at all. No big deal. She knew the apartment's layout. She and Gerta sometimes filled in for each other, so Lani had been there to help out with Nick and Connie more than once. Once she'd let herself in the door, she would go straight to the children's bathroom, clean Ellie up and get out. Fast.

She took the key. "Keep an eye on Trev?"

"Will do."

The apartment was quiet when she let herself in. The maids had been and gone for the day, leaving a faint scent of lemon polish detectable when she pushed the door open, but quickly overpowered by what Ellie had in her diaper.

No sign of Max. Lani breathed a quick sigh of relief.

In the children's bathroom, she hoisted the diaper bag

onto one of the long white quartz counters, shifting Ellie onto her hip as she grabbed a few washcloths from the linen shelves by the big tub. Returning to the counter, she pulled the changing pad from its side pocket and opened it up. Ellie giggled and waved her arms, trying to grab Lani's hair as Lani laid her down.

"You need a toy." Lani gave her the butterfly rattle, which she promptly threw on the floor. Lani played stern. "If I give you another toy, you have to promise not to throw it."

Ellie imitated her serious face. "K," she replied with a quick nod of her tiny chin.

There was an apple-shaped teething ring in the bag. Lani gave her that. She promptly started chewing on it, making happy little cooing sounds.

Lani flipped the water on and set to work. She had the diaper off and rolled up nice and tight and was busy using up the stack of cloths, wiping and rinsing and wiping some more, when her phone in the diaper bag started playing "Radioactive." It was the ringtone she'd assigned to her agent, Marie.

Her heart rate instantly rocketed into high gear.

Okay, it could be nothing.

But what if it *wasn't* nothing?

What if this was her moment, the moment every wannabe author dreamed of, the moment she got the *call,* the one that meant there was an actual publisher out there who wanted to buy her book?

She let out a moan of frustration and wiped faster. Not a big deal, she promised herself. She could call Marie back in just a few minutes. If there was an offer, it wouldn't evaporate while she finished mopping Ellie's bottom.

"Let me help," said the wonderful deep voice that haunted her dreams.

Slowly, her heart galloping faster than ever, she turned her head enough to see him lounging in the doorway wearing gray slacks and a light blue shirt.

The phone stopped ringing and she scowled at him. "How long have you been standing there?"

"Only a minute or two." He straightened and came toward her, all confidence and easy male grace. "I was in my study and I heard your voice and Ellie's laughter…." He stopped beside her at the counter. His niece giggled up at him as she drooled on her teething ring. "Give me the washcloth."

"I… What?"

"The washcloth." He reached out and took the smelly wet cloth in his long-fingered, elegant hand. "Return your call."

"No, really. I'll do this. It's fine." She tried to grab it back.

He held it away. "I have two children. I know how to diaper a baby." Ellie uttered a string of nonsense syllables, followed by a goofy little giggle. "See? Ellie knows I can handle it." On cue, Ellie babbled some more. "Make your call," he commanded a second time as he stuck the washcloth under the water. He wrung it out and got to work.

Lani washed her hands, grabbed her phone and called Marie back. She watched Max diaper Ellie while Marie Garabondi, the agent she'd been working with for just over a month now, talked fast in her ear.

Somewhere in the third or fourth sentence, Marie said the longed-for word: "offer." And everything spun away. Lani listened from a distance, watching Max, so manly and tender, bending over Ellie, doing a stinky job gently and efficiently.

And Marie kept on talking. Lani held the phone to her ear, hardly believing, understanding everything Marie was telling her, only somehow feeling detached, not fully present.

She held up her end, answered, "Yes. All right. Okay, then. Great." But it all seemed unreal to her, not really happening, some odd little dream she was having in the middle of the day. "Yes. Good. Let's do it, yes…" Marie talked some more. And then she said goodbye.

Lani was left standing there in the bathroom holding the phone.

Max had finished changing Ellie and lifted her onto his shoulder. She promptly pulled on his ear and babbled out more happy sounds that didn't quite amount to real words.

"Well?" he asked. Lani blinked and tried to bring herself back to reality. "Lani, what's happened?" he demanded. He was starting to look a little worried.

She sucked in a long breath and shared the news. "That was my agent. We have a deal. A very good deal. I just sold three books."

Max smiled. It was the biggest, happiest smile she'd ever seen on his wonderful face. And it was for her. "Congratulations," he said.

Ellie seemed to pick up on the spirit of the moment. She stopped pulling Max's ear and clapped her hands.

Very carefully, Lani set her phone down on the bathroom counter. "I'll be right back."

Max didn't say anything. He just stood there grinning, holding the baby.

And Lani took off like a shot. She ran out into the hallway of Max's apartment, shouting, "Yes! Yes! Yes! Yes!" When she got to the kitchen, she turned around and ran back again, shouting "Yes!" all the way.

Max was waiting, leaning in the bathroom doorway with Ellie in his arms, when she returned to him. "Feel good?"

"Oh, yeah." She wanted to grab him and plant one right

on him, to take his hand and lead him back to the kitchen where they could sit and talk and…

She stopped the dangerous thought before it could really get rolling.

"Nani, Nani…" Ellie swayed toward her.

She took the little sweetheart in her arms. "I'd, um, better get back. Gerta will wonder."

He was still smiling, but there was something somber in his eyes. "All right, then."

Neither of them moved.

"Nani…" Ellie patted her cheek—and then started squirming. "Dow, Nani, dow…"

Lani broke the tempting hold of his gaze. "I need to get back." He was blocking the doorway. "The diaper bag?"

He went and got it for her. "Here you are."

She took it from his outstretched hand and carried the wiggling toddler out of there, away from him.

"It's time and you know it," Sydney said the next day.

They were at the villa, just Syd and Lani, sitting at the table in the kitchen, sharing a late lunch while Trev and Ellie napped.

Everything had changed with that single call from Marie. And the time had come for Lani and Syd to deal with that.

Lani couldn't seem to stop herself from arguing against taking the next step. "But I love Trev and Ellie. And I have plenty of time to write and to take care of them."

Syd wasn't buying. "Why do I have to tell you what you already know? You'll be needing to network, to put together a PR plan. And what about that website you still don't have? And you keep saying you're going to establish more of an online presence, see if you can do more to boost the sales of those three e-books you have out."

"You're making me dizzy. You know that, right?"

"What I'm saying isn't news. It's what we always agreed. As soon as you were making enough with your writing to live on for a year, you would put all your work time into building a career. This sale does that for you."

"I know, but…"

"But what, Lani?"

Lani let out a low cry. "But it's all happening so fast. And what about Ellie and Trev? They're used to my being with them all the time. How will they take it, having some stranger for a nanny?"

"They will do fine." Syd reached across the distance between them and ran a fond hand down her hair. "They grow up, anyway. To a degree, in the end, we lose them to their own lives."

Lani wrinkled up her nose at her friend. "Okay, I get that you're trying to make me feel better. But come on. Ellie's still in diapers and Trev's four. It's a long time until they're on their own. And I know you and Rule are planning to have more children. You need me, you know you do."

"And you need to get out there." Syd set down her fork. "Listen, don't tempt me, okay? You're amazing with the kids. They love you so much—almost as much as I do. You're part of the family and I hate to let you go."

"Then why don't we just keep it like it is for a while?"

Syd refused to waver. "Uh-uh. No. You *need* to do this. And it's not like you're moving back to Texas or anything. You'll see them often, every day if you want to."

"Of course I want to see them every day. I *love* them. I love *you*."

"And *I* love you," Syd said. "So much. I'm so crazy happy for you."

Lani's throat clutched and her eyes burned.

"Oh, honey…" Syd grabbed the box of tissues off the windowsill and passed them to her.

Lani dabbed at her eyes. "Somehow, I didn't expect it to be like this. To get what I've always wanted—and just feel all weepy and lost about it."

"It's all going to work out. Change is a good thing."

Lani shot Syd a sideways look. "Keep saying that."

"You'd better believe I will—until you stop trying to go backward and move on."

Lani pushed her plate away, braced her elbows on the table and rested her chin between her hands. "Unbelievable. Seriously. And yeah. Okay."

Syd chuckled then. "Okay, what?"

"Okay, you can find a new nanny."

"Excellent. You're fired, as of today. And I'm perfectly capable of watching my own children until I find someone else." In the old days, before she'd married Rule, Sydney had worked killing hours at her law firm in Dallas. A full-time nanny had been a necessity then. Now, Sydney had projects she took on, but her schedule was flexible and she enjoyed being a hands-on mom. "And Gerta's terrific. I know she'll be willing to accept a nice bonus and keep an eye on all four kids if I get desperate."

"*I* can help if you get desperate."

"The main thing is you're a full-time writer and you're getting out on your own."

"Yes. Fine. I'll start looking for a place. Something in Monagalla, maybe…" The southwestern ward was close to the palace. It was known as the tourist ward because room rates were relatively low there. But housing in Montedoro didn't come cheap no matter where you lived.

Syd seemed to be reading her mind. "If you need help with the money…"

"Don't even go there. I have enough to tide me over until

the advance check comes. I'm just…a little freaked out at making the move."

"No kidding."

Lani pulled her plate close again. "God. I'm a basket case. Thrilled. Terrified. Sure that Marie will be calling any minute to tell me never mind, it was all a big mistake."

Syd sipped her coffee and set the cup back down with care. "Is it a guy?"

Lani almost choked on the chip she'd just poked in her mouth. She swallowed it whole and it went down hard. "Whoa. That came out of nowhere."

"Did it? I don't think so. Something's been bothering you since the beginning of the year. I keep asking you what. And you keep not telling me. Who is he?"

Lani was so tired of lying. And Syd didn't believe her lies anyway. Still, she tried to hold out. "Syd, come on…"

"No, Lani. *You* come on. Whatever this is, it's got you really on edge. And it's got me more than a little bit worried for you."

"Don't be. I'm all right."

"No, you're not. You're kind of a mess lately."

"Gee, thanks."

"Just *talk* to me."

Lani waffled. "It's only, well, I'm afraid you won't approve."

Syd made a sound that was midway between a laugh and a groan. "Don't give me that. We've been friends for too long. There is nothing…*nothing* you could do that would make me love you any less."

Lani stared at her friend and wanted to cry again. "You are the best. You know that, right?"

"So tell me."

The words were right there. And so she just said them. "I slept with Max on New Year's Eve."

Syd's green eyes bugged out and her mouth fell open. "Max. As in Maximilian, aka my brother-in-law?"

Lani drew herself straight in her chair. "Yes. Maximilian as in the heir to the throne. That Max. You know the one."

"Oh, Lani…" Syd shook her head slowly.

Lani made a low, pained little sound. "See? I shouldn't have told you. Now you've gotta be certain I have a screw loose."

Syd's hand came down on top of hers. She squeezed her fingers tight. "Stop."

Lani turned her hand around and grabbed on to Syd's. "I know you're shocked."

"No—well, surprised, maybe. A little."

"More like a lot."

Syd gave her a patient look. "I knew the two of you were friendly…."

"Right. Just not *that* friendly. I mean, the prince and the nanny ending up in bed together. Ick. It just sounds so tacky."

"I don't want to have to tell you again," Syd scolded. "Stop beating yourself up. You like him. He likes you. You're both single. It happens. Men and women find each other. I mean, where would we all be if it *didn't* happen?" Protectively, she laid her other hand over their joined ones. "I did notice how he was always finding a reason to talk to you, always hanging around with you and Gerta and the children."

"Well, his kids were there, too."

"Lani. Let me make myself clearer. I should have guessed."

"Why should you guess? I mean, everyone talks about how much he loved his wife, about how he'll never get married again, how nobody has a chance with him."

"Nobody until you, apparently."

She pulled her hand free of Syd's comforting grip and ate another chip without really even tasting it. "It was one night, that's all."

Syd leaned a little closer. "Do you want it to be more?"

Lani hardly knew how to answer, so she didn't.

Syd kept after her. "Is he treating you like it never happened or something? Do I need to kick his ass for you?"

Lani pushed her plate away again, then pulled it back, ate a slice of pickle and teased, "You think you could take him? He's pretty fit."

"Answer the question. Has he been disrespecting you?"

"No, he hasn't. He's been wonderful. Last night, he kissed me and said he won't give up on me, even though I've done everything I possibly can to chase him away."

"Wait. Stop. I'm getting whiplash, this conversation is so confusing. He wants to keep seeing you—and you're just not interested?"

Lani pushed her plate aside for the third time so that she could bang her head on the table. Then she sat up, sucked in a hard breath and said, "No, actually, I'm crazy about him."

Syd stared at her for a long time. Then she said gently, "So give him a chance." Lani only looked at her. Syd spoke again. "This is not eleven years ago."

Lani almost wished she'd never confided in Syd about what had happened when she was eighteen, the terrible choices she'd made and the life-altering domino effect of the ugly consequences that followed. But they *were* best friends and best friends shared the deepest, hardest secrets. "I just don't want to get my heart broken, okay? Been there, done that. It almost destroyed me. I don't want to go there again."

"The way I remember it, you broke up with Michael Cort because you wanted more than just safety in a man…."

"Yeah, I know that, but—"

"Save the *buts*. I don't get this. A big part of the reason I went to lunch with Rule that first day I met him was because *you* told me to get out there and give another guy a chance. You knew how many times I'd been messed over, and that I was scared it was only going to happen again. But you pushed me to see that you don't get what really matters without putting yourself out there, without risking big."

"Well, I'm having a little trouble right now following my own advice."

"Just think about it."

"Are you kidding? I do. Constantly. I just made the big sale. I'm living my dream. But all I can think about is this thing with Max."

The apartment, in an old villa on a narrow street in Monagalla, had one bedroom, a tiny kitchen nook and a six-by-ten-foot balcony off the living room that the land-lady called a terrace. From the terrace you could see the hillside behind the building, and a forest of olive and rubber trees and odd, spiky cactus plants. Lani took the place because the old Spanish-style building charmed her. Also, it was available immediately at a good price and it was only a short walk from the front door up Cap Royale to the palace.

One week after she got the call from Marie, she moved in. She had all the furniture she needed, courtesy of Rule and Sydney, who had led her down into the warren of storage rooms in the basement of the palace and let her choose the few pieces she needed from the mountains of stuff stored there.

It took her two days to make it livable. She designated half of the living room as her office, positioning her desk so she could look out the glass slider at the little square of terrace and the olive trees on the hillside. And she found a housewares shop nearby where she bought pots and pans, dishes, glassware and cooking utensils. The shop had all the linens she needed, too.

At the end of the second day of fixing the place up, when she had it just the way she wanted it, she cooked herself a simple dinner in her little kitchen and she ate on the plain white plates she'd bought from the nearby shop. After she ate, she sat down at her computer and wrote ten pages and felt pretty good about them. It was well after midnight when she closed her laptop and saw the pink sticky note she'd slapped on the top: *Call parents.*

Actually, she'd been meaning to call them for days now—ever since she made the big sale. They would be thrilled for her, of course. But she'd been putting off making that call.

They loved her and they worried about her. And every time she talked to them they wanted to know when she was coming home. They didn't seem to understand that she *was* home. She'd tried to explain to them that she was never moving back to Texas. So far, they weren't getting it. Sometimes she doubted they ever would.

Midnight in Montedoro meant five in the afternoon yesterday in Texas. Her mom was probably still at her clinic. But her dad might be home. She made the call.

Her dad answered. "Yolanda." He sounded tired but pleased to hear from her. "How are things on the Riviera?"

She told him about the sale first. He congratulated her warmly and said he'd always known it would happen. And then she couldn't resist bragging a little, sharing the dollar amount of the advance.

He got excited then. "But this is wonderful. You won't have to spend your time babysitting anymore. In fact, you could come home. You know your mama and I would love to have you right here in the house with us. But I know you probably don't want to live with the old folks. You would want your own place, and we understand that."

"Well, I already have a place. I moved out of the palace and got myself an apartment."

"But you could—"

"Papi. Come on. I've told you. I don't want to leave here. I love Montedoro and I plan to stay."

"But not forever. Your home is here, near your family. And you're almost thirty. It's time you found the right man and made me a doting grandfather."

She didn't say anything. It seemed pointless to argue.

He kind of took the hint and tried to put a positive spin on what he considered self-destructive stubbornness on her part. "If you have your own apartment there in Montedoro, does that mean you're not babysitting Sydney's kids anymore?"

"Yes. That's what it means."

"Well, I'm glad for that. You have great talent. I always told you that. If you're going to take care of babies, they should be your own."

She couldn't let that stand. "I'm an excellent nanny, Papi. And I enjoyed every moment with Trevor and Ellie."

He got the message. More or less. "Well, of course, you will excel at whatever you do." He said it much too carefully.

That was the problem now, with her and her parents. In the awfulness of what had happened more than ten years ago, something essential had been lost. They continued to go through the motions with each other, but there were barriers, things they didn't dare talk about with each other—or maybe didn't know how to talk about.

She asked how he was feeling, and how Mama was doing. "Fine," he answered. "Very well." And then he told her that her brother, Carlos, and his bride, Martina, had bought a house in San Antonio. Martina's family was in San Antonio, and Carlos would be opening a new restaurant there. "Of course, your mama and I are happy for them, and you know how proud we are of Carlito's success."

"Yes, I know." She made her voice bright. "He's done so well."

"*And* they are already trying for a baby. A first grandchild is a precious thing."

A first grandchild. The words stung, though Lani knew she shouldn't let them.

After that, the conversation really began to lag. She told him she loved him and to give her love to her mother. They said goodbye.

She went to bed feeling empty and lonely and like a failure as a daughter. Sleep didn't come. She just stared up at the ceiling fan, trying to turn her mind off.

But instead, she thought about Max.

She'd had zero contact with him since that afternoon in his apartment when he'd diapered Ellie for her while she took the call from Marie. Nine days. And nothing. She hadn't seen him during the week she was still at the palace. And for the past two days, she'd put all her effort into setting up her place.

He'd made no attempt to get in touch with her. So much for how he wasn't giving up on her. No doubt he'd had enough of her pushing him away. She didn't blame him for that. He'd tried and tried and she'd given him nothing back.

She sighed. So all right. It was over between them.

Over without ever really getting started.

And, well, that was fine with her. It was better this way. Except that it wasn't.

And she was a complete coward who'd driven away a perfectly wonderful guy. Even if he was too much for her, too overwhelming, way more than she'd bargained for. Even if he was probably still carrying a torch for his lost wife. Even if it scared her a lot, how gone she was on him.

She turned over onto her side and punched at her pillow. But sleep wouldn't come. Her mind thrummed with energy. With longing. She started thinking about calling him—and yeah, she knew that was a very bad idea.

So she tried *not* to think about calling him.

And that only made her want to call him more.

She had his cell number. He'd given it to her months ago, long before New Year's, just taken her phone from her one day when they were out in the gardens with the children and added himself to her contacts.

She'd laughed and said she didn't need his number. They saw each other all the time. If something came up and she had to reach him, Rule and Sydney had his landline on autodial.

But he'd said he wanted her to have it. Just in case…

Lani reached out a hand through the darkness and felt around on the nightstand until she found her phone. She punched up his number and hit Call without letting herself stop to think about how it was too late and she'd already blown it and calling him at one-thirty in the morning was hardly a good way to reestablish contact.

Not surprisingly, he didn't answer. The call went to voice mail. She knew she should just hang up. But she didn't.

"Hi, Max. Um, it's me. Lani? Yeah, I know it's almost two in the morning, not to mention you've probably decided you're better off giving me what I said I wanted and leaving me alone. And I, well, I get that. I mean, why wouldn't you finally just give up on me? I haven't been anything but a headache lately. Why wouldn't you just…?" She stopped, closed her eyes and let out a whimper of utter embarrassment. "Okay, this ridiculousness is stopping now. Sorry to bother you. Sorry for everything. 'Night." She disconnected the call, dropped the phone on the nightstand and then grabbed her pillow and plunked it down hard on top of her face.

For several seconds she lay there in the dark, pressing the pillow down on her nose and mouth as hard as she could. But it was all just more ridiculousness and eventually she gave up, tossed the pillow aside and pushed back the covers.

If she couldn't sleep, maybe she could work. Not pages, no. Not tonight. But she did need to get going on a marketing program. She could look around online, see what resources were generally available. She needed to find a website designer. And maybe enroll in a few online classes. Things such as how to make the most of social media and how to create an effective PR plan. When the first book in her trilogy came out, she needed to be ready to promote herself and the books, and do it effectively. Gone were the days when an author could sit around and wait for her publisher to set up a few book signings.

Her phone rang as she was reaching for her robe.

Her heart lurched and then began thudding hard and deep in her chest. Sweat bloomed between her breasts, under her arms and on her upper lip. She craned her head toward the nightstand to see the display.

Max.

She dropped the robe and grabbed for the phone. "Uh, hello?"

"Gerta says you're no longer working for Rule and Sydney." His voice was careful, measured. Withdrawn. Still, that voice had the power to make her breath come uneven, to make her thudding heart pound even harder. "And I understand you've moved out of the palace."

"Yes. That's right. I'm not at the palace anymore. And Max, really, I'm sorry about—"

"I don't want your apologies."

"Um. Well, all right. I'm okay with that."

"You're okay." His tone was too calm. Calm and yet somehow edged in darkness.

"That's what I said, yes."

"You're okay and you're no longer a nanny working for my family. No longer at the palace."

Anger rose up in her. Defensive anger. She reined it in and tried to speak reasonably. "Look, I don't know what's the matter with me. I shouldn't have called you tonight. It was wrong of me to do that and I—"

"Not so."

"Excuse me?"

"You were very right to call me tonight."

"I—"

"But you were *wrong* to run off without a single word to me."

"Max, I did not 'run off.' I moved. I certainly have a right to move without checking with you first."

He was silent.

"Max?" She was sure he'd hung up on her.

"Where are you?" Low. Soft. But not in any way tender.

"I don't—"

"An address. Give me your address."

"Max, I—"

"I must tell you, I could have your address so easily without asking you. Gerta would give it to me. I could get it from Rule. And there are other ways. There are men my family hires to find out whatever we need to know about anyone with whom we associate."

"Max, what are you doing? I really don't like this. Is that a threat?"

"No threat. Only an explanation. I can find out whatever I want to know about you. But I would never do that. I care for you. I respect your rights and your privacy. So please. Give me your address or hang up the phone and never call me again."

"Max, this isn't like you. Ultimatums have never been your style."

"My *style,* as you put it, is not serving me well with you. Make a choice. Do it now." There was nothing gentle in that voice. He didn't grant her so much as a hint of the compassionate, patient Max she'd always known.

Obviously, her sweet and tender prince was being a complete jerk and she needed to hang up and forget about him. Let it be and let him go. Move on. It was only what she'd repeatedly told him she wanted.

He spoke again. "Lani. Choose."

She gave him the address.

Chapter Four

MAX was furious.

He'd been furious for a couple of days now. Ever since Gerta had told him that Lani was no longer Trev and Ellie's nanny, that she'd found an apartment and moved into it.

He left the palace by a side door and walked down Cap Royale under the pale sliver of a new moon. It took him eight minutes to reach her street and a minute more to get to her door.

The old villa was locked up at that hour of the night. But she was waiting in the vestibule, as he'd told her to be.

Their gazes locked through the etched glass at the top of the door. She opened it. He went in. She wore yoga pants and a big sweatshirt that made her look small and vulnerable, her hair curling on her shoulders, a little wild, as though she hadn't been able to stop herself from raking her fingers through it.

"This way," she said in a hushed voice, and turned for the stairs.

He caught her arm before she could escape him.

She gasped and faced him, tried to pull away. "Max, I—"

"Nine days," he whispered, pulling her closer, bending

his head to get right in her face. "Nine days. Not a word from you."

"I thought it would be better. You know, to let it go."

"Maybe it would have been. I didn't want to give up on you. I thought it mattered, what we might have had. But a man can be told no only so many times before he begins to wonder how big a fool he really is. When Gerta told me you had moved, I decided that was it. You'd been sending a message and I'd finally received it. I was done with you. I set my mind on forgetting you. Then you called me tonight. Why?"

She drew in a careful breath and let it out slowly. "Let's just go upstairs. Please."

He jerked her closer. The sweet scent of her hair drifted up to him, piercing him like knives.

"Max…" She said it pleadingly.

He wanted to be cruel to her. He wanted to make her pay somehow for being able to just go like that, just walk out of his life so easily. He wanted to get even with her for giving him a taste of heaven.

And then taking it back.

But she was right. They should go to her apartment, where they could close the door and say what needed saying without the possibility of nosy neighbors listening in. He was the Prince of Montedoro, after all. The heir to the throne should know better than to let himself be heard carrying on an intimate discussion in a dimly lit apartment foyer in the middle of the night.

He released her.

She turned again and led him up two flights. Her apartment door was open, soft light spilling out onto the landing. She ushered him in first and closed and locked the door behind them.

They were in the living room. It was small and plain—a sofa and two chairs, her desk facing a sliding door.

She gestured at the sofa against the inside wall. "Sit down."

He did no such thing. They remained near the door, facing off against each other like enemies. "Why did you call me tonight?"

She wore a look of desperate confusion. "I couldn't help it."

"Not good enough." He waited.

Still she only gazed at him, all big, dewy eyes and no answers.

He knew then that he really was a fool. Duped by the best of them. Tricked yet again. "There's nothing here for me. I understand." He did his best to gentle his tone. "It's all right, Lani. We'll do what you wanted. We'll move on. Step out of my way."

She gulped. Hard. "I… Oh, God, Max. Please don't go."

He tried not to waver. But it wasn't easy to cut her free. She'd changed his world, turned the never-ending grayness to warm, soft, beautiful light. When he looked at her, he never wanted to look away. "Give me a reason to stay."

"I…" She shut those enormous black eyes. Gulped again. "I need to…Max, I need to tell you a few things about me, a few not-so-good things." She made a sound then. Ragged, shrill. Not quite a laugh and not exactly a sob. "Scratch that. Worse than not-so-good. Straight-up bad things. I've done some really rotten, crappy, bad things. I thought I had forgiven myself. But now, since New Year's, since I had to admit how much you mean to me, I'm not so sure."

How much you mean to me. Could he count the admission as progress? He searched her face. "I knew there was something."

"I haven't wanted to tell you. I didn't think I could bear to see the disappointment in your eyes."

He dared to reach out and take her hand. Her soft fingers felt good in his, as always. They felt achingly right. Gently, he suggested, "I think that now we should sit down."

She blinked, looking slightly dazed. "Yes. All right."

He turned for the sofa and she followed obediently. Once there, he took her slim shoulders, gently pushed her down and then sat beside her, facing her, laying an arm along the sofa back behind her, hitching a knee up onto the cushions.

She did not turn to him, but sat facing front, hands folded in her lap, staring straight ahead. "When I was eighteen, I fell in love with my dad's best friend. He was forty-five and he was married—well, separated. But still. There had been no divorce. He was a writer, a novelist. His name was Thomas McKneely."

McKneely. Max knew that name. He was pretty sure he'd read at least one of the man's novels and that he'd found what he read funny and smart.

She went on. "Thomas was everything I thought I wanted someday to be. He and my dad had gone to college together. Thomas wrote humorous novels set in Texas."

"I've heard of him." Max kept his voice carefully neutral. "Go on."

"I'd known Thomas since I was a child. I'd always idolized him. He was…bigger than life, you know? Tall and broad-shouldered and handsome, always laughing and saying the cleverest things. He and his wife, Allison, often came to dinner, to the parties my parents would give. And then, in the summer after my senior year, he left Allison. He came to dinner alone one night and he was…different. Kind of sad and withdrawn. But then he looked at me and I knew he really saw me, finally. He saw me as a woman."

He couldn't resist pointing out the obvious. "His best friend's daughter? What a bastard."

"Yeah, well. I *wanted* to get something going with him or nothing would have happened, believe me."

"You were only eighteen. Barely an adult."

She shook her head slowly. "True. I didn't know my ass from up. Some people have seen enough and learned enough to be grown-ups at eighteen. Not me. In hindsight it's way clear I was asking for all kinds of trouble. But I was the baby of my family, totally spoiled, and I thought that if I wanted something bad enough, it had to be okay. So I snuck out to meet him several nights in a row. We were secret lovers. I thought it was so romantic and beautiful and he would divorce his wife and we would be together forever." She put up her hands and covered her face—and then dropped them again. "Young. I was so young. And I really was sure I knew everything, all the secrets of life and love and happiness that my parents just couldn't understand."

"And then?"

"My father found out. He caught me sneaking out and he confronted Thomas. They fought, the two of them, punching at each other, rolling around on the front lawn. My father won. He stood over Thomas and called him a lowlife child-molesting… Well, there were bad names and there were a lot of them. And I…I blamed my dad. I yelled at him that I was eighteen and a grown woman and I had a right to love the man of my choice." She fell silent, staring into the middle distance.

Max wanted to say something, to offer some kind of comfort. But he had no words right then. And when he reached out a hand to her, she leaned away from his touch.

"No," she whispered. "Don't. Let me finish this." He drew back and she went on. "I left with Thomas that night. I moved in with him. I thought we would live on love and he would write more brilliant novels and dedicate them all to me. But what do you know? The summer went by and he wasn't writing and I didn't go away to the University of Iowa as planned. We started fighting. He drank too much. I cried all the time. And then, in October, he told me that I was a spoiled, selfish child and I didn't really have anything to offer him. He went back to his wife." She looked at him then, and her eyes were defiant. "He was a bastard, yes. But he was also right about me." She smiled the saddest smile. "I went home. I didn't know where else to go. My parents forgave me. That's how they are."

He wanted to kill Thomas McKneely. But it seemed to him he'd read the man's obituary already. "I think I read somewhere that Thomas McKneely died."

She made a small sound in the affirmative. "Four years ago. A ruptured aortic aneurysm. Allison was with him right to the end." Lani eased her folded hands between her knees, hunched her shoulders and looked down at the floor. "She was a good wife to him. Truer than he ever deserved. A year after he died, I went to see her, to apologize for all I'd put her through. She was really something, so kind. She said it was all years ago, that I should put it behind me and move on."

"A good woman."

"Yeah. I heard later that she remarried and moved to Florida. I like to picture her there, holding hands on the beach with some handsome older guy."

Max waited, in case there might be more.

And there was. Eventually, she let out a long, slow sigh. "A month after Thomas went back to Allison, I realized that I was pregnant." He swore, with feeling. She gave a sad little shrug. "I didn't know what to do. I just…did nothing. I told no one. I stayed in my room most of the time. My brother, Carlos, came and tried to lecture me. He yelled and told me off, trying to make me snap out of it. I just shut the door in his face. And my poor parents didn't know how to reach me, how to help me. I never actually told them I was pregnant. They found out when I miscarried at the first of the year."

He cast about for something helpful and comforting to say, but all he could think of was, "I'm sorry, Lani. So damn sorry…"

She raked a hand back through her hair. "My parents called an ambulance. They stayed at my side. I lost the baby, but I pulled through all right, physically at least. Mama and Papi were hurt that I hadn't told them about the baby, that they found out only when I was losing it. Children and family mean everything to them. But still, they didn't accuse me or blame me. They tried to see the positive. They said that miscarriages do happen, that someday there would be other babies, that I was young and strong and things would get better in time." She lifted her tear-wet gaze to him. "I meant it when I said that they're good people. They stuck with me and came through for me and they tried to convince me to get help, tried to talk me into seeing a counselor. But I refused. I felt I was dead inside. I *wanted* to die."

He knew then what she would tell him next. "Lani, my God."

She covered her face again. "I had the pain medication they'd given me at the hospital when I lost the baby. I took it. All of it. I was unconscious when my mother found me. She called me another ambulance. It was touch and go for a while, they told me. But, well, here I am. I pulled through."

He touched her arm. "Look at me."

Once more, she lowered her hands and turned her eyes to his. "I was in a psych hospital for several weeks and I got the intensive therapy I needed right then, and for a year more after I got out, I saw a really good doctor who helped me to get well."

He didn't know what to say. So he didn't say anything. Instead, he touched her again, lightly clasping her shoulder, guiding her closer. She didn't resist that time, but melted against him. He pressed his lips to her hair.

She said in a voice barely more than a whisper, "I swear to you, Max. I thought I was over all that, over the past, over my own stupid, blind arrogance, to risk it all on a completely self-absorbed married man more than twice my age. I thought I was, well, if not over losing my baby, at least at peace with it. I thought I had forgiven myself for going against everything I've ever held true and trying to end my life."

"But you're not over it." It wasn't a question.

She put her hand against his chest and tucked her head more snugly under his chin. "I've made a good life, a safe life, with Syd and her family. Kind of, you know, living on the edge of other people's happiness. Loving Syd's children. Writing my stories, but not taking too many chances. Dating safe, kind men like Michael Cort, breaking it off with them eventually because what I had with them was never enough. But then…" She pushed away from him and looked at him. "There was you…"

He pulled her down again and guided her head back to his shoulder.

She said, "I know I tried to deny it that day in the gardener's cottage, but you *were* my friend for more than a year. And it was okay, being friends with you. It was safe, the kind of safe I've always needed, after all that happened eleven years ago."

"You mean it was okay until New Year's. Until we were suddenly more than friends."

"That's right. Then I got scared. Terrified. I've felt this

strongly for a man only once before. And now you know that didn't go well."

"I would never do what he did." He said it quietly, but a little of his earlier fury crept in. He had made his own mistakes, been the worst kind of fool. But at least he'd always kept his promises.

She had tipped her head back, was watching his face. "Of course you're nothing like Thomas. Nothing at all. Oh, Max. If you despise me now, I do understand…."

He traced the line of her hair where it fell along her cheek, his anger fading away. "You're harder on yourself than I could ever be."

She gazed up at him pleadingly. "Just tell me. Do you despise me?"

"No. How could I? You made some bad choices. Everybody does. You learned from those choices and you came through to be who you are right now. I have no problem with that. I'm only grateful you're finally able to tell me about it."

"But, well…" She put her hand against her throat.

"What?" he demanded. "Tell me."

"Oh, Max, I hate to have to say it, but you see now, don't you, why I said it would be better if we both just moved on?"

Move on now? When he was finally breaking down the walls with her? No. "I don't see that. I don't see it at all."

"But you should. You really should."

"Shh." He cradled her closer. "I don't want to move on, Lani. I want to stay right here with you."

She hitched in a sharp breath. "You really mean that?"

"I do."

She laughed then, a low laugh. There was something deeper than humor in the sound. "I think you must be out of your mind. I'm a mess. It's not pretty."

"You are something of a mess, I'll give you that—but you are very, very pretty."

She sat up and made a show of tossing her head. "What are you telling me? That at least I'll have my looks to fall back on if all else fails?"

He grinned at that, and then he said in all seriousness, "It matters to me, that you trusted me, finally. That you took that kind of chance on me. But you have to stop running away from me."

"I get so scared that I'll ruin everything—and then I ruin everything…"

He finished for her. "By running away."

"Yes. That's exactly right."

"Stop doing that," he instructed sternly.

"I will. I promise you, Max." She made a low, nervous sound. "So…we're good, then?"

He reached out, eased his fingers up under the thick fall of her hair and wrapped them around the soft, warm nape of her neck. "We are excellent." He gave a tug.

And she came to him, leaning close, smelling of gardenias and oranges. Her soft breasts brushed his chest. He felt the promise of that softness, even through the layers of their clothing. And her mouth was right there, an inch from his. "Oh, Max…"

He claimed her lips. She opened, sighing. He tasted her. He wrapped his arms around her and kissed her for a long time, sitting there on the old sofa in her plain living room.

"Lie down," she whispered against his mouth.

He admitted reluctantly, "I can't stay…"

"I know."

"New Year's was beautiful," he told her, his voice rough with the memory of it, with the reality of her right now, in his arms. "But next time, I want to go slow, to have the whole evening together."

"All right. Yes."

"That is a word I love to hear you say."

"I'll say it some more then. Yes, yes, yes, yes—and now, tonight, won't you stay just a little longer?"

She was way too tempting. So he let her guide him down to stretch out on the cushions—after which she promptly wriggled away and got rid of her shoes and then his, too. He put his feet up on the sofa and reached for her, pulling her against him so she was lying on top of him.

And she gazed down at him, eyes bright as stars now. "You were so angry when you got here. I was sure it was over, that I had pushed you too far and there was no hope."

"I'm not angry now."

"And I'm so glad. It all seems a little unreal, though. I can't believe I finally put it all out there, told you everything. And you didn't walk out. You're still here, in my apartment, holding me tight…"

"I'm here," he promised. "I'm right here." He stroked her back and smoothed her hair. "Sunday," he whispered.

She let out a low, husky laugh. "Comes after Saturday, last I heard."

"*This* Sunday, day after tomorrow…"

"What about it?"

"You, me, breakfast with the family in the Sovereign's apartments." It was a tradition. He had eight brothers and sisters. They all tried to show up for the family Sunday breakfast whenever they could manage it. In recent years, there were wives and husbands and children, too. Some Sundays it was a big group.

She pulled away enough to make a pained face at him. "Sunday with your family. I don't know. What will they all think?"

"They will be happy for me, that I've found someone special again at last."

She laid her head against his chest. "Your mother is so amazing. I'm kind of intimidated by her."

"There's no reason to be."

"Oh, come on. Some say she's the best ruler Montedoro's seen in five hundred years."

"Yes, she is."

"And she's as beautiful as she is brilliant. Why wouldn't I be intimidated?"

"She will see us together and she'll be glad. She's like all good mothers. She wants her children to be happy."

"You have to see that it could be awkward. Everyone will know for sure that you've got something going with the nanny."

"But you're not the nanny. Not anymore. So that's a non-issue—not that it ever mattered to me, anyway."

She lifted her head and gazed at him steadily. "You really do mean that."

"Yes, I do."

"I am so crazy for you, Max." Her voice was soft, full of wonder.

He guided a lock of hair behind her ear. "Hold that thought—and you are coming with me and Nick and Connie to breakfast on Sunday. Stop trying to get out of it."

"Oh, all right. Fine. I'll be there."

"Yes, you will. And tonight, dinner. I'm taking you out."

She made a breathless little sound. "A real date."

"Exactly. Be ready at seven."

For once, she didn't argue. She brushed a kiss across his cheek and whispered, "Yes, Your Highness."

He held her tighter. "You and me," he said, to make certain she understood. "For all the world to see."

"I'll be ready."

"That's the spirit. Kiss me again." She did, wrapping him in her softness, in the scent of her hair. When she lifted her head, he groaned. "On second thought, maybe I should stay a little longer...."

She brushed another light kiss against his mouth. "I wish. But I know you like to be there, in the morning, for breakfast with Connie and Nick." And with that, she slid off him, bringing another groan from him as she shifted away. Kneeling, she handed him his shoes. He sat up and put them on.

Then she followed him to the door.

"It's so strange," she whispered, her hands on his shoulders, her forehead pressed to his. "I'm almost afraid to let you go. I'm afraid that in the morning, I'll wake up and this will all be a dream."

He tipped up her chin, kissed her one more time. "It's already morning, my darling. And this is no dream."

When he was gone, Lani wandered to the sliding door and stared out at the night, at the shadowed olive trees on the hill beyond the terrace. She was smiling to herself. Eventually, she turned and went to bed, feeling light as a moonbeam, her feet barely touching the floor.

She peeled off her yoga pants and sweatshirt, took off her bra and her panties. Naked, still smiling, she climbed between the sheets and closed her eyes. She was asleep in seconds, a deep, contented dreamless sleep.

Chapter Five

"**D**inner out tonight with Max?" Syd laughed in delight.

"Shh." Lani pointed at Ellie, who was asleep on her lap.

Syd lowered her voice. "Good for you." They were sitting in the kitchen at the villa. Trev had made short work of his lunch and gone off to the playroom. "Good for both of you."

Lani stroked Ellie's silky curls. The little one muttered a nonsense word in her sleep. Lani whispered, "That's not all. He asked me to come with him and Connie and Nick to Sunday breakfast with the family. I said I would."

"Wow. The man is not fooling around."

"He's…something special."

"You really told him everything, the whole story?"

"I did. And he was wonderful."

"*You* are wonderful," Syd declared. "Remember that."

Lani grinned. "Well, you are my best friend. You have to say that."

Syd seemed to study her. "You know, it feels kind of right, the more I think about it. You and Max not only both love sitting in the library talking Montedoran history for half the night, but you've also both seen some rough times. You fell for an egotistical, alcoholic SOB who broke your heart and practically cost you everything. He lost Sophia so suddenly, so tragically." His wife had died in a waterski-ing accident. "You both deserve a big dose of happiness."

Sophia. Lani had seen pictures of her—in Max's apart-ment and in the long hallway to the throne room, which was lined with portraits of generations of Calabrettis. She'd been tall, slim and elegant. With auburn hair and hazel eyes. "It's strange about Sophia," she said. "Somehow, Max seems… protective of her, of her memory. Or maybe it's just that he never says much about her, about his life with her."

"You're worried about that?"

"I guess so. A little. It's like…there's a mystery there."

"Think how you'd feel if he never *stopped* talking about her."

Lani considered that option. "Good point. I suppose I should just admit I'm jealous of her. She was so beautiful. The daughter of a Spanish grandee. And I've heard the sto-ries. That they had loved each other since they were chil-dren, that they always knew they would marry."

"Yeah. And they married early. I think Rule told me they were both twenty. Pretty young."

"Maybe it's just that he will never get over her, really, and that bothers me. I mean, who wants to compete with a memory?"

For that remark, Syd gave her an eye-roll. "Well, you could start by not borrowing trouble. The man is showing clear intent when it comes to you. He's heard your darkest, deepest secrets and he's still hanging in. He's bringing you to breakfast with the family."

"Okay, I hear you. I've got nothing to complain about."

"The big question is do you want to be the Princess Con-sort one of these days?"

"Oh, come on."

"What do you mean, come on? It could happen. It se-riously could. You know how the Bravo-Calabrettis are.

They marry for love. If you two have that, well, wedding bells will be ringing."

"No, they won't."

"They could. They absolutely could."

"Syd, everyone knows that Max is never getting married again."

"Everyone *assumes* that Max is never getting married again. That doesn't mean he won't."

"Yes, it does. He told me so himself, months and months ago."

"Wait a minute. You two discussed getting married months and months ago?"

"Not like that, not in terms of him and me. It just came up naturally out of another conversation."

"Another conversation about…?"

"Syd, honestly. You are so pushy sometimes."

"It's part of my charm. Another conversation about…?"

Lani gave in and told her. "The Prince's Marriage Law." The controversial law decreed that each of Montedoro's princes and princesses had to marry by age thirty-three or be stripped of all titles and disinherited. The law was put in place to help ensure early marriages, like Max's to Sophia, because early marriages are more likely to be fertile and provide potential heirs to the throne. "We were in the library at night, just Max and me, and we were discussing the Marriage Law. We went on from there to talking about marriage in general. I told him how I didn't think I was even cut out for marriage, or that I would ever have children. And he said he understood, that he didn't plan to marry again, either."

Syd made a humphing sound. "That is all just so wrong in so many ways."

"It's how I feel—and how he feels, too. Not everybody wants to get married. Not everyone is cut out to be a mother."

"If anyone is cut out to be a mom, it's you. You're letting what happened in the past steal your future from you."

"Syd. I'll say it again. It's how I feel." Ellie stirred in her arms. Syd opened her mouth to argue, but Lani put a finger to her lips and pointed at the baby. They were quiet for a moment, waiting, as Ellie sighed and settled back into sleep.

Syd whispered, gently now, "People change. You might find, as time goes by, that you want a life with the right man, you want children of your own to raise. And as for Max, well, whatever he said in the library months and months ago, that was then."

"Then?"

"Yeah, *then,* when you were calling yourselves 'friends.' Everything is different now."

"Not *that* different."

"Oh, yeah. *That* different. Wait and see. And remember this conversation, because one of these days in the not-too-distant future, I'm really looking forward to saying I told you so."

After she left Syd, Lani went to the library and worked for a while. The ancient librarian, Oliver Laurent, greeted her with more enthusiasm than he'd ever shown her before. He brought her some reference books she needed on Montedoran law in the sixteenth century to help her work out a plot point. And then he congratulated her on her big sale.

"His Highness Maximilian told me about it a week ago," the librarian said. "He's quite pleased, as are we all—and really, you've been coming here to work and study for almost two years now. I think it's time you called me Oliver."

"I would like that. But you will have to call me Lani."

He said he would be delighted. And then he slid her a

sly sideways glance. "You will be sure and tell us when the books will be available?"

Lani took the hint. She thanked him for his good wishes and promised to provide signed copies to the library, to him personally and to his assistants as soon as she received her author's copies—which, she warned, would be more than a year away for the first of the three books.

At four, she went out into the gardens looking for Gerta, who often brought Constance and Nick outside after school. Gerta greeted her with a hug. Connie had a friend over. They were playing with their dolls a few feet from the bench where Gerta sat.

Lani sat next to Gerta and asked, "Where's Nick?"

"Still at school." Both Nick and Connie attended Montedoro's highly rated International School. "They have an after-school swim program now."

"That's perfect for Nicky. He can swim off some of that energy."

"He's a handful, all right. How's the new place?"

"Cozy."

"Ah. You like it, I think."

"I do. And Gerta, I…" Somehow, she didn't know how to go on.

A small smile tipped the corner of the older nanny's mouth. "You and His Highness, eh?"

Lani stole a quick glance at the two little girls. They were busy with their dolls, lost in their own world. "How did you know?"

"I have eyes. And ears. Also, you should have seen his face when I told him you were no longer Trev and Ellie's nanny and that you had left the palace."

Lani felt more than a little ashamed. "He was really angry that I didn't tell him."

"Oh, yes. He was tense and preoccupied for days. Then

last night late, I thought I heard him go out. And this morning at breakfast he was all smiles."

"We worked it out, I guess you could say. And tonight, we're going to dinner."

Gerta nodded. "He's a good man, the prince. He was the sweetest little boy, so helpful and kind. I keep hoping Nicky will grow to be more like him."

"It's the age. Most eight-year-olds are ready to run the world—or at least to knock themselves out trying to get things their way." Lani still wasn't sure of how Gerta felt about her seeing Max. "You're…okay then, with the idea of Max and me spending time together?"

"You make His Highness happy. And I did help to raise him. He may be a grown man, but to me, he's still the good little boy who always wanted to do the right thing and would tell me he loved me when I tucked him in his bed at night. So if you make him happy, I'm happy." Gerta patted her hand. "The question is, are *you?*"

"Yes, of course, I…" She blew out a slow breath. "I have to admit. It's all kind of new and scary."

"Only if you make it that way," said Gerta. "Life is short. Savor every minute."

"I'll try."

Gerta tipped her face up to the thin winter sun. "I admit it might get a little difficult when the press gets hold of it."

"Don't remind me."

"You'll be fine. Do what they all do, all the Bravo-Calabrettis. Hold your head high, show them no weakness and never let them see you cry."

Max came to get her that night in a black limousine. His driver held the door for her and she ducked into the waiting embrace of the smooth leather seat.

But she wasn't careful enough of her short black dress.

It rode way up. The driver shut the door and she tried to be subtle about tugging the skirt back down where it belonged.

Max watched her plucking at her hem, a smile flirting with those fine lips of his, looking every inch the prince in one of those suits that probably cost more than she made in a year—well, last year anyway. This year would be better due to that nice, fat advance check she was getting.

"Nervous?" He leaned a little closer. He smelled wonderful, as always, a heady combination of subtle, expensive aftershave and pure manliness.

"I feel…I don't know. Naked, somehow."

He leaned closer. "You're not. You look beautiful and all the naughty bits are covered."

She poked him with her elbow as the driver pulled away from the curb. "It's not what I meant."

He grew more serious. "You're still afraid to be seen in public with me."

She put on her seat belt. "Well, yeah. I mean, being as how you're such a complete loser and all."

He hadn't hooked his seat belt. So it was easy for him to slide the rest of the way across the plush leather. He put his arm around her. "You're mean when you're nervous. I don't care. I like you next to me, whatever mood you're in."

She liked having his arm around her, liked the feel of him, of all that hot and muscled good-smelling manliness pressed against her side. "If we get in a wreck, you could go through the windshield."

He nuzzled her neck. "I'll take my chances."

"Spoken like a man born to privilege."

He caught her ear and worried it a little between his teeth. She felt a rush of heat across her skin. "I love to touch you. I love that you're finally *letting* me touch you.…"

She couldn't stop herself. She turned to him. They shared a kiss. It was slow and very sweet. The feel of his mouth on hers was a miracle to her. She could just climb in there and swim around in all that heat and wetness. Finally, she whispered against his lips, "I'm not walking into a restaurant on your arm looking like I just had sex in the car. So slide back to your side of the seat, please."

He chuckled. But he did as she asked. "It's going to be fine. No one will bother us. You'll see."

"I know that. I've seen how careful the reporters are here." In Montedoro, the tabloid journos kept their distance from the princely family. Security was unobtrusive, but everywhere. Reporters and photographers who got out of line were quickly escorted to the French border and invited firmly never to return. "It's only…"

"Say it." He did that thing, holding her eyes, making her feel she could trust him with anything. Her life. Her future. Everything she'd almost thrown away in the past.

She tried to explain. "Everything's changed overnight. Since New Year's, I've been running away from you. Now I need to stay right here beside you. I'm not sure of how to do that yet."

He offered his hand. She took it and twined her fingers with his. His touch soothed her frazzled nerves. "I'm here." He made the two words into a promise. "Hold on to me."

She dredged up a smile for him, one that hardly trembled at all.

The restaurant was beautiful, in the Triangle d'Or, the area of exclusive shops and hotels in the harbor area near the casino. And Max was right about how they wouldn't be bothered.

Yes, people stared when she walked in on Max's arm, but then they went back to their own meals, their private conversations. The staff was right there when needed, invisible when not. And if paparazzi lurked nearby, she never spotted one.

As the meal progressed, she relaxed a little. They talked of things they always used to talk about, before New Year's. He brought her up to date on his progress with his second nonfiction book, a chronicle of Montedoro's two hundred years as a Spanish protectorate. They discussed her new contract and her plans to go to New York in a couple of months, as soon as she finished the book she was working on. She would meet with Marie and with her new editor.

Max said he would be speaking at Columbia University in April. He sipped the really excellent Cabernet he'd ordered for them. "Let's go together, combine business with pleasure."

The unreality of all of it—the two of them, out for an evening like any two ordinary people might do, casually discussing a trip together—hit her all over again. "Can we get through breakfast Sunday with your family before we start planning for two months out?"

He ate a bite of artichoke heart. "Fair enough," he replied in a neutral tone.

After that, he seemed a little subdued. Not withdrawn, exactly, but careful. She knew it was her fault, for being snippy and difficult. She knew she should apologize.

But she was feeling just edgy enough that she'd probably only hurt his feelings again. Better for him to be on his guard against her.

The lamb came. It was fabulous. They had soft cheeses with wonderful little bits of crusty bread. And the dessert cart pretty much took her breath away.

She couldn't decide.

He told the waiter, "We'll have the chocolate cake and the crème brûlée."

She saw no reason to argue. "Good choices."

He shrugged. "Someone had to make a decision."

She felt defensiveness rise, and reminded herself that she'd already been crabby enough for one evening. So she beamed a big smile at the waiter. "Put the chocolate cake right here in front of me."

They shared both desserts. She tried to have only a taste or two. But she ended up unable to resist devouring every last bite of the cake. He ate most of the crème brûlée, so she told herself they were even.

There were more stares when they left the restaurant. But really, the curious glances weren't that hard to ignore. Lani started thinking that being stared at all the time was like anything else. If it happened enough, you got used to it. Maybe eventually, she would be like Max, confident and graceful in just about any situation.

When they stood outside across from the casino and the world-famous Fountain of the Three Sirens, he asked, "Would you like to play the tables for a while?"

She answered truthfully. "I would rather be alone with you."

He put his hand at the small of her back then, the light touch possessive and also somehow tender. She sucked in a sharp breath and glanced up into his waiting eyes.

"There you are," he whispered, for her ears alone. "Good to see you again."

"All right," she confessed. "I *have* been nervous."

"Not so much anymore?"

"It's getting better all the time."

The long black car drifted up and stopped at the curb in front of them. They got in. When he pulled her into the circle of his arm, she didn't even complain about the safety issues of driving around without her seat belt.

She put her head on his shoulder. "Where are we going?"

He touched his lips to her hair. "Around the block. I have a villa on Avenue d'Vancour."

"Your villa." Just the two of them. Alone. "Perfect."

Five minutes later, he still had his arm around her. Her head was comfortably tucked into his shoulder. And they were driving in circles.

She observed, "It's a very long way around the block."

He ran his hand down her bare arm, stirring a row of happy goose bumps. "Evasion maneuvers, just throwing off any nosy reporters—here we are."

"It's beautiful." In the classic Mediterranean style, the two-story villa was yellow stucco with white trim. The driver turned the car into the side driveway that curved around to the back.

They got out onto a walkway paved in white stone. In-ground lights showed them the way, across a pretty patio to a pair of French doors. Light glowed from within. Max ushered her into a living area that adjoined a large open kitchen.

A middle-aged woman in a plain black dress came toward them. Lani recognized her. She was Max's personal housekeeper and cook. "Sir," she said.

"Hello, Marceline."

Marceline gestured at the ice bucket on the low coffee table. "I've opened the champagne and left you a few treats there on the counter, and in the refrigerator."

Max thanked her. With a quick nod, she went out the way they had come in. He shrugged out of his jacket and tossed it across the sofa. Then he turned to Lani and smiled, and she realized there was nowhere else she'd rather be than right there, with him. "Let's go upstairs."

"Yes."

He handed her the two flutes waiting on the coffee table and he took the bucket of ice and champagne. They went through a central hallway to the front foyer and up the curving white stairs.

Halfway down the upper hall, he led her into a large bedroom suite. He set the bucket down on the coffee table, took the flutes from her and poured them each a glass.

There was a terrace that looked out over the sea. "Let's go out there," she said.

"It will be chilly."

"Just for a minute."

So they went out on the terrace and admired the Mediterranean gleaming under the new moon. When she shivered, he stood behind her and wrapped her in his strong arms.

He brushed a kiss above her ear. "This was my parents' villa. They bought it when they were newlyweds, a quick and easy getaway from the palace. I was almost born here."

"Almost?"

"It's tradition that the heir to the throne should be born at the palace. My mother went into labor here. The story goes that she felt the first twinge at noon and I popped out at a quarter of one. She barely made it to the palace on time." There was laughter in his deep voice. "All of us were like that, eager to get into the world. My mother had easy pregnancies and quick births."

"Which would explain why she was willing to go through all that nine times."

"Eight," he corrected. "Remember, Alex and Dami are twins."

"Oh, well. *Only* eight—and that's just another way your mother is amazing."

"Some have remarked that a ruling princess should be more delicate."

"Jealous much?"

He gathered her closer. "Yes, I believe that they are."

She sipped her champagne and shivered in the wind off the water, even with his warm arms holding her close.

"Ready to go in?" He rubbed his cheek against her hair.

Another shiver went through her, as much from anticipation as the chill in the air. "Yes."

Inside he took her hand and they went to the bed. The covers were drawn invitingly back. He set down his flute on the inlaid night table, took hers and set it beside his.

Then he cradled her face between his two strong hands. "Am I rushing you?" He rubbed his nose against hers, breathing in, scenting her.

Her heart thrummed a deep, hungry rhythm under her breastbone. "No." Breathless. Yearning. "Absolutely not."

He pressed his cheek to hers. Already, she could feel the slight roughness, the beginnings of his dark beard. He said, "The first time I saw you was outside my parents' palace apartment. It was in mid-May, not long after you came here with Sydney. You had Trevor in your arms. You were bringing him to Sydney and Rule, I believe."

She seemed to recall that. "You smiled at me, didn't you?"

He kissed her lips, a brushing caress. "You barely remember."

"Everything was so new, so completely outside of my experience."

"I was just another Bravo-Calabretti prince among so many, eh?"

"Never."

He chuckled against her mouth. "Liar. I knew you hardly saw me. But *I* saw you. I wanted to touch your cheek, to learn the texture of your skin. I wanted to get close enough to know the scent of you."

She hardly knew how to answer. "Oh, Max…"

He took her shoulders and turned her around. "You have

no idea how rare that moment was for me. I find most people interesting. You could say I'm socially adept. It's part of my position as heir, to be good with people. But to be… swept away at the sight of a woman. No. Usually, there's a distance I feel, a need to be careful, to proceed slowly. The sense that I will never really know them, be open to them. Not with you. Right away, I knew I wanted you, wanted to be with you."

His words excited her. They also surprised her. "I had no clue you felt that way."

He went on. "The second time I saw you was in the garden by the topiary hedges, with Trevor again. I ducked away so you wouldn't see me. By then, I'd decided that I was *too* attracted to you and I would be wiser to avoid you."

"Too attracted? Seriously? How could I not have picked up on that?"

"Yes, well. I didn't want you to know."

She leaned back against him. "Ah. Right."

He linked his arms around her waist. "And then I saw you in the library and I was intrigued. I wanted to know what you were doing there, with your laptop, so serious and intent, those charming black-rimmed glasses you wore then sliding down your nose. I asked Oliver Laurent about you. He said he believed you were writing a novel."

She could feel him growing hard against the small of her back and she settled in closer, savoring the power in his arms as they tightened around her. "Yes," she said on a whisper.

"Yes, what?" His voice teased in her ear.

"Yes, I saw you there several times before you ever spoke to me. I knew who you were by then. I remember us sharing nods and polite smiles."

"I kept waiting for my interest in you to fade. I was absolutely certain it would." His palms glided up her rib cage. He cradled her breasts. She gasped, a tiny sound. He pressed his lips against her hair and whispered, "It only got stronger. Finally, I gave in to it and spoke to you."

Even through the fabric of her dress and bra, the feel of his hands on her was so lovely. "I remember that day." She held back a moan of pleasure and felt all the more aroused as he found her nipples with his thumbs. "We argued about Anastagio the Great." An early Calabretti lord, the deposed Anastagio had turned to piracy to reclaim what he'd lost. Later, he'd recaptured Montedoro from the Genoese. "I said he was a genius. You said he was a murdering thief willing to do anything to regain the power he'd lost."

"I'd never met a woman so fascinated by Montedoran history." He nuzzled her ear and continued to do naughty things to her breasts. "Through the whole of our first conversation, your eyes didn't glaze over once."

"It was a fascinating conversation."

"To you and to me, which is exactly my point."

She rubbed back against him, shamelessly. "After that first time we talked, you were always kind to me. Friendly. Easy to talk to—about books and history, about your work and mine, about the children. I knew you liked me. But that you wanted me? I swear, I didn't know, not for months and months. Even when you asked me to dance that first time, I assumed you were only being kind."

"Denial." He breathed the word against her temple.

She confessed it. "Yes. I never let myself admit what was happening between us until I had no choice."

"Until New Year's Eve."

"Yes. New Year's Eve…"

His hands left her breasts. She wanted to grab them back. But then he touched her hair, smoothing it to the side. She understood his intention and reached back to guide the dark strands out of his way. He took the zipper down. "I read you correctly. I knew I would never get near you unless you trusted me first. It took a very long time to gain your trust." He guided the dress forward, off her shoulders. It dropped to her waist.

"I had no idea what you were up to...." She looked down at the twin swells of her breasts cradled in the black lace of her bra. Her skin felt thin and acutely sensitized.

He made her burn by the simple act of running both palms so lightly up and down her bare arms. "You didn't *want* to know what I was up to."

"Max, I..." She tried to turn around to him.

He caught her shoulders and held her in place facing away. "You're not an easy woman to get close to. Still, I want you. Why is that?"

"Um, because you're a glutton for punishment?"

He chuckled then, a rough, low, exciting sound. "There could be some truth in that." And then he buried his face against her neck. He scraped his teeth across her skin and she moaned. "Take off the dress." The words seemed to burn themselves into her yearning flesh.

She eagerly obeyed him, pushing the dress down. It fell to the rug. He took her by the waist and lifted her out of it effortlessly, as though she weighed no more than a glass of champagne, setting her down again closer to the head of the bed, but still facing away from him.

He hooked a finger under the strap of her bra next and guided it down so it fell along her arm. The other received the same treatment. And then he undid the clasp. Instinctively, she lifted her hands and caught the cups against her chest.

"Let it go." A command.

By then, she wanted nothing so much as to obey him. She did. The bra dropped to the side of the bed and slid off to land near the toes of her black high-heeled shoes. She waited, her breath uneven, yearning for him to touch her breasts again.

Instead, he trailed both index fingers slowly along her sides, from just under her arms down into the cove of her waist and outward, following the swells of her hips, pausing at her panties. And then inward, tracing the elastic from each side across her lower belly. Until those clever, knowing fingers met in the middle right below her navel.

Her belly muscles twitched in anticipation.

And he didn't disappoint her. He dipped both fingers lower. She moaned at that, and moaned again when he cupped her through her panties.

He whispered, "Take these off, too." And he let go of her.

Trembling, eager, she did what he commanded. Stumbling a little as she lifted one foot and then the other to get them off and away.

He touched her, his hands on her hips again, steadying her. "Lani…" It sounded so good to her, so right, her name from his mouth. She had no idea at that moment why she had ever run from him. Here, with him, was exactly where she wanted to be.

She stood up straight again.

And he guided her hips, turning her at last, until she was facing him.

A kiss. Sweet, wet. Endless. Her breasts brushed the fabric of his beautiful dress shirt, the slight friction increasing her already considerable arousal. And her hands strayed up, her fingers sifting into his hair, clasping his neck.

Images of their one time before, at the first of the year, floated in her mind. He had seemed shier then, somehow. More careful of her, almost reverent.

Not so reverent now.

More forceful. More sure. She found she was wild for both sides of him. Forceful or tender, his caresses excited her. His kisses carried her away, made her forget all her fears and doubts and hesitations, all her past sins, until there was nothing but the sound of his voice in her ear, the wonder of his hands on her flesh.

He clasped her waist. She gave a soft cry of surprise as he lifted her, setting her down on the side of the bed.

"Don't move," he instructed.

So she sat there on the silky sheet, naked in her high-heeled shoes. He undressed swiftly, in a ruthless economy of movement, shucking everything off from his tie to his socks and silk boxers in no time at all.

His body was so beautiful, broad and strong, the muscles sharply defined beneath bronze skin. He worked out several times a week in the training yards of the Sovereign's Guard, he'd told her. *I'm a geek and proud of it. A very fit geek.*

She grinned at the memory, and kicked off her shoes.

He bent close so suddenly that she gasped. "What's funny?"

"You." She kissed him, quick and hard. "Total geek, really buff."

He caught her mouth again and kissed her endlessly, wrapping his arms around her as he did it, coming down to the bed with her, rolling until she was on top. She braced on her hands and gazed down at him.

And then he smiled. Slowly. "I have you where I want you now."

She'd ended up with her knees to each side of his lean waist and he was pressed against her in exactly the right spot. "Or maybe *I* have you…."

He slid a hand down between them. She hitched in a hungry breath as he touched her. "Wet," he said softly, appreciatively.

With a low, pleasured sound, she bent close and kissed him again.

And then they were rolling. And he was on top. She looked up into his eyes as he caressed her, making her wetter, hotter, ready for him. He groaned and he bent his head and captured her breast as below he went on caressing her.

She threaded her fingers in his hair, holding him to her as he drew her nipple into the wetness beyond his lips, as he touched her, fingers delving in. It was good. It was so sweet. Without shadows, without fear.

Right now, she was lost in him, joyfully, all her worry and hesitation about where they might go from here banished. Gone.

He rolled her on top again, pulling her down to him, kissing her, deep and slow and endlessly. And then they were on their sides, facing each other. He said her name. She gave his back to him.

Within that sweet heat pulsing between them like a beating heart, the past didn't matter and the future was of no concern. He wrapped her close, scooted back—and pulled open the little drawer in the bedside table. He took out a condom.

They laughed together, breathless and eager, as he fumbled to get the wrapper off.

"Here. I'll do it." She took it from him and managed it easily.

He said, "Well done."

And then she rolled it down over him smoothly, fitting it snugly at the base. "I do good work."

"Come here." He flipped her onto her back once more and rose up above her.

She opened to him, reaching up to bring him down to her, taking his weight gratefully, wrapping her legs around him, crying out as he entered her in one smooth, hard thrust.

"Wait." He held still, hips flexed, fully within her.

"Oh, my…"

He braced his forearms on the pillow, to each side of her head. "Still. Be still. Don't move."

"Oh, my, oh, my…"

He lowered his mouth and he kissed her, his tongue sliding inside, tasting her as deeply as he was buried in her below.

She ached with the pleasure of it. She moaned into his mouth. And still, he held steady as he went on kissing her.

Finally, when she thought she would go mad with the sheer unbearable goodness of it, with the burning need to move, he lifted his head and he stared down at her, eyes gone from iron-gray to the sweetest, cleanest blue.

She panted, dazed, gazing up at him. "Now? Please?"

His mouth twitched. "Say that again?"

She punched him on his big arm. "You are torturing me."

He was merciless. "Again."

"Please?"

"Please what?"

"Please, Max, I need to move."

"Ah. Move? Really?" And then he did it. A smooth, hard flex of his powerful hips. "Like this?"

She had no words left. Which wasn't really a bad thing. Because finally, he was willing.

He did it again. "Answer me. Like this?"

"Yes," she somehow managed to croak out.

"Say it again."

And she did. "Yes. Yes, yes, yes…"

And at last, they were moving. Moving together. Rising and falling, faster and harder. Until there was only the two of them on a high wave of pleasure, rising and rising higher, opening outward to light up the night.

Chapter Six

"**I**'m not sure about Sunday," she told him a little bit later, as they stood in the kitchen wearing matching silk robes he'd pulled from a closet, drinking champagne and eating red-hearted slices of a Montedoran orange.

He reached out, wrapped a hand around the back of her neck and brought her right up close to him. "Forget it. You're not backing out." He kissed her.

She tasted the oranges, tart and sweet, as she sighed into his mouth. "It seems a little too soon, that's all."

He looked at her patiently. "All right. I'll play along. Too soon? How do you figure that?"

She stammered out the best explanation she could think of on such short notice. "Well, I mean, we really only barely got something going between us last night. You know, in a real, sincere, both-on-the-same-page and we-want-to-be-together kind of way."

His eyes were iron-gray. But at least he wasn't scowling. Then, unfortunately, he started talking. "I'm not going to argue with you about it. I'm not going to point out that we should have been together months ago, but you needed forever to admit that this is important, this thing between us."

"But you *are* arguing."

"No, *you* are. You're going. No excuses." He offered her

a slice of orange. She pushed it away. That didn't stop him from reminding her, "You agreed to go. Keep your word. Do not disappoint me."

"You used to be so patient."

"And look where being patient got me."

"If you would only—"

"No. I mean it. There is no 'if only' here. Last night, you made a choice to tell me your secrets, to go forward with me. You said you would go to Sunday breakfast. There's nothing to argue about here. You're going."

She thought of his children then. "What have you told Nick and Constance about me?"

He looked at her sideways. "What do you mean?"

"Do they know I'm invited for Sunday morning?"

He gazed off toward the French doors. "Well, I…"

She drew in a breath and let it out slowly. "You haven't talked to them."

"I only thought—"

"Max. Come on. You *didn't* think."

He got that look, his I'm-the-prince-and-you're-not look. "We have to start somewhere."

"And we have. We went out. We're here, in your villa, sharing champagne and oranges after mind-altering sex."

His lips twitched. "Mind-altering, was it?"

"I'm only asking why you need to rush things."

"I'm not rushing. You are dragging your feet. I will tell Nick and Connie that you'll be with us for Sunday breakfast."

Another awful thought occurred to her. "You *have* told your parents I'll be there, right?" The silence was deafening. "Oh, God, Max. You haven't told them. You're bringing me to a private family breakfast—and I'm a surprise."

"It's not a formal event. It's easy and comfortable, open-ended. There's plenty of food for whoever can make it.

Husbands, wives, children, dear friends, girlfriends, boy-friends and all variety of significant others are welcome."

"Meaning you *haven't* told them."

"I just explained. It's not necessary that I tell them."

"Oh, really? How many significant others have you brought to your family's Sunday breakfast since you lost your wife?"

He set down his empty champagne flute. Slowly. "All right. You're the first."

"So it's very likely I will be a surprise. Possibly a big surprise. I don't want to be a big surprise. If you're going to hold me to this—"

"I am. Absolutely."

"Then you will tell your parents and your children that I will be there."

He picked up the bottle and poured them each another glass. "All right. I'll tell them."

She didn't know whether to be relieved—or more anxious than ever. "I still think it's too soon."

"You're going. That's that."

All her clothes were wrong.

Lani knew this because the contents of her closet were strewn across the bed and she still hadn't decided what to wear to Sunday breakfast with the princely family. Yeah, okay. She should have given it some thought before now. But she'd been busy all day Saturday writing and researching—not to mention creating her Facebook profile and fan page, setting up a Twitter account, reserving her domain name and signing up for a couple of online classes.

Who had time to think about what to wear? She stood in front of the mirror mounted on the closet door and scowled at her reflection. There was nothing wrong with her slim gray skirt and blue silk blouse—but nothing particularly right about them, either.

She'd pinned her hair up. Should she take it down?

The intercom down the hall buzzed. That would be the driver of the car Max had insisted on sending for her.

"Oh, help!" she moaned aloud. And then she grabbed her gray suede pumps and her blue faux crocodile purse and raced to the door.

The driver let her off at the palace entrance closest to Max's apartments.

The guard there checked her ID against his handheld device and admitted her with a quick nod. She hurried down one gorgeous hallway and then another, the heels of her pumps echoing on the inlaid floors. When she got to Max's door, she paused to smooth her hair and straighten her blouse. A buzzer sounded inside when she pushed the little button by the door.

The housekeeper, Marceline, answered with a polite smile and a pleasant, "Come in. They're almost ready, I believe."

"Lani. You're right on time." Max entered the foyer from the apartment's central hall, wearing tan slacks and yet another beautiful soft sweater, looking casual and confident and way, way hot—and making her certain all over again that her clothes were all wrong. He herded Nick and Connie in front of him.

Nick, in dark pants and a striped shirt, his cowlick slicked mercilessly down, complained, "If I *have* to go, let me at least bring my Nerf gun." He glanced up at his father, who shook his head. "Bow and arrow? Slingshot?" Max only kept moving his head from side to side. "This is going to be so *bo*-ring."

"You'll get through it," Max said. He really was so patient with the kids.

Nick glanced back at Max again. Something in his father's eyes must have reached him, because he stopped complaining.

Max said, "Thanks, Marceline." She nodded and circled around him and the children on her way to the central hall. Max and the kids reached Lani. "You made it," he said softly. He looked so happy to see her, she forgot all about how she hated her gray skirt and she still wasn't sure she even wanted to do this.

Connie, looking a little flushed in a darling red dress and sweater over white tights with Mary Janes, was tugging on Lani's hand. "Nanny Lani, I don't feel so good," she said in a near whisper.

"Oh, honey…" Lani felt her forehead.

Max said, "What?"

"I don't know. She's not feverish."

And then Connie said, "Oh!" Her eyes went saucer wide and she put her hand on her stomach.

"What?" Max demanded again.

Alarm jangled through Lani. "Honey, are you going to be sick?"

"I…" It was the only word Connie managed. Then she vomited on Lani's gray suede shoes.

For a moment, they all four just stared down at Lani's splattered shoes in stunned disbelief.

Nicky broke the shocked silence with a howl. "Oh, gross! Connie barfed all over Nanny Lani!" He put his hands to his throat and faked a loud string of gagging noises.

Max shot him a dark look. "Nicholas." Nicky dropped his hands and had the good sense not to let out another peep. Max gave Lani a quick, apologetic glance and then knelt and laid a gentle hand on Connie's shoulder. "Sweetheart…"

Connie blinked at him—and gagged again.

Lani's inner nanny took over. She dropped her purse, scooped up the little girl and headed for the bathroom, not even pausing to see if Max followed, hoping against hope that she wouldn't end up with vomit down her back to go with what already squished in her shoes.

She did not get her wish. Connie let loose again just as she made it to the bathroom door.

Lani gulped against her own gag reflex and kept moving. Grabbing a big towel from the linen rack, she bent with Connie in her arms and spread the towel on the rug by the tub. "It's okay, okay," she soothed as she let the little girl down on the soft rug in front of the towel. Lani's mother, the pediatrician, had always offered a towel rather than the toilet in a situation like this. Kids found it less disturbing—if it was possible to be less disturbed when the contents of your stomach refused to stay down. "Right here. Just bend over this towel. That's right. That's it. Easy…" On her knees now, Connie kept gagging. Kneeling beside her, Lani rubbed her back and held her blond curls out of the way as more came up. Lani flipped the edges of the towel over to cover the mess.

Max came in quietly and stood over them. "More towels?" At Lani's nod, he went to the linen shelves and came back with three more. He dropped to the floor on Connie's other side.

Lani kept up the soft encouragements. "That's good. Just let it happen. You'll feel better, sweetie, it's okay…."

Connie moaned and more came up. Max put down a new towel over the soiled one.

Finally, Connie sighed and slumped against her dad. "I think I'm all done." The poor little thing looked wrung out.

Lani levered back on her heels and stood. "Where's her water glass?"

"The pink one," Max said.

So Lani grabbed the pink plastic glass from the counter by the sink. She splashed in a little children's mouthwash from the medicine cabinet and then filled it halfway with water. "Here." Max reached up and took it from her. "She shouldn't drink any, just rinse—and wait a minute." Lani quickly rolled up the soiled towels and pushed them out of the way, all the time acutely aware that she herself was probably the worst-smelling thing in the room now. "Can you stand up, Connie? So you can use the sink?"

"I think so."

Max rose and helped her up. She rinsed out her mouth as Lani ran cold water from the bathtub tap over a washcloth. She wrung it out and gave it to Max, who bathed Connie's face with it.

Max looked kind of sheepish. "I had no idea she was sick."

"I *wasn't* sick," Connie insisted. "But then, all of a sudden, I *was*."

"Probably just a stomach bug." Lani stayed well away from father and daughter and tried not to think about the sticky wetness down her back and the mess in her shoes. "I think I remember Gerta saying there was some stomach thing going around at school."

"I've called the family doctor," Max said. "He's on his way." He asked Connie, "How about a little rest?"

"Papa…" Connie sighed and reached up her arms to him. He scooped her up.

Gerta appeared in the doorway. "I have your bed ready, *Liebchen.*"

Lani suggested, "Along with more fresh towels?"

"All taken care of." Gerta kept a cheerful expression on her face and didn't once glance down at Lani's ruined shoes.

"Nanny Lani." Wide eyes regarded her solemnly over Max's broad shoulder. "Sorry I got throw-up all over you."

"It's not your fault. It washes off and I'll be good as new." *And I hate this skirt anyway.* She had, however, loved the suede shoes. "Rest and get better."

"I'll take her," Gerta offered.

But Connie wanted her dad right then. She hugged Max tighter. "Papa will take me." And then, just a tad imperiously, "And Nanny Gerta, you come, too."

"I am right here with you," Gerta promised tenderly.

Max sent Lani a rueful glance. "I'll be back."

They all three went out, leaving her standing there in her ruined shoes, unsure of whether she ought to try and clean up a little or wait for Max to return.

She was just about to shuck off the disgusting shoes and rinse her feet in the tub, at least, when Marceline bustled in with a fluffy white robe and a laundry bag over one arm, a basket of shower accessories on the other. Lani's blue purse was hooked over her shoulder. "You poor girl." She put the purse and the robe on the chest that stood against the wall. "Get out of those clothes. I'll see what I can do about them."

Lani took off the shoes first. "I think these are hopeless—and watch where you step. It's all over the floor here, and at the door, and in the foyer, too."

Marceline was undaunted. "Not to worry. I will take care of everything while you're in the shower."

Twenty minutes later, with Connie safely tucked in bed and Gerta comfortably situated in the corner chair watching over her, Max went to find Lani.

She was sitting on the edge of the tub in the children's bathroom wearing his robe, her cheeks pink and her pulled-back hair coming loose around her face in the most charming fashion. Marceline had done her magic. The floor was clean and the air smelled faintly of citrus.

Lani regarded him solemnly, an elbow on her knee and her chin on her hand. "How is she?"

He took a moment to answer, indulging himself in the sight of her, in his apartment, wearing his robe. "She's resting. Gerta took her temperature. It's slightly elevated. The doctor should be here soon."

"Good, then." She rose as he came toward her. "I didn't know where to go. It seemed inappropriate to start wandering around your palace apartment barefoot in a robe." Down the hall, the entry buzzer rang. "I'm guessing that's the doctor."

"Marceline will answer it." He took her shoulders. Her upturned face was dewy. She smelled of soap and roses. "Anywhere you wander, I will find you." He tugged on a curl that had gotten loose from the knot at the back of her head. It coiled, damp and tempting, down her neck. "You were a champion with Connie."

A smile bloomed. "Nanny Lani to the rescue." She teased, "And what do you know? I think we're kind of late for breakfast with the princely family."

"Do you have to look so happy to get out of it?"

Now she played innocent. "Happy? Me? No way. Poor Connie is sick and I'm out a favorite pair of shoes—and do you think you could send someone to my apartment to get me some actual clothes to wear?"

"I like you in my robe."

"How many ways can I say 'inappropriate'?"

"Yes, I will send someone to get your clothes."

"Thank you."

"And you'll come to Sunday breakfast *next* week." The postponement was probably just as well. He'd told the children that she was coming, as he'd promised her he would.

However, he hadn't quite gotten around to giving his mother and father a heads-up on his plans. Now he'd have time to take care of that.

As usual, she tried to back out. "I'll think about next Sunday."

"Do we have to go through this all over again? Just say yes now."

"Don't boss me around." She faked an angry scowl.

He took the shawl collar of the robe in both hands and tenderly kissed the end of her nose. "Please."

"I know what you're doing," she grumbled.

"I just want a yes out of you."

"You *always* want a yes out of me."

He couldn't resist. He buried his nose against her neck, sucked in the wonderful scent of her shower-moist skin and growled, "So give me what I want."

She laughed and playfully pushed him away—and then stiffened, her laughter catching on a gasp. Turning, Max followed the direction of her startled gaze.

Nick was standing in the doorway, watching them.

Chapter Seven

A few choice obscenities scrolled through Max's brain.

How long had Nick been there? What exactly had he seen?

A teasing embrace. A kiss on the neck.

Nothing that traumatic, surely.

"Nicky." Max managed to keep his tone even and easy. "What is it?"

Nick just went on staring, his face flushed scarlet.

Max tried again. "Nicky?"

Nick opened his mouth and said in a rush, "Marceline said to tell you the doctor's here." And then he ducked from the doorway and vanished from sight.

Max called after him, "Nicky!"

Lani touched his shoulder. He turned back to her and she suggested softly, "You'd better go after him and make sure he's all right."

"Lani, I…" He let the words trail off, mostly because he felt like the world's biggest idiot. What was he thinking, grabbing her like that with the door wide open?

"Go on," she said. "Check on Nick. Deal with the doctor."

He dared to touch that sweet loose curl again. "I've made a complete balls up of this, haven't I?"

At least she smiled. "It's not the end of the world. Go on. I'll be fine here."

* * *

He went to the foyer first.

Dr. Montaigne, who'd been curing the ills of the princely family for decades, waited in a carved mahogany hall chair, his old-school black bag on his lap. He jumped up when Max appeared.

Max greeted him and led him back to Connie's room.

Connie knew the doctor. He always took care of her when she was sick. "Dr. Montaigne," she said gravely. "I've been very sick and it was very sudden and I threw up all over Nanny Lani."

Old Montaigne set his bag by the bed. "Well, well, young lady. Let's have a look at you, shall we?"

"Will you check me with your stethoscope?"

"Excellent idea. We'll start with that."

Max edged close to Gerta. "I'll be back. I need a moment with Nicky…" He ducked out as the old doctor started taking Connie's vital signs.

Max found his son in the first place he looked—Nick's room. The door was wide open and he was lying on his bed with his tablet computer. Max stood in the doorway for a moment, watching him, a cautious feeling of relief moving through him.

Nick hadn't run off somewhere to hide. He'd just gone to his room. And he'd even left his door open. Surely that was a good sign.

Max knocked on the door frame.

Nick glanced at him—and went right back to his game. It was hardly an invitation to talk. On the other hand, he hadn't asked Max to leave him alone.

Max dared to enter. He went to the bed and sat carefully on the edge of it. Nick went on playing his game. Lego figures drove an armored car wildly through a Lego city. Max watched a chain of vehicles careen across the screen and tried to come up with a credible opening.

All he could think of was, "Nicky..."

Nick played on, kicking his stocking feet against the coverlet as he manipulated the armored car on the screen. But then, finally, he did say, "What?"

"I...want to talk to you about..." God in heaven, how to even begin? He'd never realized before what a terrible father he was. On any number of levels. "...about Nanny Lani and me in the bathroom." He tried not to wince as the words came out of his mouth. One day he would rule Montedoro. Right now, he didn't even know how to talk to his son.

Nick tossed the tablet aside and sat up, swinging his feet over the edge of the bed. For a moment, Max was sure he would leap to the floor and run off again. But instead he kicked his heels against the side of the mattress and accused, "You said she was coming for breakfast."

"That's right. And she did."

"I thought that was kind of weird, Nanny Lani coming to breakfast in Grandmother's apartment with us."

"Because she isn't part of our family?"

"Well, she's not." He kicked the mattress for emphasis. "And nannies don't come and eat with the family."

"Sometimes they do. Sometimes Gerta eats with us in the kitchen."

"That's different than Sunday breakfast. You know that it is."

"Nick, I...I happen to like Lani. I like her very much." Was this going well? He guessed not.

"Papa." A swift, angry glare. "You were *kissing* her neck." He seemed to suppress a shudder. "And she's not even a nanny anymore, really. Trev told me so."

"It's true she's not taking care of Trevor and Ellie any-

more. She has another job now. She writes books. And I...
well, Nick, I like her very much."

Nick stared straight ahead. "You already said that once,"
he muttered. "I heard you the first time, you know."

"You're right. I said it twice because I want you to know
that Lani is important to me and that's why I kissed her."

"Is she your *girlfriend*?"

"Yes. That is exactly what she is."

Silence from Nicky. He kicked his feet some more. Max
gritted his teeth and waited for his son to speak of Sophia,
to say how he missed her and no other woman better try
to take her place.

What was Max going to say to that? He had nothing.
Zero. He was dealing with this on the fly and he knew he
wasn't up to the challenge. As a rule, he liked to plan ahead
before tackling sensitive subjects with the children. Frantically, he cast about for something brilliant and fatherly
to contribute, all about how of course, Lani wouldn't be
taking Sophia's place. Sophia was Nicky's mother and always would be.

Was that completely self-evident and painfully obvious?
He had a sinking feeling it was.

Then Nick said, "So. Since Connie got sick, I guess we
don't have to go to Sunday breakfast, after all."

Max said nothing. He was too busy trying to decide if
he should bring up the subject of Sophia.

"Papa? Did you *hear* me?"

"Erm, yes, I did. And no, we won't be going to Sunday
breakfast this week."

"But next week we will?"

"Next week, yes."

Nick grew thoughtful. Would he speak of his mother
now? Max prepared himself to provide gentle fatherly re-
assurance. Finally, Nicky said, "Sunday breakfast isn't *that*

bad. It's just that I'm the oldest. Lately, Connie is always wearing dresses and playing with her dolls. And Trev is okay, but I mean, he's only four. And the rest of them are babies." All right. Nothing about Sophia. Should he just let it go? "Papa, there's just no one to play with at Sunday breakfast."

"Sometimes you have to go places where there's no one to play with."

"Yuck."

Max couldn't bear this. He had to say *something*. "Nick, I just want you to know that your mother loved you very much and she will always be your mother. No one could ever take her place."

Nick sent him a look of great patience. "I know that."

"Well, good. Wonderful." He waited, but Nick said no more. So he prompted, "And…is there anything more you'd like me to explain to you about Lani and me?"

Nicky's brow furrowed. "You never had a girlfriend before."

"Does that bother you, that I have one now?"

He thought some more. "It's okay."

"You're sure?"

"Papa, why do I have to keep telling you things over and over again?" He spoke with more inflection now, and rolled his hand in a circle for emphasis.

Max took heart. The animated Nicky he knew and loved was back. Apparently he wasn't scarred for life, after all. "Sorry. Anything more you need to know from me?"

"Well, if she's not Nanny Lani anymore, what I am s'posed to call her?"

"What would you like to call her?" Was that a dangerous question to ask an eight-year-old boy? Too late now.

"Um. Miss Lani maybe?"

Not bad. Max hooked an arm around his son. "That sounds just fine to me."

"Yeah." Nick leaned into Max's hold and swung his feet some more. "Miss Lani. I think that's good." Max nodded. For a moment, the two of them just sat there, together, as Nick kicked his heels against the bed. Then Nick said, "Where *is* Miss Lani?"

And that reminded him that he'd left her in the bathroom and he'd better get moving. "She's still here. And right now, I need to go and see what the doctor says about how Connie's doing. Do you want to come with me?"

Nick looked up at him. He could see echoes of Sophia in the bow of his mouth, the tilt of his nose. "Do you think she's going to puke again?" His eyes gleamed with eagerness. Nick found bodily functions endlessly fascinating.

"Let's hope not." Max got up. "Are you coming?"

Nick slid off the bed, put on his shoes and went with him.

In Connie's room, Dr. Montaigne was finishing up. "She should rest for the day," he instructed. "Give her liquids, starting with a half glass of juice or a little clear broth. If that stays down, she can have more…." The old guy droned on. Max listened and nodded and promised to call if Connie took a turn for the worse.

Then Connie started in about how she felt "all better" and wanted French toast. Max left Gerta to the job of keeping her in bed for a while. He needed to send the doctor on his way and get back to Lani, who'd been sitting in the bathroom for at least half an hour since the *last* time he left her in there.

What a disaster. He'd probably never get her to come near the apartment or either of his children ever again.

They had to walk past the bathroom on the way to the door. He glanced in and there she was, perched patiently on the edge of the tub, reading a magazine Marceline must have found for her, that tempting curl of hair brushing the collar of his robe. She spotted him with the doctor and Nick, and waved him on.

And he realized he couldn't bear to leave her there another minute. It just wasn't right. He turned to Nicky. "Nicholas, will you see the doctor the rest of the way out?"

"Yes! And then I want to eat because I am *starving*."

"Once you show the doctor out, find Marceline. Ask her to order up breakfast for us."

"Yes, I will! This way, Dr. Montaigne."

"Thank you, young man." He trotted off in Nicky's wake.

Max detoured into the bathroom.

Apprehension in those big dark eyes, Lani set her magazine on the edge of the tub and stood. "How did it go with Nick?"

He wanted to touch her. But no. He'd learned his lesson on that score. Anyone might go strolling by the bathroom at any time. "Overall, I think it went well. He says he has no problem with your being my girlfriend. And he's decided to call you Miss Lani now. Trevor told him that you're not a nanny anymore."

"I'm glad he's all right. What about Connie?"

"She says she wants French toast."

Lani laughed. She really did have a fine laugh, rich and husky and full out. "She'll be back to normal in no time." She straightened the robe. "I had Marceline call for a driver to go to my place for clean clothes. He'll be here any minute to pick up my key."

"Good."

Nick materialized in the doorway and announced, "Marceline says she has enough food in the little kitchen to make us breakfast." The main kitchen was downstairs and served regular meals for palace guests and residents alike. But the apartment had its own small galley kitchen, too. "She said to ask is that all right with you?"

"Yes, that would be fine."

"Good. She can cook it fast so that I don't *die* from *hunger*." He put his arms out in front of him and made monster sounds.

Lani laughed.

Nick grew suddenly shy. "Um. Hi, Miss Lani."

"Hello, Nick."

He glanced hopefully at Max. "Marceline said she'll make toast with strawberry jam."

"Go on then," Max said, and Nick darted off, leaving him alone with Lani. Again, he reminded himself that he wasn't going to touch her, not even to tug on that sweet loose curl. "There's really no reason for you to stay in this bathroom. Come on to the kitchen, have something to eat."

She straightened the robe again. "It's only…it's strange enough, not being the nanny anymore, everything changing, coming here to your palace apartment for the first time as, um, well, not as a nanny. And to end up like this…" She looked down at the robe. "It's just awkward, you know?"

"Everyone knows why you're wearing a robe. And if it will make you feel better, Marceline or Gerta can loan you something until your clothes get here. Or I could scare up something else from my closet, I'm sure."

She aimed that soft chin high. "You know, you're right. I shouldn't make a big deal of this." She got her purse from the chest in the corner. "Get me out of here." And she held out her hand.

A perfectly acceptable excuse to touch her. Wonderful. He wrapped his fingers around hers.

It turned out to be a really lovely morning after all, Lani thought.

The driver came for her key a few minutes after they joined Nick and Marceline in the kitchen.

They ate Marceline's excellent French toast and were just finishing the food when the driver returned with the clothes she'd asked for. Marceline showed her to a spare room where she got out of Max's robe at last and into a fresh skirt and sweater, comfy tights and a clean pair of shoes.

As she was changing her cell rang. It was Sydney. "Where *are* you? I thought you were coming to breakfast with the family?"

"Long story. Connie got sick. I think it was just something she ate, because she's better already. But we ended up staying here, in Max's apartment."

"Spending your Sunday with Max and the kids. This thing with you two is just moving right along."

"I can't really talk now. Max is waiting."

"Are those wedding bells I hear?"

"Knock it off, Syd."

With Sydney's laughter echoing in her ear, Lani ended the call.

By then, it was almost noon. She returned to the kitchen to find Max there alone. She joined him at the table. They drank too much coffee and discussed the finer points of Montedoro's delicate relationship with France. Eventually, they went to Connie's room to check on her. She was sitting up against the pillows, drinking apple juice and insisting that she was well enough to be out of bed.

Max kissed her forehead and told her to rest a little longer.

"But I'm all well!" Connie cried.

Lani suggested a board game. They called Nick in and Gerta produced a game of Trouble, which Lani remembered playing when she was a kid. An hour flew by. They popped the dice in the board's central "magic dome" and raced each other around the board.

Nick won, which pleased him no end. He flexed his

skinny arms and beat his chest and crowed, "I am the *champion!*"

And then Connie yawned and admitted that maybe she was ready to take a little nap.

Nick wanted to go out to the garden and play with his Nerf gun, so Gerta took him out. Lani and Max stayed in the apartment while Connie slept. They sat in the front sitting room and talked.

It really was almost as it used to be, before New Year's. They could talk for hours on any number of subjects.

But then again, no. It was completely different than it used to be. Every time he looked at her, she knew it. They were much more than friends now.

Syd could joke about wedding bells all she wanted, but Lani really didn't know where this thing with Max was going. He was important to her, and he'd made it very clear that she mattered to him. But marriage? Neither of them was up for that.

And why was she thinking about marriage, anyway? Why was she letting a few teasing remarks from Syd tie her all in knots about the future? After that disastrous foray into first love with Thomas all those years ago, she'd been playing it way too safe. She needed to take a few chances again. And now, at last, she was. Best to enjoy every moment and let the future take care of itself.

Nick and Gerta came back inside. Connie woke up and Max allowed her to bring her dolls out and play quietly in the family sitting room next to the kitchen.

Lani said she had to go. Max walked her out to the foyer.

But when they got to the door, he took both her hands. "I don't want you to go. Stay for dinner. It will only be us, you, me and the children." *Only us.* She did like the sound of that. She liked it way too much. He kept on convincing her. "We'll stay in, right here. I'll have the meal sent up and Connie can take it easy."

It was just too tempting.

She stayed. They ate early, in the kitchen, the four of them. Connie had soup and crackers and announced that it was the best soup she'd ever had and she didn't feel one bit like throwing up.

Lani got up to go again at seven. She said goodbye to Nick and Connie and Gerta.

Marceline appeared with her gray skirt and blue blouse, good as new, pressed and on hangers, covered with plastic. "I'm so sorry about your shoes," she said. "But there was no saving them."

Lani wasn't surprised. "Thanks so much for trying."

Max followed her to the door.

They lingered there, whispering together.

"You sure you won't let me call you a car?"

"Don't be silly," she told him. "It's a quick walk."

"I want to kiss you," he said, leaning close, but not actually touching her. "But after what happened with Nick, I'm trying to control myself."

"Self-control is important."

"Self-control is overrated," he grumbled. "I'm holding on to it only by a thread."

"I admire your determination to behave."

"No, you don't. You're laughing at me."

She bit her lower lip to keep it from twitching. "Only on the inside—and you have to let me go now."

"But I don't want to let you go now."

She went on tiptoe and brushed a quick kiss across his beautiful mouth. "Good night, Max."

Reluctantly, he opened the door for her. She slipped out fast, before he could convince her to change her mind and stay even later.

There was a different guard on duty at the door she'd used that morning. He checked her ID and nodded her out into the cool evening. She took a path she knew through the gardens and she was down Cap Royale and hurrying to the old villa on her little cobbled street in no time.

A stranger in a gray coat stood under the streetlight in front of the building. As she passed him and started up the steps, he called, "Yolanda, hey!"

Startled that he knew her name, she paused in midstep and glanced back at him.

He lifted something to his face. She didn't realize it was a camera until the flash went off and the shutter started clicking. And then she just stood there, gaping at him as he took several pictures.

"Thanks a million, sweetheart," he said when he lowered the camera. And then he turned and ran off down the street.

She knew what he was. Paparazzo.

Her legs felt like rubber bands, all wobbly and boneless. But she managed to put one foot in front of the other, to let herself in the building, to climb the stairs to her apartment.

Once inside, she locked up, tossed the plastic-covered skirt and blouse on the sofa and then stood in the middle of the room trying to assess the meaning of what had just happened downstairs.

It shouldn't have shocked her so. She'd known this would happen if she went out with Max. But after Friday night, when no one bothered them, and then today, in Max's apartment with the children, everything so normal and ordinary, she'd let herself forget.

She tossed her purse on top of her skirt and blouse and booted up her laptop. It took only a simple search of her name and Max's and there she was, at his side in her little black dress getting out of the limo, sitting across from him in the restaurant, driving off in the limo again.

The articles that went with the pictures were short ones without a lot of detail, at least when it came to her. She was called a "black-haired beauty," and a "mystery date."

"Mystery date," she whispered aloud to herself. Was that like a blind date? A date who made you solve a puzzle? Someone you went out with and didn't even know their name?

There was more about Max, all the old stories, of his perfect marriage, the tragic loss of his forever-love. Of how true he was to Sophia's memory, how he'd never been linked to any woman in the four years since her death.

Until now. Until the black-haired beauty, the mystery date.

Lani shut down the laptop and told herself it wasn't a big deal, that she'd known this would happen. That she needed to get used to it.

But the stuff about Sophia kind of stuck with her.

Sometimes Lani felt so close to him.

But right now she was thinking that she really didn't understand him at all. She needed him to talk to her about Sophia. And because it seemed to her such an important, sensitive subject, she'd been waiting for him to do that in his own time. He never had.

Now she had to decide how much longer to wait, how much more time he needed before he might be ready. Not to mention, how much longer she could hold out before she just went ahead and asked him.

Monday morning Her Sovereign Highness Adrienne met with her ministers in the Chambers of State. As his mother's heir, Max sat on her right-hand side.

Adrienne often conferred with him during the meeting. Sometimes she would call him into her private office beforehand or afterward, to discuss any measures or upcoming decisions on which she needed input or more information. Max had a talent for research and she would often ask him to gather more data on a particular subject. Sometimes she simply wanted his opinion on an issue she needed to settle. So when she asked him to join her in her office after the meeting, he assumed she needed to consult with him on some matter of state.

He followed her through the gilded doors to her inner sanctum. She led him to the sitting area, where she took one of the sofas and he claimed a Louis Quinze wing chair.

Adrienne smoothed her trim Chanel skirt and folded her delicate long-fingered hands in her lap. "We missed you at Sunday breakfast. How is Connie?"

He wasn't surprised she already knew that Connie had been ill. Old Dr. Montaigne was under orders to inform her if one of the children needed his care. "She's doing well. It was some kind of stomach upset. Something she ate, we think. But she recovered quickly. Gerta's keeping her home today, just in case."

"I'll try to get by and see her."

"She would love that." He waited for her to tell him what she needed from him.

And then she did. "I understand you've been seeing Trevor and Ellie's former nanny."

The skin pulled tight on the back of his neck. He felt ambushed. But then he ordered his neck muscles to relax. He'd taken Lani out. That was major news in Montedoro. Of course, his mother would have heard about it. And he'd been planning to tell her about Lani anyway, and putting it off, waiting for the right moment. This, apparently, was it. "Her name is Yolanda Vasquez, but she goes by Lani."

"Of course I know what her name is, darling. And she's a lovely young woman."

"Yes, she is."

"A budding novelist, I hear, who just made her first big sale."

"From whom did you hear that, exactly?"

She answered easily. "More than one source. Sydney mentioned the sale quite proudly over a week ago. And Oliver, in the library, seems very impressed with her success."

He felt slightly ashamed of his own defensiveness. Of course, his mother would have heard about Lani's big sale—and remembered it. Adrienne had a photographic memory and could recall the most obscure personal details shared by people she'd met only briefly, in passing. He explained, "She has a three-book contract with a major New York publisher. The books are historical novels set in Montedoro. She's also self-published three other novels that take place in present-day Texas."

"Wonderful. You must introduce me so that I may congratulate her properly." There was a definite chiding quality to her tone.

He couldn't resist chiding her right back. "Introduce you? She worked at the palace for nearly two years. You've never spoken to her?"

"Please, Maximilian. It's one thing to ask the nanny if Trevor is eating all his vegetables. It's another to have a conversation about publishing with someone my son and heir is seeing romantically."

He confessed, "I was bringing her to breakfast yesterday."

"Without mentioning it to me or your father beforehand."

"You've always said we're welcome to bring someone special—but you're right. I probably should have said something. Lani asked me to tell you that she was coming. I didn't get around to it." His mother wore a skeptical look. He admitted, "All right. I wanted you to meet her, wanted you to see us together without my making a big thing of it

beforehand…but then Connie grew ill and we stayed in."
In the interest of full disclosure, he added, "Lani stayed
with us until after dinner. We played a board game with the
children. Lani and I talked about the situation with France.
She has an excellent understanding of politics and history.
The day went by much too fast."

"And on Friday night, you took her out to dinner."

"And to the villa on the Avenue d'Vancour afterward."
He shifted in the chair, though he knew he shouldn't, that
to move at all showed weakness.

"It *is* serious, then?"

"Yes."

A soft smile curved her lips. "I didn't really have to ask
if it was serious, did I? You don't have casual relationships."

"No, Mother. I don't." Actually, there had been a few
physically satisfying arrangements with discreet partners
after Sophia's death. But those were more in the nature of
transactions than relationships.

"There could be…issues with the French ministers,"
Adrienne said thoughtfully. By the terms of the treaty of
1918, two of the ruling prince's five ministers were French
nationals. And while the ruling family was officially in
charge of succession, the French government had to for-
mally approve the next prince to take the throne. When his
mother had married his father, the French had been outraged. As the heir apparent to the throne, they'd expected
her to marry a man with money and influence, preferably a
prince or a king, though a duke or a marquess would have
done well enough. His father, a moderately successful Hol-
lywood actor, had not fit the mold.

On the other hand, when Max had married Sophia, the
French ministers were all smiles. They'd considered her
the perfect bride for the Montedoran heir. She was not only

the virgin daughter of a Spanish grandee, but she brought a large dowry, as well.

Not that any of that really mattered anyway. He and Lani were on the same page about marriage.

Max said, "The French ministers will get over themselves. They always do."

"I am a bit hurt, I must confess, that you didn't come to me and tell me about this sooner."

"I'm sorry, Mother," he said automatically.

She studied him, her head tipped to the side. "No, you're not. And wasn't there some talk about the two of you last year?"

"I'm sure there was," he said resignedly, "because I danced with her." In the four years since Sophia's death, Max had made it a point to dance only with his mother and his sisters. He intended never to marry again, and dancing only with family members was one of the ways he made his intentions—or rather, the lack of them—clear to everyone.

But in September, at the palace gala celebrating his sister Rhiannon's marriage to Commandant Marcus Desmarais, Max had danced with Lani for the first time. He'd done it again at the Harvest Ball and yet again at the Prince's Thanksgiving Ball. And then, finally, he'd claimed those five dances on New Year's Eve, when everything started to change between them at last.

His mother waited for him to say more.

He gave in and explained himself a little. "I knew what I wanted over a year ago. It's taken her longer. Whatever people whispered when I danced with her, there was nothing to say to you, nothing you needed to know, until last Thursday night when Lani and I finally came to a mutual understanding that we were more than friends."

Adrienne rested her elbow on the sofa arm and gave him a slow, thoughtful dip of her dark head. "All right, then. She's important to you and you intend to continue seeing her."

"Exactly."

"I'm glad for you," his mother said, and he knew she meant it sincerely. "Glad that you've found someone, glad that you're finally willing to try again." She extended her hand across the low table.

He took it. Her grip was strong. They shared a smile before letting go. "Until I met Lani, there didn't seem to be any reason to try again."

Adrienne regarded him steadily. "As I recall, Yolanda worked for Sydney for several years…."

"Seven in total, yes—and she prefers to be called Lani."

"Lani. Of course. I understand that Lani has been an excellent nanny."

"That's right."

"And as to her family in America…?"

"Her father's a college professor and her mother's a pediatrician. They're still married to each other, and happily so from what Lani's told me. She has a married brother who's a businessman." Max knew where this was going and he just wanted it over with. "What are you getting at, Mother?"

"Darling, it's all very well to dismiss the French ministers. But is there anything in Lani's past, anything about her that might require damage control if the tabloids get hold of it?"

There it was. The question he'd been dreading. He proceeded with care. "Lani has her secrets, yes. Her regrets. As do we all. I don't know how much an enterprising journo might dig up. And frankly, I don't really care. We will get through it, whatever happens. I have no doubts on that score."

His mother's beautiful face appeared serene. But he knew her sharp mind was working away behind the smooth facade, exploring possibilities, considering options. "She must have passed our usual background check, or Rule would never have made her part of his household. So then what, exactly, is there to dig up?"

"I can't tell you that, Mother. Lani told me in confidence."

"Will she tell me—or let *you* tell me?"

"My guess would be no."

"I could…order a discreet inquiry."

"Please don't. Leave it."

Adrienne looked tired, suddenly. She asked wistfully, "You couldn't have chosen someone sweet and uncomplicated?"

"Someone eighteen and raised in a convent?" Adrienne actually chuckled at that, though it wasn't an especially happy sound. He went on, "Lani *is* sweet."

"I only want you to be absolutely certain of your choice before you tie a knot that cannot be undone."

Bitterness moved in him. He tasted dust and ashes in his mouth. His mother knew too much. She was far too observant, and so infuriatingly wise. "There won't be any knot, so that won't be a problem."

Adrienne didn't move, but the sovereign of Montedoro vanished. She became only his mother, worried for him, wanting his happiness above all. "So you're still determined never to—?"

"Yes." There was no need to go into all this again. "Let it be. I stayed true to my vows and the throne is secure and I'm free to make other choices now."

"But how does Lani feel about that?"

"We've discussed it. She understands how it will be. In fact, she has no desire ever to marry."

"How long ago did you discuss it?"

He didn't like the direction this was going. Not in the least. "It was a while ago."

"Before you became lovers?"

"You know, this really isn't a subject I want to talk over with my mother."

An amused smile ghosted across her mouth. "Think of me as your sovereign, then. Did you discuss your feelings about marriage with Lani before you two became lovers?"

He gave in and answered her. "Yes." It had been more than a year ago, as a matter of fact. "But so what? Lani knows my position and she feels the same. And what exactly are you getting at?"

"You should tell her again. It's one thing to explain to a friend how you feel about marriage, another entirely to tell a woman who loves you that you'll never share your life with her."

"That's not the way it is. I intend to share my life with her."

"But on your own terms, with no commitment."

"That's not so. I *am* committed to her, fully. In all the ways that really matter."

Adrienne only looked at him with sadness and a hint of reproach.

And the past was there, rising up between them, reproaching him all the more. She *had* tried to warn him, to get him to slow down, to see other people, to grow up a little before he rushed into marriage. And she had been right. He should have listened to her then, but he hadn't. And he'd paid the price. "I'm a grown man now, Mother. I know the right woman for me. This isn't about contracts and promises. This is about someone I want to be with who wants to be with me. Everything is different this time."

"Is it? Oh, darling, I do hope so."

Chapter Eight

Monday, Lani's plan was to write at least eight pages by two in the afternoon, and then to put in another couple of hours researching websites and web designers.

But she woke up groggy from spending most of the night wide awake thinking about Max—about how wild she was for him, about how she felt she knew him to his soul. And, at the same time, that she didn't know him at all. She worried about next Sunday and the family breakfast. She obsessed over the incident with the paparazzo, over the pictures online of her and Max together, over when her mother or father would call her and say they'd seen the pictures and…well, she had no idea what they would say after that.

She sat down to her laptop at nine.

At eleven, when she had barely written half a page, Max called. The first thing he asked was how the work was going.

She grumbled, "I've gotten stuck on a certain sentence. I think I've rewritten it twenty times."

"Leave it. Go on to the next sentence. Sometimes you have to keep moving forward."

"Good advice. Now to try to make myself take it."

He laughed, the sound warm and deep, reaching out to her through the phone, wrapping around her heart, making her so glad he'd called. "Is that whining?" he teased. "There's no whining in writing."

"Not for you, maybe. I have to whine constantly. It's part of my process."

He laughed again. Then he said, "I'll let you get back to it, but I want to see you tonight."

"Yes," she said, without even stopping to think about it. Because she wanted to see him. Because every time she saw him, she only wanted to be with him some more. And all the other stuff, all her worries and doubts? Lately, all that stuff was starting to feel like lead weights pulling her down, trying to drag her back, to keep her from finding happiness. Maybe she only needed to let go of them, to stop giving them such unnecessary power over her. "How's Connie?"

"Dr. Montaigne says she can go to school tomorrow."

"That's what I wanted to hear—and about tonight?"

"You already said yes," he reminded her gruffly. "You can't change your mind now."

"I have no intention of changing my mind."

"Now, that's what *I* wanted to hear."

"I have a request, though."

"Name it."

"I don't feel like going out. Would you come here and we could stay in?"

"I'd like that. I'll bring dinner."

"I think you just might be the perfect man."

"Hold that thought. I'll see you at seven."

She hung up, smiling, and went back to that awful, unworkable sentence. And what do you know? There was nothing wrong with it. She kept going, pressing ahead as Max had suggested, refusing to edit or second-guess herself.

By one-thirty, she had nine good pages, which got her thinking that she had to stop staying up all night worrying.

Having an actual love life could be *good* for her writing, if she would only allow it to be.

After a quick sandwich break, she did a little website research and ended up requesting more information from two designers whose portfolios appealed to her. Then she wrote a couple of totally lame tweets, because she had to get used to the whole Twitter thing. Finally, she checked email.

She had messages in the in-box of the email account she'd linked to Facebook and Twitter, messages from people she'd never heard of. Four of them came right out and said they wanted to talk with her about her relationship with the prince of Montedoro. She trashed those.

Three of them said they'd read about her sale in Publisher's Marketplace and wanted to congratulate her and learn more about her books.

Yesterday, she would have been totally jazzed that she was already getting interest. But after last night and the man with the camera, she couldn't help wondering if those potential interviewers really only wanted what the others wanted: a hot scoop on what was going on between her and Prince Max. She didn't trash those three messages, but she didn't answer them either. She just called it a day, shut down her laptop and treated herself to a long, relaxing bath.

Max arrived with a shopping bag in one hand and a picnic basket in the other. She took the basket from him and set it on the counter of her little kitchen nook.

He dropped the shopping bag on a chair, threw his jacket on top of it and swept her into his arms. His wonderful mouth closed over hers and his tongue slipped between her parted lips, and she thought that there really was no place she would rather be than held nice and tight in Max's embrace.

"I missed you," he said, after he finished kissing her senseless.

She stared up at him. She could do that endlessly. "Do you know that you have to be the best-looking guy on the planet? I love the way your brows draw together, as though you're constantly thinking very deep thoughts. And what about the wonderful, manly shape of your nose? Oh, and the scent of you. I could stand here and smell you forever."

One side of his gorgeous mouth kicked up. "Please do— but did you miss me?"

"I did."

"Tell me all about it."

"It's been awful. Twenty-four hours without you. I don't know how I survived."

"You're right," he agreed with enthusiasm. "It's been much too long."

"Though I do feel kind of bad about taking you away from Nick and Connie."

He bent close again and whispered in her ear. "Tomorrow night come up to the palace. We'll have dinner together, the four of us."

"Yes."

His lips brushed her temple, setting off sparks. "You're saying yes a lot recently. Yes works for me in a big way."

She stood on tiptoe to whisper in his ear. "Something seems to be happening to all my fears and doubts."

"Tell me. Don't hold back."

"They could be…vanishing. I feel freer without them, but a little bit naked, too."

"You. Naked. Nothing wrong with that." He tipped up her chin and caught her mouth again, starting out with a gentle brushing of his lips across hers and then slowly deepening the caress, until her senses were swimming and desire began to pool low in her belly.

She took his face between her hands and gently broke

the scorching kiss. "If you keep doing that, we'll end up in bed before dinner."

He arched a brow at her. "Would that be such a bad thing?"

She took a moment to think about it. "Hmm. You know, now that you put it that way, I have to tell you…"

He bent, buried his face in the crook of her neck and growled, "Tell me what?"

She stroked her fingers up into his silky, unruly hair. "I don't think it would be such a bad thing at all."

That was all the encouragement he needed. She let out a happy cry of surprise as he scooped her high against his chest and carried her the short distance to her tiny bedroom. She'd drawn the blinds earlier and the room was dark. He put her down on the bed, switched on the lamp and stood back to get out of his clothes.

She gazed up at him in the pool of lamplight, dazed and admiring—and then it occurred to her she was wasting precious time. She might as well get busy getting rid of her clothes, too.

So she did. She grabbed the hem of her sweater and ripped it up and off over her head. Her bra came next. She wiggled out of it as he kicked off his shoes and hopped on one foot to tear off a sock.

It became something of a competition, both of them whipping off articles of clothing and tossing them out of the way. She started laughing. And then he started laughing.

He tossed two condoms on the nightstand and came down to the bed with her. They laughed as they kissed.

And then, somehow, neither of them was laughing anymore. He was touching her everywhere and whispering her name and she held on so tight to him, her body aching with longing, stunned with sweet delight, her mind a hot whirl of wonder and happiness.

Was this really possible? This magic, this beauty? In the long years since her eighteenth summer, she had let herself give up on ever finding this kind of joy.

She'd become careful, cautious of both her body and her wounded heart. The girl she'd once been, bold and sure, afraid of nothing, had been lost to her, stolen away by her own headstrong, youthful choices, by a thoughtless, selfish man more than twice her age.

But now...

Yes. Now.

This was hope, wasn't it? This was happiness calling her, opening to her again.

She closed her eyes and she whispered, "Max."

He answered, "Lani," rough and low and tender, too.

All thought whirled away and there was only sensation, only the two of them, locked together, only the promise in her heart, the press of skin on skin, and the sweet, endless pulse of their mutual pleasure.

Sometime later, they gathered up their scattered clothes and put them on again. In the living room, he presented her with the shopping bag he'd tossed on the chair when he came in.

"What's this?"

"Open it."

In the bag was a shoebox and in the box, a brand-new pair of gray suede pumps identical to the ones she'd worn the morning before. With a shout of pure glee, still holding a shoe in each hand, she threw her arms around his neck.

He grinned down at her and she thought how young he looked, and how totally pleased with himself. "You did say you loved those shoes."

"Thank you." She went on tiptoe and captured his mouth. They shared a long, lovely toe-curling kiss. When he lifted his head, she asked, "How did you get them in just one day?"

"You'd be surprised what a little money and a lot of determination can accomplish."

Over roast chicken and *pommes rissoles*—pan-fried, herb-crusted potatoes—she told him about the man with the camera the night before and also about the suspicious messages in her in-box.

"Welcome to my world." He sipped the wine Marceline had packed with the meal. "Where your privacy will be gleefully invaded at every turn." He set down the glass. "If you can describe the paparazzo, I might be able to see to it that he leaves Montedoro once and for all."

"It's tempting. The guy really freaked me out at first. But no."

The lines between his brows deepened. "You mean you *can* describe him, but you won't?"

"It was dark and it happened too fast for me to get a good look at him. But even if I could tell you exactly what he looked like, you're right. I don't know if I would. It was awful only because I wasn't expecting it. And even sleazy photographers have to make a living."

"Not by ambush, they don't, not in Montedoro. And they know it, too. They all know the rules here. They can take all the pictures they want, snap away to their venal little hearts' content—but they have to keep their distance while they do it. The fellow last night? Completely over the line. He deserves to be sent away and not allowed back."

She ate a bite of the delicious potatoes. "Sorry. Can't help you."

He didn't look happy, but at least he let it go. "As to the emails, can you simply ignore them?"

"I deleted the ones that were fishing for information

about you. A few of them, though, look as though they might be legit, bloggers in publishing just interested in interviewing a budding author. I thought I might write them back and ask for the interview questions. When I get those, I'll have a better idea of what I'm dealing with."

"Be careful."

She promised that she would. And then she asked him about his day.

He told her about the weekly meeting with the ministers of state and then added, almost as an afterthought, "I met with my mother alone afterward."

Something in his voice warned her. "Did you talk about me?"

He held her gaze. "We did. It was all good."

Somehow, she didn't quite believe him. "Why do I think there's more going on here than you're telling me?"

He reached across the narrow table and snared her hand. "She's glad for me, that I've found someone who makes me happy."

"Well." She felt a smile kind of tremble its way across her mouth. "That's nice to hear." He looked down at their joined hands and then back up at her, a glance that seemed just a little evasive. She asked, "You're sure that's all?"

He squeezed her hand, made a low noise that could have meant yes—or could have been a tactic to avoid answering her question.

"Max. Why do I feel that you're not telling me everything?"

"Mothers worry," he gave out grudgingly. That did it. She pulled her hand free. He glared at her. "Damn it, Lani."

She schooled her voice to gentleness. "You're not telling me everything."

"It's nothing for you to worry about, take my word for it."

"I don't believe you." For that, she got an angry shrug. "Oh, Max…"

He shot her a look from under his brows. "Let's change the subject, shall we?"

Oh, she was tempted. How simple, to let it be. To move on to some other, happier topic. But when you really cared about someone, you didn't always get to just drop it when things got difficult. "I can take it," she whispered. "I promise you I can. Won't you give me a chance?" He folded his big arms across his broad chest and sat back in the chair. She kept after him. "I know I haven't made it easy for you, up till now. I know you had to do all the work and that for a very long time, I gave you so little."

"That's not true."

"Yes it is. I created a whole new meaning for the word *reluctant*. I know you understand why now, because I finally drummed up the nerve to tell you about the hardest things. It's just, well, it's taken over a decade, for me to forgive myself for Thomas, for my poor lost baby, for…all of it. The therapy I had helped. Sydney helped, by making a place for me in her life, by being the best friend I've ever had and never, ever judging me. And you, Max. I think you've helped most of all."

"My God, Lani." He leaned in at last and reached for her hand again.

Instead of giving it, she raised it between them. "No. Wait. It's important, if we want to go on together, that we're honest with each other, that you don't sugar-coat things for me. If your mother has issues with you and me together, I need to know about it."

He picked up his wine again and saw it was empty. With a low, impatient sound, he set it back down. "You have to understand. My mother is about as egalitarian as a ruling monarch could be. She wants us—my brothers and sisters and me—to be happy above all, to build relationships based on love and respect first and foremost. But it's a little different for me."

"Because you're the heir."

"Exactly. There are other things to consider when I become serious about a woman."

Serious. It was one of those words. Enormous and yet so simple, both at the same time. "You told her that you're serious about me?"

"I did. Because I am."

Her throat clutched. "That, um, sounds really good."

He almost smiled. But his eyes remained somber. "My mother has to consider our allies and their possible reactions to any woman I become close to."

Lani knew her Montedoran history. "The French, right? Her French ministers. For them, an ordinary American girl just won't do."

"Yes, the French. She said they wouldn't be happy. I said they would get over it."

"Well, they got over your mother marrying your father."

He did smile then. "You're taking this so well and you understand perfectly."

"See? You should have just told me. What else?"

"Lani, I…" He let the words trail off. She could tell he really didn't know how to answer.

And by then, she knew. A cold shiver traveled up her spine. "Scandal, right? Your mother wanted to know if there was anything about me that might make tabloid fodder."

He gave it up. "That's right."

Her chest felt tight, and her stomach churned. "And you told her…?"

"I said you had secrets, things you regretted, as we all do. She wanted to know what those secrets were. I refused to break your confidence. She said she could make inquiries. I asked her not to."

"Will she do it anyway?"

"I don't think so."

"But did she say that she wouldn't?"

"No." He stared at her so hard, as though he could pin her in place with just that look. "I don't care."

"What do you mean, you don't care?"

"Whatever happens, we deal with it. We don't let it break us."

"Someone *could* find out though, right?" she asked in a hollow voice. "Someone could dig it all up again. The whole world could read about…all of it." She shook her head slowly, back and forth and back again, absorbing the enormous ugliness of that. "I should have thought of this. I can't believe I didn't. But then, why would I ever want to face that someday the whole world could know? I thought it was more than bad enough just making myself tell *you*."

His eyes were storm-cloud gray and his lips twisted cruelly. "Are you bailing out on me? Is that what you're doing?"

She stared at him, wide-eyed and blinking, feeling like someone startled by a bright light in a very dark room. "You shouldn't continue with me. It's not a good idea for you."

"How many ways can I say it?" Shoving back his chair, he stood.

She gasped and blinked up at him. "Um. Say what?"

He turned his back to her. She sat there, not sure what to do or say, as he paced to the living area, all the way to the sliding door, where he gazed out at the night for several seconds that seemed to stretch to an infinity.

Finally, he whirled and faced her again. "I always knew there was something that kept you from coming to me. I knew and I didn't care. I just wanted to get through it, to be the one you reached for when you were ready at last, to be the one to gain your trust and know your truth. And when you finally did tell me, you didn't shock me. It all made complete sense to me, those choices you made as an eighteen-year-old girl. I didn't—I *don't*—judge you for those choices. They caused you great pain and loss and almost killed you. But you survived. They changed you. They *are* you, a part of you anyway, a part of what brought you here, to Montedoro, to me.

"I don't really care who knows, who finds out something that happened years and years ago. To me, that's just another possible storm to weather, along with all the others we have to get through in this life. What I care about is *you.* That you know you can trust me. That *I* can count on *you,* that when the latest storm has played itself out, you're still there, where I need you, at my side."

Lani pushed her chair back and got up. Somewhere in the middle of all those beautiful things he'd just said, she'd stopped feeling stunned and broken and scared. Somewhere in there, it had become crystal clear to her what she had to do.

He watched her walk toward him, those iron eyes never leaving her face. "I'll ask you again. Are you bailing out on me?"

She went right to him, right up good and close. She laid her hands on his chest, where she could feel the power in him, feel his big heart beating under her palm. "No, Max. If you're crazy enough to stick with me, I'm not bailing."

His breath left him in a rush. "Thank God." He grabbed her close, hard arms closing around her.

She felt his lips against her hair, and for a moment she let herself cling to him. Then she pushed away enough that she could look up at him again. "I want to meet with your mother, just the princess and me. I will tell her the long, sad old story. All of it."

He looked at her so piercingly, as though he was trying to see inside her head. "You would do that?"

It was strange. Yesterday, she never could have volunteered to do such a thing. But now, somehow, she could do nothing less. "I think I have to, Max. I think it's the right thing to do."

"And then what?"

"I have no idea. But if you and I are going to continue together, it only seems right that she should know. We can start with that. And after I've told her everything, the two of you can take a meeting on the subject and decide what, if anything, you need to do."

Chapter Nine

At two the next afternoon, Lani sat on a fabulous damask-covered sofa in HSH Adrienne's private office. As always, she tried not to gape at the sovereign princess, who had to be almost sixty, but still had full lips and flawless skin. There really was something magical about Adrienne Bravo-Calabretti. She brought to mind some legendary movie star of the silver screen—Sophia Loren, maybe, with that wide mouth and those unforgettable eyes.

There was tea. With scones and delicate pots of jam and clotted cream. Adrienne poured, those slim, perfectly manicured hands dealing with the fragile china pot and the gold-trimmed, paper-thin teacups without making a single clattering sound.

Otherworldly. Definitely. Beyond the whole not-gaping thing, Lani was experiencing an absolute cringing sort of terror of this whole situation. What was she thinking to volunteer to tell this incredible woman all about how stupid and destructive she'd been once? Last night, with Max's arms around her, coming here and telling all had seemed like an excellent, brave and necessary idea.

Clearly, last night, she'd gone temporarily insane.

"What do you take?" Adrienne asked.

A Valium about now would be nice. "Just a little sugar, thanks."

Adrienne moved the sugar closer to Lani's side of the low table, next to the cup of tea she'd just poured for her. Lani put in the sugar and stirred—carefully, trying not to make those annoying clinking sounds that all the etiquette books said were so rude.

Now what? When taking tea at a table, one never picked up the saucer with the cup. But when standing, the saucer was necessary to catch any drips. Did the low table actually count as a table, or…?

The princess took pity on her and picked up both saucer and cup. Lani did the same. She sipped.

Not too clattery, thank God. And she didn't spill a drop on her carefully chosen outfit of blue skirt, white shirt and short red blazer—red, white and blue; everyday, ordinary American and proud of it. She also wore the gray suede pumps. They made her think of Max, and that gave her courage. She set down the cup and saucer and doubted she would pick it up again.

Adrienne said, "I understand congratulations are in order." Lani went blank. For what? For coming here with the intention of revealing all the ways she'd screwed up her life and broken her parents' hearts, not to mention the heart of Thomas McKneely's poor, long-suffering wife? Adrienne must have read her bewildered expression. Graciously, as with the teacup, the princess came to Lani's rescue. "Three books sold at once. We're all so excited for you."

"I… Thank you," Lani managed rather woodenly. "I've had high hopes for this series of books and I'm glad they're going to be published and published well. Very glad."

"Max says they're all three set in Montedoro."

"Yes, the stories take place in the fifteenth and sixteenth

centuries. The main characters are fictional, but I try to stay true to the period, to…history as we know it."

"And these books are called…?"

"The working titles are *The Poisoner's Apprentice*, *The Sword of Abdication* and *The Crucible of Truth*."

Adrienne laughed. "I'll have you know it's never been proven that Lucinda Calabretti poisoned her husband to put their son on the throne so that she could rule through him."

"Well, it *is* fiction," Lani shamelessly backpedaled. After all, these were Adrienne's ancestors.

But Her Sovereign Highness looked delighted. "And *The Sword of Abdication* takes place in the court of Lucinda's son, Cristobal?"

"Yes, it does." Cristobal Calabretti had abdicated the throne his mother had murdered his father to get for him.

"And *The Crucible of Truth?* Let me guess. It takes place in the time of Cristobal's son, Bernardo, who certainly can't be blamed for doing what he had to do in order to regain the throne his father had turned his back on." Her huge dark eyes gleamed. "I have no idea why they called him Bernardo the Butcher."

Lani played it diplomatically. "He was a very determined man."

"We Calabrettis tend to be that way, though nowadays we are much less bloodthirsty. My husband is the same— determined, I mean. And our daughters and sons, as well. Maximilian most of all."

Max. God. For a moment there, she'd almost let herself relax. But now her throat locked up and her left leg was showing a distressing desire to bounce. She kept her foot firmly on the floor and gulped to make her throat relax. "Yes. Max is, um, very determined."

Adrienne nodded, a slow, regal dip of her dark head. "I think he will make an excellent sovereign."

"Yes."

"And whatever you've come to share with me, rest assured I would no more betray your confidence than Maximilian would." Adrienne spoke softly, with real kindness.

"I… Thank you." Lani's palms were sweating. Ridiculous, annoying tears burned at the back of her throat, forcing her to swallow again, to gulp them right down into the deepest part of her. She was not going to sit here and blubber in front of Her Sovereign Highness. "I…well, the good news is, I've never killed anyone or been arrested for bank robbery or cooked crystal meth or…" Good Lord in Heaven. Cooked crystal meth?

"It's all right, I promise you," Adrienne said in the tone people use to calm wild animals. "Take your time."

Lani wanted to cover her face, become really small, jump up and run out of there and keep on running and never look back. "I don't know where to start."

"It doesn't matter." Adrienne snared her gaze and held it so steadily. Very much the way Max often did, and suddenly the resemblance, mother to son, was so powerful, so close. "Just begin," the princess said. "I think you'll find the way. I know you will." She sounded so certain.

And really, if Adrienne Bravo-Calabretti, Sovereign Princess of Montedoro, was sure that Lani could do it, well then, she absolutely could. She said, "My father's best friend was a writer named Thomas McKneely…" And once she got going, she just kept on. On and on through all of it, her own arrogance, her pride, her complete self-righteousness, her unforgivable treatment of her own father, her certainty that what she called love justified any action; her heedless, limitless cruelty. All of which led to the loss of so much that mattered, including her baby and almost her life.

When she finished, Adrienne reached across the low

table and touched her hand. The princess spoke. She said soft, comforting things.

Lani thought that whatever happened next, it wasn't so bad, really. To simply tell the truth as it had happened, to tell it and let it stand, let it be.

Adrienne stood. Lani automatically started to rise as well. "No," said Adrienne. "Stay. Just a moment…" Lani sank back to the sofa.

Adrienne went out.

Lani heard the door close behind her. Several minutes passed. Lani sat there, wanting to go, but feeling she should wait until the princess came back and excused her.

The door opened again. She turned to look and Max was standing there.

He held out his arms to her. It was all the encouragement she needed. She got up and ran to him.

He wrapped her up tight in his warm embrace.

She clung to him, burying her head against his hard, strong shoulder. "Your mother…?"

"She said you've told her all she needed to know."

"What does that mean?"

"It means we have her blessing. The rest is up to us."

"Oh, Max." She held him tighter.

He kissed her hair. "My brave darling…"

"Brave…" The word sounded wrong to her.

"Yes. Brave."

Funny. She didn't feel all that brave. What she felt was strangely, completely free.

Chapter Ten

After that, Lani knew happiness. Weeks of it.

She got past the dreaded midpoint of *The Crucible of Truth* and forged on toward the end. Two of the bloggers who'd messaged her through Facebook turned out not to be tacky tabloid journos, after all. She gave them interviews. She worked on her web presence, hired a website designer and had two long discussions with her New York editor concerning revisions to the first and second books.

Even better than her steady progress in her career, she had time with the people who mattered to her. With Sydney, with Trev and Ellie, with Nick and Connie and Gerta. And with Max most of all.

She went to breakfast with the princely family four Sundays running. Everyone seemed to accept her, to welcome her. Adrienne treated her warmly. And Max's father, the prince consort, Evan, would smile when he saw her and ask how the book was going.

The paparazzi remained relentless. Any time she went out in public, alone or with Max, or even with the children, there was always some guy lurking nearby with a camera or a smartphone stuck to his face.

She learned to do what the Bravo-Calabrettis did: ignore them. It wasn't that hard once you got the hang of it.

And they kept their distance, which really helped. Not a one was as in-your-face as that first guy outside her building that Sunday night in late February. They all kept back, out of the way as they were required to do in order not to be packed off to France.

There were pictures on the internet, lots of them. And videos on YouTube—of her and Max out for an evening, of her shopping with Sydney, of her and Max and the children enjoying an afternoon on the family yacht.

And there were stories, in the tabloids and online. More information came out about her, specifically, about her previous job as a nanny to the children of Prince Rule, about her long friendship with Sydney, about her budding career as a novelist. The tabloids seemed to love the whole nanny angle. All the stories had headlines like The Prince's Nanny Love and Wedding Bells for the Prince and the Nanny?

Lani tried to take it all in stride. The stories about wedding bells and diamond rings kind of got to her, though. Max never talked about marriage. Neither did she. It seemed a delicate, dangerous subject in light of what they'd said to each other that long-ago night in the library.

He wasn't going to get married again. He'd said so straight out. And she'd gone and told him that marriage wasn't for her.

Only, well, something had happened to her in the course of forging her freedom from the chains of the past. She'd found a way to love again—or maybe to love for real, as a grown woman, in the way she hadn't come close to all those years ago, with Thomas.

She'd found her way to love and she loved Max. And now that she loved him, now that she was truly able to let the past go, marriage didn't seem like such an impossible proposition, after all.

In fact, marriage felt like a good thing. A *right* thing. A big step that she and Max really ought to talk about taking—not right away. There was no reason to rush it. But someday, most definitely.

She'd gone on the pill. It was nice, not to have to fiddle with condoms, and to rest a little easier that there would be no surprise pregnancy. But more and more to her, having a baby someday seemed like a good thing, the *right* thing for her.

Yes. Someday. She was sure of that now.

Her father called near the end of March. Someone had finally told him what was going on over there in Montedoro.

"Is this Prince Maximilian good to you?" her dad demanded.

"Yes, Papi. He's a wonderful man."

"You're happy." It wasn't a question. He seemed simply to know.

And that pleased her, gave her that warm and fuzzy feeling down inside. "I am happy. Very happy."

"When will you bring him home to meet your family?"

Okay, she was kind of dreading that. Just a little. She'd gone home twice since the move to Montedoro. Both times had been awkward, with her parents pushing her to move back to Texas, and her brother all over her for deserting the family, for leaving her parents without their daughter in their waning years.

Plus, well, now that she had finally found someone she was serious about, there would be the usual Vasquez Family Marriage Interrogation Squad. They all—her mom, her dad and even her overbearing big brother—wanted her to be happy. And to a Vasquez, happiness meant marriage and babies.

"Yolanda Ynez, are you still on the line?"

"Yes, Papi. I'm here. And I do plan to bring Max and

the children to meet you. As soon as we can work that out, in the next couple of months, I hope...."

He grumbled a little more, accusing her of putting him off, which was only the truth. But then he asked about her writing and she told him how much she liked her editor, about her new website and her progress on the third book of her trilogy.

And he told her he was proud of her, which got her kind of dewy-eyed. Then he said he loved her and put her mom on.

That went pretty well, at least at first. She told her mom all about how well her career was going, and her mother congratulated her enthusiastically on her success.

Then her mom came right out and asked her, "Are you going to marry this man, this prince that you're dating?"

Lani cringed—and evaded. She reminded her mother that she and Max hadn't been together that long, that it was never a good thing to rush into something as important as marriage.

And of course, her mom said, "Your father proposed to me on our second date."

"I know that, Mama, but—"

"I said yes."

"No kidding." Lani had heard the story at least a hundred times.

"You can mock me if you want to."

"Sorry..."

"All I'm trying to say is that it was the best decision I ever made."

"I know, Mama. Papi's a prize."

"Yes, he is. And a woman knows when she's found the right man."

Yeah, sure. Like I did with Thomas. "Well, Mama. *You* knew."

"What does that mean, *mi'ja?* Are you telling me you don't know your own heart? Because the heart knows. You only have to listen to it. Are you listening to your heart with this prince of yours?"

"Of course I am."

"Well, okay, then. Bring him home so that I can see if he's good enough for you."

"Oh, Mama…"

"I love you, *mi'ja.* You are always in my heart and I am so proud of you."

Out of nowhere, tears welled up. One even overflowed and dribbled down her cheek. She swiped it away. "I love you, too, Mama. Very much."

"Bring him home."

She promised that she would. Soon.

Her mother was silent. And then a few minutes later, they said goodbye.

"He's so completely gone on you," Sydney said. "Everybody sees it. But then, you're gone on him right back, so it all shakes out."

Trev and Ellie were at the villa with their new nanny that afternoon, so it was just Syd and Lani in Lani's tiny kitchen area, sharing a lunch of grilled cheese sandwiches, cream of tomato soup and tall glasses of iced tea. Lani ate a bite of her sandwich and sipped her tea and stared out the little window by the table. It provided a view of another tenant's balcony across the way, partially obscured by the crown of an olive tree.

"You're too quiet," Sydney accused. "What's wrong?"

Lani sipped more tea and watched the olive branches sway in the early-spring breeze. "I talked to my parents yesterday. They want me to come home and bring Max with me."

Sydney fiddled with her napkin, lifting it off her lap, smoothing it down again. "And this…annoys you? Depresses you? Has you feeling overcome with joy?"

"I really need to do that—go home, I mean. I haven't been back to Texas enough since we moved here."

"So give yourself an extra week when you go to New York for that business trip next month. Visit your family and take Max with you."

"It seems a little early for him to be meeting the parents."

"But you've already met *his* parents—and I don't just mean because you lived at the palace. He's brought you to Sunday breakfast several weeks in a row. That counts as meeting the parents, and you know it, too."

"Still, it's different. We live here. It's all just more natural, Max taking me to family things."

"Is this some new form of amnesia you've got now? Think back to the first time he asked you to Sunday breakfast. It didn't seem all that natural to you then. You were tied in knots over it."

"True."

"But you did it anyway. Because he's important to you and his family matters. Well, he needs to know *your* family. Take him to Texas."

There was a gray cat on the neighbor's balcony. He sat in a little splash of sun, giving himself a bath. "Okay, Syd. I'll think about it."

Sydney reached across the narrow table, took Lani's chin in her hand and guided it around so she was looking at Syd instead of the gray cat across the way. "Talk to me. Come on. You know you want to. Tell me what's on your mind, and I shall use my big brain to help you solve whatever problem is nagging at you."

"I didn't say anything was bothering me."

Syd actually shook a finger at her. "Don't be that way."

"Fine." Lani let her shoulders slump.

Sydney ate two spoonfuls of soup, taking her time about it. "Still waiting over here."

"If I take Max to Texas to meet the parents, they're going to be all over him wanting to know what his intentions are. I just cringe when I think of it. My mother is already asking me when Max and I are going to get married."

"So? I've been kind of wondering about that myself."

"Very funny. Especially since I explained to you that Max has told me he'll never get married again."

"Didn't believe it then, don't believe it now."

"I'm pretty sure he still feels that way."

"Pretty sure, huh?" Syd gave a disgusted little snort. "Has he said so?"

"We've only been—what?—together, exclusive, whatever you call it—for a little over a month."

"Not the question."

"You're getting all lawyerlike on me, you know that, right?"

"I'm going to ask you again. Since you and Max have been 'together,' has he said that he'll never get married again?"

"No. We haven't talked about it. It hasn't come up."

Syd sat back in her chair. "And what about you? How do *you* feel about marriage now that you're in love with my brother-in-law?"

"Did I say I was in love with him?"

Syd gave her that look, the one that said she was barely restraining herself from rolling her eyes.

Lani stared at her soup and her half-eaten sandwich and realized she had no appetite at all. "You're going to make me say it, aren't you?"

"No. You're going to say it because you *want* to say it.

Because it's the truth and I'm your friend and you and I, we always try to deal in the truth with each other."

"Okay. All right." She pushed her plate away. "I'm in love with Max and nowadays marriage is starting to sound like a pretty good concept to me, like a good thing to do with the person you can see yourself being with for the rest of your life. I'm even…" She let out a moan and put her head in her hands.

"Come on, sit up straight. Look at me and say the rest."

She let her hands drop to her lap again. "Dear God. I want to have babies with him. I want to help him raise Connie and Nick. I want…everything. All of it. The wedding ring and the stepkids and the baby carriage, too. I want Max and me getting old together."

"Beautiful." Syd beamed, green eyes misty. "Good for you."

"But I haven't told him any of that. I don't even know where to start. And really, as I already said, I'm thinking it's kind of soon to be bringing all that up, anyway."

"Soon?" Syd gave another snort. "You've known him since we moved here. You were friends for a year before the man even kissed you. Now you're together and it's obvious to everyone that you not only have the fireworks, you have the friendship and the mutual interests and everything else it takes to make it work. So I've gotta say that it's not in any way too soon in my book."

"That's because you're one of *those*."

"One of *whats?*"

"Oh please, Syd. You accepted Rule's marriage proposal within forty-eight hours of meeting him in Macy's. Then the two of you promptly ran off to Vegas to tie the knot. You're like my mother. Love at first sight, a marriage proposal coming at you so fast it should make your head spin— but you don't even hesitate. You just say yes."

"Tell him you love him."

"Oh, Dear Lord..."

"Trust me, Lani. It never hurts to lead with the love."

Tell him you love him.

It shouldn't be that hard, should it?

After Syd left, Lani started kind of obsessing over the idea of saying her love out loud to Max. Over how she might just tell him that very night.

I love you, Max. Four little words. Seriously. How hard could that be?

He was coming over at seven, bringing dinner. It had gotten to be a regular thing with them. Once a week at least, the two of them spent the evening at her place. Max brought the food so she wouldn't have to think about cooking after a hard day stringing words together.

How quickly the weeks had fallen into a certain rhythm. A night at her place, a couple of evenings and all day Sunday with the children. Friday or Saturday night out together, and then after the night out, the villa on the Avenue d'Vancour afterward, for slow, delicious lovemaking and maybe a little champagne.

They had it all, really, and she ought to remember that. She *did* remember that, always. She had the work that she loved. And her own place, where she could write undisturbed all day long. And a wonderful man she loved to talk to, whose kisses turned her inside out, a man who had stuck with her, refused to quit on her, during all those months she'd given him almost nothing in return.

And now?

Well, now, she simply wanted more.

She was out on the balcony when he arrived. He let himself in with the key she'd given him. She'd left the slider open behind her, so she heard him, heard that one little squeak the door always gave, heard him reengage the lock and then move to the table to put the food basket down.

He approached, his steps quiet, measured. Still, she heard them. Or maybe she only felt them all through her, in the form of a sweet shiver of pleasure and longing, as she leaned on the iron railing and stared out at the hill and the shadowed trees directly across from her.

His hands, so warm and strong on her shoulders, pulling her back against him, then easing lower, sliding over her waist, across her stomach.

She let herself lean against him with a sigh. "Max..." Already she could feel him growing hard against her back.

He kissed her temple, rubbed his cheek against her hair. She couldn't resist turning in his arms then. She wrapped herself around him and they shared a long, sweet kiss.

The balcony seemed safe enough from prying eyes. But you just never knew.

He took her hand and led her inside. She pushed the slider closed behind them and followed him, breathless, her body already humming with pleasure, to the bedroom.

I love you, Max. She stared up into his iron-blue eyes as he took off her shirt and unbuttoned her jeans.

I love you, Max, as he laid her down across the sheets. *I love you, Max,* as he kissed her and caressed her. Every touch was pure wonder, every kiss a revelation.

I love you, Max. Love you, love you, love you...

The words filled up her head as he filled up her life, her body, her yearning heart. As he blasted away her loneliness, her very *separateness.*

She felt so close to him, so right with him.

But those four little words that filled up her head?

She didn't let them out. She couldn't quite bring them to the level of sound.

Maybe it was cowardice.

Or maybe she would do it a little later, over dinner. Yes, that would be better. While they sat at the table to eat the meal he'd brought.

In time, they got up and shared a quick shower. She put on the silk robe he'd bought for her. He pulled on his trousers, and they went to the table to eat.

She opened the basket. Draped over the white napkin cradling the dinner rolls, something glittered: a diamond and onyx bracelet. "Oh, Max…"

He looked so pleased with himself, eyes shining, hair damp and curling at his temples. "Goes with the earrings." He'd given her the diamond and onyx earrings a couple of weeks before. He was always bringing her presents, usually rare research books she coveted, occasionally something pretty and far too expensive. "Here." He took it. "Give me your wrist."

She extended her arm and he put it on. The diamonds gleamed against her skin, and the onyx had a deep luster, blacker than night. "So beautiful." *I love you, Max.* "Thank you." *I love you, I do.*

He pulled her up out of her chair and she went to him for a slow, lovely kiss. "You make me happy. So very happy," he whispered against her lips.

I love you, Max. "You do the same for me."

Reluctantly, he let her go. They sat down to eat.

He waited through the meal, all the way until after they'd demolished a nice pair of caramel-glazed crème puffs, before he said, "There's something you need to see."

She peered at him more closely. Was that anxiety in his eyes?

"All right," she answered cautiously. And he got up and went over to the low table in front of the sofa. He moved a stack of books she'd left there and took a tabloid paper from underneath them. She caught a glimpse of the garish cover. It was *The International Sun*.

Her stomach did something unpleasant. She pushed her dessert plate aside.

He came and sat down again. "I was selfish. I saw you out on the balcony, looking relaxed and happy and so tempting, waiting for me. I wanted some time with you before you saw this." She only stared at him and put out her hand. He gave it to her. "Page two."

Her stomach lurched again as she stared at the cover and read the lurid headlines: "Kate's Darkest Hour," "Alien Baby Born in Perth," "Secrets of the Killer's Dungeon."

"Lani?" he prompted, sounding worried.

She tried to make light of it. "It seems there's always an alien baby being born somewhere." The effort fell flat. She made herself turn the page, where she found a color photo of her and Max by the Fountain of the Three Sirens in front of Casino d'Ambre. She wore her favorite little black dress and he looked so handsome it made her heart ache. He had his arm around her. They were smiling at each other, happy simply to be together, pretending the rest of the world didn't exist.

But it did exist. Inserted next to the picture of the two of them was a black-and-white promotional headshot of Thomas taken several years before his death. He grinned his jaunty grin straight at the camera. The headline read, Prince Max's Naughty Nanny.

"Really, really tacky," she heard herself say.

"It could be worse," he offered hopefully.

She shot him a grim glance and started reading. It was short, which was the only good thing about it, a lurid little exposé concerning the "secret love nest" she'd shared with the bestselling Texas author who, at the time of their "torrid

May-December affair," had been a married man twenty-seven years her senior.

That was pretty much the whole thing. Nothing about her lost baby, nothing about her attempt to end her life or her extended stay at Spring Valley Psychiatric Care.

Max said what she was thinking. "The rest, beyond what you see there, would be pretty hard to dig up. The medical community has confidentiality laws to abide by. Unless someone close to you who knew more started talking…"

She lifted her head from the ugly little story and looked at him across the table. "I think you're right. People did talk when I moved in with Thomas. You could say that was public knowledge. But everything else, only my doctors, my parents and my brother ever knew—and now you and your mother and Sydney and probably Rule. All people I trust who would never break a confidence."

"Then there you have it. That should be it."

"You never know, though."

"God knows that's true."

She stared down at the story again, at the picture of Thomas, who'd once torn her heart out and stomped it flat. How strange that she wasn't more upset. "I…"

"What?"

"I don't know. It was such a long time ago. I thought it would rip me apart all over again, if any of it ever came out."

"But…?"

"Well. It happened. I did what I did and I'm not proud of it. It took me years to get over it, to forgive myself. But now I *am* over it. I've moved on. Would I prefer not ever to see anything about it in the tabloids or online? Definitely. But it *is* in the tabloids. And all I can say about that is, hey. The prose may be purple, but at least what's written here is more or less the truth."

He made a low noise that was almost a laugh. "That's the spirit."

A disturbing thought occurred to her. She demanded, "Has your mother seen this?"

"Settle down. There's nothing to be upset about."

"But—"

"Lani, my mother's the one who gave it to me. Her secretary has a clerk who spends every morning scanning the scandal rags and the internet for possible stories that the family ought to be keeping in front of—for damage control. There's an art to it, I promise you. My mother's a genius at putting positive spins on negative situations."

Now she did feel a little sick to her stomach. "Oh, God. What will she do about this?"

He smiled then. "Have you *read* some of the things that have appeared in print about my family? We've been embroiled in one scandal after another since the thirteenth century. You, of all people, ought to know that. You've written three books detailing the shocking exploits of just a few of my ancestors."

She tapped the page with the story on it. "You're saying this isn't that big of a deal to her or to the family?"

"Her concern was more about how *you* were going to take it."

Now, *that* was lovely to hear. "Truly?"

He gazed at her so tenderly. "Truly."

And she got up and went over and sat on his lap. "I guess we'll get through it."

"You guess?" He smoothed her hair along her cheek. "I *know* that we will."

She kissed him for that, another long, slow one.

He trailed kisses over her chin and down the side of her throat. And then he stood, lifting her high in his arms, and carried her back to the bedroom. For a while she forgot everything but the glory of his touch, the wonder of his kiss and the joy she had in loving him.

It wasn't until much later, after he'd gone home to his children and she was alone in bed, that she began to see his lack of concern about the tabloid story in a different light.

"No," Syd said firmly. "I don't believe that. You're letting your doubts and fears override simple logic. Maximilian is a good man. He doesn't care about that old story because he's got his priorities right. He cares about *you*."

They sat in the living room of Syd's villa, just the two of them again. Ellie was napping. Trev and Sorcha, the new nanny, were out in the gardens.

Lani raked frustrated fingers back through her hair. "Of course he cares about me. And he *is* a good man, a good man who's been completely honest with me all along. But logic is on *my* side here. I'm Max's lover. If I have a shady past, so what? It's not like he's going to *marry* me. He doesn't care if all that old garbage about Thomas comes out because he's never getting married again. He won't have to explain me to the French ministers. I'll never be his princess, never have a baby who would end up in line for the throne. I'm his…refuge, his safe haven, the one he turns to when he needs to decompress. But my past, my… reputation doesn't really reflect on him. He can keep me completely separate from his position as heir to the Montedoran throne."

Syd was shaking her head. "What am I going to do with you? Just when I think that you've come so far, you come up with something like this."

"Something that makes perfect sense and you know it."

"Really, you ought to be ashamed of yourself."

"Syd, I'm only being realistic."

"Did you tell the man you're in love with him?" Silence echoed. "Well, I guess I have my answer on that one."

Lani knew her lip was quivering and there was a big, fat lump in her throat. "I just… I can't, okay? He's a wonderful guy. I'm insanely in love with him. But what we have, that's it. That's all there is. I need to learn to accept that. Or if I can't, I have to accept that the day will come when I need to move on."

"Or you could just get honest, just tell him you love him and you've changed your mind about certain things—and then take it from there."

"Eventually, yes. I will do that, of course. When I feel the time is right."

"Oh, honey…"

"I mean it, Syd. It's like this. He comes to my apartment, or I go to his at the palace. Every moment we have together is precious, rich, unforgettable. But then he goes home. Or I go home. Back to our separate lives—and that would be fine, that would be about all I could deal with, anyway. If he hadn't made me open up to him, made tell him the secrets that were holding me back, helped me to see that I really can let the past go and move on from here. He… accepted me. He *wanted* me, just as I am. And now, he's done this wonderful, beautiful thing for me. And it's changed me. I want more now, more than all that we already have, more than to be his lover and his friend. I want it all. And I just don't think that he does."

Syd wouldn't give it up. She'd always made relentlessness into an art form. "You need to get with him, can't you see that? You need to tell him all these things you just told me. You need to give the guy a chance to be what you need him to be."

"But I don't even know how to begin. It's like we had a certain contract and now I want to break it and start something he never signed on for, something he's made it clear from the first he's never wanted."

"I told you—"

"I know. I remember. Lead with 'I love you.'"

"Just do it."

"Oh, Syd. Look, I'm sorry. I know I'm disappointing you. I'm disappointing *myself,* but I'm just not ready to go there yet."

Chapter Eleven

The next day, Saturday, Max had the main kitchen pack them a picnic lunch. Then he took the children and Lani to the family's private beach in the northeastern ward of Lardeaux. They parked on the point above the beach and took the steep, narrow trail down to the water's edge.

It was still chilly for swimming, but the children wore shirts and shorts over their swimsuits. They ran barefoot at the water's edge, hunted for shells and built a cockeyed sand castle with a leaky moat.

Max loved watching them with Lani. She had such a way with them. Connie liked to whisper to her. Girl things, both Connie and Lani called whatever they whispered to each other. They refused to tell Max exactly what those girl things were. But whatever they said to each other made Connie smile and put a certain confident look in her eyes. That was enough for Max. He refrained from pushing to find out the secrets the two of them shared.

Nicky was a whole other story. He could be difficult and moody. You never knew what he might say or do. Lani always managed to take whatever he tried in stride.

That day, while all four of them labored over the lopsided sand castle, Nick grew impatient with Connie's effort to construct her own separate tower.

"It's crookeder than the big tower," he whined. "And you keep making the moat leak."

"I want my own tower," Connie insisted and patiently continued patting wet sand along the base of her wobbly tower, denting the sides of the moat as she worked.

Nick jumped up. "This is dumb. I am not going to build this castle if *she* gets to just mess it all up."

Max started to say something about how they all should work together.

But Lani spoke first. "Maybe you could give her a little help repairing the moat."

"But Miss Lani, *she* broke it."

"I did not break it," argued Connie. "I only just mooshed it a little tiny bit."

"You broke it."

"Did not."

"Did so."

"Did *not*."

Nick started to lift one sandy foot, his narrowed eyes on Connie's leaning tower.

Max spoke up then. "Nicky."

Nick put down his foot, stuck out his chin and swung his gaze to Max. A stare-down ensued. Luckily, Nicky looked away first. "I don't want to build this castle anymore." He dropped his toy shovel, whirled and took off at a run.

No one else moved, except Connie, who went on patting at her tower. Max watched his son race toward the cliffs at the far end of the beach.

Lani said what he was thinking. "Good. Let him work off his frustrations with action. Nicky's an action kind of guy."

"He's also a big butthead," Connie mumbled, patting her tower.

Max almost called her on the questionable word, but

Lani caught his eye and shook her head, mouthing soundlessly, "Leave it."

He didn't argue. She somehow always knew when to step in and when to wait it out and let the children work through a conflict on their own.

Connie sat back on her knees and stared at her handiwork. "I did kind of mess up the moat. But if I go say sorry to Nicky, he'll only be mean to me."

"Wait till he comes back," Lani suggested. "Then the two of you can fix it together."

"He'll still be mean to me."

"Are you sure about that?"

Connie admitted, "Not *completely* sure."

"So then, how about if we just wait and see what happens?"

"Miss Lani, I *hate* waiting."

Lani got up and dusted off her knees. "What, you hate *wading?* Well, I was just going to go wading." She held down her hand.

Connie frowned. "*Waiting,* not *wading.*"

"But do you want to go wading or not?"

"I do!" Connie took her hand and jumped up and the two of them ran down the sandy slope to the water's edge, laughing together.

Max watched them as they played in the foamy edges of the lazy waves, giggling and rushing backward before they got in too deep. Lani's black hair was a wild halo of curls tangled by the wind and Connie's blond mop had gone straight and stringy. The sun caught the iridescent grains of sand on their arms and legs, making nature's own glitter on smooth, healthy skin.

They were beautiful, his little girl and Lani. They were beautiful and he was happy as he'd never thought to be. Everything made sense now. His life not only had purpose, there was real pleasure now, deep and good and satisfying. Pleasure and someone to talk to, someone who loved the same things he did.

Nicky dropped down beside him. "So when are we going to eat?" He flopped flat onto his back and squinted up at the sky. "I'm *starving*." Nick was never merely hungry. "Papa?"

"We'll eat in a few minutes."

"But how *many* minutes?"

"I don't have an exact time for you. But soon."

For about thirty seconds, Nick lay quietly, panting a little from his run along the beach. Max went back to admiring the girl and the woman playing in the waves.

But Nick could never stay silent for long. He wiggled back up to a sitting position and wrapped his arms around his knees. "Are you going to get married to Miss Lani?"

Max sat very still. Maybe if he said nothing, Nick would get the hint and let it be.

Fat chance. "Papa?"

Fair enough. He would *have* to say something. "Why do you ask?"

Nicky fisted up a handful of sand and strained it through his fingers. "You said you really like her. You said it twice, remember?"

"I do remember, yes."

"Well, when a grown-up has a girlfriend and he really, really likes her, then they get married. Philippe told me so." Philippe was one of his school chums.

"Ah." Max waited. It was a complete cop-out. He had nothing. The truth was way too complex to share with an eight-year-old boy.

"So *are* you going to marry her?"

He tried, lamely, "Sometimes people are together just because they really, really like each other. Liking each other a lot is reason enough for them."

"And then they *don't* get married?"

"That's right."

"That's not what Philippe said. He said people get married. That's what they *do*."

"Not all people."

"Philippe's father has gotten married five times."

"Why am I not surprised?"

"Huh? So then, you're *not* going to marry Miss Lani?"

"I'll tell you what. If I do, you and I will talk about it first."

Nick made a face. "You don't need to talk to me about it. I like Miss Lani. You can marry her if you want to."

"Well, ahem. That's good to know."

Nicky just sat there, scowling.

Max tried gingerly, "Nick, is there something bothering you?"

Nick braced back on his hands, wiggled his toes in the sand and huffed out a hard breath. "Well, I keep trying to remember my mother and sometimes I just don't, you know?"

Sophia. He probably should have known.

Max reached out an arm and hooked it around his son's neck.

Nicky complained, "Papa!" but he didn't try to squirm away when Max pulled him close. He had that sweaty-boy smell, like wet puppies and sunshine.

At the water, Lani and Connie turned and started toward them. But then Lani seemed to register that a father-son moment might be happening. She took Connie's hand and led her off down the beach a ways. Together, they squatted and started writing with their index fingers in the shining wet sand.

Max said, quietly, father to son, "When we lost your mother, you were pretty young."

"I was *really* young. Only four. I mean, *Trev* is four."

"It's natural that you don't remember very much about her."

Nicky didn't reply at first. Max cast about for something reasonably helpful to add. But then Nick whispered, "I remember she had soft hair. And she would play with me sometimes, rolling a rubber ball in the play yard of the gardens."

"See? You do remember."

"It's not a lot. It should be more."

Max felt a certain tightness in his chest. "Whatever you remember is just right."

"Did you really, really like her, Papa?"

"I did, yes." It was the truth, for the most part. Through a good part of their marriage he had liked his wife very much. And once, a lifetime ago, he had thought what the world still thought: that Lady Sophia Paloma Delario Silva was the love of his life.

"And so you got married."

"Yes."

"Hah. Just like Philippe said."

"That Philippe," Max said wryly. "He knows it all."

Max woke in Lani's bed.

It was late, he knew that. He should have been back at the apartment hours ago. But their lovemaking had been so good and she was so soft and inviting. He remembered thinking, *Just for a few minutes. I'll just close my eyes...*

Beside him, she stirred but didn't wake. The bed smelled of her. Vanilla. Flowers. Something citrusy. Everything good.

He wanted to turn into her, pull her close, wake her with kisses.

Instead, he turned his head the other way and squinted at the clock.

Four in the morning.

He needed to get back. Sunday mornings had a certain rhythm to them. Marceline brought him coffee in bed to tide him over until the big family breakfast at nine. On Sundays, Nicky and Connie were allowed to join him in the master suite. They would stretch out on the bed with him, propped up on the pillows, and drink the hot cocoa Marceline brought with the coffee. Lani would arrive later, in time to go with them for Sunday breakfast.

"What time is it?" Her voice beside him, soft and enticing as the scent of her.

"After four. I have to go..."

"Um." She moved, turning over on her side, pressing closer.

He couldn't resist. He gathered her in. "Have to go..."

"Um..."

He stroked her sleek, warm back, sifted his fingers up into the wild, fine tangle of her midnight hair. The scent of gardenias was always stronger in her hair. "You do things to me..."

Her lips, her breath, trailing over his shoulder, caressing his throat.

He groaned. "Lani..."

And then she was moving closer still, her smooth, curvy body sliding over him, until she was on top of him, her softness pressing into him, making him burn. "Sometimes I wish you would stay a whole night."

He started to say how he couldn't.

And she said, "Scratch that. I *always* wish you would stay the whole night."

"Lani, I..." And that was as far as he got. Her lips

brushed his, teasing him, and he would rather be kissing her right then than talking, anyway.

So he did—or rather, she did. She covered his mouth with her soft, warm one and there was nothing but the sweet, heady taste of her, the glide of her naughty tongue over his teeth, the rub of her body all along his.

She moved her legs, straddling him, folding them to each side of his waist.

He groaned as he slipped right into place in the cove of her thighs. She was already wet and so very ready. Just the feel of her came very near to pushing him over the top.

Somehow, he held out, held on, as her body rose and she was sliding forward, lifting him with her as she moved. The endless kiss continued, and he caught her face between his hands so he could thoroughly plunder her mouth.

Right then, without him really realizing how perfectly she'd positioned them, she lowered her body down onto his, taking him into her, all the way in.

He groaned her name against her lips. Paradise, to be buried deep in her welcoming heat. And then she manacled his wrists with her soft hands, guiding them back to the pillow on each side of his head.

"Lani…" It came out as a plea.

She lifted her sweet mouth away from him, sitting up on him. He moaned at the loss—and also at the way the shift in position had her pressing down tighter where they were joined, deepening the connection. And then she started moving, holding his wrists in place on the pillow, driving him out of his mind with pure pleasure, her cloud of dark hair falling forward over her white, smooth shoulders.

He sought her black eyes through the darkness, held them, tried to stay with her as she took him, rocking him.

But it was pointless to hold out, impossible to last. The

sensations intensified, sparks flying down every nerve, heat popping and sizzling across his skin.

He shut his eyes as he went over, and he broke the hold of her hands on his wrists, so he could touch her, grasp the perfect, full curves of her hips and press her down even harder on him as he pressed up into her.

She crumpled onto him then, her softness covering him. As his climax rolled through him, she caught his mouth again and she kissed him endlessly, crying out wordless things, her climax chasing his.

He pressed even harder into her, and with a long, low cry, she shattered around him.

"I have to go," Max whispered, his hand on her cheek, fingers weaving up into her tangled hair.

Lani pretended not to hear him, tucking her head into the curve of his shoulder and then settling against his chest. His heartbeat slowed under her ear and she felt so lovely, so loose and lazy, her body still thrumming with the echo of pleasure, her skin, like his, sticky with sweat.

For a string of too-short moments, he just went on touching her, guiding her hair behind her ear, stroking warm fingers down her arm.

But then he took her shoulders in a tender but determined grip and pushed her away from him.

She groaned in protest, grumbling, "No..."

But he was already gently guiding her to the side, sliding away from her, easing his feet over the edge of the mattress, rising before she had a chance to pull him back.

With another groan, she buried her face in the pillow.

"A quick shower," he said, bending, brushing a kiss against her hair.

She heard the hushed whisper of his bare feet as he padded across the floor.

Not five minutes later, he was back. She sat up and watched him quickly pull on his clothes.

Smelling steamy and wonderful, his hair curly, sticking up on one side the way it did when it was wet, he bent close to give her a last, sweet kiss. "I'll send the car for you. Eight-thirty?"

Her throat ached with all the things she was holding in. Her love, her longing, the future she saw for them versus the one she had finally admitted, to herself and to Syd at least, that she wanted.

But now was not the time. Not after he'd slept too late, not after she'd shamelessly kept him there longer still, using her body to get a little bit more from him, a little bit more *of* him. A little bit more of what he didn't want to give.

We have to talk.

She tried the words out in her head and didn't like them.

We have to talk. The four little words people said when things had to change.

He arched a brow at her. "Lani? Eight-thirty?"

She forced a smile and nodded.

One more kiss. And he was gone.

She got up, pulled on the silky robe he'd given her and went out into the living area to engage the dead bolt after him. Then she brewed coffee and took it out on the balcony, into the cool predawn darkness. She sipped and stared at the tree shadows on the hill in back, planning what she would do.

She needed to wait for an evening when they wouldn't be disturbed. Tonight wouldn't do. They would be with the children all day and she would have dinner at the palace apartment, in the little kitchen, all casual and cozy, just the four of them and maybe Gerta. Later, she might stay until eight or nine, but when they were at his apartment, there was always the possibility that Connie or Nick would need him for something. She didn't want them overhearing what she had to say.

Tomorrow, they were leaving together for two days, flying to London, where he would speak at a charity fundraiser. They would return Wednesday.

She'd been looking forward to it, to the time together away from home, to the nights when he wouldn't have to get up and leave before daylight.

So then. Tuesday night maybe, after the event? If that didn't feel right, then whenever he came to her place next, she would do what Syd had said she should do. What she realized at last she *needed* to do.

She would tell him she loved him. And that she had changed. She would tell him what she wanted from him, from her life. She would do all that right away, as soon as he walked in the door, before they started talking about her day or his day or what was going on with Nick and Connie, before they made love or had dinner. She would do it and not put it off.

And then they would take it from there.

Her cup was empty. She pushed back the slider to go in and get more. And right then, on the counter, her cell started playing the theme from *Big Brother*.

Carlos? At this hour? Five-thirty in the morning in Montedoro was ten-thirty last night in Texas.

Dread coiling in her belly like a snake about to strike, she grabbed the phone. "Carlos?"

"Hey, *hermanita*." He sounded very un-Carlos-like. Hesitant. Careful. All wrong. Her big brother was always the most confident person in the room. He knew what was right and he never minded telling you. "I'm sorry if I woke you up. It's not even daylight there yet, right?"

"It's okay. I was up. I… Is there something wrong?"

And then he just came out with it. "It's Papi," he said. "You need to get home."

Chapter Twelve

Dressed in the silk pajamas he always wore when expecting a visit from the children in the morning, Max was just climbing into his bed when his cell rang. He could hear it buzzing away, over there on the chair, still in the pocket of the trousers he'd worn to Lani's.

He considered letting it go to voice mail and calling whoever it was back later. But who called at six Sunday morning? It would be a wrong number or someone who urgently needed to reach him.

Just in case it was the latter, he went over there, grabbed the trousers, fished the phone from the pocket and answered.

"Max?" Lani's voice vibrated with urgency.

Alarm jangled through him. "Lani, what is it?"

"I just got a call from my brother. My father's in surgery. Acute appendicitis. Can you believe that?" She didn't wait for him to answer, just barreled on, the words tumbling over each other in a frantic rush. "My mother's a doctor and *she* didn't figure it out. The symptoms can be a little different for older people. It doesn't seem so acute. But it *is* acute. If they'd waited any longer, it would have ruptured. He's still not okay, far from okay. They've got him in surgery—did I already say that? It's... Oh, Max, I'm sorry. I guess I'm rambling."

"It's all right. Don't apologize." He dropped to the chair and raked his fingers back through his hair. "An appendectomy then?"

"Yes. That's right."

"But it's a standard procedure, isn't?"

"I don't know. My brother made it sound pretty bad."

"Still, your father *is* going to pull through?"

A ragged sound escaped her. "I think so. I'm pretty sure. I need to fly back there, to be with them, to see Papi, to tell him how much I love him."

"Yes. Of course you do. I'll arrange for a jet." He should take her, he knew it. He should be there when she needed him. "I don't know if I can get out of that thing in London at this point..."

"Of course not. I understand." She sounded strange suddenly. A little stiff, too formal, somehow. He didn't like it. It made him feel apart from her, not family.

But then, he *wasn't* her family. He was her lover and her friend and she meant the world to him, and that was how they both wanted it.

She went on, "I mean, it's bad, but he's not *dying* or anything. At least, he'd better not. And really, Max, I only wanted you to know what was going on. As far as getting there, I can just fly commercial. You don't have to—"

He cut her off. "I will arrange for the jet."

"Oh, Max..." A tight laugh escaped her. "I don't know why I'm so freaked out. I mean, people get sick sometimes. You deal with it. It's probably mostly the guilt."

"Guilt?"

"That I haven't been back much, that I never go home. All that he did for me, all my life, especially in the hardest times. And I'm not there when he needs his whole family around him, rooting for him. Or maybe it was Carlos."

"Your brother?"

"He was the one who called me. Did I tell you that? I guess not. Carlos sounded so cautious and subdued. My brother is never subdued and…" She pulled herself up short. "There I go. Babbling away again."

"I'll arrange everything," he promised. "Two hours, tops, you'll be in the air."

"But I could so easily—"

"Don't argue. I will get you there hours ahead of any commercial flight you could find. And you want to be there fast, don't you?"

"Oh, Max. I do." A hard sob escaped her. "Yes."

"Then count on me. Pack, get ready to go, call Sydney and tell her what's happened. Do whatever you need to do. I'll be there to take you to Nice Airport at seven. Be ready."

"All right, yes. I… Thank you."

"You don't need to thank me." His voice sounded gruff to his own ears. "You never need to thank me."

"Oh, Max, I…" She seemed to catch herself. "Seven. Yes. I'll be ready when you get here."

Max arrived at her apartment ten minutes early. They were on their way to the airport at seven on the dot.

During the drive, Lani seemed distant, distracted—which was in no way surprising given the circumstances. He held her hand and gave her Gerta's good wishes. "And Connie sends a thousand kisses and orders you to take care of your papa and then be home soon."

She smiled softly at that. "Tell Connie a million billion kisses back. And of course I will do exactly as she instructed. Any message from Nicky? Wait. Let me guess.

Something along the lines of 'So can we stay home from Sunday breakfast, then?'"

"You know him too well." He wanted to be closer to her. So he unhooked his seat belt, slid over to the middle seat and hooked himself in there. "Hello." He put his arm around her. With a sigh, she leaned her head on his shoulder. Better. He breathed in the scent of her hair and tried to tamp down his apprehensions. Her father would be fine in the end, he was sure. And she would come home to Montedoro, home to him.

She glanced up at him. "Tell Nicky he gets a million billion kisses from me, too, whether he likes it or not."

"I will. Have you talked to your mother yet?"

She sighed again. "No. I'll see her soon, and she's focused on my father right now. I'm in touch with Carlos, getting everything I need to know from him. He'll tell her I'm on the way."

"The thing in London is tomorrow evening. Once it's over, I'll come to you."

Her head shot up. "You're coming to Texas?"

He eased his hand under her hair, wrapped his fingers around the warm, soft back of her neck and teased, "That's where you'll be, isn't it?"

"Yeah, but I didn't…" She seemed to catch herself.

He held her gaze. "You do that a lot lately—stop talking in the middle of sentences, as though you're editing yourself."

"I… Sorry."

"Did it again."

"I'm worried about my father."

"I know." But he doubted that was all of it.

"Max, really. You don't have to come."

"It's not a question of having to. I *want* to come." He was more and more certain that something other than her father's sudden illness was bothering her—and had been for a while now. "Unless you don't want me there…"

"No. That's not so. Of course I want you there." She was trying too hard to convince him, which only made him more certain that she really *didn't* want him in Texas with her family.

Too bad. He was taking her at her word, whether she liked it or not. "All right then. I'll be there."

Max would be joining her in Beaufort….

Lani wasn't sure how she felt about that. Glad that he wanted to be there for her, certainly.

But a little bit freaked, too. Her family wanted her to come home to Texas to stay. Failing that, they at least wanted her settled down and happy wherever she lived. To her family, settled down meant married, and she doubted they would be shy about making that painfully clear to Max.

The fact that what they wanted had finally turned out to be what she wanted didn't really help all that much. Not when she knew in her heart it wasn't what Max wanted.

Which was something the two of them were going to be talking about.

Soon.

At the airport, the driver took them right out to the plane bearing Montedoro's coat of arms. An attendant rushed forward and dealt with her luggage. Max took her on board and exchanged greetings with the flight crew.

Then he cradled her face between his hands. "They'll take good care of you. A car will be waiting in Dallas."

Now that he was leaving, she realized that she wanted him never to go. "Thank you."

"Stop saying that."

"Kiss me."

"That's better." He took her mouth gently, a tender salute of a kiss that ended way too quickly.

She trailed him to the exit.

"Call me when you arrive in Dallas," he said.

She promised she would and watched him run down the airstairs. "I love you," she whispered under her breath as he ducked into the limo. It seemed the truest thing she'd said all day. Too bad she hadn't managed to shout it out loud and proud.

Before they took off, she called Carlos. "How's Papi?"

"He's out of surgery. Groggy. Hanging in." He was still sounding strange, almost guarded, and that worried her. Was it worse than he was letting on?

"Is there something you're not telling me, Carlito?"

"Not telling you?" He spoke impatiently, with a hint of belligerence, her big brother reminding her that he was the oldest and knew best. "What do you mean?" He could be such a jerk sometimes.

She schooled her voice to a reasonable tone. "I mean, is he worse than you're telling me?"

"No, of course not."

"Thank God for that."

"Yoli Poly, you still need to come home." Yoli Poly. She'd always hated that nickname. And she didn't like his scolding tone.

"Carlos. I'm in the jet. I'm on my way. Sheesh."

"Good. You need a ride from the airport?"

"No, thanks. It's taken care of."

"She's a big girl," he teased. "She can do it herself."

"That is exactly right." She said it jokingly, but she meant every word. "And don't you forget it."

The plane took off at 8:00 a.m. Flying west, the time zone difference worked in her favor. She arrived at Love

Field at a little before noon. There was customs to deal with, but it didn't take that long.

She called Max from the limo on her way to the hospital and told him she'd arrived safely and her father was out of surgery, doing well.

"That's what I wanted to hear." His voice played through her, deep and fine, rousing way too many dangerous emotions. She promised to call him if there was any other news and he said he would be in touch tomorrow to firm up plans for joining her there. "Shall I find a hotel?" he offered.

Oh, that was tempting. Separate him from the parents and the pushy big brother. Create fewer opportunities for cringe-worthy remarks and questions about their relationship and where it might be going.

But that wouldn't be right. He mattered to her. A lot. And the people she loved had a right to know that. Plus, in her family, you didn't send out-of-town guests to hotels unless you had no room for them.

There was plenty of room at the rambling five-bedroom redbrick ranch-style house on Prairie Lane where she'd grown up. "My mother would never forgive me if I sent you to a hotel."

"There will be a bodyguard," he reminded her. "Are you sure?"

"We'll make it work."

"All right, then." Did he sound okay with the plan? He might come to her little apartment for the evening twice a week, but then he went home to a palace. He would probably be more comfortable at a decent hotel....

"Max. Just tell me. Would you rather get a hotel suite?"

"I would rather be with you."

A sweet warmth stole through her. "Well, okay, then. You'll stay at the house."

"Good."

She almost warned him that they would have separate rooms. But then again, what was so strange about that? They had yet to spend a full night in the same bed together. And never once had she shared his bed at the palace. This was pretty much the same thing, really.

He spoke again. "Lani."

"Um?"

"I miss you."

She chided, "It's been what, twelve hours since I left?"

"Maybe it's your being so far away. Whatever it is, this is the moment for you to say, 'I miss you, too.'"

She confessed it. "I do miss you." She wished he was there, in the car with her, that she could put her head on his shoulder, have the steady weight of his arm around her. Not to mention, be his wife and have his babies.

But he wasn't there. And the last time they'd talked about marriage, he'd told her he would never get married again.

She said goodbye.

When she entered her father's hospital room, Jorge Vasquez was sitting up in bed, alert and clear-eyed. At the sight of her, he grinned from ear to ear and held out his arms. "*Mi' ja,* Carlito said you were coming!"

A miracle had happened, evidently. Her father had taken a turn for the *better*.

"Papi." She went to him and he hugged her close. His grip was strong. When he let her go, she looked him over. "You seem…good. Really good."

"I'm just fine. The surgery was laparoscopic, no complications—at least so far. I've been up and walking around. They're letting me out of here today."

"Today?"

"Don't look so shocked. I'm strong as an ox and modern medicine is a wonderful thing."

"But I thought—"

The sound of her mother's voice cut her off. "Yolanda, my baby girl…" Lani turned as Iris Vasquez entered the room looking just as Lani remembered her, petite and pretty, her long dark hair threaded with silver, parted in the middle and pulled back in a low ponytail.

"Mama." Lani went into her open arms. As always, her mother smelled faintly of plain soap. Dr. Iris never wore perfume. Too many of her young patients were allergic to it. She took Lani by the shoulders and held her away enough to beam at her. "Oh, it's good to see you. Look at you. More beautiful than ever."

Lani pulled her close for another hug. "You, too, Mama."

That time, when they moved apart, her mother urged her to take a chair.

She sat down. "Carlos really had me worried about Papi."

Iris waved a hand. "Oh, I know. I told him there would be no need for you to come, but he wouldn't listen."

"No need?" Lani tried to keep her voice light, though inside she was starting to seethe.

Her mother nodded. "Right away, I knew what was going on. Textbook symptoms of appendicitis. I took your father straight to his internist and then here for surgery."

"So you're saying you caught it early?"

"Well, *mi'ja,* I am a doctor, after all. And I'm sorry to drag you all the way from the Riviera. But now, looking at you right here where I can reach out my arms and hug you, I can't help but be glad that Carlos insisted this was a good way to get you to come home."

Max was in bed when his phone rang. Lani. It was after ten in Montedoro, which meant it would be past three in the afternoon where she was.

Eager for the husky sound of her voice, he set aside

the book he'd been reading and put the phone to his ear. "How's your father?"

"Good. Really good. *Too* good."

"*Too* good? How is that possible?"

"Turns out Carlos lied to me when he said my father was practically at death's door. Apparently, he did it to get me to come home. So I get here an hour ago and my father's sitting up in bed, all smiles and so happy to see me. My mother figured out it was appendicitis from practically his first twinge of pain. The operation was laparoscopic—minimally invasive, small incisions, faster healing."

"It all sounds great—other than the part about your brother lying to you."

"I'm thinking positive. My dad isn't dying after all. The doctor's with him now and he's going home today."

"But you're angry."

"I was terrified. I want to strangle Carlos, I really do. I'll get him alone later and tell him exactly what I think of him."

"Be kind."

"Right. And you know…" Suddenly she was doing that hesitating thing again, her voice trailing off as though she wasn't sure how much she could say to him. He gritted his teeth and waited for it. "It's really not necessary for you to come here now. Everything's going to be fine and I'll be back in Montedoro in a week, two at the most."

He said nothing.

"Max? Are you still there?"

"I'm here. Are you saying that you don't want me there?"

"No, of course I'm not." The words sounded automatic and not all that sincere.

He should probably back off, leave her alone to be with her family. She'd return to him soon enough. But he wanted to go to her, to see where she'd grown up, to meet her mother and father and even the devious big brother. "All right then. I'll come directly from London, as planned."

"You scared me to death," Lani accused. "You know that, right?"

It was nine o'clock that night. Her father was resting comfortably in his own bed, her mother beside him. Carlos's bride, Martina, was in the living room on the phone with her own mother in San Antonio. Lani had dragged Carlos out to the back deck to have it out with him.

Carlos blustered, "You needed to be scared. You needed to come home." Her big brother was the same as ever. He had no shame. But why should he? He was always right, just ask him.

"You lied to me, Carlos. You manipulated me. Papi was never in any real danger."

"When there's surgery, it's always dangerous—and Mama and Papi need you. They're getting older and they need their only daughter close." Leave it to Carlos to play the guilt card early and often.

She reminded herself it was just more manipulation. "If they need me, I will be here. So far, they seem to be doing just fine."

"You are so selfish, *mi'ja*. You always have been. You do what you want and you don't care who gets hurt." Great. Two minutes alone with him and he already had the heavy equipment out excavating the pain of the past.

Deep breaths. Calm words. "What's going on here, Carlos? I mean, what's *really* going on?"

He strode out to the edge of the deck and stared off through the darkness, his broad back held stiffly, chest out. A wrestler in high school and college, Carlos never gave up until he had his opponent's shoulders pinned to the mat in a match-winning three-second hold. "Martina and I are in San Antonio most of the time now. No one's close if they need us."

She went for the positives. "Really, it's not that bad. I admit I haven't been here enough. But I will come more often, and be ready to fly back anytime it's necessary. And it's an hour flight for you."

He made a humphing sound. "You're the daughter. It's your duty to be here for your mother and father."

"Seriously?" she asked, with excruciating sweetness. "Do you even have a clue how sexist that sounds?"

He whirled on her, black eyes flashing. "You have a duty, Yoli, after all they've done for you."

She kept her head high. "Maybe I do. But that's between Mama and Papi and me. And whether or not I ought to move back to Texas has got nothing to do with why I asked you to come out here and speak with me privately. Carlos, you lied and you manipulated me to get me here. It was wrong, what you did."

He dropped into the iron chair by the railing and stared out at the backyard again. "You're getting way too damn reasonable, you know that? In the old days, you'd be crying and carrying on and calling me all kinds of names by now."

"It so happens I grew up." She waited for him to meet her eyes again. He didn't. "You need to stop thinking of me as some spoiled eighteen-year-old. I made some terrible choices and I hurt the people I love, including you. I know that. I live with that, will live with that, for the rest of my life. I hope someday you can forgive me for all the trouble I caused."

"Of course I forgive you," he grumbled. "You're my sister. I love you."

"And I love you. But, Carlos, you were in the wrong to scare me like that about Papi."

He shocked her then—by busting to it. "All right. Yeah.

It was wrong. I shouldn't have made Papi's condition sound worse than it is."

She went over and took the chair beside him. "And?"

At last, he looked at her. His eyes were softer. She saw regret in them. "I shouldn't have done it. I'm sorry. I'm sorry for…all the ways I'm being a douche. I just wanted you to come home. It doesn't seem right, you living halfway around the world."

She did long for him to understand. "I love Montedoro, Carlito. My life is there now. It's the home of my heart."

"Your home is with your family."

Here we go again. "Listen to me. You don't get to decide what works for my life. You really need to stop imagining that you do."

He looked away, then slid her a sideways glance. "This guy, this prince…"

She sat a little straighter. "His name is Max."

"There's a lot of stuff online about you and him."

"I know. And in the tabloids, too. Don't take any of it too seriously."

"There was even something about you and that SOB, McKneely."

She reached across the distance between their chairs and nudged his arm. "Don't speak ill of the dead." He made a sound low in his throat, but left it at that. She added, "It's public knowledge. What can you do?"

He held her gaze. "You're taking it well."

"Hey. I try."

"You said at dinner that the—er, Max—is coming here Tuesday."

"Well, he *was* coming to support me in my hour of need, what with my father practically dying and all…"

He scowled at her. "You made your point. Give it a rest."

"Now he's just coming to meet my wonderful family, I guess."

"Are you going to marry him?"

She'd known he would ask, and she had her answer ready. "At this point, that's none of your business."

"So then, that's a no?"

"What part of 'none of your business' was unclear to you?"

Carlos made more grumbling sounds. "I guess if you married him, you'd be a princess and live in the palace and never come home."

"Of course I would come home. I just promised I would, and more often, too. And can we worry about marriage when the time comes?" *If it ever does.*

The back door opened. Martina stuck her head out. Carlos's wife was every inch the dancer, graceful and slim, her long brown hair pulled up in a high, tight ponytail. A strong-minded, opinionated woman, Martina also had a big heart. From the first, she'd fit right into the Vasquez family. She gave Carlos a look of equal parts fire and tenderness. "Stop arguing, you two, and come inside."

The next morning, Jorge came to the table for breakfast. He winced and groaned getting down into the chair, and he only had juice and a few spoonfuls of plain yogurt. But still. It did Lani's heart good to see him sitting there, so proud of himself, so happy to have his family around him.

She had missed him—missed all of them—she thought, as she sipped her coffee and ate her mother's killer chorizo and eggs. They were dear to her and they loved her. And the emotional distance she had felt between herself and them since all the trouble eleven years ago?

Gone. Vanished. She had created that distance, she realized now. She had erected barriers against them. And now that she no longer needed to wall herself off from them, the barriers had crumbled of their own accord.

She didn't approve of the way Carlos had tricked her to get her to come home, but her brother had been right that she needed to be there. Whatever happened with Max, she would do better by her family. She would get back to Texas more often.

Whatever happened with Max...

He was still coming to be with her, to meet her family. He seemed to really *want* to come. And she wanted him there, even if it was difficult and awkward and her brother and her parents asked all kinds of leading questions, even if they came right out and demanded to know if he had marriage on his mind.

So what if they did ask? It would only prove they were braver than she was.

Carlos said, "Now that we're all here together and Papi is looking good, Martina and I have a little announcement to make."

Martina was blushing. Carlos took her hand and brought it to his lips. They shared a look of such joy and intimacy, Lani almost felt guilty watching them.

Her mother clapped and cried out, "Oh! Already? I can hardly believe it." She reached for Jorge's hand.

He took it, wrapped his other hand around it and declared, "I am a happy, happy man."

Carlos laughed. "We haven't even told you what it is yet."

Iris chuckled. "As if we don't already know."

"Could be I got a great deal on some restaurant equipment."

Iris sputtered and Martina said, "Carlos, don't tease."

And Carlos finally came out with the big news. "Martina and I are having a baby."

Iris let out another happy cry and Jorge said, "Wonderful news."

Lani added her voice to the others. "That's terrific. Congratulations."

And her mother jumped up to go hug Martina, while her father grabbed her brother's arm and gave it a hearty, man-to-man squeeze. "You have made me so happy, my son."

Lani let their gladness wash over her. She was glad *for* them, for the new life that her brother and his wife would soon bring into the world. At the same time, she was suddenly far away from all of them, remembering her lost baby, who would be older than Nicky now. There would always be a certain empty place within her, a place that echoed with longing, a place that held only regret for the life her child would never have.

But beneath the old sorrow, now there was something new. Something hopeful and scary, too. She was through with denials, through taking care of other people's babies and telling herself that it was enough. One way or another, she was ready for happiness now, ready to make a family of her own.

Max needed to know that.

And not in a week or two, when they were back in Montedoro.

Uh-uh. No more putting it off. No more making excuses for the things she didn't have the courage to say. No going along as usual with secrets in her heart, no pretending that everything was okay when it wasn't.

He was coming tomorrow. And at the earliest opportunity, she would get him alone and tell him that she loved him—was *in* love with him. And also that, for her, everything had changed.

Chapter Thirteen

The driver, Calvin, pulled the car to a stop in front of the redbrick house.

"A minute," said Max, before Calvin could get out.

"Certainly, sir." Calvin already had his door unlatched. He pulled it shut and glanced at the bodyguard, Joseph, in the seat beside him. But Joseph sat patiently, staring straight ahead.

Max gazed out the tinted side window at the graceful sweep of lawn, the long front porch and the large front door with the arched fanlight in the top. The house seemed to him so completely American, long and low, a style they called midcentury ranch. Lani had grown up here. He could almost picture her, a little girl with black braids and scraped knees, riding a pink tricycle down the natural stone front walk.

The door opened and the grown Lani came out, wearing jeans that hugged her beautiful curves and a light, lacy turquoise shirt. She closed the door behind her. And then for several seconds she just stood there on the porch, staring at the car.

He stared back at her, something dark and hot and needful churning within him. He knew she couldn't see him through the tinted glass. Still, he felt the connection anyway. Strong. Urgent. Unbreakable.

Or at least that was what he kept telling himself, even if sometimes lately she seemed to be pulling away from him.

She emerged from under the shadow of the porch roof. The spring sunshine caught deep red gleams in her black hair as she came down the walk to the car.

He pushed open the door.

She leaned in. "Change your mind about staying?" He reached out, snared her arm and dragged her inside. "Max!"

He pulled the door closed, pressed his nose to her smooth throat and breathed in the unforgettable scent of her. "I wanted a minute or two alone first."

She shot a glance at the two in the front seat. "We're not alone."

He ran up the privacy screen. "Now. Be quiet. Kiss me."

"Yes, Your Highness."

He tasted her sweetness, stroked her silky hair, considered telling Joseph and Calvin to take a long walk. But there was her family to consider. "I suppose they're waiting in there, wondering what I'm up to."

She grinned, though her eyes seemed somehow guarded. "You suppose right. How was the thing in London?"

"The usual. Long. Somewhat dull. I need to rework the speech I gave. We got several large donations, though, so I'm calling it a win. Connie sends big hugs, by the way. Nick says, and I quote, 'When Miss Lani gets back can we go to the beach again and make another sand castle and I'll be nice to Connie?'"

"Whoa. He is becoming downright sweet. You told him yes, right?"

"I said I'd check with you." He tipped up her chin. For a moment, she met his gaze, but then her glance skittered away. He demanded, "What's the matter?"

She caught his wrist, pushed it gently aside. "Later."

"So there *is* something?"

"Yes, Max. There is. And my mother just came out on the porch. We should go in."

Max liked Lani's mother. He told her to call him Max and she shook his hand and said with a smile almost as beautiful as Lani's, "I'm Iris."

Iris took the usual awkwardness with Joseph in stride. The three of them—Lani, Max and Iris—waited on the porch while the bodyguard made a quick reconnaissance of the property.

When Joseph was ready to check inside, Iris went with him in order to explain to her husband, her son and her son's wife why the large stranger with the Bluetooth device in his ear was checking in the showers and opening closet doors.

Once that was over, Calvin brought in the luggage and Iris showed Max to his room, which had a window that looked out on the front yard, a double closet and a bath just down the hall. Joseph got a much smaller room next door. Max would have to share his bathroom with the bodyguard. That was a first. He couldn't recall ever sharing a bath with another man. Luckily, Joseph was a consummate professional. He made being unobtrusive into an art form. Max foresaw no problems there.

Dinner was served at seven. There were big slabs of beef cooked on the outside grill the way Americans loved best, along with enormous baked potatoes, lots of green salad and hot dinner rolls.

Lani's dad came to the table, though he ate only a small dish of applesauce and some yogurt. Jorge Vasquez was cordial enough, but watchful, too. Same with Lani's brother, Carlos. Max could feel the men's protectiveness of Lani.

Max might be the heir to a throne, but that didn't mean he was good enough for their little girl.

During the meal, Max learned that Carlos's wife, Martina, was going to have a baby. He congratulated her. Martina thanked him and said she was very happy. Carlos took her hand for a moment and she gave him a glowing smile.

"Love, marriage, children." Jorge Vasquez looked misty-eyed. "What else is there, eh?" He aimed the question at Max, one bushy brow lifted.

"Family is everything," Max agreed with a smile. He sent a quick glance at Lani, to his left. She only nodded, her expression relaxed and neutral, but her eyes as watchful as her father's.

"I'm so glad you feel that way," said Iris, beaming. "Lani tells us you have two children already. We hope to get to meet them soon."

Already? As if he intended to have more? "Yes." He turned to Lani again. "We should plan on that."

She nodded as she had before, but didn't say anything.

And it went on through the meal, the Vasquezes taking turns dropping hints about matrimony and babies, Max knocking himself out trying to be receptive and agreeable without actually lying and vowing to get a ring on Lani's finger immediately so they could set to work providing Iris and Jorge with more grandchildren. Through it all, Lani never said a word. Max tried not to be annoyed with her, but he couldn't help thinking that it would have been so easy for her to make a joke of the whole thing, or to simply tell her parents and brother to cut it out.

After the meal, they watched a comedy on the large flat-screen television in the family room. Of course, the movie had a romance in it and when the hero proposed to the heroine, Max stared straight ahead. No way was he getting caught checking to see if Lani's mother or father was watching him, hoping he was getting the hint.

Jorge and Iris went to bed when the movie ended. Holding hands, Martina and Carlos went out the back door to the deck.

Lani said, "There's a park a few blocks away and it's a nice night. Get Joseph and we'll go for a walk."

The night was balmy and no one disturbed them as they walked in and out of the wide pools of golden light provided by high streetlamps. He'd been a little worried the paparazzi might have gotten wind of his destination when he left Heathrow. But no. Her parents' neighborhood was quiet except for the ordinary sounds of places like this: the sudden bark of a protective dog, the honk of a car horn, the whisper of the wind in the branches of the oak trees.

They walked without speaking. She seemed withdrawn, thoughtful. And he was still a little put out with her for not backing her family off during dinner.

When they reached the park she'd mentioned, she led him to a bench by a deserted grouping of swings, a slide, monkey bars and a jungle gym. They sat down and Joseph retreated into the shadows several yards away.

And she said, "There's something I've been meaning to tell you, Max. Something I really need to say."

And he *knew.* He was certain. The bottom dropped out of his stomach. "You're pregnant."

Her eyes popped wide. And then she laughed. "No."

He felt relieved. And also foolish. "Oh. Well. I'm… That's good." Did he sound like an idiot? Definitely. He shut his mouth and waited.

She got up from the bench and held down her hand. He took it. She led him to the swings and they each sat in one. For a moment, she pushed herself slowly back and forth, her head tipped up to the three-quarter moon, the swing chains making a faint squeaking sound.

Then, as the swinging slowed, she turned to him. "I've changed, Max, since I met you. Changed in so many ways I can hardly name them all. Changed way down, in the deepest, truest part of me. You've…opened me up. You've freed me. There's no other word for it. I am free now. You've accepted me, just as I am. With you, I've shared the worst of me, and still, you…wanted me, cared for me. It's meant everything, how you are, how *we* are, you and me, together." She stilled the swing and swayed there, just the slightest bit, beside him. "I know that I matter to you."

"Of course, you—"

"Shh." She reached across the space between their two swings and put her finger against his lips. At his nod of agreement not to interrupt, she withdrew her hand. "I don't know why we don't say it to each other, why I've never said it to you when I've known it for weeks now. Longer. Known it even back when I was set on denying it. For all those months when we were 'just friends.'"

He had the strangest feeling—weightless and drowning, both at once. He wanted to stop her, wanted to drag her back somehow to the safety of what they were to each other now, of all they'd had together in the past month.

But she refused to stay safe. "I don't know why we don't say it, Max. Maybe because to say it leads on to the next step and the next step is one you're not willing to take. But, well, I have to say it. Are you listening? Tell me you're listening."

"Damn it, Lani."

She stilled the swing completely. "I'll say it anyway. I love you, Max. You're everything I could ever want in a man. Are we clear on that?"

"Lani, I—"

"Max. Are we clear?"

I love you, too. You're everything to me. How hard could it be to tell her? "Yes. We're clear."

She looked at him so sadly. But he didn't need her sad look to tell him how completely he had disappointed her. "I need to…say the rest." She sounded breathless now. And not in a good way. "I know I told you once that I would never get married, never have children. I meant it, at the time. And you told me the same about yourself. You do remember that." It wasn't a question.

He answered it anyway. "Yes, of course I do."

"Well, for me, everything's different now. For me, the world is wide open again and I can be happy. I can love you and marry you, be your wife, help you take care of your beautiful children, give you more children…"

He needed to stop this. But of course, he knew he couldn't. He knew it was already too late. So he gave her what he had, which was the truth. "I will never get married again. And I don't believe in having children outside of marriage. However, if you became pregnant, I would love and accept the child."

"I told you, I'm not pregnant. I'm very careful about contraception, so you can stop worrying about that."

"I'm not worrying. I just wanted you to know."

"Ah." She stared at him for a long time, her eyes bright with unshed tears.

He couldn't bear the silence. "I told you from the first that I wasn't looking for a wife." Defensive. Gruff. God, he hated himself.

"Yes, you did. You told me you would never marry again. What you didn't tell me is why. Why won't you take a chance on a real future with me? How is it that you've opened me up, given me the ability to love again, to dream again? And you remain the same. Closed off. Unchanged."

"But I'm not unchanged. You mean everything to me."

One tear fell, shining and pure, sliding slowly down her cheek. "You never talk about Sophia."

"Lani—"

"No. Don't cut me off. Don't redirect me. I just need to know. Is it what people say? That you've had the perfect, forever love and nothing can ever come close so you're never even going to try?" She shook her head. "That doesn't make sense to me, somehow. It doesn't feel true. You never say anything about her, nothing. No fond memories. Nothing about the good times you shared, or the hard times you got through together. You are silent on the subject of Sophia. What was it with her that makes it all such a mystery, that has you swearing off ever really trying again?"

He didn't know where to start. He didn't *want* to start. "Just because I don't want to get married again doesn't mean I'm not trying."

She tipped her head to the side, studying him. "Okay. Maybe I was unfair. You *are* trying. Up to a point. But after that point, uh-uh. You're done. And see, that's the thing. You pried me open like a can of peaches, you know? You got inside my head and my heart and you found out all the bad stuff. I gave it to you and you took it with an open heart. I knew that it would make you despise me. But it didn't. You were wonderful, tender, so completely accepting. I want to do that for you. I wish you would let me."

"Lani." He stood from the swing so fast that she gasped. "Stop."

She gazed up at him as the swing bumped against the backs of his calves. And then she laughed. It was the saddest sound he'd ever heard. "You saw how it was with my parents and my brother. They want happiness for me, and I'm like them, as you've helped me to discover. I want what they want for me—a husband, a home, a family. And they're going to keep after you. They want you to tell them that you're ready, or at least close to ready, to give me what I want."

"Are you saying you want me to leave you here and go back to Montedoro?"

She gazed up at him, the moon shining in her tear-wet eyes. "No. I want you to stay. I want you to stick it out. But I'm warning you, it's not going to be a whole lot of fun for you if you do."

They were at an impasse. What she wanted now for her life and her future, he would never give her. What she needed to hear from him, he would never say.

He should go home. But there was a bloody fool within him who couldn't bear to lose her, who refused to surrender the field. "I'm not going anywhere, not until you're ready to come home with me."

She kept staring at him, steadily. "I want more than this, Max. I want everything, all of you. A lifetime together, to live with you and Nicky and Connie, to sleep the whole night in the same bed with you, to be in that bed with you on Sunday morning when the children come in for cocoa. The right to be there, as your wife, when you need me the most."

There was no point in telling her again that she'd never get that from him. "Let's go back to the house." He held down his hand.

She took it without the slightest hesitation and she said softly, "It's not going to be pleasant."

"What isn't?"

"None of it. You'll see."

They stayed in Texas, at her parents' house, for a week. The Vasquez family treated him with kindness and a wry sort of affection. And they never stopped working on him to declare his intentions concerning his relationship with Lani.

He could have left. He knew that. Maybe he *should* have left. But something in him held on, refusing to let go. He knew if he left her there it would be over between them.

He did not want that. He wanted things as they had been: the two of them, free to live their separate lives, connected, but freely. Committed to each other not forever, not because of some ancient words recited before a priest, but anew every single day.

She used to understand that. He was furious with her for changing. And he felt somehow bested by her at the same time.

But he was not going to leave her in Texas without him at the mercy of her family. They would be bound to convince her that he wasn't the one for her, that she needed to move home to Texas and find a nice American man, a man ready, willing and able to put a ring on her finger and baby in her belly.

After the conversation that night on the swings, she treated him as she had before—up to a point. She held hands with him and kissed him now and then, quick, chaste kisses. Alone on the back deck with him in the evening, she would laugh with him over the things that had happened that day. They might get into some debate over a minor point of Montedoran law. In front of her family, she showed him affection and tenderness.

But beyond safe discussions of her father's quick recovery and the final turning point in the last novel of her Montedoran trilogy? Nothing. He knew that was very much his fault. He wanted to speak more intimately with her, but that was too dangerous. It would only lead back to that night on the swings, to what she wanted that he didn't, to why he was holding on when she needed more and more was not something he would ever share with her.

As to physical intimacy, there was nothing beyond the

occasional fond touch, her hand in his, those infrequent chaste kisses. Even before that night in the park, he hadn't expected to make love with her there, in her father's house. But he'd hoped that maybe they might sneak away to a hotel once or twice....

So much for that idea. She had been right. It was not pleasant, being so close to her and yet feeling that she was somehow a million miles away from him. It was a lot worse than not pleasant, actually. It was a whole new way of living in hell.

And yet he stayed. He couldn't make himself give up and go.

Four days in, the paparazzi found them. So for the final three days, every time he left the house, there were photographers waiting. That first day they showed up was the worst. They came running up the walk at him, waving microphones. So he gave them an interview right then and there. It was like being interviewed by Lani's parents. Just about every question added up to: Was he there to propose and had she said yes?

He answered as vaguely as he'd answered the Vasquezes.

That appeased them enough that most of them went away. There were still the lurkers, the ones who tried to get shots of him and Lani from a distance whenever they were in open view, but it was bearable. He ignored them.

The Vasquezes seemed to take the whole thing in stride. They laughed about it over dinner and teased Max that he should just marry Lani and make all those reporters happy.

The final days in Texas went by at last. They flew home on Tuesday, leaving the house before dawn. Carlos and Martina had gone home to San Antonio two days before. But Iris and Jorge got up early to say goodbye.

Lani promised she would return in a few weeks, just for a day or two, when she flew to New York at the end of the month. There were hugs and kisses and Lani and her mother cried.

Jorge hugged Max and whispered, "You treat my daughter right."

And Iris grabbed him next. "Just be happy together," she commanded in his ear. "That's all we ask."

And then, at last, they were out of there, rushing down the stone walk to the waiting car.

He thought it would get better once they were home in Montedoro, that they would slip back into the happy, fulfilling life they'd shared before.

But it wasn't the same. She started actively avoiding him. She was too busy to have him visit her apartment in the evenings. She came to the palace to see Sydney and her family, and to be with Gerta and the children after school. But if he tried to join them, she always had some reason that she had to be going.

They were all over the tabloids. The journos made up all kinds of ridiculous stories about the trip to Texas. The headlines gave a whole new meaning to the word *absurd*: "Prince Max and the Nanny: Their Secret Engagement" and "The Prince's Cinderella Bride" and "The Naughty Nanny Snares the Prince." He wanted to talk to her about those stories, to laugh with her over them. He wanted to go with her and the children to the beach on the weekend. He longed to make love with her for hours.

None of that was happening.

Sunday, she said she couldn't make it to the family breakfast. The next week was the same. The children and Gerta saw her practically every day, but if he appeared when she was with them, she would simply get up and leave. She wouldn't spend the evening out with him and she just didn't have a free moment when he might join her at her place.

He never got a chance to talk her into making that trip to New York with him. How could he? He never got a chance to talk to her at all.

On April 20, he flew to JFK, spent the night at the Four Seasons and then spoke at Columbia University the next day. That evening, he had dinner with his brother Damien and Dami's fiancée, Lucy Cordell. Lucy and Dami lived together right there in Manhattan, where Lucy was attending fashion school. Max tried to be good company, but mostly he just wished Lani could have been there. He arrived home on the twenty-third to find that she had left that morning. Gerta told him she would spend two days in Manhattan, then go on to Texas to see her family.

She returned the following Tuesday.

And by then, he'd had enough. They needed to talk.

Wednesday, he called her. She let the call go to voice mail. He left a message for her to call him back. She did no such thing. Thursday, she came to see the children. He tried to get her alone for a moment, but she'd learned a thing or two about evasion since that February morning when he'd caught her in the garden and dragged her to the gardener's cottage.

At the sight of him, she was up and out of there. He almost took off after her. But the children were watching and he didn't want to alarm them. He still had the key to her place and he considered the pros and cons of letting himself in and refusing to leave until she talked to him.

But even desperate for her as he was becoming, he could see the wrongness of that. A woman's home, after all, was her castle. A man was not allowed to simply break in to get to her.

Next, he thought he might take up a position in front of her building and not budge until she talked to him.

Was he moving into the realm of stalkerdom? Probably. He could see the headline now: The Naughty Nanny's Stalker Prince.

It had to stop.

And he knew what to do to stop it. He'd always known, but he'd been holding out, hoping she wouldn't make him go that far. His bluff had failed. He *would* go that far if there was no other way to get near her.

When he called her Thursday evening and got her voice mail, he said, "All right. I will tell you about Sophia."

She called him back five minutes later. "I'm here. Come on over."

Chapter Fourteen

Lani sat on the worn sofa and he took the chair. He stared across the low table between them, drinking in the sight of her in old jeans and a worn white T-shirt that clung to her glorious curves, her hair a cloud of dark curls on her shoulders, just the way he liked it best.

All he wanted in the world was to get up and go over and sit next to her. Such a simple thing. But her expression warned him against such a move.

He thought of the night that she'd told him about her past. Of how furious he'd been with her, how he'd demanded she make a choice: give him her new address or never call him again.

How had they gotten here from there? How had it all turned around, their positions reversed? Now he was the one forced to make a choice while she looked at him with cool reserve behind her eyes.

When she spoke, her tone was gentle. "You don't have to tell me. You can just go."

But he couldn't go. It wasn't an option. He'd missed her too much. If telling her about his marriage would a make a difference between them, he would do it. Besides, in the past few weeks, without her, he'd had way too much time to think.

He'd kept the reality of his marriage to himself for so long. To do so had become second nature. Also, in spite of everything, he'd felt a certain allegiance to Sophia's memory, a duty to maintain the long-held fiction that she'd been an ideal wife.

He said, "I should have told you long ago. I see that now. I...*want* you to know."

She drew a slow breath. And then she nodded.

And he began, "I married Sophia convinced that we were born to love each other. That we were meant to be together forever. I was my mother and father's son in every way then. I believed in marriage, in true love between two people, love that lasts a lifetime. The problem was I didn't know the real Sophia."

Lani shifted on the sofa. "How so?"

"After we were married, I found out that Sophia had been out to catch a prince. She wanted become a princess. She wanted one of her children to rule Montedoro. She went after that goal with single-minded purpose. Later, she confessed that her family had encouraged and coached her to that end. She was to marry the heir to the Montedoran throne."

Lani's cool gaze warmed—at least a little. "Oh, Max. I'm sorry."

He shrugged. "From the first time I met her—I believe we were both nine—she hung on my every word. Already I was interested in history, in writing. She listened, rapt, as I told her stories about my ancestors. She found me fascinating, or so I thought. For a decade, as we grew to adulthood, she treated me like her king. She laughed at my slightest attempt at a joke. When I kissed her, she always seemed about to faint from sheer excitement."

"You're telling me she played you and you fell for her act?"

He tried not to wince. "You have to realize, we weren't together all that often. Never long enough or often enough for me to start seeing that maybe the Sophia I knew and the real Sophia weren't one and the same. She always claimed she loved to hear me talk, that just to be near me was enough for her. I was young and inexperienced and arrogant, too. I became absolutely certain it was true love. I believed that she adored me and we were a perfect match."

Lani shook her head slowly. But she didn't speak.

He went on with it. "I proposed to her when we were both eighteen. She instantly accepted. My mother and father tried to get me to slow down, tried to convince me to wait, to grow up a little, to see other girls. But I was a one-woman man and I wouldn't listen. I knew that Sophia was my great love."

"So you got married in a fantasy wedding of state when you were both twenty."

"That's right. And as soon as the ink was dry on our marriage license, Sophia changed. Suddenly, talking politics made her want a long nap. We no longer found the same things funny. She had no interest in the college studies I was finishing up, or in traveling with me to my speaking engagements. Reading and discussing books bored her. She preferred to sleep till at least noon, and I couldn't stand to stay in bed once the sun was up. As soon as we were married, there was essentially no way the two of us connected."

"Was she unhappy?"

"She never admitted she was. She claimed that she looked at it simply, that we were married and that was that. She *liked* me, she said. She wanted my babies, and she was proud to be the wife of the heir to the throne. When I told her how, to me, she'd changed completely, and that *I* was unhappy, she only frowned and told me to stop being silly about it. We got along well together, she said. She just didn't get what my problem was."

"You were miserable the whole time you were married to her?" Lani was incredulous. "Is that what you're telling me?"

"No, not the whole time. After a few years, it wasn't so bad."

"But what does that mean, it wasn't so bad?"

"I grew numb, you might say. And then, when Nick was born, it got a little better. Sophia and I both wanted children. Parenting was something we both valued, something, at last, that we had in common. We were a family, and that was a good thing. Then we had Connie. I was actually happy by then, fond of Sophia and grateful for my children. I learned to accept that I would never have the kind of marriage I'd planned on, never have the closeness my parents share."

Lani kicked off her shoes and drew her feet up on the sofa. "But, Max, people still talk about the two of you, about the perfect marriage you had, about how well matched you were, how blissfully happy you were together...."

"So? They had it wrong—but not completely wrong. By the end, I *was* happy with her, with our life together. And it was fine with me, that the press made up a pretty story about how much in love we were. Just as you're my *naughty nanny* and my *Cinderella bride,* Sophia and I were *soul mates.* From the beginning, the story was that we were exactly like my parents, that we shared a great love."

"But it was a lie...."

"I was the heir. Divorce wasn't an option. And even if I hadn't been the heir, I would have stayed in my marriage, because I personally believe that marriage is forever. In so many ways, Sophia was an excellent wife. After I accepted that she wasn't going to change, I wanted to make the best of the situation. So did she. For once, the press cooperated. To the world, we were the perfect couple. Beyond occasional reports about the total happiness we shared, they pretty much left us alone."

Lani seemed lost in thought. And then she asked, "Were you there when she had the accident?"

"No. I stayed in Montedoro with the children while Sophia took a long weekend at Lac d'Annecy in the French Lake District with her sister Maria and their brother Juan Felipe."

She looked at him expectantly. "But how did it happen? I know I could do a little research and get all the facts. But, Max, I would rather hear it from you."

So he told her what he knew. "Sophia was skiing and the line went lax. She just went down. They circled the boat back around to get her, but there was no sign of her. Juan Felipe and Sophia's bodyguard both jumped in to save her. Her skis bobbed on top of the water, but she was nowhere to be found."

"They never found her?"

"A fisherman spotted her body days later in a secluded inlet, floating near the shore. Her life jacket was missing. The cause of death was drowning. But she'd taken a serious blow to the forehead, from one of her skis, they said. The theory was that the head injury had disoriented her. In her confusion, she took off the life jacket and eventually she drowned."

"It's so sad and senseless."

"What can I say? Yes, it was. And after she was gone, I found that I missed her terribly. I began to see that I had been happier in my marriage than I ever realized. I began to…idealize what we'd had. I missed her so much, missed her presence, her steadiness, what I saw as her commitment to our life together. I grieved. In the end, in spite of everything, we *were* partners in life. I really believed that what we'd had, together, what we'd built together, our marriage…I believed it had meant something, that, in spite of the rocky start, the two of us had made a good, rich life. By the time she died, I'd gotten over the way she'd tricked me at the beginning. I'd fallen in love with her all over again."

Lani was watching him so closely, studying his face. "There's more, isn't there? It…wasn't what you thought, somehow."

He only looked at her.

And she whispered, "You said you *believed* that your marriage had meant something, not that it actually did."

He couldn't stand to draw it out a moment longer. He went ahead and told her. "She betrayed me."

Lani gaped. "I don't… What?"

"Six months after she died, I found out she'd been in love with another man for the whole time she was married to me."

"No…"

"Yes. Sophia had a lover—a longtime lover. In fact, she and that other man were lovers through most of our marriage, from her first trip back to visit her family in Spain a year after our wedding, until the other man died, which happened almost a year to the day before Sophia drowned at Lac d'Annecy."

Lani made a low, disbelieving sound. "But how did you find out?"

"I was cleaning out her desk and I found his letters—old-fashioned letters on plain white stationery, the kind no one writes anymore. But Sophia's lover did. Later, I went through her computer, looking for emails or instant messages from him. None. Just those letters. Over a hundred of them. They were tucked away in a hidden drawer, along with his obituary torn from a Spanish newspaper."

Lani's sweet face had gone pale. "Oh, my God, Max."

He went ahead and told the rest. "I locked the door so no one would disturb me and I read them all, every one of those letters. His name was Leandro d'Almas. He was a friend of Sophia's brother, of Juan Felipe, and Sophia had known him since she was a child. D'Almas held a minor title and he had very little money. He never married. She would go home to Spain a few times a year and they would be together in secret then."

Lani asked softly, cautiously, "Nicky and Connie, are they...?"

"Mine. D'Almas had some medical condition that eventually killed him. He was sterile and his letters were full of his frustrations that he couldn't give her children, that her children were mine. He also went on and on about his love for her, about the things they had done together in the past and what he would do to her and with her the next time she could get away from me and come to him."

"Oh, Max..."

"Those letters were tearstained, folded and refolded, tattered, read and reread. Sophia had cherished them. She should have destroyed them, but she didn't. I'm guessing she couldn't. They held her true heart. The heart I never understood, never saw, never knew...because I didn't know *her*. Even when I thought that we had come to something workable and strong and lasting together, over time—even then, it was just a lie that I told myself. I didn't know my wife at all."

She caught her lower lip between her neat white teeth. "Is that what you're afraid of with me? That I'll betray you? That if you marry me, I'll take a secret lover and lead a secret life behind your back?"

"No. Of course not."

"Are you sure?"

"Yes. Of course I'm sure."

"Then I just don't get it."

"Get what?"

"Well, Max, you wanted a real marriage more than anything. We could have that, together, you and me."

He longed to get up and circle around the table, to sit on the sofa with her, wrap his arms good and tight around her, to breathe in the wonderful scent of her hair. But he stayed in the chair. "I just can't, Lani. I can't do it again. I don't believe in marriage anymore, not for me, anyway. I can't…lock myself in that way. I want us both to be free to go at any time—so that every day we're together, we know, we're certain, that with each other is where we really want to be."

"But you're throwing away the very thing you've always yearned for. Oh, Max. What kind of sense does that make?"

He only shook his head. "I don't know. No sense at all, I suppose. But still. I mean it. I can't do it. Not again. Not even for you. Why can't you understand?"

That soft mouth trembled. He could see the pulse beating in the base of her throat. And then she unfolded her legs and stood.

He willed her to come to him.

But she only went around the low table and over to the sliding door. She stood there, staring at her own darkened reflection in the glass.

Finally, she seemed to draw herself up. She turned to him. "I'll tell you what I see." Her voice was soft suddenly. Soft and resigned. "I see that you can't get past what happened with Sophia. You can't get beyond the lies that she told you, that she *lived* with you. I see that you loved her twice—when you married her and then later, after the children came."

"And both times it was a lie."

"Oh, Max, no."

"Yes. It was a lie."

"All right. I get how you would feel that way. But I see… gray areas, too."

"What do you mean 'gray'?" he demanded gruffly.

"I just… Well, I think she must have loved you, too. Not enough for you, I know that. But enough to mean that you and she knew happiness together."

"No," he insisted. "How can you say she loved me? She loved *him.* With me, it was all a lie.…"

"I just don't agree with you. Yes, she lied to you. But there was also a certain truth in what you had with her. You were partners, raising a family. She gave you two beautiful children. Maybe you never knew the secrets of her heart, but I think there was goodness in her. If there wasn't, you never could have loved her."

"How can you defend her?"

"I'm not. I think what she did was totally wrong. I'm defending *you,* my darling, defending the marriage you made, the trust that you kept. As for Sophia, she's gone. You'll never be able to confront her. You need, somehow, to make peace with her memory."

"How can I make peace? I loved an illusion."

"I don't think so, Max. You didn't know everything, but that doesn't mean the love you had for her wasn't real."

"I was a blind idiot and she was a…" He let the sentence trail off unfinished. For Nicky and Connie's sake, he refused to speak the ugly word he was thinking.

Lani stared at him so tenderly, unspeaking, for an endless time. And then finally, she said, "I'm sorry for you, for her, for all of it. But what you've just told me doesn't change the fact that I want a lifetime with you. I want you for my husband. Not because you're a prince and I want to be a princess. Not because you're the heir to the Montedoran throne. There is no one else waiting in secret for me.

You're the one for me, Max. I want to marry you because I love you. Because we're good together. Because I love Nicky and Connie and I want to be there for them, while they're growing up. I want to be your wife, Max. I want to give you everything you always wanted from Sophia. But I can't do that. Because you don't trust yourself or me."

"That's not true. I trust you absolutely."

"No, you don't. If you trusted me, you would put your fear aside, take my hand and make a life with me. Deep in your heart, I think you still want what your parents have, a good marriage that can stand the test of a lifetime. But you won't let yourself have that. You're too afraid it will all go wrong all over again." Those big dark eyes pleaded with him. They begged him to swear that he *did* trust her, that he was ready to get past his fears and give a life with her a chance.

But he couldn't do that, not in the way that she wanted it. And right then, at that moment, he saw what he'd been so stubbornly refusing to see. In this, in the question of marriage, there really was no middle ground for either of them. She wanted what he couldn't give her. And it was wrong of him to keep after her, to keep pushing her to come to him on his terms. He was not the man for her. He needed to do the right thing, to let her go. There was nothing more to say about it.

He took her key from his pocket and set it on the low table. "I hope you find what you're looking for."

Her mouth was trembling again. With a soft cry, she turned her back to him. "I can't bear this. Just go now. Please."

That at least, he could give her. He strode to the door and pulled it open. "Goodbye, Lani."

She didn't answer him.

He went out, shutting the door quietly behind him.

* * *

Lani whirled when she heard the door click shut.

Her eyes blinded by hot tears, she ran over and locked it. Then she threw herself down on the sofa and let the tears have their way, let the ugly, painful sobs take her.

An hour or so later, she went online and tortured herself a little more looking at pictures of him, and pictures of the two of them together. She read the crappy tabloid stories about their relationship and groaned through her tears over the lurid headlines.

More than once that night, she picked up the phone to call him, as she'd been doing every night since they returned from Texas together more than three weeks ago. What could it hurt? she kept asking herself. To call him and tell him she was willing to do things the way that he wanted. That she couldn't bear being apart from him for another minute. If he wouldn't marry her, she wanted them to be together, at least.

But she couldn't do it. Couldn't make that call.

In loving him, she'd learned to love herself so much better than before. To respect herself and her principles. She was her mother's daughter to the core, one of those people who still believed that true love and marriage went together. It wouldn't work for her to try to be someone else. It would only make the inevitable ending more painful.

That Sunday afternoon, Max took the children to the beach. They built a crooked sand castle and ran in the waves.

When they sat down to eat the picnic Marceline had packed for them, Connie asked him why Miss Lani couldn't come with them.

He did his best to ignore the ache in his chest at the mere

mention of Lani's name and told his daughter gently that he wasn't seeing Miss Lani anymore.

Connie crunched on a carrot stick. "But I see her all the time. I saw her Friday. She came out into the garden with Aunt Sydney and Trev and Ellie. We were all together and she let me brush her hair."

Jealousy added a knot in his stomach to the ache in his heart. He was jealous of his own daughter, for getting to be with Lani, to touch Lani, when he had to make himself stay away.

Nicky said, "Papa means he dumped her. She's not his girlfriend anymore."

Connie gasped. "Papa! You dumped Miss Lani?"

He put a soothing hand on Connie's little shoulder and gave Nick a stern frown. "I did not dump Miss Lani. It didn't work out between us, that's all."

"You broke up with her," Nick accused.

"You shouldn't have done that," Connie pouted.

Was he suddenly in the doghouse with both of his children? "Ahem. It didn't work out between me and Miss Lani. Sometimes that happens. There is no one to blame." God. He sounded like a pompous ass.

Nicky peered at him, narrow-eyed. "I knew it already. I've known it for days and days."

"Erm, knew what?"

"That you and Miss Lani broke up."

"How did you know?"

"You're different, that's all." Nick sipped from a bottle of Evian. "Back like you used to be."

Connie announced, "Well, at least Miss Lani can still see *me*."

Max asked Nicky, "Like I used to be, how?"

Connie put in dreamily, "She likes me and I like her. We have our girl things."

Nick said, "You know, like this." And he made a blank sort of face. "All serious and maybe kind of sad."

Connie crunched another carrot. "She would never stop seeing *me*."

Serious and sad? Did Nick have it right?

Max told Connie, "I'm glad that you and Miss Lani are still friends."

Connie wrapped her arms around his neck and kissed him loudly on the cheek. "I'm glad, too."

He turned to Nick. "And I promise I will try not to be so serious and sad."

Nick shrugged. "It's all right, Papa. That's just how you are, I guess. You were always that way. Except, you know, with Miss Lani."

A week went by. And then another. He saw Lani now and then. In the garden. In the library. They would nod and smile politely at each other and leave it at that.

It hurt every time he saw her. A deep, fevered kind of ache. But at least then he felt something.

Because his son was right. He'd gone back to his old ways, to living his life at a distance, as though there was an invisible barrier between him and the rest of the world. The familiar numbness he'd known for so long had claimed him again.

Most of the time, he simply went through the motions. He felt alive only in snips and snatches: when he held Connie on his lap and read her a story. When he helped Nick with his studies. Or when he caught sight of Lani and gave her a false smile and his love for her welled up, hot and hungry and alive.

Other than those brief flashes of intense feeling, he was his old self in the worst kind of way.

His mother got him alone after a Monday meeting with her ministers and asked him what had happened with Lani.

She knew, of course. She always did.

He told her it was over and he didn't wish to speak of it.

"May I make a suggestion?"

"No."

She suggested anyway, "Consider putting your pride aside. Stop punishing yourself for making the wrong choice once. Think of your children, of all you gained by that wrong choice. And move on. Ask Lani to marry you. Let yourself be happy."

"This has nothing to do with pride, Mother. And Lani and I are finished."

She didn't argue further. But he saw in those legendary dark eyes that she thought he had it all wrong.

On the last weekend in May, his sister Alice married real estate golden boy turned international investor Noah Cordell in Carpinteria, California. Most of the family attended.

Max went and took the children and Gerta. The wedding was held in the big Spanish-style house at Noah's estate. Alice came down the curving staircase, arms full of Casablanca lilies, wearing a daring white wedding gown that fit her like a second skin and dipped to the base of her spine in back. The spectacular dress had been designed by Noah's talented younger sister, Lucy, the one who was engaged to Damien.

Max felt a jolt of aliveness when Alice stood with her groom and said her vows. They were happy, Alice and Noah. Happy and willing to take the biggest risk of all, to bind their lives together.

Most of his siblings had taken that risk. Only his two youngest sisters, Genevra and Aurora, remained single—

and Damien, too. Dami and Lucy planned to wait a while to marry, until Lucy had gotten through at least a couple of years at fashion school. But then Max overheard Lucy laughing and saying she didn't know how long she could wait to be Dami's bride.

So there you go. Before you knew it, they would all be happily married. Except for him.

Because he was both prideful and cowardly, and completely unwilling to take a chance like that again. He was willing to trust neither himself nor the woman he loved, just as Lani had said.

Noah's sprawling estate not only had one of the finest horse stables in America and extensive equestrian trails and fields, it also had artfully landscaped gardens rivaling the ones at home in Montedoro. To escape the crowd in the house for a while, Max left Nick and Connie in Gerta's excellent care and wandered outside, where the weather was California perfect and trees shaded the curving garden paths. Lost in his thoughts, enclosed in the usual bubble of numbness, hardly noticing the beauty around him, he walked past the infinity pool and down one path and then another.

Until he rounded a curve and there she was: Lani. Sitting on a small stone bench beneath a willow tree, her back to him, her long black hair dappled in sunlight and leaf shadow.

Max stopped stock-still on the path as the world instantly flashed into vivid three-dimensional life. Everything glowed with color and light. He smelled dust and eucalyptus and the haunting sweetness of some unknown flower. He heard birdsong. Something rustled in a patch of greenery to his left. And from back the way he'd come, the sound of voices and laughter drifted to him.

And then she turned her head. He saw her face in profile.

It wasn't Lani.

The vivid world subsided into dull reality once more.

The woman saw him, gave him a nod.

He returned her nod and walked on by.

It happened again that night. He caught a glimpse of black hair and the sweet curve of a woman's shoulder. The world exploded into life.

Until he moved closer and saw his mistake. Only another stranger. The bubble of numbness descended as before.

He didn't start wondering if he might be going insane until after he was back at home and it happened three more times: a woman in the marketplace buying oranges; another at a formal dinner in the palace's state dining room; a third in the library.

Each time everything flashed bright. The world pulsed with vibrant intensity—and then flattened away to grayness once again.

He was an intelligent man. He got the message. Not only did his mother and his children think he was crazy to let Lani go, even his subconscious was out to teach him a lesson now.

Max was just stubborn enough that he might have soldiered on in his gray bubble, telling himself it didn't matter if he'd lost his mind, he'd messed up on forever once and he couldn't afford to risk it again.

But then he started dreaming of Sophia.

In the dream, she wore her favorite white tank bathing suit and she stood on a narrow ribbon of pebbled beach at the lake where she'd drowned. She shaded her eyes with the flat of her hand, her mouth twisted in exasperation, glaring at him. "For such a smart man, you have always been so stupid. Go. Have the love you've dreamed of at last. Live. Live until you die." And then she dropped her hand and dived into the water.

He ran in after her, shouting her name. But no matter how he splashed about and called for her, there was no sign of her. She was gone.

Until the next night, when he would dream the dream again.

After the fourth night he had the dream, even he knew he could hold out no longer. Love and life were calling him.

And they were never going to shut up until he finally gave in and answered.

Chapter Fifteen

On the third Friday in June, just as night was falling, Lani finished the final book in her Montedoran trilogy. Satisfied with the ending at last, she saved her work. She was just closing her laptop when the intercom buzzer sounded from downstairs.

She got up and went to see who was there. "Yes?"

He said only her name. "Lani."

Her hands went numb and her heart stopped dead—before recommencing beating so fast and hard she felt certain it would batter its way right out of her chest. "Max?"

The old intercom crackled. "May I please come up?"

Had someone died? If Connie or Nick… No. She'd seen them both just yesterday. They were fine. She wouldn't accept any possibility but that they remained so.

"Lani. Please?"

Numb hands shaking, she buzzed him in. And then she undid the locks and opened the door and stood there on the landing, her heart going a mile a minute, listening to his swift footfalls growing louder as he came up the stairs.

She leaned over the railing and watched him run up the second flight to her floor, his chestnut hair as unruly as ever, a little too long, curling against the collar of his blue shirt. She knew how soft those curls would be, the way they wrapped so sweetly around her index finger.

He looked up and saw her. "Lani." His eyes in the light from the stairwell were more blue than gray. And did he have to be so handsome it hurt her just to look at him?

She retreated, backing across the landing and through the open door of her apartment. He reached the landing and came for her, matching her backward steps with his forward ones, until they were both over the threshold.

"Lani." He reached out, grabbed the door and pushed it shut behind him, closing them in together.

She was breathing too hard, her poor overworked heart going faster than ever. "I don't... Is everyone all right?"

He just stood there and stared at her. He seemed to be breathing as hard as she was. "God. Lani."

"Tell me. Nick and Connie...?"

"Fine," he said. "Everyone's fine."

She put her hand to her chest in a vain attempt to calm all the pounding in there. "Then what's happened?"

And he reached out and took her by the arms. His touch sent shivers dancing across her skin. She gasped. And he said, "Yes." And then again, "Yes." His voice wrapped around her, deep and rich and so well-remembered. It made her throat clutch just to hear it. "Alive," he whispered. "With you I am alive." He pulled her closer, bent nearer and breathed in deeply through his nose.

"Max." She made herself say his name louder, more firmly. "Max, what in the world is going on?"

"Tell me I'm not too late."

"Too late? It's a little after nine, I think."

"I don't mean the time." He gripped her arms tighter. "Is there anyone else?"

"Anyone...?" She gaped at him. "You mean another man?"

"Yes." His straight brows drew together. He looked angry. Or maybe terrified. "Is there another man?"

"Uh, no." She shook her head.

He mirrored the movement, his head going back and forth in time with hers. "No." He glared. "You said no."

"I did, yes. I said no. There is no one."

"Lani." Desperate. Pleading. "Lani…"

And then he pulled her even closer and he kissed her.

Oh, dear sweet Lord, his kiss.

How had she kept going without his kiss?

Her thoughts were a jumble. Her body was on fire. Her heart ricocheted against her ribs.

And she couldn't stop herself. She slid her hungry arms up over his hard, warm chest and wrapped them around his neck, pulling him closer, sighing in surrender against his parted lips.

When he lifted his head, he said, "It's no good without you. I keep seeing you everywhere. But then it's not really you, just some stranger with black hair. And then I started dreaming of Sophia."

"Sophia? You're not serious."

"Yes, I am. She kept saying, 'Go. Have the love you've dreamed of. Live until you die.'"

She blinked up at him. "Sophia. In a dream…"

He nodded. "I know. Madness. I've been wondering if maybe I've gone round the bend. But I've come to the conclusion that I'm still reasonably sane. I'm just stubborn and full of pride. And scared. Yes, I am. Scared, most of all. But I do love you, Lani. I trust you completely." He touched her hair, guided a dark curl behind her ear. It felt so good. Heaven on earth. His hands on her skin again, caressing her. At last.

And he wasn't finished. "I love you so much. I love you and my life is one big, gray cave of numbness without you.

I love you and my children love you. My mother thinks I've been an idiot. She told me to stop being stubborn, to put my pride aside and ask you to marry me."

She hitched in a sharp breath. "Your mother said you should marry me?" She stared at him, stunned. "But the French ministers—"

"Don't worry about them. They'll come around, they always do." He reached into the breast pocket of his blue shirt. "I want only you, Lani. I love only you. You're the one I saw in my heart, always, even before I knew you. You're the one I should have waited for. But I didn't wait. And still, there was good in that, just as you said all those endless weeks ago. There was Nick and Connie. And I was true to my wife even if she wasn't true to me. I kept my vows. And life went on."

"Oh, I'm so glad you see that now."

"I do. It's what you said. What else is there but to let the bitterness go? I swear it to you. I'm done with letting my pride and my anger rule my life. I trust you, Lani. And I trust my own judgment in choosing you."

"Oh, Max…"

"You are my hope for the future, Lani. You are everything bright and true and vivid and alive. I want to be with you. *Truly* with you. I want to be your husband, if you'll only have me." His legs gave out.

Or so she thought at first as he was slowly sinking to the floor. She put her hands over her mouth and let out a soft cry.

And then he was there on one knee right in front of her, reaching up to take her left hand. "Marry me, Lani." He slipped a ring on her finger—an impossibly beautiful ring, with three giant sapphires surrounded in diamonds on a platinum band.

Her eyes blurred with tears. "Oh, Max…"

"I know it's taken me way too long to come to this, to come to you," he whispered, his voice gruff with emotion. "I know I've hurt you."

She touched his upturned face. "You've only ever been honest, I know that. I never faulted you. I just wanted more."

He pressed a kiss in the heart of her palm. "And now, if you'll have me, if it's not too late, I want to *give* you more. I want to give you everything, all I have. My life, my love. Forever."

"Oh, my darling…"

"Be my bride, Lani. Marry me."

"You mean this?" she demanded breathlessly. "You *want* this?"

He didn't waver. "More than anything. Marry me, Lani."

There was only one answer by then. She gave it. "Yes."

He swept to his feet and wrapped her in his arms. "Say it again."

She laughed. "Yes, Max. I will marry you. I will be your wife."

And he grabbed her closer, claiming her lips in a kiss that promised all the joy she'd never thought to share with him. "Together," he whispered.

She nodded. "You, me, the children…"

"Through the good times and all the rest," he vowed. "From today onward. No matter what happens, we will get through it. As long as I have your hand in mine."

* * * * *

JOIN US ON SOCIAL MEDIA!

Stay up to date with our latest releases, author news and gossip, special offers and discounts, and all the behind-the-scenes action from Mills & Boon...

 millsandboon

 millsandboonuk

 millsandboon

It might just be true love...

MILLS & BOON
True Love

Romance from the Heart

Celebrate true love with tender stories of heartfelt romance, from the rush of falling in love to the joy a new baby can bring, and a focus on the emotional heart of a relationship.